D0585927

THE JANUS MAN

Who is Janus, the man who looks both East and West?

Tweed must solve the secret of his identity before it is too late. The terrible fact is that he knows Janus has to be one of his own European sector chiefs – Hugh Grey, Guy Dalby, Harry Masterson or Erich Lindemann.

The murder of one of Tweed's agents triggers the desperate search which takes Tweed to Hamburg, Lübeck – the Baltic port perched on the border with East Germany – then on to Copenhagen and Oslo, and back to the lonely flatlands of East Anglia.

As time runs out, Tweed realizes he may also be tracking a mass murderer – that an appalling scandal in London must be avoided at all costs. Then, from East Germany, the order goes out – *Kill Tweed* . . .

Aided by foreign correspondent Bob Newman, Tweed continues the chase, employing his own unorthodox methods to bring together the strands of an insidious conspiracy. But who is Diana Chadwick, the girl with a nostalgia for the 1930s – and why does Tweed insist she is the key witness? And what is the role of the strange Dr Berlin, reputed to be the Albert Schweitzer of today?

Colin Forbes has written his most gripping, true-to-life epic in *The Janus Man* – a spellbinding novel.

By the same author

COVER STORY
TERMINAL
THE LEADER AND THE DAMNED
DOUBLE JEOPARDY
THE STOCKHOLM SYNDICATE
AVALANCHE EXPRESS
THE STONE LEOPARD
YEAR OF THE GOLDEN APE
TARGET FIVE
THE PALERMO AMBUSH
THE HEIGHTS OF ZERVOS
TRAMP IN ARMOUR

THE
JANUS MAN

Colin Forbes

COLLINS
8 Grafton Street, London W1
1987

William Collins Sons & Co Ltd
London · Glasgow · Sydney · Auckland
Toronto · Johannesburg

BRITISH LIBRARY CATALOGUING IN PUBLICATION DATA

Forbes, Colin, *1923-*
The Janus Man.
Rn: Raymond Harold Sawkins
I. Title
823'.914F   PR6069.A94

ISBN 0-00-223102-6

First Published 1987
Reprinted 1987
© Colin Forbes 1987

Photoset in Linotron Times
by Rowland Phototypeseting Ltd
Bury St Edmunds, Suffolk
Made and printed in Great Britain by
William Collins Sons & Co. Ltd, Glasgow

FOR JANE

CONTENTS

Prologue

East Anglia in July. 2 a.m. Carole Langley walked by herself along the lonely road elevated above the surrounding flatlands of the Wash. She was half a mile from the village of Plimpstead.

It was a warm night, a cloying warmth. The moon had come out from behind the cloud bank, illuminating the deserted fields on either side stretching to the dim horizon. Eighteen years old, an attractive blonde, Carole felt a little nervous. The stillness of the flatlands seemed to hold a hint of menace.

'All right,' she had told her boy friend, Rick, 'if that's what you want you'd better look elsewhere. And, no thanks, I'll get home by myself . . .'

'Please yourself,' Rick had told her, his voice slurred with a little too much liquor. 'Girls are like buses. There's always another one coming along. I might even find one inside . . .'

Saying which, he'd gone back into the old house where the party was still in full swing. When she'd accepted the invitation Carole hadn't known Peggy's parents were away, that the young crowd would have the house to themselves. The trek to the bedrooms had started early.

And I'm bloody sure some of them were on drugs, she told herself as she trudged along the road in high heels. She wished now she'd brought walking shoes in a bag. But how was she to know it would end like this – letting Rick bring her back in his car had definitely not seemed a good idea. Not along these deserted roads where the distance between houses – let alone villages – was measured in miles.

She saw the car coming a long way off. It was incredible the distance you could see across the Wash. Two headlights not dipped – like a couple of monster eyes. Impossible to identify the make of car.

The road – like all roads in that part of the world – curved and changed direction frequently. Sometimes she saw the powerful beams broadside on, then the car would swing round a curve and the monster eyes, gradually growing larger, would stare straight at her. The pallid light of the moon began to fade, moving behind the clouds. The lights of the car grew stronger.

Who could be out by the Wash at this hour? Most people would be in bed. Even back where I came from, she thought savagely – and they could keep that. My mum will kill me, she worried as the ache in her feet grew worse. She'll be waiting up. Of course! And when she didn't hear the sound of a car stopping she'll want to know what happened. I'll tell her Rick's car wouldn't start. That's it . . .

She felt better for a moment, but only for a moment. The oncoming vehicle was beginning to bother her. She walked slowly past an isolated copse of trees and wondered whether to hide until the car had passed.

Damnit, I've got to get home. It will probably just drive on past me . . .

The headlights came round the last bend and headed down a straight stretch of road towards her. She paused, remembering the copse of trees. The only hiding-place for miles. He must be able to see her now. The bloody lights were glaring full on her face. Why didn't he dip them?

She stopped, made up her mind, slipped off her shoes and prepared to run back to the shelter of the trees. Moving at speed, the driver rammed on the brakes, halted a few feet from her. In the glare of the lights she couldn't see what was happening – but she heard the sound of a car door opening and closing. The sound of footsteps approaching with a steady, purposeful tread.

She waited no longer. She turned and ran for the copse, feet flying over the smooth road surface. Behind her the steady footsteps followed. As she ran she fumbled in her handbag for the torch she always carried. It was some kind of a weapon.

She turned off the road, clutching handbag in one hand, torch in the other. She had the sense not to switch it on – that would make it easier for whoever was coming to spot her route. The precaution was her undoing.

Her left foot caught in the root of a tree and she sprawled on the grass full length. Spinning to one side, she lay on her back and switched on the torch, aiming it upwards. That was when she began to scream.

In the torchlight she saw the blade of the huge knife. Saw it as it descended towards her breasts in a powerful arc. Like some madman performing a ritual sacrifice. The knife entered her body and was drawn downwards, like a butcher carving meat. The scream died to a moan of horror. Then Carole Langley died and the heavy silence of a Norfolk night also descended.

That was two years earlier. The importance of the macabre event was not realized. Not until two years later by a man called Tweed.

Part 1

Suspicion

One

Summertime in Regent's Park. Like being in the country, Monica thought as she walked with Tweed. Their feet treading the soft grass, the sound of children's voices as they played. All was right with the world. But it wasn't.

Tweed walked with hands thrust inside jacket pockets, staring straight ahead through his glasses. She knew what that meant. A crisis. Tweed was disturbed. His first words confirmed her insight.

'For the first time in ages I'm frightened, really frightened.'

'Ian Fergusson's murder in Hamburg?'

'That, of course. The time for mourning comes later.' A grim note in his quiet voice. 'The implications behind the murder are what scare me stiff.'

'Explanation?'

She linked arms with him, expressing sympathy, support.

'Only six people in the world knew Fergusson was en route for Hamburg. The two of us.' He paused. 'Hugh Grey, Guy Dalby, Harry Masterson and Erich Lindemann.'

'You can't mean one of the sector chiefs? They've all been with us for years . . .'

'Which makes it more serious still. The greatest crisis we've ever faced.'

'Somebody had left the minutes file drawer in Central Registry unlocked. Anyone in the building could have sneaked a look at the file recording the decision to send Fergusson . . .'

'Camouflage.' Tweed's tone was bitter. 'I wrote the minutes of that meeting. I omitted all mention of the decision. There was no reference to Fergusson going anywhere at all . . .'

'Strictly against the regulations,' she twitted him, seeking a lighter mood.

'And done quite deliberately – to protect Fergusson . . .'

'Why?'

'I don't know,' Tweed confessed. 'Some sixth sense. The fact remains. Anyone checking the file wouldn't know a damned

17

thing about the Hamburg assignment. Clearly someone left the file unlocked to cover themselves. They must have been disturbed – maybe by a cleaner. They obviously never had time to read the minutes.'

'It's still hard to believe . . .'

'The most deadly things in life are . . .'

'Why are you so sure whoever unlocked the cabinet was disturbed?'

'If he'd had time to read my minutes he'd have locked it again – realizing his attempt at camouflage hadn't worked.'

'It's a pretty bloody creepy thought – an enemy inside the citadel. What are you going to do? Does Howard know?'

'I said *six* people. Howard was away in France at the time, which is why I chose that moment to despatch Fergusson. I'm going to Hamburg myself,' Tweed added casually.

He unlinked her arm, took his hands out of his pockets and walked faster. She knew his mind was churning the problem, working out the angles. She waited a few minutes before she posed her next question.

'Secretly, you mean? Without letting anyone know?'

'On the contrary. I'm calling a full meeting of all sector heads to announce the fact. Fergusson's murder is a tragedy. But that comes second to tracking down the fly in the ointment.'

Typical of Tweed to reduce such an appalling prospect to an everyday cliché. Monica was equally appalled at his strategy.

'You're telling them – knowing one of them will pass it on that you're going to Germany?'

'Which is the object of the exercise – to try and find a lead to the identity of who caused the death of Ian Fergusson.'

'Isn't this trip going to be very dangerous?' Monica queried. She was careful to keep the anxiety out of her voice as they wandered back towards Park Crescent. The green of the park spread away on all sides. No scene could have been more peaceful, she thought: such a contrast to what they were talking about.

'So the PM thinks.' Tweed turned down the corners of his mouth. 'You'd think I'd accepted Howard's job the way she clucks over me like her pet hen . . .'

'Why did you turn down her offer? You'd have run the outfit far better than Howard ever will.'

'Because I had to deceive – almost betray – too many of my staff when I was involved in the Adam Procane business.' He went on speaking quickly as though he found the topic distasteful. 'You won't believe the condition she laid down before she sanctioned my going . . .'

'Try me . . .'

'I have to take a bodyguard with me. A bodyguard! I was forced to accept to get permission.'

'Who is coming with you – and I'm jolly glad she did insist . . .'

'Bob Newman. He's got ideal cover – being a foreign correspondent. He can turn up anywhere and people assume he's after some story. The PM still wanted all background details about him before she consented. I think what did the trick is that he once had SAS training – the complete works – to do a story on them.' Tweed checked his watch. 'He should be landing at Heathrow just about now on his way back from Paris . . .'

'He disappeared for quite a while after the Helsinki thing. What has he been doing with himself?'

'Brooding, I gather – brooding over his wife's murder by the GRU. Maybe he's had an affair or two. I hope so – but I doubt it. He is in a bitter mood. Sounded cold and remote when I spoke to him over the phone when he reached the Paris Embassy. He accepted the job at once. Which surprised me . . .'

'Probably the perfect bodyguard . . .'

'And he will carry a gun, which I don't much like. The PM's idea again. The German people in Bonn have agreed. They're issuing a special weapons permit. Kuhlmann of the Federal Police fixed it. He's worried about the killing of Fergusson. He thinks there's more behind the murder than has come to light. I really wish I was just going on my own. I hate fuss.'

'And now?'

They had left Regent's Park and were waiting to cross the road to Park Crescent, the Georgian scimitar-shaped curve of buildings, one of which houses the SIS HQ.

'Now,' replied Tweed, 'we set up the meeting of sector chiefs . . .'

*

19

Which one?

Tweed sat at the head of the long table in the conference room, looking at his four colleagues – seated two to a side – while they waited for him to open the proceedings of the emergency meeting he had called.

Not a man with less than fifteen years' service. Now he felt he no longer knew them at all. One of these men – friends as well as colleagues he had regarded them – had sent Ian Fergusson to his death in Hamburg. The loyal Scot he could always count on. Tweed felt a sudden revulsion.

One of the waiting faces was a mask. A carefully contrived personality built up over the years to hide his true role. His true purpose in life. Treachery. Which one, he asked himself again?

He cleared his throat and four pairs of eyes watched him.

'Gentlemen,' he began, 'I am leaving for Hamburg. I have taken over personally the investigation into the death of Ian Fergusson.'

He paused, checking their reactions. His tone was matter-of-fact. Like a man discussing a routine piece of business.

'There is more to this affair than has come to light . . .'

Again he paused, looking at each man in turn. He could detect no clue in their expressions – but that he hadn't expected. It was Hugh Grey who responded first, sector chief for Central Europe.

'Who will be in charge while you're abroad?'

Was there a hopeful note in his question? Grey, thirty-nine, was the youngest. Slim in build, he had recently remarried for the second time and his main residence was a farmhouse in Norfolk. He also had a tiny *pied à terre* in Chelsea.

Clean shaven, he had darkish hair and a pink baby face. He gave the impression of being a lightweight, a man who could talk a lot and say very little. Very self-assured, ambitious, physically restless, his easy manner concealed an alert brain and a ruthless dedication to his own self-interest. And he had a way with women, a certain type of woman. The opposite sex found him either charming or they detested him.

'Howard,' Tweed replied. 'Due back from Paris tomorrow to take up normal duty . . .'

20

'You're travelling alone to Germany?' Erich Lindemann enquired.

'Yes,' Tweed lied promptly.

There, it had started already. The web of deceit with his closest colleagues. Rather like Procane all over again. But this time there was a difference, Tweed reminded himself. He was beginning what could be a long and dangerous search for the odd man out sitting at this very table.

'Is that wise?' Lindemann pressed. 'After what happened to Fergusson?'

Erich Lindemann. Forty-eight. Head of the Scandinavian sector, which included Denmark. Known to the others – behind his back – as The Professor. A thin-faced man who looked older than his years – the dark grey hair also thinning. Dry in appearance and manner, unlike Grey he used words sparingly.

Born in Copenhagen, his mother had died early and his father remarried an Englishwoman. Brought up in Britain since he was ten years old, his accent had not a trace of his Danish origins. He was, Tweed considered, the most cautious of the four men. Only when all the ground work had been laid would he move – then he moved with the speed of light. An austere bachelor, he had been compared by Howard to Field Marshal Montgomery.

'Never tasted a decent claret in his life,' Howard had once summed him up.

'That would help him in his work?' Tweed had enquired.

'You know what I mean. Bloody brain-box and cold as ice. Like a grand master of chess, our Erich . . .'

Harry Masterson shot his cuffs clear of the sleeves of his dark blue business suit and waved a hand as he spoke.

'Presumably while you're checking out Fergusson we all carry on as usual? I'm due to leave for Vienna, as you know. My people get slack if I'm not there to boot their asses.'

'Business as usual,' Tweed agreed. 'You get off to Vienna as planned . . .'

Masterson. Forty-six. A head of hair as black as coal, neatly brushed with a centre parting. A large head, strong features, a commanding personality. A snappy dresser with a string of girl friends. Divorced by his wife when caught in a position which could hardly be described as a compromise. Impatient, he was

21

the dominating character among the five gathered round the table. Chief of the Balkan sector.

'Good hunting in Hamburg,' he wished Tweed. 'Get the bastard who fixed up poor Ian. You will, of course . . .'

'We'll have to see,' Tweed said. 'And unless there are some questions I propose closing this brief meeting.'

He glanced at Monica, who sat silent at a small table by the wall, pencil poised over her notebook from which she would later prepare the minutes of the meeting. It was a role she took over when Tweed wanted no distraction. But her main reason for being there this time was quite different.

Tweed looked at Guy Dalby who so far had not contributed a word. A reserved man of forty-four, chief of the Mediterranean sector, he had a compact frame and his dark brown hair looped over his forehead in a catlick. He spoke now, terse and to the point.

'What do you think was the motive behind Fergusson's murder?'

'No idea. That's what I'm going to find out . . .'

Tweed rose from the table, pushed his chair under it and made the announcement in a casual tone.

'Before you go about your normal duties I'd like to see each of you in my office later this morning. Separately, please.'

It was a faint hope – that in private conversation he might notice something about one of them which seemed out of place. A very faint hope indeed.

Two

Bob Newman flew into Heathrow aboard Flight AF 808 from Paris. He liked the Airbus – you had plenty of space. The stewardess watched him as he unfastened his safety belt. She wouldn't have minded going all the way with the Englishman.

In his early forties, she guessed. An easy manner, a strong face but the eyes and the mouth hinted at a sense of humour. He would, she was sure, have been fun. He nodded to her as he left the aircraft and walked up the narrow corridor towards Arrivals.

It felt strange – setting foot in England again for the first time in a year. The memory of his late wife, Alexis – killed by the Russians in Estonia, a faraway nowhere place on the Baltic – flooded back. The pleasant side of a marriage which had gone sour, which had been on the verge of the final break-up, filled his thoughts as he went through Passport Control.

The seated official looked at him twice. He had been recognized. Well, he was used to that. You couldn't become one of the most successful foreign correspondents in the world with your photo plastered across God knew how many papers and not expect recognition. Something he could do without.

Settled inside a taxi on his way to his flat at Chasemore House in South Ken, Newman's relaxed expression changed. He gazed out of the window grimly. A wasted year of his life, drifting round Europe, never able to settle anywhere for long, refusing to take on any of the many assignments offered.

So why had he taken on this weird job of acting as bodyguard – for God's sake! – to Tweed? Because it might give him a chance to do damage to the other side? Newman didn't ever delude himself – it was because the offer gave him a *purpose* in life.

He didn't like the fact that he would be carrying a gun. A crack shot – the SAS had seen to that – Newman had never shot a man in his life. Not yet, he thought bleakly.

Also the job intrigued him. He liked Tweed, admired him as a real pro. He'd worked with him before more than once. Why, he wondered, had Tweed himself accepted the idea of protection? It was out of character. As the cab carried him closer to his flat, all that Newman knew of what lay before him was they were going to Hamburg. Had something happened there already? Well, he'd find out soon enough.

23

Three

'What did you think of their reactions, Monica?' Tweed asked.

The two of them were alone in his Park Crescent office at the HQ of the SIS. Beyond the net-curtained windows was a view across towards Regent's Park. Tweed stared at the view, not seeing the sunny day as he sat behind his desk.

'The problem is I don't know any of them well enough. They're all newly-appointed, brought in out of the field to replace the men who held their jobs before. That was a clean sweep you made. How did Howard take your pushing out the Old Guard?'

'Not happily, of course. A couple of them were drinking companions at that toffee-nosed club of his. But the PM gave me only two options. Take on Howard's job – or bring in a younger team. She thinks it's time a younger generation took over at sector chief level. And I chose them. The trouble is I made a major error of judgement – to say the least – with one of them. Which one is the draconian question . . .'

'I'd hoped you would replace Howard himself . . .'

'I've already told you why not.'

Tweed's tone was abrupt, dismissing a topic he didn't want to discuss any further.

'How are you going to start in Hamburg? You haven't anything to use as a lead as far as I can see . . .'

She broke off as the phone rang. Her expression glowed when she heard who was on the line. She handed the receiver to Tweed.

'It's Bob Newman. Calling from his flat. He's just arrived from Paris . . .'

'That you, Bob?' Tweed's tone was businesslike. 'Look, we won't talk over the phone. Welcome back. Can you get over to see me? Good. Noon will do fine. Mind how you cross the road. You look right first, now you're back from the continent! See you . . .'

'He sounded a bit remote,' Monica commented. 'Not his usual buoyant jokey self.'

'The main thing is he's agreed to act as chaperon,' Tweed grimaced. 'I love the idea of having a chaperon . . .'

'Don't forget the PM's instructions. She said Newman must be next to you wherever you go . . .'

'Do stop nagging . . .'

'And you didn't tell me how you're going to start off when you get to Hamburg.'

'Visit the hospital where Fergusson died. Apparently he said a few words which made no sense to the doctor. They might make sense to me. Then a few quiet words with Ziggy Palewska.'

'The Polish refugee who settled in Hamburg? What's Ziggy got to do with anything – apart from the unsavoury way he makes his money?'

'That was why Fergusson went to Hamburg – to see Ziggy. He'd sent me a message saying he had urgent and serious news. Now, before you wheel in Hugh Grey, tell me what you know about him.'

Tweed sat back in his chair, clasped his hands in his lap and behind his horn-rimmed glasses he closed his eyes. Monica was used to this exercise. Her chief was using her as a sounding-board to clarify his own thoughts. She spoke from her phenomenal memory without referring to her card index of staff.

'Hugh Grey. Remarried an attractive brunette called Paula six months ago. Just about the time he was appointed sector chief for Central Europe. Under your reorganization that sector includes West Germany, Holland and Belgium. Penetration zones where he runs underground agents are East Germany, Poland and Czechoslovakia. Speaks fluent German, French and can get by in Italian and Spanish. Headquarters, Frankfurt-on-Main.'

'A bit more about his domestic background, please.'

Tweed was motionless, his eyes still closed, his mind concentrated totally on Hugh Grey.

'Paula Brent – that was her maiden name – is twenty-nine. Which makes her ten years younger than Hugh. She has built up a thriving pottery-making business based in King's Lynn. She makes up the designs herself, has a growing export market.

25

Especially in the States. Very bright girl, Paula. A stunner to look at. Lives a lot of the time at Hugh's farmhouse out on the Wash in Norfolk. The export deals are made over the phone. Then suddenly she's flying off to LA. Getting back to Hugh, he's madly sociable. Throws dinner parties at the farmhouse when he's home on leave. Enough?'

'For now, yes.' As an afterthought Tweed added, 'I do know Paula. Very independent type. The best sort of new businesswoman. And would you ask Hugh to come and see me now? Stay at your desk while we're talking . . .'

'Only one more question,' Tweed said to Grey, 'and then we can let you get on. Hamburg is your sector. Fergusson was killed in Hamburg. Is something stirring in your part of the world?'

'I thought we'd get to that.' Grey smiled his moon-like smile. He sat upright in his chair and radiated self-confidence. 'If I knew why Fergusson was sent there – as you pointed out, it is my territory – I might be able to help . . .'

'Just answer the question.'

'Everything has quietened down since Gorbachev took over – I get the impression the word has gone out. No incidents . . .'

'You wouldn't call the killing of Fergusson an incident?' Tweed enquired.

'It surprised me very much.' Grey paused to adjust his display handkerchief in his breast pocket. 'I was going to say my impression is Gorbachev wants all quiet on the western front while he consolidates his position at home. He's the development we've been waiting for – the new generation taking over.'

'Which fits in with the gospel according to Gorbachev. New times are arriving. For your information, Mikhail Gorbachev is Stalin in a Savile Row suit. That will be all.'

Monica waited until Grey had left the room, the smile wiped off his face. She turned down the corners of her mouth.

'Saucy bugger. You squashed him beautifully. He's after your job, you know . . .'

'I know.' Tweed was frowning. 'That's a negative comment on Grey. Give me a positive one.'

'Funny man. Acts like a playboy. But in the field he rides his

26

agents harder than any other sector chief. No mistakes is his motto. No second chance.'

'Which is why I gave him the job. Now, Erich Lindemann. We can just squeeze him in before Bob Newman is due. Résumé, if you please.'

'Erich Lindemann. Headquarters, Copenhagen. Penetration zone, Northern Russia. Born bachelor. Speaks German, Swedish and Danish. The very opposite to Grey. I've been to his flat in Chelsea. Neat as a pin. His study walls are lined with God knows how many books. Venerated by his men – he's so careful of their lives. The most reliable of the lot, I'd say. That's it.'

The interview with Lindemann was brief. The chief of the Scandinavian sector arrived wearing a sports jacket with leather patches on the elbows, sports slacks and a casual shirt. He nodded to Monica without speaking and sat in the waiting chair, resting his arms on the chair arms.

'How are things in Scandinavia?' Tweed asked amiably.

'Too quiet. The Kremlin is cooking something unpleasant to serve up to us. I've known this sinister quiet before.'

'The quiet before the storm?'

'I would say so, yes. May I make a suggestion?' Lindemann asked.

'I'm listening.'

'If you don't like the atmosphere in Hamburg, catch the first flight to Copenhagen. I'll be waiting there for you.'

'Would you care to elaborate on that, Erich?'

'I don't think so.'

'Then I'll bear it in mind. Thank you.'

Something curious about Lindemann's personality, Tweed said to himself as the door closed. Without saying much he projected such an aura of force and power he still seemed to be in the room. He had no time to pursue the train of thought. The phone rang and Monica told him Newman was waiting downstairs. The time was exactly noon.

'After what you've told me I don't like it one little bit,' Newman said emphatically. 'This trip to Hamburg smells like a trap. And you could be the main target – not Fergusson . . .'

'I know,' Tweed agreed.

'Then why the hell walk into it? Send someone else – a couple

27

of men with back-up. They travel on separate flights and meet up. The Hauptbahnhof would be a good place . . .'

'Because I think you're right. It's me they want.'

'You need a holiday. You're not thinking straight. I haven't the experience you need . . .'

'You did pretty well on your own inside Estonia – which was inside the Soviet Union. We're only going to West Germany. And I have the worst problem I've ever faced.'

'You have that in spades. One of your top deputies is working for Lysenko – because it will be General Lysenko of the GRU who is behind this manœuvre. Unless they've sent him on holiday to Siberia . . .'

'My information is Lysenko is controlling all anti-West European operations from Leipzig. He's one of the very few of the Old Guard Gorbachev has promoted. The rumour is they've established a close personal rapport . . .'

'There you are,' Newman said, lighting up a cigarette. 'And Lysenko's one ambition after what you did to him last year will be to discredit you – at the least. And now you tell me he has an ally inside this very building. He may well try and kill you . . .'

'I don't think he'd go that far. The news is Gorbachev wants a period of quiet – while he packs the Politburo with his own supporters. Killing me would create a storm.'

In that assumption Tweed could not have been more wrong.

Four

'Sit down, Lysenko. How is your plan progressing?'

It was typical of Mikhail Gorbachev that he kept the question terse and came straight to the point. The master of the Soviet Union sat in a large chair at the head of the long oblong-shaped table in his office inside the Kremlin, the section which tourists never see, an old, four-storey building deep inside the ancient fortress.

Dressed smartly in a dark grey, two-piece business suit, he

shifted his bulk restlessly, his large hands playing with a pencil. His whole personality exuded an aura of physical and mental energy as he studied the GRU general.

'I have just arrived from Leipzig with the latest news . . .'

'I know that. What *is* the latest news?'

'The trap to lure Tweed to West Germany has been sprung. A close associate of Tweed's, Ian Fergusson, took the bait. He arrived in Hamburg when he heard a Polish refugee had urgent news . . .'

Lysenko, in his sixties, stockily-built and with a slab-like face, kept his explanation as short as possible. The General Secretary had a short fuse where wafflers were concerned.

'Erwin Munzel, the East German executioner, killed him – made it look like an accident. Tweed won't accept that . . .'

'You've left a bit out. Who is this Polish refugee? And did Fergusson meet him before he had his accident?'

'Yes, he did. The refugee is Ziggy Palewska, a piece of rubbish. He lives off providing information to whoever will pay for it . . .'

'And where does he get information from?'

'Other refugees he's friendly with. As you know, Schleswig-Holstein, the part of Germany closest to Denmark, is crammed with refugees who fled from East Prussia and other places after the Great Patriotic War . . .'

'I know that. Did Fergusson meet him?'

'Yes. Munzel organized the permanent accident shortly after Fergusson had left Palewska's place in Hamburg.'

'This Munzel . . .'

'Erwin Munzel, General Secretary . . .'

'I know the name. His father was a Nazi, an SS General?'

'That is so . . .' Not for the first time Lysenko marvelled at the remarkable range of Gorbachev's detailed knowledge. He wanted to know everything – about everybody. Not a comfortable feeling – but Gorbachev was not a comfortable man to sit down with. Lysenko felt the moisture growing on the palms of his hands.

'And this professional assassin, Erwin Munzel. Also a bit of a Nazi, I hear.'

'He is one of us though . . .'

'No German is one of us.' Gorbachev's expression froze.

29

'But if we can point them the other way – against the West, so be it. An expert on accidents, our lackey, Munzel?'

'He's quite brilliant.'

'He had better be when he deals with this Tweed. The new policy is apparent – I emphasize *apparent* – arm's-length friendship with the Americans while Reagan is president. After that, we'll get someone softer. No American president in my time will be as tough and realistic as Reagan. In the meantime, no serious incidents to destroy the illusion.'

'The death of Tweed will look like an accident,' Lysenko assured his chief. 'But it is essential to our plan. Only Tweed could detect the major operation under way to demoralize Britain – and maybe even defeat all our efforts.'

'Then he must go . . .' Gorbachev paused and Lysenko pushed back his chair. 'Keep your backside in that chair, I'm not finished,' Gorbachev growled. 'Is Balkan still in place? It should make your job easier – knowing what Tweed is doing almost before he knows himself.'

'Balkan is the best agent we've ever had. We can't miss so long as he is in London. Plus his other function.' Lysenko waxed enthusiastic. 'Balkan is the most audacious manœuvre we have ever pulled off. Tweed would go berserk if he discovered the truth. He would never believe it possible . . .'

'Time you flew back to Leipzig to oversee the operation. Is Markus Wolf still useful? He's held that job a long time now.'

Gorbachev was referring to the chief of East German Intelligence based in East Berlin. He watched Lysenko closely, searching for any doubt in tone of voice or expression.

'I cooperate with Wolf very well . . .'

'You *direct* Wolf,' Gorbachev corrected him. 'Never forget he also is another bloody German.' Seated, he waited until Lysenko had almost reached the exit door before he barked out the warning.

'You could get over-confident where Tweed is concerned. I was rereading his file last night. That man is very clever – so, very dangerous. Go!'

Five

'Guy Dalby . . .' Monica again recited her résumé from memory. '. . . head of the Mediterranean sector. The largest of all the territories. Zone of operations includes France, Spain, Italy, Turkey, Portugal and Switzerland. HQ in Bern. Our best linguist. He speaks French, German, Spanish, Italian and Arabic. Also the best admin man. Very methodical. Well organized in his job – and his private life. Penetration areas Libya and the Middle East. Our most well-informed man on terrorists, even outside his own zone. That's it.'

'His private life – so well organized, you said,' Tweed asked.

He sat back again in his chair, eyes almost closed. He had returned from having lunch with Newman at Inigo Jones, a restaurant where the tables were arranged so you could have a private conversation without fear of being overheard. And no one else Tweed knew frequented the place.

'Married to a French girl. Lives in Woking, Surrey. It has the best train service in the country for commuting to London. Also he can drive across country to Heathrow without touching London – which makes it easier for him to slip abroad unnoticed. Has no friends among his neighbours. They think he's an accountant with his own practice. Perfect cover.'

'The perfect man?' Tweed commented with a touch of irony. 'Tell him I'd like a word . . .'

Dalby, dressed in a conventional grey suit, walked in and sat down without a glance at Monica. He whipped the catlick higher up his forehead and waited, leaving Tweed to make the opening move. Typical Dalby tactic.

'Guy, why did you ask what was the motive behind Fergusson's murder during our meeting this morning?'

'Track down the motive and you're close to the people who did the job. Howard is back a day early, by the way. He'll be up to see you soon I think.'

'Thank you for the warning.' Tweed, Monica noted, was at his most ironic. And he already had the information. Newman

31

had told him over lunch that he'd seen Howard aboard the same flight which had brought him from Paris.

'What is the atmosphere like in your sector, Guy?' Tweed continued. 'You'll be on your way back to Bern soon, I take it?'

'By a late flight this afternoon. To Geneva, then on by train to Bern. The atmosphere?' Dalby cocked his head to one side in a bird-like gesture Monica knew so well. 'Very odd. I was going to ask to see you, but you got in first. The other side has withdrawn most of its top agents back behind the Curtain. Something is up . . .'

'A conference with Gorbachev so he can drum into them his new strategy?'

'Perhaps.' Dalby sounded unconvinced. 'The last time they did this it was the prelude to a major operation. I don't like it – I've put all my people on top alert. They're getting in touch with every contact they know. Someone must know something. I'll be glad to get back into the field.'

'And how is your wife?'

Monica bent her head over her file and had trouble keeping a straight face. A typical Tweed ploy when he was puzzled – to switch the conversation abruptly from one topic to another. 'Going fishing,' he called it.

'Renée has gone back to Paris. We're separated. There's a full report on Howard's desk. I have two men following her . . .'

'I wouldn't worry overmuch. She was thoroughly vetted. I'm sorry to hear it though . . .'

'I'm not. The French have funny habits. She couldn't keep her eyes off other men. At parties. In a restaurant. I tackled her and we had our last flaming row. Packed her bags and off she went. I'll be glad to get back to some real work. Is that all? Can I go now?' Dalby asked perkily.

'Why not?'

Monica waited until they were alone before she spoke. Her voice was full of disapproval.

'I'm not a bit surprised about Renée. I suppose he didn't catch on earlier because he's away so much.'

'And what does that catty remark mean?'

'That she was promiscuous. I saw her twice in London clinging on the arm of a man – a different one each time. You could

32

tell what she was doing with them the way she walked and looked.'

'I'm sure you could. As you know, I'm catching the plane to Hamburg, so we'd better get on. Masterson is last on the list . . .'

'Harry Masterson is fun,' Monica began. For the first time she didn't sound as though she were speaking by rote. She really has a crush on him, Tweed thought as she continued her description.

'Chief of the Balkan sector. Headquarters, Vienna. Zone covers Austria, Yugoslavia and Greece. Operates in the most dangerous penetration areas – Hungary, Roumania, Bulgaria and the Ukraine. Speaks German, Serbo-Croat, Greek and Russian. A gay dog since his divorce – even before it . . .'

No note of disapproval for Masterson, Tweed observed.

'. . . has a succession of girl friends. All of them in this country, all of them British. Very careful not to get involved once he leaves for Vienna. Very popular with his agents – he'll take any risk he asks them to undertake. Has been behind the Iron Curtain seven times before you stopped him. Can hold his drink. At a party I once saw him – he was loaded – walk into the street with an unopened bottle of champagne perched on his head. He walked along the centre white line, arms outstretched like a tightrope walker. All for a bet . . .'

'Your enthusiasm wouldn't be running away with you?'

Monica wouldn't stop. She continued in full flood. 'Lives in a lovely old cottage at Apfield near Chichester. Mixes with the yachting crowd but wouldn't set foot on a boat. Hates them and says so. That's a tribute to his personality. Boaty people are very sensitive about their hobby. He doesn't give a damn. "Bloody boats," I once heard him say at Cowes, "they never stay in one place." They made him a member. Can you believe that?'

'If you say so, Monica. Call him. Let's get it over with. I'm beginning to feel I'm conducting a series of interrogations.'

'Isn't that exactly what you *are* doing?' she asked and picked up the phone.

'The general situation in the Balkans?' Tweed asked and watched Masterson through half-closed eyes.

33

'Bloody boring. Nothing doing. Can't understand it. Never known the roubles go to ground like this before. Something sinister in the wind. I'll damned well dig out what it is . . .'

'Go to ground, you said. What exactly does that indicate?'

'It indicates what I said. All enemy agents have dived into their burrows like a bunch of flaming rabbits. You can walk down the Kärntnerstrasse in Vienna and back up again all day without seeing one suspicious character. That's suspicious in itself. Vienna is the espionage centre of Europe east of Geneva. The place is losing all its character . . .'

'Slow down, Harry. I've got the picture. What does that picture suggest to you?'

'They're preparing something really nasty, of course. Pull out, lull us into a state of spending our time in the bars. Then, bingo! Launch the operation. Always the same technique. Moscow got into a rut years ago. I keep telling you that. So what do I have to do to convince you? Take out an ad in *The Times*?'

'It could be the new leadership assessing the situation . . .'

'Assessing my ass! We'd better brace ourselves, Tweed – and you'd better watch your back on that Hamburg jolly. From what I hear the only big feature recently has been the killing of poor Ian Fergusson. Hamburg is what it's all about. Not that Hugh Grey has caught on yet. Too busy dusting off Howard's chair before he plants his poncy behind in it. God, I'd hate to work under him. Come to think of it, I wouldn't . . .'

'He's got a tricky job,' Tweed pointed out when he could edge in a word. 'That's the sector where you can't tell one German from another – East or West . . .'

'So, why didn't one of his feelers warn him Fergusson was on to a one-way trip? I'd have known if he'd been heading for the Balkans.'

'Which is your way of saying you don't much like each other.'

'I hate the guts he doesn't have . . .'

'On that punch-line maybe we'd better end this chat. You'll never better it,' Tweed assured him.

'You watch your back!'

Masterson, his ruddy complexion flushed beneath the coal-black hair, waved a minatory finger at Tweed, gave Monica his quick salute and was gone. Through the door without opening it was Tweed's impression.

'Isn't he marvellous?' Monica cooed, her own face flushed a pinkish tinge.

'I believe that bit about walking the white line with the champagne bottle now,' Tweed told her. 'So, we've seen the lot. Any clue as to which one sent Fergusson into the abyss?'

'Nothing I spotted. Did I miss something?'

The door opened again and Masterson reappeared. He closed it and stood staring at Tweed as he spoke.

'I hope you took me seriously. I meant it. I know what I'm talking about. I'm pretty sociable – and that party at Grey's farm . . .' He stopped. 'Oh, hell, you've had a bellyful of me.'

Monica made a fuss about being busy when Masterson had left the room for the second time. Tweed watched her as she moved files around and then reached for the phone.

'Hold that call,' he said. 'Now, tell me what all that was about. Some party at Grey's farm out on the Wash. What party?'

'It was a couple of years ago. July 14.' She looked embarrassed but Tweed waited, compelling her to go on. 'Grey had a birthday party. Paula acted as hostess – his wife had pushed off and he and Paula were living together . . .'

'Get to the point. Who were the guests?'

'The four men who are now sector chiefs. Masterson, Dalby and Lindemann. It was Grey's birthday. He asked them all to come for dinner. They happened to be on leave at the same time. So, it seemed an ideal opportunity.'

She stopped and studied Tweed's expression. He looked amused. 'You're thinking I was one of their main topics of conversation?'

'They might have asked you to join them . . .'

'Why should they? They were all lower down the ladder – men in from the field and in search of relaxation. I'd have put a real damper on their having a free-and-easy time. They need something to get the tension out of their systems. How is it you remember the date so well?'

'July 14? Bastille Day.'

'Of course. And all this time you've kept quiet – thinking I'd be offended?'

35

'How was I to know how you'd react? It wasn't a piece of information which affected our work. If it had been, I'd have let you know soon enough.'

'I'm sure you would. Now, let me have the tickets for Hamburg, foreign currency, travellers' cheques, etc.' As she took a folder from a locked drawer he threw the question at her.

'During my recent interviews, did you notice any common link?'

'They've all worked in the field. None of them are desk types who haven't a clue as to what it's all about . . .'

'True. Go on.'

'That's it,' Monica said, her brow crinkled.

'They all have just one European language in common which they all speak fluently. German.'

'Is that significant?'

'How do I know what is significant? It's early days yet . . .'

The phone rang, Monica answered and spoke briefly, then pulled a wry face.

'Company?'

'Yes. Your favourite person. Howard is on his way up now.'

'I really wouldn't have thought this Hamburg affair required your august presence,' Howard pontificated in his most lordly manner. 'Let Hugh Grey handle it – after all, the incident did occur in his sector.'

'The incident, as you call it, involved the death of one of my top men. A second-hand view isn't good enough.'

'I'd hardly call Hugh second-hand. You make him sound like a used car.' Howard chuckled and glanced at Monica expecting a tribute to his wit.

'I'm catching a Lufthansa flight. It's all arranged. And the PM has sanctioned the trip . . .'

'Oh, my God!' Howard clapped a theatrical hand to his domed forehead. 'Not another of her bloody directives, I trust?'

'Your trust is misplaced.' Tweed sat back in his chair and stared bleakly at his chief. 'And I suspect Fergusson was on to something big – otherwise, why murder him?'

'Don't let's over-dramatize, old boy.' Howard, six foot tall, wearing a new made-to-measure chalk-stripe suit, perched his behind on the arm of an easy chair. 'We don't know that for sure – from what Hugh has just told me . . .'

'Hugh knows damn-all. I'm keeping the wraps on this one.'

'Hugh's a good chap,' Howard protested. 'And I heard in Paris from Pierre Loriot the quiet streets are empty. The Russian laddies have all gone home – doubtless to listen to Uncle Mikhail and make their number with him.'

'Pierre said that?' Tweed leaned forward, intrigued by Howard's news. The reference to 'quiet streets' was parlance for the Soviet embassies located in discreet areas. 'That was his report,' Tweed pressed. 'What was his opinion?'

'There has to be a difference?' Howard studied his manicured nails, his plump face smug.

'Well, was there? You tell me.'

'I suppose you could say there was a subtle shade of difference. Pierre did say the pregnant silence – his phrase – worried him. Just his opinion though. Pierre isn't happy without something to worry about. Keeps him late at the office – away from that awful wife in Passy. He'd read the telephone directory rather than go home before ten . . .'

And so would you, matey, Tweed thought, but didn't say so. It was well-known Howard's relations with his rich wife, Cynthia, had become distant. 'Clear out of sight,' was Monica's comment.

'If there's nothing else . . .' Tweed began.

'Think that's all.' Howard stood erect, straightening his tie. 'Sorry about Fergusson, and all that. Goes with the territory, of course . . .'

'Not with my territory,' Tweed shot back as Howard strolled to the door and left the room. He looked at Monica. 'Hamburg next stop . . .'

Six

July 10 1985. Flight LH 041 arrived at Hamburg dead on time at 1255 hours. Tweed peered from his first-class seat through the window as the machine descended through a grey vapour.

37

The greyness dissolved, Germany spread out a few hundred feet below.

He studied the jigsaw of cultivated fields and plantations of firs and pines. Narrow sandy tracks led inside the woodlands from the outside world. Peninsulas of housing estates poked into the fields, then the countryside was inundated by the urban tide.

More trees as the plane dropped lower. He remembered this approach to Hamburg, one of his favourite German cities. A stranger would never realize he was passing over the city. In the seat behind him Newman was not peering out of the window. His eyes were flickering over the other passengers, searching for anyone taking an interest in Tweed. They landed.

Tweed was the first passenger to walk down the mobile staircase, Newman the third. They had travelled from Heathrow as though they had never met. Tweed was standing by the carousel, waiting for his two cases, when Chief Inspector Otto Kuhlmann of the Federal Police joined him.

'Got a light?' Kuhlmann asked in German, holding his cigar.

'I think I can accommodate you,' Tweed replied in the same language. He lowered his voice as he flicked on the lighter and the German bent forward. 'I have two cases, as you suggested over the phone . . .'

'Point me to the first one. I'll take that.'

When the first case appeared Kuhlmann leaned forward and heaved it off the moving belt. He then had trouble relighting his cigar with Tweed's lighter. The second case appeared, Tweed grabbed it, accepted the lighter from Kuhlmann and they walked away together from the crowd gathered round the carousel.

Anyone watching would have assumed the two men had travelled together on Flight LH 041 from Heathrow. Outside the reception hall Kuhlmann led the way to an unmarked police Audi, they both climbed into the back and the driver left the airport.

'That little manœuvre may have covered your arrival,' the German commented as they drove along tree-lined streets. Entering Hamburg was like driving into the country.

'*May* is the operative word. Where are we going first? I have a reservation at the Four Seasons . . .'

'Living high?'

'The best hotel is the last place the opposition will expect to find me. And I have an escort following in a cab. Robert Newman, the foreign correspondent.'

Tweed produced a photo of Newman from his wallet which Kuhlmann hardly glanced at. He took a deep drag at his cigar and shook his head.

'I'd have recognized Newman without a picture. I saw him back at the carousel. I was going to check his presence with you. If it's OK by you the first stop is the hospital where Fergusson was taken to and died. The doctor may be able to tell you something. Anyway, you're safe in Hamburg . . .'

'Let's just say I'm in Hamburg.'

The flight had still been in mid-air when the call to an apartment block in Altona, a Hamburg suburb, came through from London. The caller – from a booth inside the Leicester Square Post Office, which is actually off Charing Cross Road – spoke in German.

'Tweed is on his way. Flight LH 041, departed Heathrow 1120 hours, arrives Hamburg 1255 your time. Have you got that?'

'Understood. He'll be met at the airport. We have good time. Thank you for calling. Now we can have a limo waiting.'

Martin Vollmer, who occupied the Altona apartment, broke the connection, waited a moment, then dialled a number in Flensburg, Schleswig-Holstein, on the Danish border.

'Tweed is coming . . .'

The wires continued to hum through a complex communication system across North Germany. Like a tom-tom beat the same message was repeated again and again. 'Tweed is coming . . . *Tweed is coming* . . . TWEED IS COMING . . .'

By the time the flight had crossed the European coastline and LH 041 was over the mainland the phone rang in the bedroom of Erwin Munzel at the Hotel Movenpick, Lübeck. The blond giant had sat by the instrument for over an hour. He snatched up the receiver.

'Tweed is coming . . .'

The brief conversation ended, Munzel, registered under the name of Kurt Franck, left the hotel immediately and walked

39

on to the main part of Lübeck situated on an island encircled by the river Trave. It was a hot day, the air was torrid as he boarded a bus for Eichholz.

Wearing jeans and a polo-necked cashmere sweater, he checked his watch as the bus left the island, drove over a bridge and headed east through a dull suburban district of four-storey apartment blocks.

In less than ten minutes he got off at the terminus. He had reached the border with East Germany – the no-man's-land which is a death-trap. A coach-load of American tourists escorted by the usual talkative guide stood staring east with all the fascination of ghouls observing a traffic accident.

Munzel pushed his way through to the front and gazed at the distant watch-tower. He checked his watch again and waited until it was 1.30 p.m. precisely. Then he pulled a red-coloured handkerchief from his pocket and slowly wiped the sweat off his high forehead. He repeated the gesture three times.

Inside the watch-tower one of the three guards stared through a pair of high-powered binoculars. He felt he could reach out and touch Munzel's forehead. Putting down the binoculars on a table he reached for the phone.

'That's Munzel reporting in,' he remarked to his companions.

The wires began humming in the DDR – the German Democratic Republic. East Germany. Within minutes, General Lysenko, seated at a desk next to Markus Wolf in the basement of a building in the centre of Leipzig picked up the phone when it rang.

He listened, said 'yes' or 'no' several times, then replaced the instrument. Typically, he kept the chief of East German Intelligence in suspense while he lit a cigarette fitted with a cardboard holder.

Markus Wolf, in his sixties, sat like a graven image, his horn-rimmed glasses perched on his prominent nose. Wolf had the patience of a cat playing with a trapped mouse.

'Tweed is coming . . .' Lysenko told him eventually.

'So, we wait . . .'

'He has taken the bait. He has arrived in Hamburg. Soon we'll hear he has arrived in Lübeck.'

'After a while, possibly. I know Tweed. He is the most cautious and wary counter-espionage chief in the whole of the West. Do not expect too much . . .'

'I expect Munzel to kill him.'

'Probably. Let us be patient. We must be even more patient than Tweed. The one who wins this duel will be the man with the greatest stamina . . .'

'You are a pessimist . . .'

'No, just a realist.'

The first man to receive the news from the phone box inside the Leicester Square Post Office, Martin Vollmer, waiting in his apartment at Altona, had made one further phone call after contacting Flensburg. Which is why a taxi with its *Frei* light doused had followed the unmarked police car from the airport to the hospital.

He parked at some distance from the Audi as Kuhlmann climbed out, followed by Tweed. He watched them enter the hospital and settled back to wait further developments. He was so intent on observing what happened beyond his windscreen that he omitted to check his rear view mirror.

Leaving the airport building, carrying his case, Newman at once noticed something odd. His whole experience as a foreign correspondent had trained him to spot the out-of-the-ordinary. He saw the Audi transporting Tweed turn out of the airport. Looking for a cab he also saw the taxi lacking the *Frei* sign illumination.

The odd thing was the vehicle was occupied by the driver alone. The coincidence was that this driver decided to leave the airport without a fare at the precise moment the Audi drove off.

Getting inside the next waiting cab, he handed the driver a ten-deutschmark note. 'That's your tip,' he said in German. 'And I may add a bonus. Just follow that black Audi, please. You'll be helping the Drug Squad,' he added.

Newman kept a close eye on the Audi. This action automatically made him observe the cab which appeared to be following it. As they turned into the kerb by the hospital Newman warned his driver to stop immediately. This placed his vehicle a dozen metres behind the other cab now parked by the kerb.

41

He paid off his driver, stooped to pick up his case and noted the registration number of the waiting cab. Then he walked into the hospital. Immediately his nostrils were assailed by the aroma of hygienic cleansing liquids. Newman detested all things medical. Still, he consoled himself as he entered the reception hall, it was in the line of duty. Damnit!

'I can have that cab driver picked up,' Kuhlmann suggested when Newman finished his brief report. 'We'll grill the hell out of him . . .'

'If I might make a suggestion,' Tweed intervened. 'Don't alert him. Have him followed, identified – if possible. But on no account should he be intercepted.'

'You're blown,' Kuhlmann warned. 'That driver could be our only lead to who organized the tracker – and from the airport. That is very serious. After the precautions we took. I'm telling you.'

Kuhlmann was short, broad-shouldered, had a large head and a wide mouth, his thick lips clamped on his cigar which was unlit. Dark-haired, his eyebrows were thick and his manner and speech suggested a very tough character. In his forties, Newman estimated.

'Not to worry,' Tweed said. 'And let's play it my way. Low profile. Incidentally, normally this would be a case for the local police. How was it they brought you in?' Tweed turned to Newman. 'Chief Inspector Kuhlmann is from the Federal Police in Wiesbaden.'

'Because they have a bright police chief here,' Kuhlmann told them. 'Name on the deceased's passport rang a bell. He put it through the computer at Cologne. Fergusson came up as one of your people. So, I phoned you. Which is why I'm here, why you are here. This case could have international implications . . .'

'Then the BND could get involved.' Tweed sounded bothered as he referred to the German counter-intelligence HQ at Pullach just south of Munich. 'Low profile,' he repeated.

'Let's go see the doctor who attended Fergusson,' Kuhlmann said impatiently. As they walked down a clinically spotless corridor he continued explaining. 'Two uniformed policemen on night patrol saw Fergusson's body floating up against the

42

lock-gates leading from the Binnenalster to the Elbe. Hauled him out with a boat-hook, found he was still alive, rushed him to this hospital. He died an hour later . . .'

'How did he come to get into the water?' Newman asked.

'Blow on the side of the skull. Could have slipped, caught his head on the stone wall before he hit the water, so they say. Accidental death would have been the verdict.' Kuhlmann chewed at his cigar, unhappy that he couldn't light up inside the hospital. 'Accidental death,' he repeated. 'Except your people don't have accidents. Here's the doctor's office. Schnell is his name. Speaks good English. Take your choice of language.'

Dr Schnell, a small, plump-faced man, wearing a white coat, rose from behind his desk and Kuhlmann made brief introductions, then launched straight into his interrogation.

'How did Ian Fergusson die?'

'He stopped breathing . . .'

'That's not funny. Tweed here was a close friend of his.'

'I had no intention of treating this tragedy humorously, Mr Tweed. But it's up to the pathologist to answer that question. Fergusson's body has been transferred to the morgue.'

'I quite understand.' Tweed paused, glancing at a dark haired nurse who stood behind Schnell, an attractive girl in her late twenties. 'Who was present when he was close to death?'

'Myself and Sister Bruns. That is why she is here.'

'He was still alive when he was brought in, I gather. Did he say anything? No matter how unimportant it might seem, I need to know everything – if he spoke.'

'Well, yes he did.' Schnell picked up a pencil and turned it slowly between sensitive fingers. 'It made little sense to either of us, I'm afraid . . .'

'He spoke in English or German?'

Tweed's gaze encompassed both Schnell and Sister Bruns who was watching him closely. He had the strong impression the girl wanted to speak but was inhibited by Schnell's presence.

'In English – which we both understand. He was in a bad way – the blow on the side of the head plus being half-drowned when the two policemen dragged him out. So he was pretty incoherent. I may not even have heard correctly . . .'

'Try and tell me,' Tweed coaxed.

'He had trouble getting the two words out which he repeated – if, I emphasize, I really did understand. First he said "Berlin". He repeated the name of the city twice. Then he repeated a man's name – "Hans" – and that, I'm afraid, is all he said . . .'

'You agree?' Tweed turned to Bruns and stared hard at her as she shook her head. 'There *was* something else?'

She took a deep breath. Beneath her uniform her breasts heaved. 'He was trying to say something *before* "Berlin". I'm quite sure of it . . .'

'Just having trouble speaking at all,' Schnell objected.

'No!' Bruns was vehement, holding Tweed's gaze. 'He said the word three times – and three times he tried to say something before it. Then when he said "Hans" he tried to say something else. After "Hans". Again it happened three times. I could not possibly be mistaken . . .'

'Really?' Schnell was ironic.

'I am quite sure of what I say. My hearing is very acute and I was watching him closely. Believe me, Mr Tweed, I am right.'

'I believe you,' said Tweed.

At the morgue Tweed stared down at the white sheet covering the body of a man lying on the dissecting table. Kuhlmann had introduced Martin Kosel, the pathologist, an ascetic-looking man in his fifties who might have been displaying furniture for sale. Kosel pulled back the sheet and exposed the head and neck.

'That's Ian Fergusson,' said Tweed. 'He can't have been in the water long . . .'

'I couldn't comment before I've completed my examination,' Kosel replied, covering the corpse with the sheet again.

'But you will,' Kuhlmann growled. He produced a folder, shoved it under the pathologist's nose. 'Federal Police. We need an educated guess. Now. Assuming you are educated . . .'

'I resent that . . .'

'Noted for the record. The pathologist showed resentment. Now, let's get to it. When we checked his personal effects his passport was hardly damp . . .'

'It was inside the breast pocket of his jacket,' Kosel pointed out. 'And he was wearing a raincoat buttoned to the neck . . .'

'A lightweight raincoat. His wallet, tucked inside his other

44

breast pocket wasn't even moist. And the police patrol dragged him out when he was half-submerged under the water. I'd say he was found within five minutes of being dumped into that outlet from the Binnenalster. They came as close as that to catching the killer.'

'Killer?' Kosel protested. 'I haven't established the cause of death . . .'

'You think he walked off the edge for an early morning swim? He was found floating by the lock-gates not five minutes' walk from the Jungfernstieg landing-stage on the Binnenalster. That whole area is well-lit by street lamps . . .'

'Maybe he was drunk . . .'

'Fergusson never touched alcohol,' Tweed remarked mildly.

'So cancel that one,' Kuhlmann said.

'The corpse smells strongly of alcohol – whisky I would say.'

'So, we can make some educated guesses?' Kuhlmann grasped Kosel by the arm and smiled grimly. 'You're doing fine. Keep it up. Now, let's come to the blow on the side of the head.'

'Encrusted with dried blood. He could have hit his skull on the stone wall when he went in.'

'Sure!' Kuhlmann waved his cigar like a conductor's baton. 'He's crossing the bridge near the lock-gates. He climbs over the rail, then dives head first for the wall. Is that really what you're saying? That it is even physically possible?'

'It would seem unlikely . . .'

Newman intervened. 'He was a first-rate swimmer, too. If he had fallen in he'd have found a way out.'

'That information is useful,' Kosel responded primly.

'Your unofficial opinion would be also useful,' Kuhlmann pressed. 'Other people's lives may be at stake. Or do you want this place to be standing room only?'

'I can't be pressured . . .'

'Try me,' Kuhlmann challenged. 'We can take what's lying under that sheet away from you – bring someone in from Wiesbaden.'

'If he never drank . . .' Kosel paused. He frowned as he looked at Tweed. 'It is beginning to seem someone made it look like an accident. The front of his clothes was soused with alcohol . . .'

45

'That's it,' said Kuhlmann. 'Take this card, keep it to yourself. Send your report to that address when you've done what you have to do.'

'Wiesbaden? It must be submitted to the Hamburg chief of police . . .'

'Hans Lenze, who is a close friend of mine, who knows I'm here, who told me about you. Do it any way you damn well wish – but that report goes to Wiesbaden. Now, let's get out of here and go look for fresh air.'

Seven

'Hans!' Newman waved his hand in a gesture of disgust. 'There must be a million men with that name in Germany . . .'

'If that is what Fergusson really said,' Tweed replied and wandered over to the window, then stood there, sipping his glass of cognac. He drank rarely but the sight of Ian Fergusson lying in the morgue had shaken him.

Vier Jahreszeiten. The Four Seasons Hotel. One of the finest hostelries in all Germany. They were ensconced inside Room 412, Tweed's room, almost the size of a small de-luxe apartment. The view from the window was magnificent. The sun was shining in the late afternoon, reflecting with a glitter off the lake, the Binnenalster, beyond the road running below the window.

Tweed stared out over a line of trees in full foliage – a room on the fourth floor gave a clear view of the water where white single deck passenger craft cruised towards the landing-stage at the end of the lake. Little more than a few metres from where Fergusson's body had been found in the water at five in the morning.

'What else could he have meant?' Newman asked and finished off his cognac. It gave off a better aroma than bloody hospitals and all things medical he disliked so much.

'That could be the key to the mystery,' Tweed replied. 'Maybe we shall know more tonight when we visit St Pauli . . .'

'The Reeperbahn? Anything can happen there after dark. I'll stick close to you. No argument.'

'Agreed.' Tweed had a dreamy look as he continued to watch the fussy water-buses plying back and forth. 'Fergusson came here to see Ziggy Palewska. I think he saw him the night he was killed.'

'What makes you think so? And who is this Ziggy person?'

'Because of this.' Tweed produced a small black notebook, one of the personal effects handed to him at the morgue. It had been found inside Fergusson's buttoned back trouser pocket and its pages were crinkled from exposure to water. He prised apart two pages and showed them to Newman. The notation, written in small neat script, was brief.

Ziggy. Berlin. Hotel Jensen.

'So, Ziggy told him something about the Hotel Jensen in Berlin. I've never heard of it.'

'Neither have I. And you asked about Ziggy. His father came from Poland. He married a girl from East Prussia – that is, Ziggy's mother. Both parents are dead. Near the end of the war they fled from Königsberg – as it was called then – with Ziggy who was only ten years old. They ended up in Schleswig-Holstein, the German province – or *Land* – which was flooded with refugees. That fact has dominated Ziggy's life – not always for the best.'

'Which means?'

'The positive side – from my point of view – is he has always kept in touch with the underground network which links the refugees. He can be an invaluable source of information. But he is very tricky. Thinks only of money. He'll work for anyone who pays – sometimes for both sides at the same time.'

'Sounds like a one-way ticket to eternity . . .'

'Oh yes, he walks a tightrope. So far with great cunning and skill. The time may come when he falls off . . .'

'That could be a long drop,' Newman commented.

'The final drop, I fear. Tonight I intend to put more pressure on him than I've ever done before. He must know something.'

'And the negative side?'

'He's mixed up in various squalid activities. Porno movies.

47

Even drug-trafficking. Swears he only trades in marijuana – but I have my doubts.'

'A piece of the world's flotsam. Floating on the surface. Like scum? The Reeperbahn sounds just his cup of tea. Kuhlmann said he'd have a gun for me when we meet later . . .'

'I don't like guns. I don't know why I agreed when Kuhlmann made the suggestion on the phone to London. On the other hand . . .'

'You don't know what you're walking into. Maybe Kuhlmann does. Has he really told us everything?'

'I doubt it. Likes to hold something back. As bad as me,' Tweed remarked, and Newman knew the cognac was working. It was the first time since he'd returned from Paris that Tweed had cracked anything approaching a joke. 'Let's go for a walk. I always find when I get abroad I have to force myself out of a hotel. It's too easy to act the hermit . . .'

Newman had the room next to Tweed's. He made the remark as they went down in the elevator.

'It's in a hotel like this I'm glad I made all that money out of my bestseller, *Kruger: The Computer That Failed*. A foreign correspondent can work a whole career and never see money like that. I really got lucky . . .'

In the reception hall Tweed paused to examine the tapestries on the walls, the fine long-case clocks adorning the place, the superb rugs laid on the floor. They walked out of the entrance, turned right along the Neuer Jungfernstieg, the tree-lined promenade by the lake.

'It really is the most beautiful city,' Tweed commented. 'Look back at that colonnade which runs behind the hotel. We cross here.'

'We're going somewhere definite?'

'My feet seem to be heading in one direction – towards the Rathaus . . .'

In the pure warmth of a sun shining out of clear skies the two men strolled past the end of the lake, past the landing-stage where tourists queued for giant ice-cream cones. A holiday atmosphere, thought Tweed, and Ian Fergusson lying in the morgue.

They turned down the Alsterarkaden, an arcaded walk alongside a canal-like stretch of water leading from the lake.

Fashionably-dressed women stood gazing into high quality shops. Tweed crossed half-way over the bridge and stopped in the middle, looking down.

'It's such a clean city,' he observed.

'Show me,' the growly voice behind them said, 'show me how any man could dive in there at five in the morning and hit the side of his head on the wall. He'd have to be a bloody acrobat . . .'

It was Kuhlmann, of course. Newman had an idea they'd better get used to the Federal policeman surprising them. He stood gazing into the water, holding a brief-case in his right hand.

'These goddamn pathologists,' Kuhlmann continued. 'If they'd stop playing God for a while, get out in the fresh air, even take a look at the scene of the crime. Then they might understand what this business is all about. And in the fresh air you can smoke a cigar. Tweed, it was murder. I don't have to wait for that dumbo's report. Even you can see that, Newman.'

'What's it like round here at five in the morning?' the Englishman asked.

'Quiet as the grave – which is why Fergusson found his grave within feet of where you stand. I checked back with the two patrolmen who hauled him out. Jogged their memories a little. A yellow BMW drove across that bridge over there minutes before they walked down here. And, Newman, I have your gun inside this brief-case. Plus a hip holster. 7.65 mm. Luger. You can handle it?'

'I've practised with it, yes . . .'

'Get close to the border and you may get plenty for real . . .'

'And why,' Tweed enquired over his shoulder, 'should we find ourselves near the border, Otto?'

'You never can tell.' Kuhlmann shrugged. 'You're exactly thirty miles away from a Soviet tank battalion now . . .'

'And the Luger,' Newman enquired. 'Do I have a permit?'

'Take this.' Kuhlmann produced a folded sheet from his jacket pocket. 'You get into a shoot-out, show this to the state police. They won't like it but they'll check with Wiesbaden – confirmation will come back fast.'

'Which will keep me out of gaol?'

'No guarantee.' Kuhlmann grinned, a wide grin showing

49

all his teeth. 'Depends who you shoot, the where and the when . . .'

'You're such a comfort . . .'

'Who knows? I'll probably be pretty close to you. Use your own judgement. Your reputation is good. How else do you protect our friend? Now, if you've finished staring at that stretch of water, let's get back to the Four Seasons. I'll hand over the weapon – with ammo – in your hotel room.'

They took a cab to the St Pauli district from a stand near the Jungfernstieg landing-stage at ten at night. Tweed had told Newman he didn't want the cab driver to be able to say they had come from the Four Seasons.

'And things don't warm up in Ziggy's place till getting on for midnight. If my timing is right, he'll be there, but not yet involved in his nefarious enterprises . . .'

The taxi cruised along the Reeperbahn, the neon of the nightclubs a weird glow in gathering dusk, then turned right into the side streets. Newman caught sight of a street sign which read Seiler-strasse, and then lost all sense of direction.

They alighted in little more than a wide alley, Tweed paid off the driver, and led the way with a confident tread. How he was able to find the place Newman could never fathom. In the late afternoon, at Tweed's suggestion, Newman had gone shopping, purchasing German clothes – shirt, tie, sports jacket, slacks, and a pair of socks and shoes.

'A couple of Englishmen might be too much for Ziggy,' Tweed had explained. 'If what I suspect happened, I will have a hard time getting him to talk . . .'

At that early hour – for the Reeperbahn – the alley was almost empty. A few sailors from a Spanish ship, resplendent in walking out uniform, strolled aimlessly, looking for trouble without too much certainty as to what brand of trouble they were interested in.

Followed by Newman, Tweed mounted two worn stone steps, pushed open an ancient wooden door and walked into a blast of Louis Armstrong trumpeting *On the Sunny Side of the Street.* Sleazy nightspot, Newman assumed, and then found he was wrong. He stared in amazement.

A powerful smell of oil and resin assailed his nostrils. He

appeared to have entered a ship's chandler's office. Tackle of all types for ships was stacked round the walls of the cellar-like room. The place was lit dimly by oil-lamps and coils of rope like snakes in the gloom hung from the cracked ceiling.

The music, Louis trumpeting endlessly on, came from various hi-fi speakers slung at crooked angles from the walls. Ziggy Palewska sat on a three-legged stool behind a bare wooden table, the surface smeared with a variety of dirt. He looked up and his face froze when he saw Tweed.

'Ian Fergusson is dead,' Tweed said, drawing up a ramshackle chair to face the Polc across the table. 'He came here, talked with you, left – and was murdered. I'm not pleased, Ziggy, so don't, please, waste my time . . .'

'I don't know any Ian Fergusson.' He looked at Newman. 'I have not seen this man before, Mr Tweed.'

Ziggy Palewska was short in stature. He made up for his lack of height by his width. Both facially and bodily he reminded Newman of a monkey. Impossible to guess his age. His brown hair was thinning over his rounded skull. His skin was worn and gnarled, like that of a veteran seaman. His eyes shifted rapidly from one visitor to another. He spoke German with an atrocious Polish accent.

'I see.' Tweed tapped his fingers on the table. 'This is going to be difficult – maybe dangerous – for you. I don't like losing one of my finest operatives. I don't like that at all. I thought you would be able to help me by telling me how he spent his last hours on earth. I know he visited you. So you have already lied to me. And you pronounced his name rather well – for an English name you claim not to know. And my friend is Heinz. The trouble with Heinz is he has a short fuse. I'll ask you once more – tell me what you told Fergusson when he came to see you . . .'

'The name means nothing. I'm a ship's chandler . . .'

'And I'm Chancellor of Germany,' Newman interjected.

'That's rude . . .'

Tweed surprised Newman by the swiftness and ruthlessness of his tactics. Normally he showed infinite patience in coaxing information from a suspect. He looked quickly at Newman.

'Heinz, can we turn up Louis Armstrong louder? A wonder with the trumpet, Mr Armstrong.'

Newman, looking very German, trod heavily towards the control panel for the hi-fi. He turned up the volume even louder. The oil lamps flickered, the lamps wobbled with the crescendo of vibration, the dark shadows across the ceiling moved and assumed new shapes. Newman casually extracted the Luger, leaned against a free space of wall and studied the weapon, pointing it at the roof.

'Oh, Christ! You wouldn't . . .'

Ziggy half-rose from his stool. Tweed slapped the flat of his hand on the bare wooden table top. A sound like a pistol shot.

'Sit down. That's better. We wouldn't what? What time did Ian Fergusson arrive here?'

'About three in the morning. After . . .' He stopped in mid-sentence.

'After you had completed various illegal transactions,' Tweed said amiably. 'Like a bit of trafficking in drugs. Who told you what to say to Fergusson?' He leaned over the table as he spoke. 'Start talking. Now!'

'The blond giant . . .' Again Ziggy stopped in mid-air.

'Oh, I see.' Tweed looked at Newman. 'The blond giant is back in the picture.'

'You know the bastard?' Ziggy asked.

'What name does he use with you?'

'Schmidt.'

Newman laughed unpleasantly. 'Schmidt. Of course.'

'I swear to you he did.' Ziggy was suddenly becoming voluble and the words poured out. 'I had never seen him before. He was a big brute. He threatened me if I didn't tell Fergusson what he told me to say to him . . .'

'How did he threaten you? Quickly,' Tweed rapped out.

'He was going to burn me.' He pointed to a corner. 'See those two drums of petrol? He brought them here. He said if I didn't do what he said he'd empty them, lock me in and throw a lighted match inside. He knew there was no other way out except for the front door. He must have checked the place out before he came to see me. He left those drums to remind me of what would happen. He said it would look like an accident. These slums burn down all the time, he said. He called my place a slum . . .'

'I wonder why?' Newman shouted.

The hi-fi sound – rather cracked – filled the place with its crescendo. Tweed looked at the drums. Beyond them an oil lamp shivered as the glass lamp rattled against the brass holder. It was a nightmare Newman had created. The table shook under his hand. Like being aboard a ship in a rough sea.

'Turn it down, for God's sake,' Tweed called out. He waited until he could speak in a normal voice. 'When did this Schmidt call on you?'

'A few hours before Fergusson arrived. He knew he was coming. I had to tell Fergusson – after getting money from him to make it convincing – about Dr Berlin in Lübeck. That he was the man who knew about the East German network in the Federal Republic. That there was a man at the Hotel Jensen in Lübeck who could tell him more. But I didn't know the man's name – only that he is at the Hotel Jensen. That was all.' Some of his normal cockiness came back as Tweed watched him. 'How much is that worth? A good few hundred marks, I'd say . . .'

'He paid you how much?'

'Five hundred . . .' Ziggy stopped once more in mid-sentence. An ashen colour had replaced his normal pallor. Not a man who took long walks, Newman was thinking, still holding the Luger.

'I see.' Tweed kept his tone judicial. 'For five hundred marks. Less than two hundred pounds. You sold Ian Fergusson's life . . .'

'I had no idea . . .'

'Of course you didn't.' Tweed stood up. He leaned over the table close to Ziggy, dressed only in an oil-stained sweater and a pair of stained corduroy slacks. 'You do realize you could be charged by the German police as an accessory to murder?'

'Oh, God, no.' The Pole shrank back from Tweed looming above him. 'I've helped you many times. I can help you again . . .'

'You might just do that. You still have that concealed cine-camera in the back wall inside the cupboard – the one you use to take porno movies? Don't play with me, Ziggy.'

'I do have a camera. Yes.'

'So, if this Schmidt comes back you could arrange with a bit of help to have him photographed?'

'I wouldn't dare.' He cast a sideways glance at the large petrol drums standing against the wall.

'Then you could always stand your trial for complicity in the murder of Ian Fergusson . . .'

'I'll do what I can. Promise. Can I have a bit of money?'

'Your thirty pieces of silver?'

Tweed thrust his hands inside the pockets of his lightweight Burberry. Newman had never seen him look so grim. Ziggy's eyes dropped, he threw his pudgy hands out in a gesture of despair.

'What else could I have done . . .'

'You could have kept your mouth shut about Fergusson coming to see you.'

'The blond was going to burn me . . .'

'And I won't tell you what will happen if you tell anyone I've been here to see you. Now, you can atone a little for what you have done. Describe this blond giant. Nationality?'

'German.' Ziggy hesitated. Tweed continued staring. 'He was a Saxon. Nasty people, the Saxons. I could tell that from the way he spoke German. I think he's from the East. I can't describe him . . .'

'Why not? He was standing in front of you. There's not all that much space in this den of iniquity.'

'I can't!' Ziggy protested. He glanced at Newman who was still leaning against the wall, still holding the Luger. 'He wore a woolly cap – like sailors wear – pulled down over his head, huge tinted glasses and a silk scarf pulled up over his chin . . .'

'Yet you say he was blond,' Newman pointed out.

'A tuft of the blond hair protruded from the back of his cap when he was leaving. He was over six feet tall, built like a house.'

'Age?' Tweed demanded.

'Thirty. Thirty-five. I couldn't say. I'm going by how he spoke. He had a big nose. Clean-shaven. A killer. That I'm sure of. Which is why I was so frightened . . .'

'Stay that way. Stay frightened. Of us,' Tweed advised and turned on his heel without another word.

Eight

At one o'clock in the morning they sat in Tweed's room at the
Four Seasons, drinking black coffee ordered from room service.
A double room, it had a separate sitting area, divided off from
the sleeping area by a graceful arch.

'Did we learn much?' Newman asked. 'And when we came
out of that Pole's slum I noticed Kuhlmann standing in a
doorway alcove, cigar unlit . . .'

'I know. I wonder when he sleeps? Yes, we learnt what poor
Ian Fergusson was trying to tell me. Berlin isn't the city at all
– he's the mysterious Dr Berlin who, I understand, spends a
part of the year in the ancient city of Lübeck on the Baltic.
And that links up with Ian's reference to *Hans*.'

Tweed finished his cup and refilled it. Newman guessed he
was being tantalizing. He liked to keep people guessing.

'All right,' he said, 'tell me how it links up. I'm damned if I
see any connection . . .'

'Not easy.' Tweed settled himself in his arm chair. 'Ian was
trying to say *Hansa* – maybe Hanseatic. In the twelfth century
a number of northern ports formed a protective association –
they reckoned there was strength in alliance. So they formed
the Hanseatic League. Lübeck was a leading member of that
League. Hamburg, too, for that matter. Ian was pointing the
finger at Lübeck, specifically the Hotel Jensen . . .'

'All being information provided via Ziggy by Blondie,' Newman pointed out.

'Yes, but Ian wouldn't have known that. And what do you
know about the recluse, Dr Berlin?'

'As much as anyone, I imagine. I once interviewed him – at
his house on Priwall Island near Lübeck. As a young man of
eighteen he started out in Africa – Kenya, I think. He looked
after the natives, a second Dr Schweitzer up to a point. That's
over twenty years ago . . .'

'And how did he come to settle in Lübeck?'

'That's a weird story. Berlin didn't want to talk about it too

55

much. I did get out of him that he disappeared from Kenya and the locals thought a wild animal had got him. He made treks into the jungle and had a mission station in a remote spot. Eighteen months went by. Everyone assumed he was dead.'

Tweed sat absorbing the data as Newman refilled his own cup. He drank half the strong black liquid and put down the cup.

'You're intriguing me,' Tweed prodded.

'He turned up in Leipzig – behind the Curtain in East Germany. As you mentioned, he's something of a recluse, a secretive man. I was lucky to get that interview, short though it was. He'd been treated at the School for Tropical Diseases for a rare complaint. Recovered, he crossed over to the West and turned his energies to helping refugees in Schleswig-Holstein. His parents had come from what is now East Germany. After he arrived in the West he said he had slipped across the border. The East German lot said he'd been permitted to go where he liked because of his international reputation. End of story . . .'

'Not entirely satisfactory,' Tweed observed. 'What does he look like?'

'Has a black beard. He first grew that in Kenya. A fanatic for work, he couldn't be bothered wasting time shaving each day. And while I was in the Lübeck area I stumbled over something else you might find intriguing.'

'Try me.'

'In summer – at just this time of year – there's a British colony afloat at Travemünde, the port on the Baltic near Lübeck.'

'Afloat? What does that imply?'

Newman grinned. 'Thought that would get you. They live on a collection of yachts and power cruisers. While at Travemünde they moor at the marinas – for the summer, as I said. And where do you think they hail from? Kenya. They're old hands, relics from the British Empire. Summertime, they sail from the Mediterranean to the Baltic to escape the tourist crowd which infests the Med. Wintertime, they sail up through the Kattegat, down the North Sea, through the straits of Gibraltar and back into the Med for the warmth. Mostly to the Greek islands, some berth in Port Said, others get as far as returning to Mombasa in Kenya through the Suez Canal.'

'They sound a curious crowd . . .'

'They are! Straight out of Maugham and Noel Coward. The one place they don't like is Britain.' Newman changed his voice, mimicking a plummy falsetto. "My dear, the place has changed so much you'd never recognize it. Simply awful." And they never pay one penny tax.'

'How do they manage that? I think I can see but . . .'

'They're careful never to be resident in any country for more than a few months. That's why I said afloat. They wander over the oceans – literally ships in the night. Some of them are pally with Dr Berlin . . .'

'Odd that – for a recluse.'

'Not really,' Newman explained. 'They have common roots – so far as they have roots at all. The old days in Kenya. Berlin himself told me that.'

'What does he do for money? How does he live?'

'Well. In a word. Rumour hath it that certain American foundations support his refugee work.'

'I'd like you to check on this Dr Berlin, Bob. Gives you a good reason for what your role is . . .'

'That means going to Lübeck.'

'Which is my next port of call. Literally.' The phone rang. 'Who can that be?' Tweed wondered. 'And at this hour?'

'Ziggy here, Mr Tweed. I'll prove I am trying to help. While you're in Hamburg you should contact Martin Vollmer. He has an apartment in Altona. Here is the address . . .'

Tweed scribbled the instructions on a pad. As he finished he heard a click. Ziggy had gone off the line. 'And that was Ziggy Palewska,' he told Newman. 'I was just going to ask him how he knew I was at the Four Seasons.' He flung down the pencil. 'I find it uncanny. Everyone seems to know where I am, where I'm going to before I get there. Gives me an eerie feeling.'

'Get some sleep,' Newman advised, standing up. 'I'm bushed. In the morning everything will seem different.'

In the morning as they sat at breakfast Hugh Grey walked into the dining-room.

'I didn't ask you to contact me,' Tweed said quietly as Grey sat facing them.

'I came in on the late flight last night. Howard asked me to

57

look you up, see how you were coming along and all that . . .'

'I'm not an invalid,' Tweed said coldly.

'Oh, you know what I mean.' Grey was full of bounce, his pink face flushed with good health. 'After all, this is my territory, so it's the least service I can render, to do the honours and all that. I say, any chance of a pot of coffee? Steaming hot is how I like it. First thing in the morning, need something to get the old motor humming . . .'

'The old motor appears to be humming only too well . . .' Tweed reluctantly summoned a waiter, gave the order. 'And the coffee is always steaming hot here. This is the Four Seasons . . .'

'Not a bad doss-house, I agree . . .'

Oh, Jesus, Tweed muttered under his breath. He forced a trace of a smile. 'You know Robert Newman?'

'I'll say. Old drinking buddies . . .'

'Once,' Newman replied. 'At a bar in Frankfurt. You spilt a double Scotch over my best suit . . .'

'Must have been half-smashed . . .'

'You were all of that.'

'We'd had a long meeting.' Grey turned to Tweed. 'Remember? Eight hours non-stop. Crisis time.'

'I do recall it, yes,' said Tweed and continued eating.

'That was the night that attractive blonde girl was raped and murdered,' Newman remarked. 'They found her floating in the Main the following day. A horrific one, that.'

'Which caused the hold-up when we were leaving Frankfurt Airport,' Tweed said. 'The most thorough interrogation I've ever been subjected to. Made me realize what it's like to be in the other chair. Hugh, talking of Frankfurt, you'll be on your way back there today, I take it?'

'Trying to get rid of me?' Grey smiled broadly. 'You're saying you can cope on your own?'

'I might just manage.'

'Found out anything about Fergusson? Can I be of assistance?'

'No to both questions.'

'Dead end?' Grey poured himself coffee.

'It was for Fergusson . . .'

'You do sound grim this morning. Not at all chipper . . .'

'Under the circumstances, I'm hardly likely to feel chipper, as you put it. And I did ask you about your future movements.'

'Sorry. Wrong mood. Under the circumstances. Frankfurt here I come. This afternoon. I get the feeling I'm *de trop* – as the French so delightfully put it.'

He paused, stared at Tweed expectantly, as though waiting for contradiction. None came.

'Ziggy Palewska was cremated at four this morning.'

Kuhlmann made his announcement standing in Tweed's bedroom, hands clasped behind his back, cigar in the corner of his mouth as he watched both Tweed and Newman who were sitting in arm chairs. The man from Wiesbaden had appeared as soon as Hugh Grey left the dining-room.

He had asked for a quiet word and they had taken him up to the bedroom. Tweed stared back at the German whose expression was bleak. Newman kept his own expression blank and left Tweed to do the talking.

'What the devil does that mean?'

'His place of business – if you can call it that – went up in flames. That heavy wooden door you pushed to get inside to see the Pole last night jams. Palewska was trapped inside. Burnt to one black cinder. An accident, the state police are saying . . .'

'But how could it happen?'

'You tell me. You were there a few hours earlier. Notice anything especially inflammable?'

'There were two drums of petrol in one corner,' Tweed said slowly. 'The room was full of stuff which could catch light – once a fire started. But how would it start?'

'I thought you might tell me. People who live in that stinking alley say he used to turn up the hi-fi full blast. Had a passion for Louis Armstrong, they say. The eye-witness descriptions make a good horror story . . .'

'What kind of a horror story?' Newman asked, feeling he should say something.

'Imagine a fiery inferno. Flames shooting sky-high. And that bloody hi-fi still blasting out Louis on his trumpet. Turned as high as it would go, they said. Any comment?'

'I don't think so,' Tweed replied. 'You tell us . . .'

'Place was lit by oil lamps. So, the vibrations topple one of those oil lamps by the petrol drums. There was a big explosion which was probably one – maybe both – of the petrol drums. People who work nearby told me the oil-lamps alone worried them. When he had that hi-fi going they'd sit talking with Ziggy, watching the damned lamps shivering on top of whatever he'd perched them on. The thing which puzzles me is those petrol drums – a neighbour saw them earlier that evening. Never seen petrol in there before.'

Kuhlmann sat down and waited. He expected a reaction – and he had seen both of them leaving Ziggy's place the same night. Tweed grunted, cleared his throat.

'What are you saying was the cause of this new tragedy?'

'State police call it an accident – subject to the report from the arson brigade. That's the second so-called accident involving you in less than twenty-four hours. First Fergusson, now Mr Ziggy Palewska. Maybe we have a specialist in town.'

'A specialist in what?' Tweed asked.

'Murder made to look like accident. I've already put that *modus operandi* through the computer. I'm waiting for the result.'

'We were there, as you say, earlier in the evening. And I did notice the petrol drums . . .'

Tweed gave Kuhlmann a brief outline of their visit, omitting a great deal. No reference to Lübeck or Dr Berlin. Kuhlmann never took his eyes off him as Tweed spoke in a matter-of-fact tone.

'So,' the German said, 'there was a definite link between Fergusson and Palewska? Why would Fergusson fly to Hamburg to see a man like that?'

'Because he has been one of my contacts over the years. You realize there is a limit as to how much I can tell you?'

'No limit on murder.' Kuhlmann pointed his cigar at Tweed. 'Fergusson was murdered – that I *know*. Fergusson had visited Palewska an hour or two before he's found floating. Now Ziggy goes up in smoke. That's a direct link if ever I met one. Who was that man who joined you for breakfast?' he asked suddenly.

'Hugh Grey. I neither expected or wanted to see him. He's a nuisance . . .'

'His face is familiar. Care to enlighten me a little more on Mr Hugh Grey?'

'Not really.' Which was a pointless answer. Tweed was aware that Kuhlmann would also put Hugh Grey through the computer. But he was playing for time. 'Someone else you might put through that computer of yours,' he suggested. 'A blond giant – over six foot tall. Ziggy told me he was the man who brought those petrol drums. No name, so I don't know where you'd start . . .'

'With a fuller description.'

'I asked Ziggy for that myself. The blond wore a woolly sailor's cap, large tinted glasses and a silk scarf pulled up over his chin. Oh, yes, he had a large nose . . .'

'That's one hell of a description. Tell me everything else Ziggy said about this blond.'

Tweed told him. Kuhlmann took out a well-used notebook, wrote a few words in it, put it back in his pocket and stood up.

'You'll be staying in Hamburg – both of you?'

'Is that a request?'

'A question . . .'

'We shall be staying in North Germany for the moment. More than that I can't be sure of . . .'

'Stay here long enough and one of you could end up having a very nasty accident . . .'

'What is it with Kuhlmann?' Newman asked when they were alone. 'Two major crimes – if he's right – have been committed in Hamburg. Surely the Hamburg state police should be handling the case? And he looked very pleased about something when he left.'

'Normally the Federal Police wouldn't get within a mile of it,' Tweed agreed. 'But from something he said at the morgue he's pally with the local police chief. That helps the Federals a lot in Germany. Also, I suspect he hasn't told us all he knows. And that look of satisfaction stems, I'm sure, from the arrival on the scene of that blond giant who visited Ziggy. *He* thought he smelt of East Germany – I'm sure Kuhlmann has the same idea. That would bring in Wiesbaden overnight. And Otto is one of the best men they have. He's supposed to have the ear

61

of the Chancellor – an open sesame to anywhere in the Federal Republic . . .'

'Before Kuhlmann marched into the dining-room, I was going to ask you, is Hugh Grey as big an idiot as he seems.'

'No. It's a pose which has fooled a lot of people. He finds it useful. Abroad he's a foreigner's idea of a typical Englishman – so they underestimate him. At home, when he's playing politics with Howard, his old boy network act goes down well.'

'A regular stinker, as they used to say. Now what do we turn to next? Visit Martin Vollmer at Altona, that contact Ziggy phoned you about early this morning?'

'I think we'll give Vollmer a miss. I want to get out of Hamburg today, poke around on our own for a bit. This is a dense area . . .'

'Dense?'

'Office jargon for a zone crammed with enemy agents. The Old Guard used to call it a full pack – they played a lot of cards. I suggest we pack our bags, pay the bill quietly and catch the 11.15 Copenhagen Express for Lübeck.'

'The Hotel Jensen?'

'Exactly. And the mysterious Dr Berlin.'

Nine

By train from Hamburg Hauptbahnhof it was a forty-minute run non-stop to Lübeck. In his anxiety to leave the city, Tweed had arranged it so they arrived at the Hauptbahnhof fifteen minutes before the express came in.

They bought single tickets, crossed the high bridge over the tracks and descended the staircase to the platform. To pass the time, Tweed paced up and down the platform with Newman. On the open bridge above them Martin Vollmer stood watching them.

A thin-faced man with pale eyes and small feet, he waited until they had boarded the express – until the express started moving north. He then ran to the nearest phone booth and dialled a number.

In his bedroom at the Hotel Movenpick in Lübeck Erwin Munzel, alias Kurt Franck for registration purposes, again sat by the phone. He snatched up the receiver on the second ring.

'Franck speaking . . .'

'Martin here. From Hamburg. Aboard the 11.15. Copenhagen Express. Bound for Lübeck. Arrives 12.05. Accompanied by companion. Tweed is coming . . .'

Munzel slammed down the phone without a word of thanks. Hotel telephones were tricky – you never knew when a bored switchboard operator was listening in.

He had arrived in good time back in Lübeck. After paying his final call on Ziggy Palewska he had caught the 7 a.m. express from Hamburg. The train's ultimate destination was far distant Oslo – via Copenhagen and the Elsinore train ferry which transported it across the arm of the Baltic to Sweden.

Accompanied by companion. That had been a cryptic warning – Tweed was not travelling alone. Well, that was OK. He'd be at Lübeck Hauptbahnhof to take a good look at this companion. He extracted a picture of Tweed from the inner lining of his executive brief-case, a glossy head-and-shoulders print. 'I'll know you, my friend,' Munzel said to himself, replaced the photo and stretched out on the bed. From the Movenpick it was no more than a five-minute walk down the road to the station.

Inside the phone booth Vollmer dialled another number. While he waited for his connection he took out the ticket he had purchased for Puttgarden. He crushed the unused ticket and dropped it. He had stood behind Tweed at the ticket window to hear his destination.

'Dr Berlin's residence,' a throaty voice said. He was through to the mansion in the Mecklenburger-strasse on Priwall Island.

'Martin speaking. Tweed is coming . . .'

'Await further instructions.'

The connection was broken before Vollmer could respond. *Bighead*, Vollmer said aloud and slammed down the phone. Back to Altona. To await further instructions. From Balkan. The man he had never seen.

*

Aboard the Copenhagen Express they had a first-class compartment to themselves. They sat in corner window seats, facing each other. The express thundered north across the North German plain, through neatly cultivated fields of ripening wheat. The land stretched away under a clear blue sky. It was going to be another lovely summer's day.

'This must be the most dangerous problem you've ever faced,' Newman remarked as he lit a cigarette. 'One of your four sector chiefs is a rotten apple.'

'I'm afraid so, Bob. That is the only fact I have to go on so far . . .'

'Any suspicions? Grey, Dalby, Lindemann, Masterson?'

'None at all. They have all been vetted up to their eyebrows. They come out pure as driven snow. It's rather depressing.'

'And you still think General Vasili Lysenko is behind it?'

'I don't think. I know. I can sense his fine Russian hand. All the hallmarks of the supreme professional . . .'

'How do you propose to go about it – smoking out Lysenko's tame hyena?'

'I suggest you concentrate on finding out everything you can about Dr Berlin. The philanthropic guardian of refugees intrigues me. The fact that he lives on the border. You know the history of Priwall Island?'

'No,' said Newman.

'Once in Lübeck I met a British ex-tank commander who served under Monty. He told me a memorable story. At the end of the war he was at the head of his armoured unit – in the very first tank to reach Travemünde and be ferried across to Priwall Island. He was racing the Russians to seize the whole strategic island – which controls the seaward entrances to Lübeck on its east and west coasts. He was exactly half-way across that island when he saw a Soviet tank approaching from the other direction. The Red Army tank commander held up his hand to halt our chap. The British tank commander did the same thing – held up his hand to stop the Red Army in its rush to seize Lübeck itself, even take over Denmark if they could. And that was where the border was drawn. At the precise point where those two tank commanders met . . .'

'So that's why Priwall Island is cut in half – with the Soviet minefield belt extending across its middle?'

'Exactly. At least the western channel to Travemünde is under Western control. So passenger ships from Sweden and Finland can cross the Baltic and berth there. It's one of the weirdest spots on earth. And that, I remember reading, is where Dr Berlin has his residence,' Tweed remarked.

'The odd thing is he only spends part of his time there. He's like a grasshopper. I remember some of the old Kenya hands used that very word. Hops all over the world, they said. But no one knew where . . .'

'Then you'd better find out. I think we are coming in to the outskirts of Lübeck. I wonder what it holds for us?'

The taxi ride from the Hauptbahnhof to the Hotel Jensen was only a few minutes. They could have walked it. Approaching the bridge crossing the river on to the island Lübeck sits on, they passed a curious pair of medieval towers, leaning precariously and topped with witches' hat turrets.

'The famous Holstentor,' Tweed remarked. 'Lübeck's trademark. That and marzipan . . .'

They met the blonde-haired woman as they carried their cases inside the Jensen. In her early forties, Newman estimated, she was tall, slim and had a pointed chin and startling blue eyes which stared straight at him.

He stood aside to let her pass and she smiled, still staring, then disappeared into the outside world. Newman looked back at her and the man behind the reception counter grinned.

'You know her, sir?' he asked in English.

'Unfortunately, no. She's staying here?'

'Oh, yes. A guest each year during the summer season. That is Diana Chadwick. A very popular lady . . .'

'With any normal man, I should imagine . . .'

'I shouldn't say it, perhaps.' The man paused and smiled again. 'Very popular with most men, yes. But not always so popular with the members of her own sex. They fear the competition, I sometimes think.'

'Diana Chadwick,' Newman repeated while Tweed filled in his own form. 'I've heard that name somewhere . . .'

'She used to be a famous society beauty in Africa many years

65

ago.' He smiled a third time. 'Not too many years, I hasten to say . . .'

'Not Kenya by any chance?' Newman asked.

'I think possibly it was Kenya. Go to Travemünde, ask some of the British boating crowd there. She spends a lot of her time with them. Thank you, sir,' he said to Tweed, and pushed the pad towards Newman for him to register.

General Lysenko had insisted they moved their centre of operations to a fifth-floor office in the seven-storey concrete block of a building in Leipzig. He stood by the window now while Markus Wolf arranged his files brought up from the basement.

'I felt like a bloody mole trapped underground in that basement,' he snapped. 'We're likely to be here sometime, I take it.'

'Munzel can move very quickly,' Wolf replied in his slow deliberate voice. 'Witness how he dealt with the British agent, Fergusson, and that piece of garbage, Palewska. On the other hand, with a man like Tweed he will take his time. Patience is so often the key to success, I find.'

The Intelligence chief glanced at Lysenko to see if he had got the message. No, he hadn't, he decided. He explained at greater length.

'First, Munzel has made his second report via the Eichholz watch-tower. He has signalled the arrival of Tweed at the Hotel Jensen in Lübeck. We spun out a string for Tweed to follow – and he is following it. Second, Munzel will want to study his target, get to know his habits, his way of going about things. Only when he has a complete picture of Tweed will he strike. And in any case, Balkan will soon arrive in Lübeck. Our eagles are gathering . . .'

'There is a time limit.'

'No, General, there is no time limit.' Wolf's graven image of a face became bleaker. 'From my informant inside the Berliner Tor in Hamburg I hear both the deaths of Fergusson and Palewska are regarded as accidents. That shows Munzel's great competence. It is only this pest of a Federal policeman, Kuhlmann, from Wiesbaden, who is unconvinced. A clever man, Otto Kuhlmann . . .'

'He may have to be eliminated . . .'

'God forbid!' Wolf was appalled. 'An intimate of Chancellor Köhl himself? I understood from you the General Secretary warned there must be no incidents – only accidents.'

'And yet,' Lysenko sneered, turning away from the window, 'you tell me Munzel is an expert on accidents . . .'

'Bonn would never believe Kuhlmann had an accident. More than that, Kuhlmann would smell Munzel as coming from the DDR a mile off. Fortunately he has no suspicions in that direction.'

'And why is Munzel known as The Cripple? He's as fit as a Nazi storm-trooper. Looks a bit like one.'

'Because he often adopts the guise of a cripple on a mission. Who suspects an apparently blind man? Or a man in a self-propelled wheelchair? It is some such technique he will use when he eventually deals with Tweed. Now, if you don't mind, I'll continue arranging my files . . .'

'Ah, the files. Yes, do be sure they are in order,' Lysenko urged in a sarcastic tone.

For the next week Tweed seemed to Newman to have lost his sense of direction and purpose. They wandered round the island of Lübeck in the sunshine and the heat which had become torrid. Lübeck was full of holidaymakers, which worried Newman. Too many crowds.

Mostly Germans, they sat at pavement cafés, drinking and chatting. The Jensen was a small, well-run establishment and Tweed's window overlooked the twin towers of the Holstentor across the river. Across the road from the hotel pleasure boats moored and picked up passengers for river cruises. It was a lazy, relaxed atmosphere.

Tweed spent some time talking with the Jensen's manager, a man who liked the English and was both shrewd and knowledge-able about conditions on both sides of the border. Newman got to know the blonde woman, Diana Chadwick, who wore her hair short and reminded him of pictures he'd seen of girls in the '30s before the war.

'You simply must come to Travemünde,' she said to him over a drink outside the Jensen as they sat at a pavement table. 'There is the most divine crowd there. Boaty people

67

and tremendous fun. You'll get an idea of what life used to be
– when every day we enjoyed ourselves. None of your creepy
machines – computers or whatever they're called . . .'

'They *are* called computers . . .'

'And if you live in England now they have you all listed in
one of their beastly machines. No privacy any more. Just like
a police state, I say. Credit cards and all that. Came from
America, of course. Everything awful comes from America. I
hate the place.'

'You have been there, then?'

'Once. New York. Those dreadful canyons. Why go to Ari-
zona – or wherever the Grand Canyon is? New York is full of
them. I did have the most marvellous time, actually. Everyone
asked me to lots of parties. But I felt I was an exhibit. "Look,
we have a Brit. girl. Isn't she quaint? Love to hear her talk –
so different from us." ' She finished her Bloody Mary and said
yes, she'd love just one more. 'So different from us,' she
repeated. 'Thank God, I thought. Who'd want to be like you?'
She smiled and studied her companion. 'Bet you think I'm the
most awful snob. Which I am, of course . . .'

'You mentioned Travemünde,' Newman reminded her. 'Isn't
that where Dr Berlin lives?'

'Only part of the year. He's away at the moment. Expected
to join the fun any time . . .'

'Where is he then?'

'God knows. He goes off without telling a soul where. But he
has his refugee work. He's bonkers over that. Can't understand
why. People must cope on their own. I've always had to . . .'

'Where were you born?' Newman lifted his glass to her.

Diana Chadwick had slim, well-shaped legs, a small waist
and a good figure, not over-full. She wore an attractive summer
dress with polka dot design, a high neck and a pussy bow. Very
feminine. Her bone structure was well-defined, a straight nose
above a firm mouth suggesting character, a trait reinforced by
the pointed chin.

Her most striking feature was her sapphire blue eyes which
held a hint of wickedness which also showed when she smiled
and stared direct at Newman. He thought he could listen to her
soft voice all night long. Above all it was her personality, her
air of cool assurance which appealed.

'Hampstead, London,' she said, knocking ash from her cigarette into the tray. 'My father was in the Colonial Service – so we moved around the world from place to place. My education was, to say the least, spotty. A term in Kuala Lumpur, another in Hong Kong, then on to Nairobi in Kenya. Both my parents were killed in a car crash when I was eighteen. By nineteen I was married. It was in Kenya where I first met Dr Berlin. He wasn't much older than me – but even by then he had become a legend.'

'Quite a coincidence – that you should bump into him again here in Lübeck of all places . . .'

'Mr Newman.'

'Bob will do . . .'

'Diana. Bob, would you by any chance be interviewing me – doing a piece on Relics of the Empire?'

'I'd hardly call you a relic . . .'

'You're dodging the question.' She waved her cigarette – held in an ivory holder – at him, took the sting out of her remark with her smile.

'No, I'm just enjoying talking to you. I haven't written one piece for a newspaper in over a year . . .'

'Why not? All that money from your bestseller make you lazy?'

'My wife died . . .'

'I'm sorry to hear that. I have a gift for saying the wrong thing. I'm sure people ask me to parties to hear me put my foot in it. I say the most outrageous things. I'm going to say one now. Are you looking for a new woman?'

'I might just be doing that . . .'

Her complexion was flawless, Newman thought. Her skin was dead white. On the chair beside her rested a wide-brimmed elegant hat of straw. Another touch of the 1930s. And the tropics. No girl worth her salt ever exposed her skin to the rays of a Nairobi sun.

'Then again,' she said lightly, 'you might be after an interview with Dr Berlin. Very difficult. I might be able to help you if that *is* what you're here for . . .'

'Thank you. I'll bear your offer in mind. Why are you staying at the Jensen when your friends are out at Travemünde?'

'To get away from them, of course!' The wicked smile again.

'I like to be on my own from time to time.' She glanced down. 'Damn! I've got some drink on my frock . . .'

Frock. Newman had only read the word in novels written twenty years or more ago. A German at the next table, a tall blond man of thirty or so, handed her a glass of water.

'Thank you so much,' Diana said. 'That's just what I need . . .'

'Glad to be of service. Any kind of service . . .'

'Oh, yes?' Her expression froze and she used a paper napkin dipped in the glass to dab at her dress. The German pushed back his chair, grinned again at her and strolled off.

'A regular charmer,' Newman observed.

'That's Kurt Franck. I saw him arrive at the Movenpick, carrying his bag inside. No, I don't know him. I know *of* him. He's started hanging round the crowd out at Travemünde, trying to ingratiate himself with them. I think he's a con artist – probably lives off dowagers. Gigolo . . .'

Newman looked up as Tweed emerged from the hotel. 'Off somewhere?' he asked.

'Thought I'd take a walk through the town. It's like a furnace inside.'

Newman introduced him to Diana Chadwick. Tweed took her hand and noticed its beautiful shape, long-fingered and not too wide. The lightest tone of pink nail varnish. None of your blood-red horror.

'And are you also on holiday, Mr Tweed?'

'Trying to relax, have a bit of a restful time. For a change.'

'I'll come with you for that walk,' Newman said, pushing back his chair. 'Stretch my legs . . .'

'Maybe you would care to accompany us, Miss Chadwick?' Tweed suggested. 'A little feminine company would cheer me up no end.' He caught Newman's expression. 'Probably have the same effect on Bob, too.'

'I'd love that.' She stood up and pulled on her wide-brimmed hat. 'Two escorts . . .' She was openly flirting with Tweed. 'I count this my lucky day . . .'

It went on like that for another ten days; Tweed mooning round the island, looking at the ancient buildings restored to their medieval glory, strolling along the river banks where trees overhung the placid water while power cruisers and more humble rowing boats moved in the torrid atmosphere as the heatwave continued unabated.

'What the hell do you think you're up to?' Newman demanded as they sat one afternoon in Tweed's bedroom, gazing out of the window at the jostling crowds below. 'You told me to hold back on checking Dr Berlin, you haven't made a single positive move to find out what is going on. Two men were murdered back in Hamburg – or have you forgotten?'

'No!' Tweed's tone was curt. 'And I was very fond of Ian Fergusson, so your comment is not welcome . . .'

'Sorry, but I'm getting restless . . .'

'You have Diana to while away the days . . .'

'She spends half her time with you . . .'

'Not my choice. Hers.' Tweed was amused. His tone changed. 'If *you* are getting on edge, what effect do you think it is having on the opposition? Fabius Maximus, the ancient Roman general, called it masterly inactivity . . .'

'You mean this is deliberate?'

'Oh, quite deliberate. I have been led to Lübeck on the end of a carefully paid-out rope. I get here. I do nothing. Imagine the pressure building up on the opposition. Soon they must show their hand.'

'If it works . . .'

'It will work. I know my friends across the border.'

Ten

'What the bloody hell is Tweed up to?' Lysenko paced round the spartan room on the fifth floor of the building in Leipzig. 'You tell me!' he shouted at Wolf, seated behind his desk. 'You and your patience . . .'

'I must admit his behaviour . . .'

'His lack of it . . .'

'I was going to say . . .' Markus Wolf, a tall, heavily-built man who towered over Lysenko, stood up, thrust his hands inside his trouser pockets, and also began walking. 'I was going to say,' he repeated, 'that I'm beginning to be puzzled. Munzel has reported daily over the phone via Hamburg. Apparently Tweed does nothing except act like a tourist. He hasn't even been near the Lübeck-Süd police complex outside the town. And Balkan is now in place . . .'

'We gave him the lead to Dr Berlin through Palewska – a totally reliable contact from his point of view. He hasn't gone near Travemünde – that is, if Munzel is to be trusted and is doing his job.'

'Erwin Munzel,' Wolf said stiffly, 'is the best we've got. I chose him personally for this assignment . . .'

'Munzel is a sadist.'

'Well, he may have his peculiar side. I grant you he enjoys his work. But the point is he is first-rate at his work.'

'Then what are we going to do?' raved Lysenko. 'Soon I shall be getting a phone call from the General Secretary. What do I say to him? Tweed has come, Tweed is having a good holiday. Mikhail Gorbachev will appreciate that, I can tell you . . .'

'Gorbachev is your responsibility,' Wolf said sharply.

'And killing Tweed is yours. You are in the front line . . .'

'Oh, I do realize that,' Wolf said ironically. 'Leave all the dirty work to the East Germans! Then if anything misfires the Kremlin has clean hands on the international front. So far, Tweed has stayed in crowded areas – always accompanied by that foreign correspondent, Newman. He doesn't go out after dark and eats dinner at the Jensen's restaurant where he's staying. What chance do you think Munzel has had?'

'That's your problem. You're in charge of the executive side of the operation. You are using your own people. My role is that of observer. I repeat, what are you going to do?'

It had become *you*, not *we*, Wolf noted cynically. He adjusted his heavy horn-rim glasses, sat down behind his desk and re-read the latest report while Lysenko prowled and fumed.

'As I said,' he began eventually, 'Balkan is in place . . .'

'And that was my idea years ago,' Lysenko reminded him. 'One of the most audacious manœuvres my organization has carried out. A bigger Philby at the centre of Tweed's outfit . . .'

'Whose identity I have protected,' Wolf replied waspishly.

'Agreed. But we must use him to the fullest extent – take a risk if we have to.'

'We'll speed things up,' Wolf decided. 'I'll get a message to Munzel. But I'm never happy about rushing things.'

'It is your decision,' Lysenko replied artfully.

'And I am capable of doing just that – taking a decision. We will get things moving within the next few days . . .' Wolf put his hand on the receiver and lifted it.

'Dr Berlin has arrived, Bob,' Diana said. 'He is holding one of his parties and you are invited . . .'

Mid-morning. They were sitting at one of the sidewalk tables outside the Jensen having a pre-lunch drink. It had become part of their daily routine. To sit and chat in the warmth before the great heat built up. Diana wore her straw hat tilted at an angle to shade her face. She looked up as Tweed came out.

'You're invited to a party, Tweedy . . .' Newman hid a smile. She was the only person he'd ever known get away with calling him that. Tweed sat down and began cleaning his glasses on his handkerchief.

'That's nice. Thank you. Tell me about it . . .'

'Oh, you don't thank me. It's Dr Berlin's party as I was just explaining to Bob.' She looked at Newman with mock severity. 'I have to tell you there are conditions. No interviews. You will be the only reporter there . . .'

'I expect one of the locals will sneak in,' Newman replied.

'They won't, you know! There will be guards on the gate. Dogs will patrol the grounds. You will have to show proof of identification before they let you in. Preferably your passport . . .'

'Sounds like a concentration camp,' Tweed observed amiably. 'I would like to know more before I accept – if that doesn't sound ungracious. Where will the party be held, what time, what day?'

'The day after tomorrow. Three o'clock in the afternoon we turn up. You can both escort me. The venue is Dr Berlin's mansion on Priwall Island opposite Travemünde. In the Mecklenburgerstrasse – that's the main road which runs like a ruler on and on until you reach the border. Full stop then!'

'I know,' said Tweed, and noticed the surprise she showed.

73

'I have been studying a map of the area,' he explained. 'How do we let Dr Berlin know we accept?'

'Oh, you can leave that to me.' She paused to swallow the rest of her drink. 'I give you both solemn warning you probably won't actually meet your host. He's very shy and reserved.'

'You mean we won't even see him?' Tweed asked.

'Oh, he'll be on the lawn. But probably surrounded by cronies. He doesn't expect guests to approach him – not even to thank him. In fact,' she made a moue, 'he positively dislikes it . . .'

'How long has he been on Priwall Island?' Tweed asked casually.

'No idea.' Diana adjusted the angle of her hat. 'Now, if you two don't mind, I think I'll trot along and let him know you're coming. He'll be so pleased . . .'

'Can't you phone him?' Newman suggested.

'Not the done thing. Besides, I have a tiny present to give him. I always do that when he turns up at Priwall . . .'

'I'll walk you to the station . . .'

Newman stood up with her but she shook her head and gave him a warm smile. Tapping him on the wrist with her rolled sunshade, she followed up this gesture by opening the shade which was brightly coloured. She was in one of her devilish moods and spun round in a circle like a ballet dancer.

'Hate that slow old train. I can drive over in my runabout – the sturdy old Volkswagen. 'Bye, both. See you here for dinner tonight . . .'

'She's quite a girl,' Tweed said, watching her until she vanished up a side street.

'She must be – to get you inside that safari jacket . . .'

Diana had insisted Tweed wasn't dressed for the climate. She had coaxed him inside a shop and made him try on three safari jackets. To Newman's amazement he had bought one and followed it up with the purchase of a straw hat.

'That girl has you in the palm of her hand, Tweed.'

'I like her.' Tweed lowered his voice. 'But now I have a job for you. Check Diana Chadwick's background with a fine-tooth comb. I want to know her history since the day she was born in Hampstead – just assuming she was born in Hampstead.'

*

74

In his bedroom Tweed's manner changed completely. He tossed the straw hat on the bed while Newman watched, took off the safari jacket and slung that after the hat. He closed both of the windows and now the room was quiet, the noise of the traffic coming in to Lübeck over the bridge muffled.

'I didn't realize you were sceptical about Diana,' Newman commented.

'I'm sceptical about everybody.' Tweed paced slowly round the room, assembling his thoughts. 'They may be using her simply as a conduit, of course.'

'Conduit?'

'Yes. Surely you realize what has happened. I've worn them down, forced them into making the first approach. There will be someone at this party held by Dr Berlin who wants to get a good look at me – at the very least. Get started, Bob. Everything you can dig up on Dr Berlin . . .'

'That could be a tall order. According to Diana he doesn't encourage people to get close to him.'

'Which is interesting in itself. I've an idea your best bet could be the floaters – those strange British ex-colonials who live on boats and commute annually between the Baltic and the Med.'

'Has something else happened? You seem more animated . . .'

'As a matter of fact, yes. The loaded pause is ended, I suspect. I told Monica to let Howard know I was staying here at the Jensen. Harry Masterson rang while you were having your drink with Diana. From Vienna. I have to go to a phone booth at the station and call him back at exactly noon. He has some information he doesn't want passing through the hotel switchboard. He made it sound very urgent . . .'

'I'll come with you.'

'We'll walk over to the Hauptbahnhof in a few minutes. Also, and this is a strange coincidence, Erich Lindemann then phoned. He's travelling down from Copenhagen to meet me at Puttgarden, the ferry point this side of the Baltic . . .'

'When?'

'Late this afternoon. I'll give you the details later. He also has information. Refused to give me even a hint on the phone. A very cautious chap, Erich.'

75

'So, one way or another everyone is converging on Lübeck. Two of the four suspects, anyway. Have you still no idea who it is? Hugh Grey, Masterson, Lindemann or Dalby?'

'Not a whisker of an idea.' Tweed rubbed his hands together. 'The main thing is things are moving. I have an idea that from now on the pace will go on accelerating.'

'Monitor here,' said Tweed, confined inside the phone booth at the Hauptbahnhof. 'What news about the deal?'

'Prefect calling. Details of the deal pretty confidential. I take it you are outside, old boy?'

Unmistakably Harry Masterson, his bluff voice booming, and he had responded to the schoolboyish identification Tweed had devised. He disliked it but any operator listening in who understood English well would think they were a typical pair of Britishers.

'I'm outside,' Tweed assured him. 'How is the deal going?'

'They won't conclude without a ten per cent reduction in the price . . .'

'That's steep. Have to think about it.'

'Oh, another thing . . .' Masterson spoke as though it was just a minor matter. '. . . a gentleman you ought to know about is heading for your part of the world. Nicknamed The Cripple. He came over near Gmünd. That report is not new – only just heard about it. So he could be already with you. A formidable competitor.'

'I agree.' Tweed felt his facial muscles stiffen. 'Suppose I should say goodnight, Vienna . . .'

'*Wiedersehen.*'

'What's the matter?' Newman asked as they strolled out of the station into the glare of the midday sun. 'You look as though you've seen a ghost. Bad news?'

'Some people would say the worst. Ever heard of a man from East Germany known as The Cripple?'

'I have now. Who is he – or she?'

'He. Their most professional assassin. Believed to be responsible for the murder of at least seven of our agents. He specializes in making his killings look like accidents. We have no description and no photo of him. Harry Masterson said he came over the border at Gmünd in Upper Austria recently and is headed this way. May already be here . . .'

'That's a hell of a long way round to get to Lübeck. He had to cross part of Austria and the whole of Germany.'

'Which was clever. If you want to escape across the Iron Curtain this is not the place to do it. The border is too heavily guarded. You'd find it much easier to slip over the Austrian frontier. The same applies if they want to send a man into the West. We may have very unpleasant company on our door-step.'

'At least Masterson has warned us . . .'

'And that was a funny thing. He was supposed to be calling from Vienna. I'd have sworn it was a local call – made from somewhere nearby . . .'

'Probably a freak line . . .'

'Probably.'

They caught the 15.33 express from Lübeck bound for Copen-hagen which would land them at Puttgarden at 17.11. The train was fairly empty and Tweed gazed out of the window with interest as the train forged north. More flatlands, but now few signs of habitation. Wild-looking countryside with fields of crops when they left Lübeck behind after a glimpse of the blue Baltic.

'You could lose yourself up here and they'd never find you,' Newman remarked.

'It gets wilder when we cross over to the German island of Fehmarn,' Tweed said. 'The track crosses Fehmarn Sound on to the island over a bridge. Puttgarden, the ferry terminal for Denmark, is at the very tip of the island. I think we're coming up to it now.'

The express slowed, rumbled slowly over a long bridge. Newman peered out and below the intensely blue Baltic was choppy. The brilliant sunlight glittered like mercury off the wave crests. It moved on to the island and Newman saw the point of Tweed's remark.

High dense grasses waved in the breeze and there was no sign of human habitation as far as the eye could see. An atmosphere of desolate loneliness hung over the island which – even in the sunlight – pressed down on the landscape.

The express lost speed again and soon it was crawling alongside the platform of Puttgarden station. Not a hint of a town or even a village. Just the endless platform.

As they descended to the platform Newman glanced to his left, to the north. In the distance, beyond the locomotive, what looked like an immense shed yawned, a dark cavern. Above the entrance was hoisted a huge metal shield-like cover. He was looking at the waiting train ferry, open and ready to receive the express.

'I can't see Lindemann,' Newman observed.

'Patience. We'll walk up and down the platform . . .'

'Who are those people?'

Newman pointed to a small group who had left the train and were standing by the road outside. About a dozen passengers, no more.

'They're waiting for the local bus to Burg. That's a nowhere place,' Tweed commented. 'Only a handful of houses and shops – but the largest hamlet on Fehmarn. Ah, who have we here?'

Newman hardly recognized Erich Lindemann as he alighted from the express. He wore a Norfolk jacket, corduroy slacks, a deerstalker hat and, perched on the bridge of his nose, a pair of crescent-shaped glasses. Shrewd grey eyes stared at Newman over the top of the lenses. His whole appearance was changed and he looked the very image of The Professor.

'You've come up on the same train as us – from Lübeck?' Newman asked, puzzled.

'That is how it would appear to anyone observing us.' Lindemann smiled wryly. 'As soon as the express train arrived I boarded it at the front, walked half-way through the train until I found you, then I got off. Shall we stroll up and down – I'm catching this express back to Copenhagen and it leaves at 17.25. That gives us less than ten minutes.' He turned to Tweed. 'In view of the news I bring I am glad you have Newman with you. Keep him by your side at all times . . .'

'What news?' Tweed asked. He raised a hand to his hair which was blowing all over the place. The air was fresh with a salty tang and a powerful breeze came in off the Baltic.

'For months I have been trying to discover the identity of the man who controls the army of enemy agents infesting West Germany. All of them East Germans, of course. Yes,' he continued in his precise way as they walked, 'I know that is strictly speaking the job of Hugh Grey, but our territories overlap. All these ferries crossing the Baltic – here and at Lübeck . . .'

'What have you found out?' Tweed enquired.

'His code-name. Balkan. I know it isn't much. But I have also heard Balkan has arrived in Lübeck very recently. I thought you should be warned.'

'Where does this information come from, Erich?'

'I can't identify my informant, of course. Let us say I made a quick flight to Oslo recently. An interesting city – and of course just north in the mountains is the great NATO base.'

'I see . . .' Tweed was silent for a short while. He was pretty sure he knew what Lindemann was saying. Norway. In the far north there was a curious area close to the Barents Sea where a section of the Norwegian frontier ran next to Soviet Russia. It would take a brilliant agent to cross from Russia – but Lindemann was a brilliant sector chief.

'This Balkan,' Tweed continued, 'have you even the hint of a clue as to where he comes from?'

'Not the trace of a hint. I am told that only Lysenko himself is privy to his real identity. That gives you some idea of the power Balkan wields. Life and death, according to my informant. There is one other thing. He has been in place, holding that position, for a long time – probably many years . . .'

'Strange we've never heard of him before . . .'

'No, that's understandable. One other tiny item.' Lindemann was pacing slowly between Newman and Tweed. 'Lysenko changes the code-name at intervals. But he has been called Balkan for some time. I was also told he is very mobile.' He checked his watch. 'And that, Tweed, I am afraid is it. I'd better board my train in a minute . . .'

'Thank you for coming, Erich. And for the information. I sense we now have movement by the opposition . . .'

'Don't forget my offer,' Lindemann said as he opened the door of an empty compartment. 'If things get overheated down here, phone me and I'll meet you in Copenhagen off the express. Don't fly. Oh, it's possible Balkan is based in Oslo.'

The door slammed shut before Tweed could react. They decided to go for a walk along the country road since their train back to Lübeck wasn't due. Newman glanced back at the express which was still standing in the station and then a bend in the road hid it from view.

'Lindemann is all brainpower,' Newman remarked as they bent their heads against the wind.

'And a man of many parts. You'd never dream that when he was a few years younger his main relaxation was amateur theatricals. He could have made his living on the stage, I heard . . .'

'I didn't recognize him immediately when he came out of that compartment. He's still pretty good at disguising his appearance. I was also intrigued by the few snippets he's picked up about this Balkan. It's a thin comparison, I know, but he reminded me of someone else we've heard about recently . . .'

'Are we thinking on the same lines?' Tweed wondered aloud.

'Dr Berlin . . .'

'Exactly. Why?'

'Lindemann said Balkan has held his position for a long time, that he is very mobile. Diana told us Berlin is like a grasshopper, jumping all over the place. No one knows where he disappears to. Also he lives like a hermit, won't normally be interviewed. He gave me mine a couple of years ago to shut the others up, I'm sure. The weird thing is when I was talking to him I felt I'd met him before . . .'

'The trouble is one fact blows a hole right through such a theory. Diana Chadwick. She knew him way back in Kenya – that was twenty years ago. He can hardly have been Balkan then.'

'I suppose you're right.'

They walked in silence, each man mulling over his thoughts, for some time. Tweed checked his watch and said it was time to get back to the station. They were on board the train, travelling south, again in an empty compartment, when Newman said it.

'Tweed, we've got a lot to think about – and do. I have to check the backgrounds of Diana Chadwick and Dr Berlin. And all at once there are developments coming thick and fast. The party on Priwall Island the day after tomorrow. This business of the mysterious Balkan turning up. *And*, the imminent arrival of the killer Masterson called The Cripple . . .'

'Should be enough to occupy us when we get to Lübeck,' Tweed agreed.

He didn't realize it, but he had just made the understatement of the year. The situation at Lübeck had exploded.

Eleven

'All hell has broken loose at Travemünde.'

Kuhlmann, wearing the same sober dark grey suit, stood by the window in Tweed's bedroom at the Jensen, staring at Newman and Tweed. Beyond the window dusk was gathering, a purple glow hung over Lübeck, the street lights had an eerie, dream-like quality.

'And how did you know where to find me?' Tweed asked.

'Had you both followed to the Hauptbahnhof in Hamburg. My man watched you board the Copenhagen Express. First stop Lübeck. A phone call to police HQ here at Lübeck–Süd. Your hotel registration comes through. The Jensen . . .'

'And what has happened at Travemünde?' Newman interjected.

'Another horrific murder of a foreign blonde girl. Rape and then sheer butchery. Found in the woods on Priwall Island. A Swedish girl. Another foreigner. That makes it Federal business.'

'You keep saying "another",' Newman commented.

'Six months ago in Frankfurt a Dutch girl was found in the early hours of the morning on the banks of the river Main. Same *modus operandi* – if you can dignify such manic frenzy with the term . . .'

'Could you be a little more specific?' Tweed pressed.

'Good job you've just had your dinner. All right, let's get a little more specific. First, both are blonde girls. This maniac slaughters them with a broad-bladed knife – really cuts them to pieces like a butcher chopping a side of beef. Then, for God's sake, he rapes them. Out at Travemünde they're barring their

81

doors, battening down the hatches at the marinas. Panic isn't the word for it.'

'Surely you're making a very general assumption,' Tweed persisted. 'Look at the distance between Frankfurt and here . . .'

'I had the dubious pleasure of seeing both corpses in the morgues. It's the same killer. So, now we check on who was in both cities at the time of the killings. Surprise, surprise! Both of you were . . .'

'That's a bit ridiculous,' Tweed said mildly.

'Puts me in a funny position, Tweed. Word comes from the lady at the top in London direct to Chancellor Köhl in Bonn. Would he allocate his best man to keep a fatherly eye on you . . .'

'Fatherly eye. Oh, for God's sake,' Tweed protested.

'Haven't finished.' Kuhlmann removed his cigar and grinned to lighten the atmosphere. 'Now I have you down on the list of suspects . . .'

'You can't be serious,' Newman broke in.

'I'm serious about checking who was in both places at the wrong time. All hotel registrations in Lübeck and Travemünde are now being collected up to send to Cologne. One hell of a job, but it has to be done. The Cologne computer then cross-checks with the list of people in Frankfurt six months ago. That way we should end up with something . . .'

'You hope,' said Newman.

'I hope,' Kuhlmann agreed. 'And now I have to get over to the morgue. The pathologist here works faster than that snail we had in Hamburg. I'll have a report by the morning . . .'

'When was the Travemünde murder committed?' Newman asked.

'First indications say last night. Some of the *Wandervogel* fanatics back-packing it through the woods found her middle of this morning. Girl by the name of Helena Andersen. Ring any bells?'

'No. Should it?'

'Just that she happens to be the daughter of an ex-Cabinet Minister. So the lines are buzzing between Stockholm and Bonn. Let you know about that pathologist's report in the morning . . .'

*

Tweed had a couple of cognacs sent up from the bar after Kuhlmann left. He raised his glass to Newman, took a sip and set the glass down on a table.

'I'm getting to be a regular toper on this trip,' he remarked.

'Are you thinking what I'm thinking?'

'Tell me what's inside your sceptical mind and we'll see.'

'Kuhlmann correctly placed us in the locations of both these ghastly murders. He doesn't know there is a third possible suspect to add to his list. Hugh Grey. He was in Frankfurt – that was the night he spilt whisky over my best suit. And when he came to see us at the Four Seasons in Hamburg over breakfast the topic of that murder in Frankfurt came into the conversation. I mentioned it myself.'

'The same thought crossed my mind. It could be worse than you realize. Mind you, it's a very long shot. I was there for a conference of the four newly-appointed sector chiefs. Not only was Hugh in Frankfurt. Harry Masterson and Guy Dalby attended the same meeting along with Erich Lindemann . . .'

'But you spoke to Masterson on the phone from the Hauptbahnhof here at midday. That was when Masterson warned you about The Cripple heading this way. And,' Newman reminded him, 'Masterson was speaking from Vienna . . .'

'But it didn't sound like it. I told you it sounded far more like a local call.'

'Then there's Erich Lindemann.' Newman paused while he sipped at his cognac. 'We only have his word he climbed aboard the express at Puttgarden. Supposing he did board the train at Lübeck just before it left?'

'Go on.'

'We didn't actually see Lindemann leave on the express when it rolled on to the train ferry prior to crossing the Baltic to Denmark. It was still in the station when I looked back as we walked out of sight of it along that country road . . .'

'Your scepticism is reaching unprecedented heights. Flights of fancy, Bob. To change the subject, I think tomorrow we might spy out the land at Travemünde before we attend Dr Berlin's party the day after.'

'It would be an ideal moment,' Newman replied.

'Ideal? I'm not with you . . .'

'That's because you're not a newspaper reporter. Think of

83

the atmosphere out at Travemünde. A brutal, motiveless murder has occurred. Kuhlmann himself made a reference to the boat people battening down the hatches. They'll all be jumpy – but ready to talk their heads off about the murder to almost anyone. In daylight at any rate. There's a ghoulish element in human nature. I predict we'll get to know more people in a day than we would normally in a month.'

'You could be right. Well, we'll see . . .' Tweed's thoughts seemed to be miles away and he gave the impression of replying automatically.

'What's the matter?' Newman asked.

'Your flights of fancy. They're crazy, of course, but I find them disturbing. If by a million-to-one chance you were right it opens up vistas infinitely more horrific than the murder itself . . .'

'It was the same bastard – the Frankfurt maniac.'

Kuhlmann made the statement as he walked with Tweed and Newman past the crooked gate towers towards the station the following morning. He had caught them leaving the Jensen on their way to Travemünde.

'How do you know for certain?' Newman asked, shielding his eyes against the glare of the sun.

'Two things. The Frankfurt pathologist's report came in over the teletype. The local pathologist checked his own findings against it. We were up all night while he did his job on that Swedish girl. His report checks with the one from Frankfurt. It looks like the same weapon was used to carve her up.'

'What kind of weapon?' Tweed asked.

'Wrong word, really. Comes to the same thing. A chef's knife is the opinion of both pathologists. The kind of knife you find in any reasonably well-equipped housewife's kitchen.'

'Not much help,' Tweed suggested.

'No bloody help at all.'

No one said anything more until they were entering the booking hall. Tweed went to the window to buy the tickets to Travemünde, leaving the other two outside a bookshop.

'What do you expect to find at Travemünde?' Kuhlmann asked.

'I'll know when I see it. This second murder is a complication we hadn't expected . . .'

'Fourth murder,' Kuhlmann corrected. 'The Dutch girl in Frankfurt. Ian Fergusson in Hamburg. Followed by Ziggy Palewska. Now this Swedish victim. The body count is rising, Newman.'

'Reminds me of East Anglia, the area round the Wash,' Tweed said, looking out of the window.

They had left Lübeck and its suburbs behind and the local train was passing through open country. Newman looked up from a newspaper reporting the Swedish girl's murder.

'Does it? In what way?'

'Look at those long green banks beyond those fields. They are just like the dykes at the edge of the Wash. The locals in East Anglia actually call them "banks". And these flat fields below the railway line. Again, just like the Wash country-side.'

The train stopped and Tweed hurried out on to a high platform elevated above the surrounding countryside. Newman followed, closed the door, looked around and then called out to Tweed who was half-way towards the exit. They were the only passengers to alight and the train was moving again.

'Hey! This isn't the right stop . . .'

A huge platform sign carried the legend *Skandinavienkai*. Scandinavian Quay. He had to walk fast to catch up with Tweed who was descending a flight of steps to a main highway below. To the east Newman gazed at a complex of docks beyond a large staging area.

By the wharfside was moored a large white passenger liner, and close to that a huge car ferry. The rear maw was open – reminding him of Puttgarden – and a great queue of vehicles was lined up waiting to drive aboard. Private cars, campers, big trucks.

'That's the liner waiting to leave for Sweden,' Tweed informed Newman. 'You can see from the name on the hull . . .'

'Why get off at this stop?'

They were walking along a wide pavement by the side of the main highway. The verge was lined with a dense wall of trees which blotted out the view to the docks. Shrubberies of wild roses grew at the edge of the verge and it was very quiet under the sun beating down on them.

'It's only a short walk into town,' Tweed said, his legs moving like pistons, his body leant forward. Tweed in full cry, Newman told himself. Weeks of doing very little and then some development would electrify him. 'I checked it on the map before we started out,' he went on. 'The next stop is Travemünde Hafen. The harbour area. Beyond that is Travemünde Strand, people tanning themselves on the beach and all that nonsense. Burning themselves red, unable to sleep for nights. What they call having a good holiday. Approaching the town this way, I can get the feel of the place. Look, we're close now . . .'

The single spire of a church speared the azure sky. Beyond it other buildings began to appear. They were leaving the dock area behind. Tweed was dressed in his new tropical drill slacks, his safari jacket.

'Hoping we meet Diana?' Newman joshed him.

'These clothes will help me merge into the background. You must admit I look as though I'm on holiday . . .'

'Tweed, you could never look as though you were on holiday.'

'If anyone asks what I do I'll say insurance. Just so you know.'

'An executive of the General and Cumbria Assurance Co – your dummy outfit back at Park Crescent?'

'Only if I have to. This must be Travemünde.'

Standing well back from the waterfront was a row of old double-storey buildings. The usual assortment of cafés, restaurants and souvenir shops. Holidaymakers, mostly German, drifted along in the aimless way of men and women not sure what to do next. Many of the buildings had the steep gables characteristic in that part of the world.

'Let's cross the road when we can,' said Tweed. 'You can do your reporter act, get people talking . . .'

'While you listen . . .'

'And watch.'

The waterfront was a tangle of masts, a variety of vessels were moored to the bollards, jammed in hull to hull. Yachts, pleasure craft, the odd expensive-looking power cruiser looming above the small fry. At a nearby marina landing stages projected out into the channel between Travemünde and a forested shore a short distance away. Tweed pointed at the forest.

'And that will be Priwall Island.'

'I know. I came here once to interview Dr Berlin . . .'

'And the small car ferry takes no more than a few minutes to cross from here to Priwall . . .' Tweed hardly seemed to hear a word Newman said. He was like a dog which has picked up the scent. '. . . When you leave the ferry you walk straight into the Mecklenburger-strasse. There are houses – including Berlin's mansion – on the right. They face the forest laced with a network of paths – the forest where that poor Swedish girl was found almost at the edge of the water. What was her name? Helena Andersen. That was it. They say the murderer must have been disturbed. He was going to throw her into the channel – there was a trail of blood where he'd dragged her through the undergrowth.'

'How do you know all this?' Newman enquired. 'You couldn't pick that detail up from a map . . .'

He was watching a sleek white liner approaching from the Baltic. It cruised through the channel where there didn't seem to be room, blanking out the island briefly, but it made safe passage and sailed on towards the docks.

'A combination of listening to Diana,' Tweed said. 'Asking the odd question. Then linking up what she said with the map. Let's explore the marina so you can do your stuff.'

'And you seem to know a lot more about the Helena Andersen killing,' Newman probed as they strolled through the crowds towards the marina.

'Kuhlmann phoned me while I was shaving before breakfast. He called from the local police station here. He'd been over every inch of the ground himself early this morning. Otto never sleeps as far as I can see. Here we are. After you . . .'

'Thanks a bundle.'

Newman surveyed the marina, the various craft moored hull to hull. You could step from one craft to another. He walked down a landing stage towards a large sloop, a sixty-footer, he estimated. A slim woman in her sixties sat in a captain's chair, a pair of rimless glasses perched on her nose as she sat reading a hardback. *Gone With the Wind*. This was probably a good place to start. She looked up as Newman approached, removed the glasses and laid the book in her lap.

Slim, she had dark hair, thick and silky, cut short, and aristocratic features. A handsome woman, there was a cynical twist to her mouth, an air of competence, increased when she spoke in an upper crust accent.

'Robert Newman? I am right? Recognize you from pictures in the papers. Welcome aboard. Take a pew. Your friend can come, too. Come to hear all the gory details? So you can write up a really lurid story? Blood on Priwall Island. There, I've given you your headline . . .'

'I might use it.' Newman settled himself in a canvas chair while Tweed lowered himself gingerly into its twin facing the waterfront. 'This is my friend, Tweed . . .'

'And I don't think you miss much either – not with those eyes.' She stared hard at Tweed who smiled faintly. 'Care for some coffee? Ben, the hired help, will provide . . .'

'Ben will provide coffee – but he's not the bloody hired help.'

A white-haired man with a weatherbeaten face appeared at the top of a companionway. Six foot tall, he was thin and wiry and stooped in the way Newman had noticed tall sailors were apt to. Blue eyes studied the new arrivals above a great beak of a nose.

'Coffee for three?' Ben asked. 'Make up your minds, do . . .'

'Yes, please,' Tweed said promptly. 'No milk or sugar for either of us.'

'Black as sin? And there's plenty of that on Priwall.'

The head disappeared and Tweed slipped a Dramamine in his mouth. The damned boat wouldn't keep still, which made the mainland seem to move. The water was only choppy but he knew he'd feel queasy if he didn't take precautions.

'Sin on Priwall?' Tweed enquired.

'And walking over there along the waterfront,' the aristocratic woman commented.

Tweed had already seen Diana Chadwick strolling towards the marina. The wide-brimmed straw hat, the elegant movement of her body were unmistakable.

'Diana Chadwick,' Tweed prompted.

'You know her?' Their hostess crossed her legs and her cream skirt dropped into its natural pleats. 'I'm forgetting my manners. I'm Ann Grayle. My husband was in the Diplomatic Service. I buried him in Nairobi five years ago. Always said when that happened I'd take a lover. The right man never turned up. Not until now.' She stared at Newman, a hint of amusement in her pale grey eyes.

'Diana Chadwick,' Tweed prompted her again before Ben arrived with coffee.

'A promiscuous tart.'

'The noun alone expresses your meaning,' Tweed said mildly.

'Oh, if that's the way of life someone wants, who am I to object? The veteran of a hundred beds. Especially back in Africa. Her husband was the last person to know – as always . . .'

'He did get to know?'

'No, which is the point of my remark. He died with his illusions *intact*. Which is more than his wife was. A bank director, pillar of the club, so popular no one had the guts to say a word to him. He was gored to death by an irritable rhino. That was supposed to have happened to Dr Berlin. But they *found* the body of Luke – Diana's spouse. If you know her you could have a good time. They do say she's an expert. All that experience . . .'

'He – Luke – left her well off?' Tweed enquired.

'Penniless. Oh, I know – a bank director. You'd think he'd be a good provider. Didn't leave a sou. Lived up to his very last penny. Hunting big game is an expensive pastime.'

'How does she survive then?' Tweed asked.

'That's the mystery. She always has plenty of new things to put on her back. Of course, she's a good friend of Dr Berlin. Creepy old horror in my opinion . . .'

'You mean he provides her with an allowance?'

'Now I didn't say that, did I?' Mrs Grayle sat erect in her chair. 'Unlikely, I'd say. Berlin is as mean as muck. Good, here at last is Ben. Not that we need him – but the coffee is essential.'

Tweed could have guessed Ann Grayle was a diplomat's wife. She carried an air of authority of a woman used to organizing other people's lives. And woe betide the wives of the junior staff if they didn't know their place.

'I heard you slandering Diana,' Ben remarked as he served

89

the coffee. Tweed drank some quickly to make sure the pill had gone down.

'Eavesdropping again?'

'You don't seem to realize how your voice carries. They could have heard you in Lübeck.' Ben sagged into a chair and turned to Tweed. 'And I'm sure Diana doesn't live off Dr Berlin.'

'Ah!' Ann Grayle's eyes lit up. 'She has a defender. I wonder what service she rendered Ben to get him on her side?'

'You have the mind of a sewer,' Ben stated calmly.

'That's because the world is a sewer.'

'You said Luke's body was found and implied Dr Berlin's wasn't,' Tweed remarked.

'Which is perfectly true. They did find a blood-stained jacket in the bush, but no positive identification that it ever belonged to Berlin. The next thing we hear is he's turned up in a hospital for tropical diseases in Leipzig.' She frowned over the rim of her cup. 'And I recall that was about the time that funny Russian attaché paid a visit to Nairobi. Caused quite a stir. We'd never seen a Bolshevik before.'

'You seem to have a good memory,' Tweed coaxed. 'Could you remember his name?'

'Began with an "L".'

'Lysenko?'

'Yes! That was it. We all gave him the cold shoulder. Never knew why he came. He vanished again after about a week.'

Tweed finished his coffee, refused another cup, and said they wouldn't impose on Mrs Grayle any longer. She rose to her feet.

'And I thought we'd be chatting about that horrible murder . . .'

'Maybe I could come back soon?' Newman suggested.

'Welcome any time. Except between two and four. Always have a nap then. Keeps me young. Bring Tweed with you.' She smiled, a dry smile. 'Diana is waiting for you.'

The large sleek white power cruiser Tweed had observed Diana Chadwick boarding was berthed at the edge of the marina, nearest to the opening to the Baltic. She was sitting on deck shaded by a parasol, reading a German fashion magazine.

'Well,' she greeted them, throwing aside the magazine, 'has the cat torn me to pieces?'

'Mrs Grayle?' Newman asked.

'Who else. She hated me in Nairobi. She detests me in Cannes. She loathes me in Lübeck. Apart from that, we get on terribly well. Plonk yourselves. That swing couch is comfortable.'

Tweed sat down and thanked God he had swallowed the Dramamine. The large power cruiser, *Südwind*, bobbed slowly up and down, insidiously. The added movement of the swing couch was not welcome.

'Midday!' Diana was in fine form. 'We can have a drink. A drop of cognac? Maybe two drops . . .'

Newman looked round the vessel while she served the drinks and said, 'Down the hatch!' It would travel a long distance; fully fuelled, was capable of traversing the North Sea. He lifted his glass and asked the question.

'All this is yours?'

'God, no! Wish to heaven it was. Belongs to Dr Berlin. He lets me sleep on it, even live here if I want to. In return, I clean the brass trimmings. Even swab down the deck when I've the energy. Take a look around if you like. I'll stay up on deck and sip my poison.'

Newman led the way up into the wheelhouse and closed the door. Tweed gazed at the instrument panel, peered closer at the various dials. His eyes lighted on the transceiver, a high-powered instrument of the latest kind.

'You can see the waveband Berlin tunes to,' he pointed out to Newman. 'See that tiny scratch mark? Let's check it . . .'

'I didn't know you were mechanically minded.'

'I did a signals course once. I'll turn down the volume – then Diana won't hear . . .' He switched a dial, then adjusted the waveband control. There was a crackle, followed by a voice talking in a foreign language, a continuous flow of words.

'Interesting,' said Tweed.

'What the devil is it? I don't recognize the language.'

'Russian. I know just enough to be able to tell what the gist is. It's the Soviet marine control. Weather forecast for the Baltic and the North Sea. Not German – so not from the DDR.

91

It has to be coming from Kaliningrad. Very intriguing. Let's turn it back to where it was . . .'

'This job could go a long way.'

'How far? You know more about boats than me.'

'Several hundred miles.'

'Do me a favour, Bob. Show me how to operate it. I've messed about with cruisers on the Broads, but it was a long time ago . . .'

He listened while Newman explained the functions of the various instruments. The reporter went over everything three times until he was sure Tweed had absorbed his instruction.

'And if you ever have to take a boat like this out, remember one thing if you forget everything else . . .'

'Which is?'

'Keep your eyes glued for'ard – what lies ahead of you. OK. Look back at the stern occasionally. But it's what's ahead you have to watch. And in misty conditions that means the radarscope. You seem to have mastered that.'

'I think I hear voices. We'd better get back to Diana.'

Her voice warned them as they opened the door, calling up to them in a voice which carried a note of strain. They had a visitor.

'Gentlemen,' Diana called out, 'we have company. May I introduce you to an acquaintance. Kurt Franck.'

The tall blond German, clad in windcheater, jeans and a leather belt round his middle, his feet shod in trainers, waved a large hand in welcome.

Twelve

'Champagne?' Franck lifted an opened bottle from a table and hoisted it like a flag. Diana had produced four tulip glasses. She sat in her chair, legs crossed, her expression wary.

'Bit early,' Newman replied in German.

'Never too early for champagne! Sit down everyone. Think of a toast . . .'

Newman sensed Diana disliked her unexpected visitor, the

92

man who had provided a glass of water when she spilt drink on her dress outside the Jensen. Franck, self-assured as the devil, had taken over the cruiser. Without waiting for Tweed to react he poured four glasses. Tweed sat next to Diana with his back to the sun where he could observe the German. Franck raised his glass and gazed at Newman who sat down and reached for his glass.

'I have thought of a toast.'

'Well, come on then! We want to drink . . .'

'A toast to the swift hunting down of the maniac who killed Helena Andersen . . .'

Franck froze, his glass in mid-air. His heavy face seemed to grow heavier as his ice-blue eyes stared at Newman. There was a sudden atmosphere of tension aboard the *Südwind*.

'I find that a macabre toast . . .'

'It was a macabre murder. Cheers!' Newman winked at Diana. 'Down the hatch.'

'I'll drink to that,' she said.

'Of course . . .' Franck sat down and splayed his powerful legs. 'You are a newspaper reporter, so you spend your life grubbing for the dirt . . .'

'Franck!' Diana said sharply.

'That's OK,' Newman said easily. 'The killing of that Swedish girl was a pretty dirty business.'

'But doesn't your conscience ever prick you?' Franck persisted. 'Poking your nose into people's private lives . . .'

'It certainly wouldn't bother me if I were investigating you,' Newman told him cheerfully. 'What do you do for a living, anyway? Unless the answer is embarrassing.'

'And why should it be embarrassing?' An ugly note had crept into the German's tone.

'Tell me what you do and we'll know the answer.'

'I'm a security consultant. I protect people's privacy – instead of invading it.'

'That's an interesting job.' Newman sipped a little more champagne, frowned and put down his glass. 'What company?'

'I work independently. Freelance . . .'

'He chauffeurs rich old ladies,' Diana said with a hint of a dry smile.

'Is that so?' Newman commented. 'Sounds a profitable . . .

occupation. Some rich dowagers like a handsome young chap at their beck and call . . .'

'What exactly does that mean?' Franck's left fist clenched on the arm of his chair and his tone was savage.

'Now, now,' Tweed intervened. He leaned forward towards Franck. 'I'm having difficulty placing what part of Germany you come from.' He waited, a look of cheerful anticipation on his face.

'Why do you want to know that?'

'I make a hobby of locating local accents. Just a foolish hobby of mine.' He smiled genially. 'You don't mind my asking?'

'Now we're getting personal,' Franck replied brusquely.

'I'd have said Saxony,' Newman interjected.

Franck pushed back his chair, stood up and loomed over Newman. The Englishman placed his glass on the table, stretched out his legs and crossed them at the ankles.

'I find your manner obnoxious,' Franck announced. 'And you don't seem to appreciate the champagne . . .'

'Obnoxious? I thought we were having a friendly conversation. As to the champagne, it's lukewarm and a rather inferior brand, now that you bring the subject up . . .'

'Bollinger? An inferior brand?'

'I'm afraid they saw you coming. The bottle may be Bollinger, the contents most certainly are not. Were you thinking of leaving us?'

'You and I will meet again, Newman.'

'Anytime.' Newman gave a broad grin. 'Anytime at all . . .'

Franck turned on his heel, and strode off the cruiser. The gang-plank trembled under his weight, under the heavy thud of his feet. He disappeared amid the tangle of masts in the direction of the Priwall ferry.

'Well,' said Newman, 'that saved him answering the question where he comes from. I must have said something that disagreed with him.'

'I find him creepy,' said Diana. 'And I don't want any more of his bloody champers.' She hurled the bottle over the side. 'He used the fact that he'd given me that glass of water at the Jensen to come aboard the other day. Thinks he's a real charmer. That women will queue up to spend the night with him. I simply love the type. A real lady-killer . . .'

94

'Maybe you're nearer the truth than you realize,' Newman told her grimly.

'Munzel has reported contact with Tweed,' Wolf told Lysenko as they wandered through the stark streets between the concrete blocks of rebuilt Leipzig. 'That means he is close to making his move to liquidate him.'

'How recent is the report?'

'Within the past few hours. His contact with Tweed was late this morning at one of the marinas at Travemünde.'

'How does Munzel safely make such a report?' Lysenko demanded. 'I emphasize "safely".'

'We have perfected our communications systems over the years.' Wolf was irked by this constant questioning of his organization. 'Specifically, in this case, Munzel phoned a West Berlin number from Travemünde. A lawyer who specializes in handling any legal problems between families in West Germany with relatives in the East. Bonn trusts him implicitly.'

'So you say. So far the message from Munzel has reached West Berlin. What then?'

'The lawyer has his office within five minutes' walk of Checkpoint Charlie. After receiving the call from Munzel he carries the message in his head and crosses into East Berlin. From there he uses a direct line to me here in Leipzig.'

'I suppose it is foolproof,' Lysenko said grudgingly.

'You'll just have to take my word that it is. Munzel says he has no doubt he can accomplish his mission within days. At the first opportunity, and those were his very words.'

'So, we are in the hands of The Cripple . . .'

'He succeeded in Hamburg brilliantly. Fergusson and Palewska were dealt with. Both executions have been accepted as accidents, as I told you earlier.'

'The sooner the better. The General Secretary will be calling for a progress report any moment. I can feel it in my bones.'

'So, you will be able to report mission accomplished.'

'The question is,' Tweed said to Newman as they finished their dinner at the Jensen, 'who is telling the truth? Ann Grayle, who calls Diana promiscuous – or Diana herself, who says the Grayle woman is a bitch?'

'Does it matter?' asked Newman.

The restaurant was quiet at 10.30 p.m. and night had fallen outside. They had stayed late at Travemünde, crossing by the ferry to Priwall Island. Diana had pointed out the mansion where Dr Berlin lived. The high wrought-iron gates had been closed with few signs of activity in the grounds beyond.

Two rough-looking individuals had stood close to the gates, gazing at them as they passed. 'A couple of the security guards,' Diana had explained. 'Dr Berlin has a fetish about his privacy.'

They had walked on down the Mecklenburger-strasse – ruler-straight as Diana had described it. Various residences on their right, interspersed with the occasional café. To their left the forest spread away towards the channel with a network of footpaths running through it. It was very peaceful, the only sound the distant siren of a ship. They approached a section with six police cars parked by the forest.

'Is this the spot?' Newman asked.

'Yes, this is where Helena Andersen was murdered,' Diana said and shivered.

The police had cordoned off a large area with ropes strung from poles. Newman caught a glimpse through the trees of a line of policemen advancing slowly, beating the undergrowth.

'It's horrid. Let's go back,' Diana had suggested at this point.

Newman finished his coffee. 'Did you get anything from your recce of Priwall Island?'

'Nothing that helps. We'll see what happens at the party tomorrow. And now I do have an idea. You know that area behind the hotel we walked round the other day. I fancy a breath of fresh air . . .'

'I'll come with you. And I can see you have something special in mind.'

'I'm going out alone – for a stroll past the church.'

'Not on . . .'

'Wait. You follow at a discreet distance. Keep out of sight. We need someone we can question – hand over to Kuhlmann if necessary.'

'It's dangerous. That area in the old town is a labyrinth.'

'We must try something, flush them out. I'm leaving now.'

Tweed paused on the steps leading down into the street. People still sat at the tables, drinking, chatting, joking. It was

96

a warm night, the air humid and oppressive. He wiped moisture from his forehead, walked out and turned left along the An der Obertrave, the street running alongside the river on the far side.

Despite the heat, Tweed wore his shabby, lightweight Burberry raincoat. His right hand felt the rubber-cased cosh inside his pocket once given to him by a friend in Special Branch. Normally Tweed would never have dreamt of carrying a weapon, but he had the feeling this trip was dangerous. He was still being led on a rope paid out to him length by length.

He passed the medieval salt warehouses on the opposite bank, their steep gables silhouetted against the Prussian blue of the night sky. Then he turned left again up a side street leading to the church. Lübeck climbed the side of a hill from the Trave river, the ascent was steep, the street little more than a wide cobbled alleyway and quite deserted. Now he had left the river a sudden sinister silence pressed down. No more voices from the holidaymakers. It was as though a door had closed on the outside world.

Tweed trudged slowly up the uneven pavement and for a moment he thought he was entirely alone. Then he heard the sound behind him. Faint at first, it gradually grew louder, coming closer.

Tap . . . tap . . . *tap* . . .!

He paused, took out his handkerchief, mopped his brow, glanced over his shoulder. It was only a blind man. The tapping sound was the tip of his white stick following the edge of the ancient stone kerb. He passed under the blurred glow of a lamp at the entrance to one of the alleys leading off the street.

A bulky figure, trilby hat jammed low over his forehead, a pair of wrap-around, tinted glasses concealing his eyes and the upper part of his face. A bulky figure which walked with a stoop, his suit old and baggy.

Tweed resumed his walk up the incline. His hearing was acute and something was bothering him. The tapping of the stick was more like a series of quick *thuds*. As though instead of a rubber tip the end of the stick was heavily weighted . . .

Only a blind man. Tweed swore inwardly at his own stupidity. The man following him steadily up the deserted street was a

97

cripple. The Cripple had at long last made his appearance – the man Harry Masterson had warned him against.

Tweed felt the palms of his hands grow moist. His mouth tightened. He resisted the temptation to hurry up to the top of the street. At least his ruse had worked. But, oh God, this was the first time he had walked alone since landing at Hamburg Airport. It gave a terrifying insight into the closeness with which he had been watched by the opposition. And Lübeck was so near the border.

Get a grip on yourself. Your people in the field live like this all the time. Never free from fear. You've worked in the field yourself for years. What the hell is wrong with you? Too much time spent behind a cosy desk back at Park Crescent?

Suddenly he felt cold. The expression on his face had not changed but the nervousness was gone. He wiped his right hand dry inside his Burberry pocket. Then he conducted a difficult manœuvre, still walking. Concealing most of the cosh inside his hand, he whipped off the Burberry and folded it loosely over his arm. Like a cloak.

He had reached the top of the street, a T-junction. He turned into an equally dark street called Kolk, just below the tower of the church which loomed above a vertical wall. Kolk was a short street. Leading into the maze of the old town. Tweed paused outside the entrance to a bar. Over the entrance was the legend *Alt Lübeck*. A small bar furnished with dark wood, stools by the counter, dim lighting. He dismissed the temptation to seek sanctuary and walked on.

Tap . . . tap . . . *tap*! Very close now. The blind man had turned the corner into Kolk, had increased the length of his stride, was very close now. Then the tapping stopped. Tweed turned round. The huge silhouette in the shadows had hoisted the loaded stick, was bringing it down in a wide arc.

'He stumbled in the dark, missed the edge of the kerb, caught his skull against the stone paving, smashed it like an eggshell. There was drink on his breath . . .'

The wording of the police report recording his death flashed across Tweed's brain. He pressed himself against the wall, protecting his back, timed it carefully, grabbed at the descending stick with his right hand, felt the stinging pain. He grasped the stick with both hands.

His attacker held on, shoved forward with the end of the stick, aiming it at Tweed's belly. Tweed's powerful wrists took the strain, and they wrestled for the weapon. Tweed knew he was at a disadvantage. His attacker had a strong grip on the handle of the stick. It was only a matter of seconds before Tweed lost his grip, then the second attack would come, a flailing blow again aimed at his skull.

Newman hit the attacker from behind with a Rugby tackle, the full force of his rush knocking the assailant sprawling in the cobbled street. Newman sprawled with him. His opponent bent his right leg at the knee, rammed his foot forward. Newman felt the steel-tipped boot hit his jaw. He was stunned.

Tweed was handicapped by Newman's sprawled body. He was stepping over it when the killer leapt to his feet, using one gloved hand to give himself extra impetus. He tore off down the street and vanished. A police car's siren sounded, came round the corner, jammed on its brakes as its headlights beamed on Newman.

'Where is he?' Kuhlmann roared.

The Federal policeman had jumped out of the front passenger seat. He addressed the question to Tweed who was standing while Newman still lay in the street.

'That direction . . .' Tweed pointed. 'Heaven knows where after that. It's like Hampton Court Maze . . .'

'Description?' Kuhlmann half-turned to the uniformed driver. 'Give me that mike.' Tweed noticed the radio car had a very high aerial.

'Six foot tall,' he said quickly. 'About a hundred and eighty pounds. Trilby pulled low over head. Shabby dark suit. Tinted wrap-round glasses – discarded by now, I'm sure . . .'

'And blond hair,' Newman added, climbing slowly to his feet.

'Could you see his hair?' Kuhlmann queried. 'With the hat?'

'Blond hair,' Newman persisted.

Kuhlmann spoke rapidly into the microphone, spelling out the description. 'Blond hair,' he ended. 'Probably – that is, the hair colour. Seal off the island now,' he continued in staccato tone. 'Close all the bridges. Road-blocks. Check all cars . . .'

'And motor-bikes,' Tweed added. 'I thought I heard one start up.'

Kuhlmann included motor-bikes, handed back the mike, then he lit a cigar before he rasped, 'What do you think you were up to, Tweed? Walking the streets – at night, too, for God's sake – by yourself . . .'

'He wasn't by himself,' Newman contradicted. 'I was following him. And we nearly got him . . .'

'And he nearly got Tweed . . .'

'Are you all right?' Tweed asked Newman.

'Bruised shoulder. The most minor memento I could have expected.' He bent down and picked up the weighted stick.

'I'll take that.' Kuhlmann held out his hand. 'And careful how you handle it. Fingerprints . . .'

'Don't waste your time,' Tweed advised. 'He wore gloves.'

'You had a pretty rough few minutes,' Newman said to Tweed as he brushed dust off his jacket.

'Oh, I don't know. A bit of excitement gets the adrenalin stirring.' He looked at Kuhlmann. 'How did you happen to be in this area?'

'I persuaded the state police to watch you. Unfortunately they waited for me to drive from the local police station to the patrol car which had you under surveillance . . .'

'You want to know where you might find the owner of that walking stick?' Newman suggested.

'What do you think?'

'Hotel Movenpick. Name of Kurt Franck. No guarantee that he's your man. We never got a good look at his face . . .'

'I'm on my way. Call you later at the Jensen . . .'

Balkan was on the move. 11.30 p.m. on the beach at Travemünde Strand. He stared straight ahead, like a sleep-walker. His feet made a slushing sound as they trudged through the sand. Lights glowed in the distant multi-storey Maritim Hotel. Most holidaymakers were indoors, drinking in the bars, dining late.

There was only one other person on the long beach. A blonde girl, clad in a two-piece bathing costume, soaking up the peace, the last warmth of the day. Iris Hansen had a date with her new German boy friend. They'd arranged to meet on the beach at midnight and then go dancing.

Iris, her long blonde hair trailing like a waterfall down her

100

nude back, lay stretched out on a towel, leaning on one elbow.

She listened to the gentle lapping of the Baltic on the edge of the shore. Dreamy. A long way off the sound of laughter, the drumming beat of pop music. All night long. That was what he'd promised. They'd dance all night long.

She'd spent three weeks in Travemünde, three glorious baking weeks. To hell with Copenhagen. This was the life. Better than she'd ever hoped for. She just wanted it to go on and on. She heard the slushing sound of feet treading the sand, looked up.

'Oh, it's you. Hello, there . . .'

He stood over her, one foot on either side of her prone body. She raised an eyebrow, then dropped her eyes. Why not here? Now the only sounds were the lapping water, distant laughter and music. She looked up and her eyes widened in horror. Oh, God. No!

He held the broad-bladed knife in his right hand. Held it high above his head. She opened her mouth to scream and he planted a naked foot over her mouth, stifling the scream. Then the blade descended in a wide arc. It entered just above her breasts. And ripped down. And down. And down . . .

'Kuhlmann here . . .'

Listening to the phone in his bedroom, Tweed detected a note of disappointment. He sat down in his dressing gown and identified himself.

'Your Kurt Franck wasn't at the Movenpick,' Kuhlmann informed him. 'Yes, he's registered here. He came into the bar for a quick drink just before he left. Time 20.00 hours. Half an hour before you walked out of the Jensen. No go . . .'

'Why not?' Tweed asked.

'Said to the barman he was going out to meet a new girl friend. I checked his dress. He was wearing jeans and a white polo-necked sweater. No shabby two-piece suit. And then I checked the parking lot. He doesn't have a motor-bike. Travels around in a hired BMW. Yellow job . . .'

'Did you say yellow?'

'I did. Why?'

'Nothing. I didn't catch the word first time . . .'

'So it looks like he's out on the town – maybe for the whole night. Not our boy, I'd say. At least today is ending quietly. Be in touch. If anything develops . . .'

Thirteen

The phone began ringing in Tweed's bedroom. He swore in the bathroom, his face covered in lather, put down the old-fashioned razor he'd used for years, grabbed a towel and ran into the bedroom. Always when he was shaving. The bloody phone. He lifted the receiver.

'Hugh Grey here. Not too early for you, I'm sure. Bright as the proverbial lark, eh, Tweed?'

Grey sounded horribly buoyant and Tweed could just imagine his plump face, the ruddy flush of his skin, the eyes sparkling with enthusiasm. It was a bit much, first thing in the morning.

'What can I do for you?' Tweed asked, wiping soap off his chin.

'I've heard about last night. A nasty experience for you. Not what you're used to . . .' A reference to the fact that Tweed's place was behind his desk. 'Can I send in the troops?' Grey went on energetically, 'I like to be supportive. Some back-up. OK?'

'No,' said Tweed. 'Thank you, but no,' he said emphatically. 'And I'm quite all right, thank you. Leave things the way they are. Anything to tell me?'

'Not over the phone. Business is very active. Results expected shortly. I'll keep London informed. Don't forget – you need anything, call HQ at Frankfurt. Keep chipper. 'Bye for now. My three minutes is nearly up . . .'

Tweed put down the phone and sighed. The jargon got on his nerves. *Can I send in the troops?* What did Grey think he was? A bloody field marshal commanding an army? He went back into the bathroom to finish his shave.

He knew the real purpose of the call. To inform Tweed that he was on the ball. Grey must have an informant inside Lübeck

102

– maybe even inside police HQ at Lübeck-Süd. He'd heard about the scuffle in Kolk damned fast. But Lübeck was on the border – an obvious place to watch closely.

He told Newman about the call over breakfast at an isolated table. The reporter finished chewing a piece of roll before he commented.

'How did Grey know you were here?'

'Oh, they all know. I'd much sooner the two of us handled the problem on our own – but I had to let Howard know where they could contact me. New boys, only six months as sector chiefs – I have to be available if something tricky crops up. Hugh Grey is just so bouncy first thing . . .'

'You have to admit he's efficient. This is his sector. The fact that he knows what's going on so quickly is a tribute to his organization . . .'

'You're right, of course. Well, we have something positive to look forward to this afternoon. Dr Berlin's party. Diana is late for breakfast.'

'She told me she was sleeping on the *Südwind* last night. It saves her driving back and forth. We get there a bit early and pick her up off the cruiser before crossing to Priwall. She's going to introduce us to people at the famous party. I'd like to get there really early,' Newman went on, 'if that's OK by you. I want to interview Ann Grayle at greater length. That lady talks . . .'

'Endlessly. And we have company. Kuhlmann has just walked in. Something tells me we have a busy day coming up . . .'

The breakfast room at the Jensen was at the back of the hotel. You helped yourself from a buffet. Kuhlmann took a plate, piled on four rolls, a quantity of butter, three canisters of marmalade and sat down.

'I've been up all night,' he announced. There was a pause as he broke a roll in two, plastered it with butter and marmalade, consumed it rapidly and ordered coffee. 'A litre of it . . .' He looked fresh and alert, his thick black hair was neatly combed, but his chin was a black stubble. It reminded Tweed of Harry Masterson who, by midday, had a blued chin, the five o'clock shadow at noon, as Masterson called it. 'I should grow a beard,'

103

he often joked, 'but then anyone could pick me out a mile off . . .'

Kuhlmann devoured his roll, swallowed a whole cup of coffee, refilled it. Newman lit a cigarette, studying the German. His sixth sense told him Kuhlmann had news.

'Why up all night?' he asked. 'Get anywhere with Franck?'

'Forget Franck. Another blonde has been carved up and raped. Sometime round midnight . . .'

'On Priwall Island again?' Tweed asked quietly.

'No. On the beach at Travemünde Strand. Incredible. That he was able to get away with such butchery on an exposed beach . . .'

'Who was the victim?'

'An Iris Hansen. A Dane from Copenhagen. Personal assistant to a senior civil servant. So now Bonn has the lines buzzing between there and Copenhagen – and the calls are still coming in from Stockholm about Helena Andersen. The poor devil of a pathologist had just finished putting Andersen's remains together when we presented him with another parcel of meat. His phrase. He worked through the night. Out at Travemünde panic has turned to frenzy. Men are going out buying hunting knives, rolling pins, anything that can be used as a weapon . . .'

'Two murders,' Newman mused. 'Both blondes . . .'

'Three,' Kuhlmann amended. 'The Dutch girl at Frankfurt six months ago. It's the same killer. He proceeds with his grisly work in the same way. Don't ask me to go into details until I've settled my breakfast. You should have seen the Hansen girl lying on the beach. She, too, must have been attractive . . .'

'Must have been? Past tense,' Newman queried.

'He slashes their faces, cuts off . . . Never mind. You can always go and see her in the hospital for yourself if you're thinking of following up the story. Want me to sign a chit?'

'Not just now. Thanks all the same. Is there any connection between the three killings?'

'The connection I need is who was in Frankfurt six months ago and is here now.' He looked at Tweed. 'The two names the computer has come up with so far are you and Newman.'

'Except that you know both of us were in the middle of Lübeck at 10.45 p.m. I thought you said Iris Hansen was killed round midnight . . .'

'I did. We parted company about 11 o'clock. At that hour it is a fast drive to Travemünde. No traffic. Twenty minutes and you're in Travemünde Strand.'

'So both of us are suspects?'

'I have to report all the facts to Wiesbaden.' Kuhlmann took his time demolishing the last roll, then his wide mouth broke into a cynical grin. 'But the night man here on reception told me when I came in this morning you both went to your rooms at 11.10. He happened to check the clock. No one can get out of this place without passing him. You both have watertight alibis . . .'

'How very fortunate,' Tweed replied coolly. 'And now you've had your fun, maybe I could ask a favour? I need a totally safe phone to make several calls.'

'Police HQ, Lübeck-Süd,' Kuhlmann said promptly. 'It's outside town. There's a room there with a scrambler phone. I'll drive you there now. And you've got that look on your face.'

'What look might that be?'

'A very worried man. Something disturbing has struck you.'

Lübeck-Süd. Not at all what Newman had expected. A huge modern fourteen-storey complex of buildings, joined together and with a black central tower. All perched on top of a small hill, looking down on slopes of trim green lawns decorated with rosebeds.

Kuhlmann drove off the main highway past a one-word sign. *POLIZEI.* He parked the car outside, led the way into the entrance hall and showed his folder to a police officer in shirt-sleeves inside a glass box to the left. They exchanged a few words and the officer handed Kuhlmann a key.

Kuhlmann took them by elevator to the tenth floor. Half way down a long corridor he handed Tweed the key in front of a closed door which, unlike all the others, had no number.

'Newman and I will find some coffee in the canteen at the end of the corridor. Come and join us when you're finished. That phone inside there is one of the safest in the whole Federal Republic. It's used by the BND,' he ended, referring to counter-espionage.

Inside Tweed found a small bare room, walls lined with steel

105

filing cabinets, a table, two chairs. A white telephone sat on the table. He pulled out one of the chairs, made himself comfortable and dialled a Frankfurt number from memory. A girl answered immediately, repeating the number he had dialled and adding the digit nine.

'Hadrian calling,' Tweed said. 'The Hadrian Corporation. I'd like to speak with Mr Hugh Grey.'

They were using Roman emperors this month for the call-sign – Howard's idea, of course.

'I'm afraid he's away negotiating a deal for a few days,' the girl responded.

'When might I get him?'

'He didn't say. I don't think he knew himself.'

'Thank you . . .'

Tweed broke the connection. Grey could have called him from anywhere in West Germany – München, Stuttgart, Cologne. Anywhere. And it was strictly against the rules to ask for a contact number. A rule Tweed himself had laid down when he had tightened security six months earlier.

He next dialled Harry Masterson in Vienna. The same reaction. Masterson was out of town. No, they had no idea when he'd be back. Patiently, Tweed went on. He dialled Bern, to speak to Guy Dalby. A third negative. He sighed. The last one now – Copenhagen.

The girl answered in perfect English, which was just as well. Tweed spoke no Danish.

'He is not here at present. If you would care to leave a message?'

'No message . . .'

Tweed stared at the phone. Zero out of four. There was nothing strange about it. He had personally trained all four to get out of their offices, into the field, to keep close personal contact with their agents. In a way it was a good sign. So why was he so disturbed?

He found Kuhlmann and Newman sitting at a table in an empty canteen. The German said would he like some coffee? Tweed shook his head and sat down as Kuhlmann continued what he had been saying to Newman.

'. . . So a team of psychiatrists is on the way from Wiesbaden. I could do without those gentlemen. Most of them are nutcases.

Their reports – the bits you *can* understand – read like the ravings of madmen. Which doesn't help – considering we're all hunting someone who has to be stark raving mad . . .'

'Or a sadist,' said Tweed.

'Which comes to the same thing. They draw up a profile – a portrait of the personality of the killer . . .'

'I'm beginning to build up my own profile of him,' Tweed remarked. 'How can we most easily get to Travemünde from here?'

'By using me as a chauffeur. I'm on my way there myself.'

'Oh, thank God you've come, Tweedy. I rang the Jensen but they said you'd gone out. Isn't it too horrible . . . another girl . . . and a blonde again . . . I'm blonde . . .'

Diana Chadwick was shaking as Tweed arrived on board the *Südwind*. She ran forward as he stepped off the gangplank, threw her arms round him and sank her golden head into his chest. He patted her back, squeezed her, realized for the first time how slim she was. She cried a little. Tears of relief. Then she released him, dabbed at her eyes with an absurdly small lace handkerchief, and drew herself erect.

'I'm making a perfect fool of myself. Do forgive me. Let's have something to drink. Coffee? Something stronger?'

'Why not coffee. Under the circumstances?'

'You're so right. Alcohol will make me go to pieces again. Come down into the galley with me while I make the coffee. I don't like being alone for a second at the moment . . .'

He followed her down the companionway into the galley, perched on a narrow leather couch and looked around while she busied herself with the percolator.

'I was actually on deck here when that girl was killed,' she said.

'How do you know that? You heard something?'

'Oh, nothing horrible – like screams. But it's all over the town. The fact that she was killed about midnight. I was sitting watching the lights, waiting to feel sleepy.' She turned to face him, leaning against the counter while she waited for the coffee to be ready. Her face looked whiter than ever.

'Actually, Tweedy, I did hear something about a quarter past midnight. I didn't think much of it at the time . . .'

107

'And what was that?'

'The sound of a dinghy crossing the channel from the beach on this side to Priwall Island . . .'

'Diana . . .' Tweed was leaning forward, watching her intently, his eyes alert with interest behind his glasses. '. . . exactly what do you mean? A dinghy doesn't make any noise.'

'I'm not explaining this very well.' She brushed a lock of hair back over her finely-shaped forehead. 'I mean a dinghy equipped with an outboard motor. I even saw its wake – quite a distance beyond the marina. It disappeared behind a headland on Priwall Island. I thought it was a bit late for someone to be going home and then it went out of my mind – until I heard the news this morning.'

'Have you told the police?'

'God, no! They never stop questioning you.' She was leaning back so the curve of her hips showed clearly against the close-fitting white dress she wore. 'Coffee's ready,' she said and poured two cups. They went back up on deck.

'It's so claustrophobic down in that galley,' she said.

Tweed recognized the symptoms. She couldn't stay in one place for long. The symptoms of shock. They sat in the chairs on deck, the sun shone down, and she had no protection to shade her face. Badly shaken, Tweed said to himself. Understandable. But why this intense degree of shock?

'Will Dr Berlin be cancelling his party this afternoon?' Tweed wondered aloud. 'In view of what has happened?'

'Oh, no, I'm sure he won't. He's a wonderful man, but he is hardly aware of what is going on outside his own private orbit. I noticed that when I first met him in Kenya.'

'How did you first come to know him?'

'I must have been no more than eighteen. Everyone worshipped him – the work he was doing to help the natives. He had a hospital in the bush. Today everyone thinks of him as a second Dr Albert Schweitzer. He was a bit out of touch with the real world from what I've read. I drove a truck with medical supplies into the hospital in the bush. I was very idealistic in those days.'

'And now?'

'I suppose I've seen too much of men to be idealistic any more. It can be a curse being a blonde. They all think . . . well,

108

you know. Dr Berlin isn't like that though. He's only interested in his work, his work for the refugees now . . .'

'But surely the refugees who fled from East Prussia and the other territories after the war are settled, have made a life for themselves?'

'On the surface, yes. Underneath, it can be very difficult. Divided families on both sides of the border. He negotiates with the East Germans at times. They accept him as a neutral, probably because his parents were born in Leipzig.' She gave Tweed a fresh cup of coffee.

'That's enough about me – and Dr Berlin. Why is Bob Newman hobnobbing with Ann Grayle? I saw him over there walking on to her landing stage . . .'

'You know these reporters. Always love talking to people, hoping for something they can turn into a story . . .'

'I spent the morning, Mr Newman, going through my bags looking for my gun,' Ann Grayle said as they sat on the deck of the sloop, drinking gin and tonic.

'And did you find it?'

'Look.' She reached down for her handbag, opened it and handed something to Newman, leaning forward so he caught the faintest whiff of perfume. She really was a very attractive woman he thought to himself.

Resting on the open palm of his hand was a Browning automatic .32 calibre. He recognized the weapon. Manufactured at Herstal, Belgium.

'Careful, it's loaded,' she warned.

'You have the experience to use it?'

'I was a crack shot back in the old Nairobi days. A woman left alone while her husband was working needed some protection. The natives could turn on you without warning.'

'And if someone crept aboard this sloop after dark?'

'I'd shoot him point-blank.'

There was a crisp, whiplash in her tone. As he handed back the gun Newman had no doubt she'd do just what she said. She slipped the Browning back inside her handbag and crossed her shapely legs, watching him as she spoke.

'I see your friend, Tweed, is being entertained by Goldenlegs. Is he a widower? He'd better watch it.'

'Goldenlegs?'

'A bit crude perhaps, but it sums up her best assets – and how she uses them . . .'

'I don't imagine Dr Berlin has much interest in women,' Newman said, changing the subject.

'Your imagination would be wildly wrong. I know he poses as the great Father Figure, the second Albert Schweitzer. But take my word for it, he likes attractive girls. You'll see some of them at his party. He has them carefully vetted before they're admitted into the august presence.'

'Vetted? You're joking . . .'

'I'm not used to being contradicted. Vetted is what I said. His chief assistant, Danny Warning, checks their backgrounds before any girl is allowed near Dr Berlin. They're on the lookout for reporters slipping through the security. I can't imagine why you've been invited . . .'

'Maybe because I did once interview him. You've kept your friendship with Dr Berlin since those long ago days in Kenya?'

'Since Nairobi I haven't exchanged a word with him – nor have the rest of the old crowd. He keeps us very much out of his new life.'

'Why?'

'I've no idea. He wasn't sociable back in Kenya. But then the bush hospital took up most of his time in those days.'

'You said none of the old crowd knows him any more. What about Diana Chadwick?'

'Goldenlegs is the one exception. She helped him with the hospital years ago. I suppose they struck up some kind of relationship that has lasted. Mind you, in case you think I'm the perfect bitch, I'm sure her friendship with Dr Berlin is purely platonic, as they used to say.' She stood up. 'And now I'm going to throw you off the sloop. I have my hair to wash – that beastly atrocity last night has upset me. And I see Tweed has torn himself away from Diana and is coming over to see you. Have a good time at the party. It will be an eye-opener . . .'

Fourteen

The ferry to Priwall Island was like a barge with steel walls and a raised ramp fore and aft. It was crammed with passengers and carried about half-a-dozen cars. One of the crew was chatting to Tweed while Newman and Diana stood near the prow.

'That tall building over there is the Maritim Hotel,' the crewman told Tweed. 'There's a flashing light at the top after dark to mark the entrance to the channel. You can see the old lighthouse – that red structure this side . . .'

Tweed estimated the hotel was well over twenty storeys – far and away the tallest building in Travemünde or Lübeck. The Baltic was choppy with wavelets under the burning sun, but the crossing took less than five minutes.

'Looks like we have a maniac on the loose,' the crewman continued. 'Two girls raped and slashed up in less than twenty-four hours. It's going to affect the season if we're not careful. I heard a number of holidaymakers have paid their bills and left.'

'How do you know they were raped?' Tweed enquired.

'It's all round the town. People talk of nothing else. I'll have to go now . . .'

The ferry slowed, bumped against the shore, the forward ramp was lowered and cars and passengers on foot began disembarking. Tweed was about to follow when the voice spoke in his ear.

'Interesting that Dr Berlin doesn't allow anything to disturb his arrangements. A couple of girls carved up,' Kuhlmann went on, 'a trivial incident.'

'You are coming to the party?' Tweed asked as they walked off and started down the Mecklenburger-strasse. He was again struck by the peace of the island, the abundance of trees.

'I may put in an appearance later. Take a good look at the security. God takes good care of himself. Have fun . . .'

It started immediately at the entrance to the mansion. Tweed was startled to see Newman holding up his arms while two guards patted his body, checking for weapons presumably. Another guard was checking Diana's handbag. Tweed joined the queue and heard Newman's comment loud and clear.

'Hell's bells. You think we're boarding an aircraft? Where are the metal detectors? And if you've got the American President here your security is lousy. Where are the dogs?'

There was confusion. The queue froze. A short, heavily-built man with a bald head which gleamed in the sun hurried up to the guards. He addressed Newman.

'I am Danny Warning, chief of security. Who are you?'

'Newman. Robert Newman. And I *was* invited to this San Quentin circus you're running . . .'

'You said something about dogs,' Warning said nastily.

'To sniff us for explosives. Do the job properly or not at all,' Newman went on sarcastically.

Warning turned to another guard who held a clipboard and a pen. 'Robert Newman,' he snapped.

'Yes, sir. He's on the list . . .'

'You have some form of identification?' Warning demanded as he turned to face Newman again. 'Driving licence? Passport?'

'In a pig's eye . . .'

A tall thin man came running across the vast expanse of lawn. Tweed realized Newman's voice must have carried clear to the distant mansion looming in front of more trees. The thin man grasped Warning's arm.

'It's all right. I recognize him. No fuss . . .'

'I have my job to do,' Warning snapped again.

'Dr Berlin sent me to tell you. No fuss,' he repeated.

'You may proceed,' Warning said.

Newman looked over his shoulder to where Diana stood watching him with a quirky smile. He beckoned her forward and shouted at the top of his voice.

'Come on! Don't worry. If Danny Warning tries to search you I'll kick his teeth in . . .'

What the hell do you think you're doing, Tweed wondered at the back of the crowd of waiting people. He watched Diana stroll forward, Newman take her arm and lead her across the lawn. When Tweed reached the open gateway he stopped and waited for the guards to check him. For the first time he noticed the thin man had a walkie-talkie. As Warning stepped forward the thin man again laid a hand on his arm.

'Let Mr Tweed through. He is an honoured guest.'

'Thank you,' said Tweed.

Warning's dark eyes, blank of all expression, scanned Tweed, then he snapped his fingers. One of a dozen waiters touring the lawn with trays of glasses came forward.

'Champagne here, sir.' He indicated a line of glasses. 'Or Chablis or Beaujolais . . .'

'Champagne, I think. Thank you,' Tweed said again and wandered towards the large mansion perched on a slight eminence. It was probably built before the First World War, he guessed. The trim lawn was crowded with groups of chattering guests. Newman and Diana came up to him.

'And what was all that about, Bob?' Tweed asked coldly. 'We didn't come here to be conspicuous.'

'A test. First, I don't like being pawed by Dr Berlin's goons. But mainly to see how much he would take. How badly he wanted us to attend his shindig . . .'

'You're brighter than I'd thought,' Tweed admitted. 'And His Highness is up there, I think . . .'

They had their first view of Dr Berlin.

In front of the three-storey mansion – running along its full width – was a raised terrace. A broad flight of stone steps led up to it from the lawn. At the foot of the steps stood a group of men in civilian clothes who were obviously guards, barring the way.

A large oblong table covered with a white cloth stood in the very centre of the terrace. A dozen people sat at the table, nine men and three attractive girls, two brunettes and a redhead. At the far side of the table in a central position sat a bulky figure with a black beard.

He sat very still, a grey beret pulled down over his head. A cloak of the same colour was thrown over his shoulders and draped over his body despite the torrid heat. But the looming hulk of the mansion behind threw a shadow over the terrace.

Dr Berlin wore large tinted glasses and he was holding up a pair of binoculars aimed at the entrance gateway. Tweed sipped

113

at his champagne as he studied his host from a distance of about fifty metres. Newman smiled cynically before he spoke.

'One thing I'll give him – he's well-organized.'

'What makes you say that?' asked Diana.

'That sudden switch of attitude on the part of bully-boy Danny Warning puzzled me. I see what happened now. From his elevated position Berlin can see through those field-glasses clear to the gate. He recognized me. And by his left hand on the table is a walkie-talkie. He can issue instructions to every guard on the premises through that. How did you manage, Tweed?'

'Received as an honoured guest . . .'

'You can see why now. He saw you through the binoculars – and for my money this is a damned weird set-up.'

'I can see the "how",' Tweed said slowly. 'What I don't see is the "why" – *why* he should be so interested in inviting me here so he can see me . . .'

'Or so you can see him,' Diana interjected flippantly.

'And this is as close as we get,' Newman remarked.

Across the lawn was strung a thick rope slung from poles rammed into the grass. The area beyond was empty of guests and more guards in civilian clothes patrolled up and down behind the rope.

'You know what I think they were checking me for?' Newman remarked to Diana as they strolled back into the crowd. 'A camera. You said he didn't like his picture being taken. Now I wonder why?'

'He's just naturally shy. Hates publicity. There are very few photographs of him in existence. He wouldn't even let me snap him. We've lost Tweed,' she said suddenly.

Tweed was still standing where they had left him, taking polite sips at his glass while he apparently admired the mansion. But all the time he was studying Dr Berlin. His host swivelled the field-glasses and the twin lenses focused directly on Tweed. Aware of the scrutiny, Tweed held his ground, staring back.

Apart from manipulating the binoculars the man rarely moved. Others at his table chatted away to each other, drank and refilled their glasses, ate from plates piled with some kind of edibles and seemed to be enjoying themselves. Dr Berlin put the binoculars down on the table, still staring at Tweed

114

through the tinted glasses, his hands hidden behind two large coffee pots.

Difficult to see his expression at that distance. The beard didn't help. The sheer lack of motion in the man fascinated Tweed, who stood equally still. There was no one else near him as he remained staring at the terrace, one hand in the pocket of his safari jacket, the other holding his glass.

He felt a soft hand grip his forearm and he knew without looking round it was Diana. She tugged gently, urging him to join her. He waited a moment longer, gazing at the terrace. The side of her face touched his. He felt the soft outline of her breast against his upper arm. 'Come on, Tweedy,' she whispered.

He let her lead him away, into the crowds, weaving her way until they reached Newman who was standing alone, his expression grim. He looked relieved as they came up to him.

'There,' Diana said, 'I've rescued him. He's safe now.'

'Safe? What on earth are you talking about?' Tweed asked.

Newman replied. 'Do you realize that standing out there in the middle of the lawn on your own you made the perfect target?'

'Stuff and nonsense . . .'

The hot, airless afternoon drifted past. Waiters brought an endless supply of trays stacked with food, with more glasses of wine. Tweed studied the other guests. Smartly-dressed men and women. Middle class. But Germany these days was almost one great middle class. Local businessmen and merchants with their wives. Doubtless a few marzipan kings. Lübeck was famous for its marzipan.

Some faces he recognized from his prowls round the marinas. The sailing buffs. But no one he could see from the old Kenya brigade.

'Fun, isn't it?' Diana said. 'I love parties . . .'

'Must have cost him a mint of money,' Tweed replied. 'Where does Dr Berlin get his money from?'

'Various organizations which support his activities to help the refugees. Most of the guests here will have contributed to one association or another. They feel they are all right, so they give something to help the less fortunate . . .'

'I wonder if anyone audits his books?'

'Cynic!'

The party broke up suddenly in a riot of confusion at exactly six o'clock.

The three of them were standing near the entrance gates – which had been closed – when the fleet of cars pulled in at the kerb. Kuhlmann himself pushed open the right-hand gate, followed by a team of men in plain clothes.

Danny Warning tried to stop him. Kuhlmann shoved his identity folder in the stocky security chief's face. He pushed him aside roughly, shouting orders to his companions.

'This is private property,' Warning rasped.

'And this . . .' Kuhlmann shoved a piece of paper in his face, 'is a warrant to search the grounds and the premises. Get out of my way or you're arrested . . .'

A sudden hush fell over the crowd of guests. A sea of faces turned as Kuhlmann marched across the lawn towards the mansion. With a gesture he summoned Tweed, Newman and Diana to follow him. The team of men with him spread out, taking guests' names.

They broke out beyond the crowd and Tweed stopped as Kuhlmann wrenched up the rope with a savage jerk. Tweed grasped both Newman and Diana by the arm as Kuhlmann moved across the open lawn.

'Look,' said Tweed. 'The terrace . . .'

Dr Berlin's special guests still sat at the oblong table, all faces turned towards Kuhlmann. But there was a gap in the centre. Dr Berlin's chair was empty.

'Diana,' Tweed said urgently, 'is there any other way out of this place?'

'Only the drive alongside the lawn . . .'

As she spoke Tweed heard the sound of a car's engine driving past them down the drive concealed behind trees towards the Mecklenburger-strasse. He turned and began running for the gates. Diana was amazed at how fast he could move. Newman ran after him and Diana followed.

Tweed reached the gate as a black Mercedes with tinted windows swung out of the drive and past the gates heading for the ferry. He ran after the vehicle, thanked God he was wearing the safari jacket Diana had persuaded him to buy. He kept on running and in the distance he saw the ferry was about to leave. He paced himself, running more steadily, covering a lot of ground.

He was in time to see the Mercedes – which had a tinted rear window – driving aboard the ferry. He kept on running. The silhouette of a man sitting in the rear turned and looked back. Tweed had a vague impression of a head wearing a beret, a black beard. Dr Berlin gave him a little wave and then the ramp was raised and the ferry departed for Travemünde.

Tweed stopped running, swore aloud, stood panting to regain his breath as Newman and Diana caught up with him.

'He got away,' said Tweed, wiping sweat off his brow.

'You look furious,' Diana said. 'Why?'

'The bastard waved at me. But it's not that. I know that man. I've seen him before. Talked to him. I'm sure of it.'

'That's impossible,' Newman objected.

'I know him,' Tweed repeated. 'That little wave he gave me. Give me time. I'll remember . . .'

Fifteen

They boarded the ferry when it returned. Diana walked by herself to the bows and stood, arms folded, gazing at Trave-münde. Tweed stayed back amidships with Newman.

'Let her alone,' he advised, 'something has upset her. When we get off I'll take her back to the *Südwind*. She said something significant recently and I'm damned if I can recall what it was. Maybe talking to her will bring it back . . .'

'In any case you like her,' Newman remarked drily.

'And how will you spend your time?' countered Tweed.

'I have to report on the party to Ann Grayle. I promised her I would.'

'Then you must do your duty,' Tweed replied with a blank expression.

He had noticed a change in Newman's attitude to women since his return to London from the year in France. During his

117

time abroad, Newman had told him, he had wandered round France on his own, trying to forget the bizarre murder of his wife in Estonia. He'd had nothing to do with women while in France. Now, gradually, he was returning to normal. His preoccupation with Ann Grayle proved the point.

'Why do you think Kuhlmann organized that raid on Dr Berlin's home?' Newman asked.

'No idea. One thing is for sure. The operation was Kuhlmann at his best and most ruthless. He exploited the element of surprise to the limit. The choice of timing.'

'I don't follow you . . .'

'Six o'clock in the evening. On the dot. He let the party get well under way. Everyone – including the guards – would be in a relaxed mood. Kuhlmann struck when they were at their most vulnerable. And that includes the guests.'

Tweed remained silent until the ferry was slowing prior to landing. He made his request as a throwaway remark.

'One thing I'd like you to do. Find out where Diana gets her money from. She has no visible means of support, as they say.'

'Ann Grayle has a pretty acid answer to that one . . .'

'Try that man she has on board. Ben. I must be off now. We can meet back at the Jensen . . .'

Diana was waiting for him just beyond the lowered ramp. She looped her arm inside his. Under her wide-brimmed hat her face looked even whiter than usual and he sensed her nervousness. It was the hottest hour of the day. The sun beat down on Travemünde, the ground gave up the heat it had absorbed during the day, the air was foetid.

'Will you come back with me to the boat, Tweedy?'

'Of course. We can have a talk. That was a somewhat shattering end to the party . . .'

'And I'm responsible. Wait till we get to the boat and then I'll explain.'

'Champers do you?' she asked as they walked over the gangplank.

'Splendid idea. You're full of them.' Tweed's mood had become jocular. 'Let me uncork the bottle. Then we won't get half of it on the deck instead of inside us.'

He followed her down the companionway and she opened

the fridge, produced a bottle and held it up for his inspection. 'Dom Perignon? Appeals?'

Tweed took the bottle and began peeling off the foil. She placed glasses on the working top, crossed to the leather couch and perched on it, her legs coiled beneath her like a cat.

'Oh, look,' she said, 'there's an envelope propped against the cupboard. Be a darling and open it for me. Later . . .'

Tweed had already noticed the envelope. Expensive paper. Her name was typed in capitals. DIANA CHADWICK. He opened the bottle, poured into the two tulip glasses she had placed on the counter, and carried them over to the couch. She eased her way to one end.

'Sit with me. I'm a bit edgy . . .'

'Get some of this down. You'll feel wonderful. Cheers!'

'Cheers!' She drank the whole glass, he refilled it, and she drank half the contents of the fresh glass. The sparkle came back into her deep blue eyes. 'Now, I'll tell you. A very grim policeman came aboard early this morning. Grim, but I liked him. If that makes any sense. A man called Kuhlmann. He reminded me of a human powerhouse. Could I have a drop more?'

'That's what it's for.'

'He's very clever, this Kuhlmann. No one else could have persuaded me to tell him what I did.'

'And what did you tell him?'

'About that dinghy with the outboard I heard crossing over the channel from the beach after midnight . . .'

'I said you ought to tell the police.'

'I know.' She was playing with a lace handkerchief. She looked up suddenly at Tweed. 'I also told him Dr Berlin has an outboard-powered dinghy, that the one I saw – the wake as I told you – was heading for the marina where he keeps his dinghy. That, I am sure, is why the police raided the party. I feel awful about it now.'

'Surely a lot of people have that type of craft?'

'I suppose so . . .' She drank more champagne and went vague.

'Let's have a look at your letter,' Tweed said briskly.

He stood with his back to her, masking what he was doing. He picked up the envelope between the flat of his hands.

Fortunately, the flap had been hastily closed and came open easily. He extracted the folded message with his fingertips, opened it and read the brief message which bore signs of being hastily typed. Even the signature was typed. He read it aloud to her.

' "Will be away for a while. Look after *Südwind*. Expenses waiting at bank. Berlin." ' He spoke over his shoulder. 'Can I keep this for a bit?'

'Why not?'

He slipped the folded sheet back into the envelope and slid the envelope inside his breast pocket. When he turned round she was lying back, her head resting on the cushion, staring up at the cabin roof. He sat down on the couch again.

'Diana, I can't quite understand it. He must have had this typed and delivered earlier this afternoon – which means he knew he would be leaving . . .'

'Not necessarily. That big Mercedes has everything inside it – including a desk flap and a small portable typewriter. He could have typed that while they were crossing on the ferry. Then he could have given it to one of his assistants, dropped him off when they landed so he could deliver it here while we were waiting for the ferry to come back.'

'He types himself?'

'Yes. He's always typing little notes with instructions.' Her eyes were sleepy as she watched him. 'He has many talents people don't know about. He plays the piano well. His favourite composer is Chopin. Stay the night with me here, Tweedy.'

'I was coming to that.' His tone was businesslike. 'After two murders nearby – and like those poor girls, you are also a blonde – you are not spending one more night aboard this cruiser. You come back to the Jensen and sleep there in your room. Is that clearly understood?'

'It's nice to have someone who cares. Yes, it is understood. I promise.'

'Then we'd better find Newman and get back to Lübeck . . .'

'After we've finished the bottle . . .'

She stretched out her right leg and rested it on his lap. He squeezed her ankle with his free hand, then shook his head as she raised herself and moved towards him.

'I'm fond of you, Diana, but I'm fully-occupied with a job which must be done. And I have a wife . . .'

'Bob told me you were separated from her – have been for a long time.'

'Newman talks too much. We'll finish the champagne and then go . . .'

'An insurance job? You help people who are kidnapped – or who might be. Wealthy people . . .'

'That's right. I can't talk about it. Drink up . . .'

They collected Newman from Ann Grayle's sloop. Diana waited at the end of the landing-stage, keeping well away from what she called 'that Grayle woman'.

It was only a short walk to the station, Travemünde Hafen. Aboard the empty train Diana sat by herself further along the coach, staring out of the window.

'She's upset,' Tweed explained to Newman, and told him about the letter and the outboard dinghy she had witnessed crossing to Priwall Island, the facts she had reported to Kuhlmann.

'A lot of people must have those dinghies,' Newman objected. 'I've seen at least a dozen of them.'

'That's what I said to her. There's something she didn't tell me – but I think she told Kuhlmann. Hence the raid. I think we've lost Dr Berlin for some time, maybe for good. And I've remembered what Diana said that seemed important – but not when she said it.'

'What was that?'

'Later . . .'

Tweed had spotted Diana leaving her seat and coming back to their part of the coach. She seemed quite different, her mood was impish, her walk light-footed. She sat down opposite Tweed.

'Sorry,' she said.

'For what?'

'Being so ill-mannered – going off on my own. I had the Black Dog perched on my shoulder – isn't that what Churchill used to say? I read it in a book. I had a decision to make . . .'

'Nothing to be sorry about,' Tweed assured her. 'Want to tell me about your decision?'

121

'Yes. I told that Federal policeman, Kuhlmann, more than I told you. That was why I had the raid on my conscience. I think you should both know what I did tell him. Especially since what happened when the police raid took place – the way Dr Berlin drove off at speed.'

'Clearly he wanted to avoid the police,' Tweed remarked.

'I told you Kuhlmann could be very persuasive. I told him I'd phoned Dr Berlin at his home just before midnight. He never goes to bed before two o'clock. He was always up late in the old Kenya days.'

She hesitated, dropped her eyes, and Tweed frowned at Newman to stop him speaking. Diana asked Newman for a cigarette and took a deep drag after he had lit it. She stared straight at Tweed.

'There was no reply. I'd called his private number which goes straight through to his study . . .'

'Maybe he was in another part of the house – it's a big place.'

'Which is exactly what Kuhlmann said. After trying the private line I called the house number. Danny Warning answered it. When I asked for Dr Berlin he said he was in his study and didn't want to be disturbed. Oh, God, I must be wrong.'

'The fact remains,' Tweed said, 'your calls proved Dr Berlin was not at home at just about the time Iris Hansen was killed on the beach.'

Sixteen

'I'm flying back to London,' Tweed announced. 'In the strictest secrecy. They'll know I've arrived at Park Crescent when I walk through the front door.'

He was pacing his bedroom at the Jensen with slow deliberate steps when he told Newman. He stood very erect and there was a hardness in his voice which startled Newman.

'What has happened?' he asked. 'I'm coming with you . . .'

'You are not. You stay here to guard Diana Chadwick. I shall catch the express to Hamburg tomorrow, go straight from

122

the Hauptbahnhof to the airport, buy a ticket and board the first flight.'

'I'll ask you again. Why this sudden turnabout? I know you came here because you suspected you were being led into a trap – and you wanted to spring the trap yourself . . .'

'I have learned things since which make me realize the crisis facing me could be infinitely worse than I suspected – the most appalling crisis Park Crescent has been confronted with since I joined the service. If I'm right – and I hope to God I'm not – I can't see how the situation could be resolved without a terrible scandal. Don't question me. I could be wrong.'

'You were going to tell me,' Newman said quietly, 'what it was that Diana said that was important.'

'She said, I quote her exact words, "or so you can see him". She was referring to the fact that I was puzzled why Dr Berlin should want to see me. She turned it round the other way.'

'You're talking in riddles . . .'

'And I am referring to a really gigantic riddle.' Tweed sat down and his whole manner changed. 'Now, Bob, find out any more about how Diana lives – the source of her income?'

'Ann Grayle started on about Goldenlegs again but I cut her short. Then she stopped being catty. She told me there is a strong rumour Dr Berlin supports her with an allowance – a very generous allowance. More than enough to live on. She looks after the *Südwind* – and his other power cruiser, the *Nordsee*, berthed at that marina on Priwall Island near the ferry. Ann marked its position on this map.' He handed a folded sheet to Tweed.

'*Another* cruiser? How big is this *Nordsee*? Did she say?'

'Very big – the twin of the *Südwind*. Capable of travelling long distances – and in rough weather. Berlin himself crews whichever vessel he takes out. He's often absent for long periods. No one knows where. A friend of Ann's swore he once saw the *Südwind* at a marina in Oslo.'

'What is he doing on these extended voyages?'

'Contacting various European organizations which provide him finance for his work with refugees. There are quite a few in Scandinavia – I know that from my own travels . . .'

'And who pays for all this? The mansion on Priwall Island,

123

the two large power cruisers. Those things eat money – even in a marina,' Tweed remarked.

'The charitable organizations I've just mentioned. I gathered from Ann Grayle Dr Berlin has a hypnotic effect on the more liberal element. His influence extends as far as the States. He's a power in the land.'

Tweed looked unhappy. 'All you're telling me makes it seem I could be right in my bizarre theory. And I want to be wrong. You simply must not let Diana out of your sight while I am away. She is blonde, remember – as were all the victims.'

'And how long will you be away?'

'A matter of days, I expect. No one must know where I've gone. If you find yourself under pressure, say "Copenhagen". And one man must not know above all others. Otto Kuhlmann.'

'Why Kuhlmann?'

'Because there is one other man who was present in Frankfurt when that Dutch girl was killed, and also here when Helena Andersen and Iris Hansen were hacked to pieces.'

'Who is that?'

'Otto Kuhlmann.'

'That phone call was negative,' Markus Wolf reported to General Lysenko in his fifth-floor office in Leipzig.

'In what way? Get to the point.'

'Munzel carried out an initial attack on Tweed. He does that sometimes – to get the measure of his target. The attack was not conclusive owing to the intervention of the British foreign correspondent, Robert Newman . . .'

'Tweed is still alive and well? Is that what you are trying to say to me in your devious way?' Lysenko demanded.

'Tweed still exists, yes. For the moment. Call it a trial run. The elimination of Tweed will proceed as planned . . .'

'Balls!' Lysenko gave full vent to his fury. 'And I have to fly back to Moscow to report to the General Secretary. He will be most pleased, I am sure.'

'Please pass on to Comrade Gorbachev my warmest regards.'

'That will make him the happiest man in the Soviet Union. I think we may have to substitute someone more effective for Munzel . . .'

Wolf removed his horn-rimmed glasses and stared at

124

Lysenko. He seemed quite unruffled by the news, by Lysenko's outburst. He chewed on a corner of one of the handles of his spectacles.

'Munzel is the best – as the General Secretary well knows. I shall go ahead with the next stage in the operation while you are away . . .'

'I shan't be away long,' Lysenko said savagely. 'So what do you expect to achieve? And something else worries me greatly. I told you Munzel is a sadist. Who do you think might be responsible for the ferocious killings of those two blonde girls in Travemünde?'

'I cannot accept scandalous implications about a member of my staff . . .'

'Implications be damned! If it were Munzel, if Tweed turned the tables and proved it – and unmasked his identity. God! Can you imagine the propaganda he could make of that?'

'It won't happen . . .'

'I find that statement immensely reassuring.' Lysenko's tone dripped with sarcasm. 'I am not prepared to leave it at that.'

'What do you mean?'

Wolf rose from his chair, replaced his glasses and glared at the Russian. They were on the verge of a major confrontation. Lysenko rumbled on, refusing to give an inch. He hammered his clenched fist on the desk.

'Balkan is in the area. Contact him. Ask him to investigate these killings with all energy. Any development, report to me in Moscow. Understood?'

'If you insist . . .'

'I don't insist. It is an order.'

'And am I permitted to tell you my next move?'

'Hurry up.' Lysenko checked his watch. 'I shall be late for my flight to Moscow.'

'I have already sent the instruction to Munzel, who has, for a short while, gone underground . . .'

'What instruction? I said I was in a hurry.'

'He is to kill Newman, Tweed's protector. Then kill Tweed. Both at the same time if possible. Both will appear to have been accidents. A mutual accident . . .'

'Get Balkan to check those blonde murders,' Lysenko said and left the room.

*

125

The taxi transporting Tweed and Newman pulled up outside Lübeck-Süd police HQ. Tweed had phoned Kuhlmann before they left the Jensen and the man from Wiesbaden was waiting in the entrance hall.

'The scrambler phone is ready for your use,' Kuhlmann said as they ascended in the elevator. 'Newman and I will wait in the canteen as before.'

Tweed entered the same bleak room, locked the door and sat at the desk. He thought for a moment, then lifted the receiver and dialled Monica's number at Park Crescent. She answered almost immediately.

'Hadrian here, Monica. Any developments? This is a safe phone – as far as any instrument is these days.'

'Nothing to report. Except an absence of calls from anyone. I find that strange, a bit nerve-wracking. It's good to hear your voice.'

'I agree it's abnormal. But it might fit in with a theory I'm developing – so don't worry,' he reassured her.

'Any instructions?'

'Yes. I'm coming back – but no one must know. And this is priority one – contact all four sector chiefs. Order them to return to London base. They must be available by nine in the morning the day after tomorrow.'

'All four? There could be problems . . .'

'I said priority one. They must be found, they must arrive.'

'They will be. Take care . . .'

He replaced the receiver. Before leaving the room he took a deep breath, aware that his expression could be grim. He strolled into the canteen, sat down at the table where Newman and Kuhlmann were talking over coffee.

'Satisfactory?' Kuhlmann enquired.

'Up to a point. We'd better get going. And thank you for the use of the phone . . .'

'Kuhlmann has something to tell you,' Newman interjected.

'Oh, yes?'

'Dr Berlin returned to his mansion as soon as the search had been completed. That was after all of us had left. I heard on the phone from the local Travemünde police station.'

'Are you going to interview him?'

'No authority. I can't go back. The warrant was to search the premises and grounds, note down all the guests' names. We did find one interesting item. High-powered transceiver hidden behind a bookcase in the library. Range would permit messages to and from Kaliningrad. That happens to be a major Soviet communications centre.'

'Illegal? You said it was hidden,' Tweed commented.

'Not at all. And Danny Warning, that toad of a security chief, said it was expensive equipment – so it had to be concealed from burglars.' He lit a cigar. 'I don't like that Warning. I can't do anything more.'

'Can you do anything about Kurt Franck?' Tweed asked.

'If I could find him – which I can't – negative. Neither of you made a positive identification. He checked out of the Movenpick, drove off in his hired BMW. Vanishing trick. See you.'

Waiting outside in the night, which was warm and humid, for their cab, Tweed stared into the darkness. He spoke suddenly.

'Guard Diana well, Bob. She could be the key to this mysterious business – the murders of Fergusson and Palewska in Hamburg, the enigma of Dr Berlin. And something much bigger.'

'Since you keep on about my guarding her you wouldn't care to tell me why?'

'She could be a witness,' Tweed said. '*The* witness . . .'

The following morning, his bag packed, Tweed phoned Kuhlmann at police HQ. The German came on the line and sounded impatient.

'I'm throwing out a dragnet across North Germany – looking for Franck. What is it?'

'I just wondered whether there were any developments on the Dr Berlin front.'

'You psychic? He's disappeared again. Early this morning. I had him tracked to Lübeck airfield – that's close to the border. He was flown off in a light aircraft. The flight plan filed was for Hamburg and Hanover . . .'

'Thank you. I won't hold you up any longer.'

Tweed replaced the receiver, looked at Newman sitting in one of his bedroom chairs and clapped his hands together.

127

'You look pleased with yourself,' Newman commented.

'Not really. Kuhlmann tells me Dr Berlin has flown off from Lübeck – from that airfield I spotted on the map. We must visit it when I get back. What are you going to do today?'

'Diana is restless, edgy. She wants us to go out to Travemünde. Which suits me. I want to have a word with that chap, Ben – Ann Grayle's friend – on his own . . .'

'Don't forget. No one must know I've left Germany.'

'You're pretty conspicuous in that safari jacket. I'll come with you to the station. Diana will wait till I get back. So stop fussing.'

At the Hauptbahnhof Tweed joined a small queue for tickets. A plump individual walked up behind him and also stood waiting. Newman, pretending to look at a paperback, tried to recall where he had seen the man before.

Tweed bought a one-way first class ticket to Bonn and hurried to his platform, carrying his white suitcase. Newman continued watching as the plump man bought his own ticket, then made for a phone booth.

Inside the booth he dialled the number of Martin Vollmer's apartment in Altona. Vollmer came on the line at once.

'Gustav here,' the plump man said in a throaty voice. 'Tweed is leaving Lübeck by train. Bought a one-way ticket for Bonn.' He described how Tweed was dressed.

'I'll report to Balkan. I'll also check at Hamburg. Just to make sure . . .'

Newman followed the plump man who shoved his ticket inside a pocket. He walked outside the Hauptbahnhof, climbed behind the wheel of a parked BMW and drove off. He remembered now where he had seen him. He was one of Danny Warning's guards who had patrolled the grounds at the party.

The wires began humming again.

'Tweed is coming to Bonn . . . to Bonn . . . *Bonn* . . .'

Aboard the Hamburg Express, Tweed found an empty compartment on the train which was very quiet. He took his large white case, bought the previous day in Lübeck, with him to the lavatory and locked the door. Unfastening the white case he took out the smaller blue one and opened that. He performed the athletic process of changing into a dark blue business suit.

128

Then he put the safari jacket and the tropical drill slacks inside the white case and closed it.

Opening the door, he glanced along the deserted corridor, opened the window of the exit door and waited. The train reached a point where it travelled along an embankment. At the bottom a tangle of high weeds grew; beyond the empty fields stretched away. Perching the case on the edge of the window, he gave a great heave. The case shot out, landed amid the weeds. He closed the window, went back to the lavatory for his blue case and returned to his compartment.

Hamburg Hauptbahnhof. Martin Vollmer stood on the same bridge overlooking the platforms where he had weeks earlier watched as Tweed and Newman boarded the Copenhagen Express. His lips moved in tune with his thoughts.

'Safari jacket, TD trousers, white case . . .'

He was watching the platform as the train came in from Lübeck. A handful of passengers trailed off the coaches and wandered to the staircase. Vollmer shook his head as the express moved off again, then walked to the nearest phone booth and dialled a number.

'Martin here. Tweed still aboard express for Bonn . . .'

Tweed was the first passenger to leave the train at Hamburg. He walked faster than his usual pace, and he had taken off his glasses. Climbing the staircase, he headed for the taxi rank.

'The airport,' he informed the driver and settled back in his seat. He glanced back twice through the rear window as the cab proceeded along the boulevard-like highway leading to the airport. No sign of anyone following.

Tweed sensed there was a dragnet out searching for him. They were probably using Markus Wolf's favourite technique – the leapfrog method. Station watchers at intervals along the target's known route. A technique almost impossible to spot – provided the target obliged by travelling the route they expected.

At the airport he bought a single first-class ticket to Heathrow for Lufthansa Flight 042, departing 13.40, arriving 14.05, local times. He was arriving in London twenty-four hours ahead of when he was expected. There was plenty to do before the meeting of the sector chiefs scheduled for nine the following morning. One appointment he hoped to make was crucial.

Seventeen

'Good God, man, where have you sprung from? You're not supposed to be here until tomorrow.'

He *had* to bump into Howard as soon as he entered Park Crescent. Tweed swore inwardly as Howard followed him up the stone steps and into his office. Monica looked up from her desk and stared. Tweed hung his Burberry on a hanger and sat behind his desk as Howard closed the door and perched his right buttock on the edge of the desk. He folded his arms and glowered at Tweed.

'And what, may I ask, is all this nonsense about summoning all four sector chiefs from Europe to a conference?'

'An essential part of my strategy to find the odd man out . . .'

'Which is so enlightening. And, of course,' Howard continued in his most upper crust tone, 'you yourself chose what you deem to call the odd man out . . .'

'Which increases my responsibility for tracking him down . . .'

'Masterly understatement,' Howard commented. 'To put it into the vernacular, your head is on the chopping block . . .'

'That's enough.' Tweed stood up behind the desk, his manner cold. 'I repeat, I take full responsibility, but I'm damned if I'm taking lectures from you. In case you've forgotten, you also checked the vetting reports.'

'Did you make any progress in Germany?' Howard had slid his bottom off the desk and stood stiffly. 'And may I remind you we have junior staff present?' he snapped, referring to Monica.

'Senior staff. She's been here longer than you have. As to progress, a little. The game is at an early stage. I move at my own pace. I'm also short of time.'

Howard dabbed his Roman nose with a silk handkerchief,

130

tucked it back in his cuff, and became more conciliatory, regretting his outburst.

'Are you all right? No damage, I trust? I heard you were involved in a scuffle in Lübeck.'

How the devil did he know that? Then Tweed remembered Lübeck was in Hugh Grey's sector. Of course. Grey would report back every titbit to curry favour with Howard.

'That was a minor incident. Probably of no significance. I would like to get on now. If you don't mind . . .'

'On my way. My desk is piled up like Everest. Doubt if I'll get to the club this evening . . .'

Monica waited until the door closed. 'The bastard!' she burst out. 'Your head on the chopping block, indeed. What does he think we're running? The Tower of London?'

'I do need every minute,' Tweed told her. 'If possible, I'd like an appointment with that psychiatrist we once used. And I don't mean the nutcase Howard sends people to. That sensible chap in Harley Street. Foreign-sounding name.'

'Dr Roger Generoso . . .'

'That's the chap. No, don't phone him for a second. I also want to drive out to Norfolk. That will have to be this evening. I want a chat with Hugh Grey's wife, Paula. I got on rather well with her when we last met. Fix up Generoso first, then Paula. She stays at the farmhouse most of the time if I remember rightly.'

'Had an appointment cancelled. You were lucky, Tweed. Trouble again for the General and Cumbria Assurance?'

Dr Roger Generoso was of medium height, well-built, middle-aged, had a rounded head and thinning hair. His manner was matter-of-fact. He listened to Tweed for ten minutes, making notes on his pad.

'That's about it,' Tweed said. 'What do you think?'

'A man leading a double life,' Generoso mused. 'One life here, the other on the continent. Keeps them both in separate compartments. Now under great pressure – and you propose to increase that pressure to expose his villainy as head of a kidnap gang. I think you're treading on thin ice.'

'Why?'

131

'Depends on whether you crack him. Put in simple language, we have a man with two sides to his head. That represents the two sides of his life. The danger is schizophrenia . . .'

'A schizo?'

'In common parlance, yes. It's as though he has a dam erected inside his brain. On one side, one life, on the other his secret existence. The danger is if the dam breaks, if one side floods into the other. Then anything could happen.'

'I read a book on Kim Philby once,' Tweed remarked. 'He drank like a fish, but still never gave himself away.'

'A good example. The alcohol saved him. Release from all the tremendous tension he laboured under.'

'So heavy drinking could be a sign?'

'Quite definitely.'

'This could be a very serious case,' Tweed said cautiously. 'If the pressure was exceptional might he resort to murdering women at random – in a rather bestial way?'

Generoso swivelled in his chair and studied Tweed. 'I didn't realize you were talking about an extreme case. There have been instances such as you describe. Very difficult to detect. The murderer might well appear perfectly normal most of the time – which is why some of my less perceptive colleagues have been known to let out of prison inmates who should be kept there for life.'

'Supposing he had a consistent tendency to kill and mutilate blonde girls?'

'You are in trouble, aren't you? Yes, to use your own word, a schizo. Surely the police should be informed?'

'They have one of the ablest men on the continent assigned to the case. It just so happens that his investigations and my own overlap. At least, they may. I'm simply not sure of anything. Are there any indications – habits – whereby such a schizo might be pinpointed? Might give himself away?'

'Oh dear, what a question.' Generoso leant back in his chair and stroked his head with one hand as though seeking to locate a clue. 'He's likely to be obsessive in some direction.'

'What kind of direction?'

'Maybe excessively neat. Fussy about small things. Can you describe the man you suspect?'

'There's more than one of them.'

132

'Doesn't help. I'm working in the dark.'

'So am I,' admitted Tweed. 'What about manifestations of character?'

'We might be on firmer ground there. Schizophrenics sometimes display an overweening self-confidence, verging on arrogance. We come back to Philby. I'm sure he only started out as a crusader. Later it was the game which hypnotized him – the delight in fooling people.'

'And if he thought the net was closing round him – that he was in danger of being exposed, identified? Would he panic?'

'Unlikely. These people can be devilish cunning. He'd feel sure he could always outwit his adversaries – because he was so much cleverer than them. That might cause him to step up the challenge . . .'

'Kill more girls?'

'I fear so.'

'And would he,' Tweed persisted, 'keep away from women?'

'Not necessarily. He might do the opposite – to divert suspicion. It's difficult for the layman to appreciate just how fiendishly clever a split personality can be. He's very like an actor – playing two roles. Another characteristic I'd count on would be insufferable conceit, a feeling of great superiority to all other human beings. That might not show,' he warned.

'Getting back to putting pressure on him – to crack him?'

'There you are on very dangerous ground. Supposing we are talking about an extreme case – someone who is going round killing these blonde girls at intervals in time. Step up the pressure, you could step up the killings. His method of release from tension, his way of countering the pressure. And that, Tweed, I fear, is all I can say . . .'

'When you send your fee to General and Cumbria please address it to me personally.'

Generoso accompanied him to the door of his consulting room. He made the remark as he opened the door.

'Take care. If you are right, you could be in great peril . . .'

'Paula Grey is available,' Monica announced as Tweed closed the door of his office. 'She sounded oddly pleased that you were coming to see her.'

'I don't understand that. On the few occasions we've met we

133

have got on well, but you make it sound as though she were relieved . . .'

'I think she is. She runs her own business, as you know. She has a pottery works in Wisbech with a small staff of girls. She does well, I gather . . .'

'You had quite a chat with her then?'

'She seemed glad to have someone from the outside world she could talk to. You're going to see her now?'

'I'm driving out in a few minutes. I suppose all four sector chiefs are turning up for tomorrow's meeting?'

'I have passed the instruction. The girl in Bern said she might have trouble contacting Guy Dalby. I told her he had to come hell or high water. How did it go with Dr Generoso?'

'Disturbing,' Tweed replied, and left it at that.

It was early evening as Tweed drove his Ford Cortina (second-hand) into the outskirts of King's Lynn and turned left on to the A17 away from the town. He was heading west now, west for the lonely flatlands of the Wash.

Tweed liked driving on his own. It gave him a chance to think, to sift all the information which had been fed into his brain during his recent trip to Germany. He even whistled a little tune as he drove on and on with very little traffic about.

He had a photographic memory for routes. He only had to drive somewhere once and, no matter how remote his destination, how devious the route, he could always remember where and when to turn. He turned now, right off the main highway to Boston and on to a deserted country road.

The road was elevated above the surrounding countryside and he could see for miles, a scene of desolate solitude. Hugh Grey's farmhouse was located some distance from the village of Gedney Drove End, about a third of a mile from the vast open waters of the Wash.

He passed through a sleepy hamlet with a church standing apart from the few houses, an old church with a towered entrance gate and a general air of neglect. Then he saw the dyke, a high bank the colour of deep purple in the evening light. Below him on his left lay Gedney Marsh. Only the dyke held back the inundation of the sea. He was reminded of the countryside he had looked out on travelling with Newman on the train from Lübeck to Travemünde. He pulled up outside the farmhouse, a single-storey, L-shaped building with a tiled roof.

As he pushed the front gate he heard through the open windows music from a record player. Stravinsky's *Rite of Spring*. He pulled at the bell and looked round. The garden was a mess, the beds full of weeds, the lawn uncut for several weeks. He pulled at the bell again, waited for maybe fifteen seconds and the heavy wooden door opened. Paula Grey, dressed in spotless cream-coloured slacks and a pleated blue blouse with a mandarin collar, stood staring at him.

'You're earlier than I expected. Sorry, that sounds awful – do come in. Coffee? Or something stronger?'

'Coffee would do nicely. How are you?' he asked as she led him into an oblong-shaped sitting room furnished with chintz arm chairs, two settees and chintz curtains.

'Very glad of your company . . .'

She kissed him on the cheek and plumped up cushions in an armchair. The place was typical Hugh Grey, Tweed thought as she sat him down. 'My little place in the country,' as he referred to it. All chintz and sporting prints on the walls.

'I'll get the coffee. Won't be a sec. I'll turn off Stravinsky . . .'

'I like it . . .'

'Turn it down a bit, then.'

She did so, walked across to a desk, picked up a leather-bound notebook and slipped it into a drawer, turned the key quickly and shoved it into her pocket with her back to him. She smiled and disappeared behind a door beyond which Tweed had a brief glimpse of a modern kitchen.

He got out of the chair, crossed the room quietly and, as he had thought, the lock on the drawer had not closed properly. He slid it open, took out the notebook and skipped through the pages. A diary with entries here and there in neat handwriting. Her pen was still on the desk top.

H. says he's going abroad . . . Portman followed him to Heathrow. Boarded plane for Frankfurt . . . Returned unexpectedly today . . . Portman watched Chelsea flat all night . . . still no sign of other woman . . . paid Portman retainer and expenses in cash . . . H. says he is going abroad again . . .

135

Tweed closed the diary. Paula might return at any moment. He put the diary back in the drawer, almost closed it, then took a tenpenny coin from his pocket. He fiddled with the coin, closed the drawer the last quarter-inch as the lock snapped up and was in position. When she returned with the tray he was sitting in the arm chair, gazing out of the rear windows over fields of ripening wheat towards the great barrier of the dyke.

'I'm so glad you've come to see me,' Paula said as she came in with a tray. She paused. 'Oh, it's not bad news . . .'

'Hugh is in fine fettle,' Tweed said quickly. 'I thought that Monica made that clear when she called you.'

'She was a bit vague, but I know with the sort of insurance you handle security is paramount. Cream?'

'I think I'll indulge – just for once. No sugar. That would be overdoing it. Hugh will be back in London tomorrow – maybe you've heard?'

'No. He's so discreet. Never talks about his work.'

Paula was about five foot nine, slim, a good figure, a brunette with her raven black hair shaped to her neck. An attractive girl of twenty-nine, she was exactly ten years junior to her husband. She had a long face, excellent bone structure and an air of independence. She crossed a very good pair of legs.

'So I should see something of my wandering husband? Or is it another quick visit?'

'I'm going to give him a week's leave. He doesn't know that yet. You can call him at the office after midday tomorrow. He has to attend a policy meeting earlier.'

'That will be nice. His week's leave. Just so long as he doesn't want to ask half England to join us for dinner. He's incredibly sociable. Never happy unless he's surrounded with friends. Most of whom I do not like.'

'Friends from the old days?' Tweed suggested as he drank her excellent coffee. She perched on the edge of her hard-backed chair, her lively grey eyes watching him. She moved agilely but with grace. Tweed felt sure she was an expert horsewoman. Very sophisticated but unspoilt, and very quick on the uptake. He'd have to watch his step.

'That's right, Tweed,' she replied, talking to him like an old friend. 'The usual problem of a second wife, I suppose – and probably mainly my fault. Tell me – if you can – what is Hugh's

136

new job since you promoted him six months ago? Even a hint would help.'

'It's a bit confidential . . .' Tweed paused. 'He now has a high executive position and is responsible for some pretty big insurance policies. Mostly with individuals – some of them famous names you'd know at once if I could identify them, which I can't . . .'

'Insurance against kidnapping?'

'Something like that. He's also involved in delicate nego-tiations under certain circumstances . . .'

'With kidnap gangs when someone has been snatched? Isn't it a trifle dangerous?'

'I didn't say that.' Tweed smiled to take the sting out of the reply. 'We have a lot of experience and Hugh is one of my best men.'

'He's very ambitious, you know . . .'

'And he must learn to walk before he can run. Something is bothering you, Paula.'

'Not really.' She clasped her shapely hands and pushed them towards him. 'I'm a very lucky girl, really. I live in the country, which I love.'

'And how is the pottery business doing?'

'Making pots of money.' She grinned wickedly. 'Pardon the pun. I'm taking on more staff. Does Hugh have to work late a lot – when he's over here, I mean?'

'At times, when the pressure is on, we all have to.' Tweed found he was enjoying fencing with Paula. I know what's at the back of your bright little mind, he thought. Her next words confirmed his perception.

'Do you have many meetings with him at his flat in Cheyne Walk? What he will call his *pied à terre*.'

'It's a good place to discuss something confidential – after office hours. The cleaners can make it tricky at Park Crescent.'

'Stay for dinner, Tweed. I'm a good cook. I've got a marvel-lous bottle of Chablis,' she coaxed. Her eyes were a challenge.

'I'd love to, but I have to get back.' He looked at the piano in a corner. 'Hugh plays that?'

'We both do . . .'

'Who is his favourite composer?'

'Grieg. Every time. Would you like to see the house? Come

137

on. Then you can think again about my invitation to dinner . . .'

The kitchen was furnished in the new style Tweed found so tedious. Rustic. Pinewood cupboards and working surfaces. She had it well-organized. He stood staring at a row of knives behind a leather belt attached to the wall. No sign of anything that could be called a chef's knife. The type of knife used to slash Helena Andersen and Iris Hansen to parcels of meat at Travemünde.

He heard her open the fridge behind him. When he turned round she was uncorking a bottle of Chablis. She poured two glasses, handed him one. 'I feel lonely tonight. You'll drink a glass with me. I never drink alone. Here's to success in solving your latest problem.'

They clinked glasses and he watched her over the rim. She was staring straight back at him, then she put down her glass.

'Why did you come all this way out to see me?'

'We have a place at Wisbech we use for meetings. Since I was going to be in the district, I thought I'd call in on you,' he lied.

'I see. Show you the rest of the house . . .'

There were three more rooms. The main one was equipped with a double bed. Paula peered through the rear window looking out towards the dyke. Night was falling, a dark shadow like a wave crawling in over the flatlands between the dyke and the farmhouse.

'It can be creepy out here in winter,' she remarked. 'When the fog comes rolling in from the Wash.' There was a sombre note in her voice, but only briefly. 'Let's continue the tour.'

There was Paula's workroom and the third bedroom had been turned into a study for Hugh. A large and very modern safe stood in one corner. Paula indicated it with her glass.

'He keeps all his policies and papers locked away in that. He is very careful about never leaving anything on view. I have to keep out of here when he's working. Now, the dining-room – and that's it. Our castle . . .'

'We can seat eight,' she explained. 'How is Harry Masterson?' she asked suddenly.

She had this habit of throwing a question, as though hoping

138

to catch him off balance. Why the interest in Masterson, Tweed was wondering.

'Full of energy as always. Never lets anything get on top of him . . .'

'Harry's great fun. When we had them all to dinner a couple of years ago – that was when Hugh and I were still living together before we married – Harry was the life and soul of the party. He's a riot.'

'When was that party?'

'God! Now I've put my foot in it. You weren't invited. I played hell with Hugh but he said you were up to your eyes and couldn't get away . . .'

'Par for the course,' Tweed said easily. 'Who else came?'

'Oh, besides Harry there was Guy Dalby and Erich Lindemann. Can't say I was too keen on Lindemann. Bit of a dry stick – and he seemed to have something on his mind. Polite enough but didn't say a lot. Guy was OK. Especially after he had three cognacs with coffee.' She stopped, put her hand over her lips. 'I'm talking too much. I do. But I thought, my God, if he's stopped by the police driving home. Oh, you asked when was the party. July 14. Hugh's birthday. Now, must you go?'

'I'm afraid so. On the understanding I can come back . . .'

'Any time. Get Monica to phone first – I might be at the pottery. I stay there half the night when I lose track of time. It's pitch-black,' she said as she opened the front door. 'Do you mind driving in the dark?'

'As a matter of fact, I find it restful. Take care of yourself. And Hugh will be back soon.'

He kissed her on the cheek and she kissed him back. As he drove off she stood in the light of the doorway, waving.

Tweed drove back a different route, continuing on along the road which would eventually take him back to King's Lynn. His purpose in visiting Paula had been to get a good look at Grey's home. You could tell more from a man's surroundings than you could from talking to the man in question.

And Hugh Grey was one of the four men in question he thought grimly. His impression was of a comfortable home which had a lived-in feeling. No cold formality. Magazines scattered idly about the sitting-room. Stacks of paperbacks on the bedside tables in the main bedroom. His headlights, which stretched a long distance, picked out a signpost by the roadside. He pulled up.

Footpath. The sign pointed along a narrow track leading towards the dyke. He was about a quarter of a mile from Grey's farmhouse. He drove off again and didn't stop until he was inside the car park at the rear of The Duke's Head Hotel. Carrying his case, he walked down the narrow lane to the side entrance, booked a double room and dumped his case.

Returning down the single flight of stairs to reception he made arrangements for a late dinner, then went back to his room. From the directory he found the number of the local police station. His call was brief and they explained to him the easiest way on foot to the station.

Leaving the hotel, he walked back through the car park. Ten minutes later he went inside the police station on the corner of St James' Street and St James' Road. Inspector Cresswell was waiting for him inside his office. He offered a chair and coffee, which Tweed accepted gratefully.

Cresswell was a short, sturdy man of about fifty with dark hair and a calm manner, the type of policeman who took everything in his stride, who was surprised by none of the vagaries of human nature he encountered. Tweed showed him his fake Special Branch folder.

'You should be in London,' he remarked. 'We need more people like you there.'

'It's been offered.' Cresswell shook his squarish head. 'I've refused three times. Of course, it would mean promotion, a lot more money. But I'm a Norfolk man. I know the folk here. I'm happy. Why risk changing things?'

'Very wise, I'm sure. I'm investigating a major case. I can't, unfortunately, give you the details . . .'

'That's all right, sir. How can I help?'

'I need to know whether there have been any random murders of girls during the past few years on your patch. Specifically, the murder, followed by rape, of blonde girls. The victim would have been brutally savaged with a knife – butchered horribly.'

Cresswell leaned back in his chair, folded his arms and pursed his lips. Tweed waited patiently. They didn't hurry in this part

140

of the world, which was probably a more sensible way of going about things.

'There have been more of these murders, if I may ask?' he enquired in his deliberate manner.

'Yes. From what you say you can tell me something?'

'A girl called Carole Langley. A little over two years ago. She was foolish but she didn't deserve such a ghastly end. She was walking home from a party – out near the Wash. Had a quarrel with the boy friend who drove her there. So she hoofed it. That was her fatal mistake. Her body was found by a patrol car sent out in the middle of the night – after a call from her parents worried that she hadn't got home. I was on duty myself that night, just like tonight. I went out with the car. I'll never forget what I saw by the light of my torch. Butchered was the word you used. Carole Langley was slashed to pieces, then raped.'

'You apprehended the killer?'

'No. It's still on file. Don't think we'll ever solve that case – not unless we get a repeat performance, which God forbid.'

'And she was a blonde?'

'Yes, she was. A very attractive girl. She came to a police dance once. Not the sort you'd forget. Lively personality. A hideous waste . . .'

'Any suspects?'

'To start with, yes. The boy friend was immediately at the top of the list. But a dozen witnesses placed him at the house where the party had taken place until six in the morning. We hauled them in for drugs – marijuana. That was why Carole left.' Cresswell smiled drily and mimicked Cockney. 'And they say virtue is rewarded. There ain't no justice.'

'What do you think?' Tweed probed.

'Could have been someone from miles away. The A17 from Boston runs close by. A commercial traveller, as they used to call them. Anyone.'

'Can you look up the exact date?'

'Don't have to. July 14. Two years back as I said.'

'You have a good memory . . .'

'Bastille Day. I'm a history buff. Read nothing else.' Cresswell's eyes studied Tweed shrewdly. 'You come up

141

to Norfolk out of the blue. Ask me a lot of questions. And the type of murder I have on my books sounds similar to something you're investigating. Have you found anything up here?'

'What time did the Langley killing take place?'

'Between two and four a.m. – that was as close as the quack could place it. He's probably right – it fits in with when she left the party and when the parents phoned us.'

'Thank you for your help.' Tweed stood up and put on his Burberry. 'If you don't mind, I haven't eaten for hours and they're keeping dinner for me at The Duke's Head.'

'Nice hotel.' Cresswell rose to accompany his visitor to the door. 'You didn't answer my question. Have you found anything up here?'

'I regret to say, no. Not a clue . . .'

Tweed arranged for a call at 5.30 a.m. By six o'clock he was on the road, driving south-west away from the flatlands and into rolling, hilly country with woodlands. As he sat behind the wheel he saw nothing except the road ahead. His expression was grim. He was facing a situation far worse than he had ever anticipated, far worse than he had encountered since he had first entered the service. A bloody nightmare.

Eighteen

It was 8 a.m. exactly when Tweed walked into his office at Park Crescent. Monica looked up from her desk in surprise as he took off his raincoat, hung it up and walked quickly behind his own desk.

'You're early. I didn't expect you until just before nine . . .'

'Have any of the others arrived for the meeting?'

'Not yet. I've asked George to tell me on the quiet as each of them clock in. How is Paula?'

'In a very strange mood. Something's worrying that girl. I wish I knew what it was . . .'

He told her briefly about his visit to the farmhouse, his later meeting with Inspector Cresswell at the King's Lynn police station. She sat very still, taking in every word.

'You do see what it means,' he ended. 'Taken in conjunction with what has been happening way out at Travemünde?'

'There can't be any connection between all these horrible murders. The one in Norfolk must be a coincidence . . .'

'How far can you stretch coincidence? All four of them – Lindemann, Grey, Masterson and Dalby – were at the meeting I held in Frankfurt six months ago. Later, when they had presumably gone to bed, a Dutch girl was hacked to pieces and raped. Two years ago, on the night of July 14, the same four were having dinner at Hugh Grey's farmhouse out near the Wash. I gather the party went on late . . .'

'How late?'

'I don't know. There was a limit to the questions I could put to Paula, but we'll have to find out. That same night – or in the early hours of the morning – this poor girl, Carole Langley, was cut to pieces and raped. Now the same thing has happened twice at Travemünde. And I'm in an impossible position – after my visit to Dr Generoso.'

'Why?'

'Do I have to spell it out in words of one syllable?' Tweed snapped. 'To expose the odd man out I need to exert unrelenting pressure on all four, hoping I can make the rotten apple crack. But Generoso warned me that more pressure can cause a schizo to increase his activities – to commit more murders.'

'You sound irritable,' Monica commented. 'Have you had your breakfast?'

'Just coffee from the thermos you gave me – supplied by the hotel. They gave me sandwiches but I can't drive and eat . . .'

Monica reached for the phone, gave the doorman a brief order, replaced the receiver. 'They're getting fresh sandwiches from that place round the corner. You eat before you preside over that meeting . . .'

'There isn't time . . .'

'I'm postponing it until 9.15. You eat first.'

'That might be a good idea,' Tweed mused more calmly. 'If they have to wait twiddling their thumbs it will make them wonder what is happening.'

'Can I sum up?' Monica suggested. 'Stick to the facts – as

143

you're always telling me. The facts are Ian Fergusson travelled to Hamburg to meet Ziggy Palewska. Only the four sector chiefs knew of his journey, his destination. So one of them must have informed the other side. *That* is a fact. All the rest is speculation. How could any of the sector chiefs reach Travemünde in time to commit those two murders? Why in heaven would they go there to do their grisly work – knowing you were in the area?'

'There could be a reason, which I don't want to reveal yet – in case I'm wrong. My theory is so bizarre. But coming back on the plane from Hamburg I studied a road map I bought at the airport. Any of them could have driven to Schleswig-Holstein. That means they'd have to be out of touch with their sector HQ.'

'Even Harry Masterson? All the way from Vienna?'

'Yes. The autobahns. There's one from Salzburg through München. And Harry drives like Jackie Cooper.'

'Why this concentration on driving? There are airlines . . .'

'People can be seen at airports. An unlucky chance meeting with someone who knows you. No, it would be by road . . .'

He waited as George brought in a wrapped packet of sandwiches and a pot of coffee on a tray. Monica produced plates, shoved ham sandwiches in front of him, a paper napkin, then poured the coffee. She wouldn't allow him to talk until he had eaten.

'That does feel a lot better,' he admitted.

'You're hopeless on an empty stomach. Now, just before you start the meeting, what are we going to do?'

'First, you check with all four European HQs – Frankfurt, Copenhagen, Bern and Vienna. Find out where each sector chief was during the past two weeks. After the meeting,' he went on briskly, 'I'm giving the four of them a week's leave.'

'Not for their health, I'm sure . . .'

'I want to visit them at their homes, see their surroundings. I've just done that with Hugh Grey's place – although I also need to see him at his flat in Cheyne Walk. The only way I can get a clue as to who it is hangs on the psychological approach.'

'Which means?'

'Using the data I learnt from Generoso, I need to find out what my four chosen disciples are really like. I've never actually

144

seen them on their home ground. That was a mistake. We vet them, build up files – but I need to get to know them as human beings, get them talking. One of them just may let something slip.'

'Time for your meeting. Feel more up to it?'

'This is going to be a grim meeting – for me. The point is I must in no way give even a hint of my suspicions.' Tweed stood up, straightened his polka dot tie. 'Oh, yes, I can handle them. That happens to be my job.'

His tone was brisk, his manner almost jaunty. Monica smiled – the four men waiting in the conference room were going to be put through the wringer. Tweed rampant.

'Gentlemen,' Tweed opened from his chair at the head of the table, 'I am not satisfied with your performance. Your reports from the field are skimpy – give no idea of the atmosphere out there . . .'

'My report did,' Grey interjected, full of confidence, his moonlike face flushed pink. 'All quiet on the western front . . .'

'Please don't interrupt. Your turn will come.' Tweed stared at Grey for a moment and then continued, his manner business-like. 'I have told you all before, atmosphere – what the Germans call fingertip feeling – is the key to what the Russians are up to. I expect you all to remedy your slackness at this meeting. You first, Guy.'

Dalby, head of the Mediterranean sector, the catlick of brown hair looped over his forehead – was it his trademark? Tweed wondered – opened a file. He spoke rapidly, his dark eyes darting round the table.

'My people are puzzled. All normal contacts – informants – have dried up. Some have vanished from their usual haunts. I have issued instructions for an all-out drive to find out where the opposition agents are. They, too, have vanished. Atmos-phere? I have the impression we are looking at a smokescreen. I want to break through the fog, find out what is being prepared behind it. That is my report.'

'Forget the facts for a moment,' Tweed said. 'What do you *sense* is going on?'

'Preparations for some major operation. We must watch out, be on the alert.'

145

'Any ideas now – you said at the last meeting you'd try to work it out – why Fergusson was murdered.'

'A trap. To get you to fly to Hamburg. They will try to kill you.'

There was a shocked hush round the table. Dalby never minced his words, never went all round the mulberry bush like Hugh Grey. Tweed glanced down the left-hand side of the table at Lindemann, who sat beyond Hugh Grey. He had his array of four different-coloured pencils, was scribbling away, so presumably Dalby was blue. A curious habit.

'Erich,' Tweed called out, 'your impressions, please.'

'Hard facts are what we need. I have some. Balkan has arrived in the West. Has probably set up his HQ in Grey's sector. Came in via Oslo. The action is starting in the North.'

Harry Masterson, who faced him, leaned forward, his manner bluff, full of confidence. 'And who the bloody hell is Balkan?'

'Code-name for their controller in the West,' Lindemann replied.

'You seem to know a lot – from your off-side sector . . .'

'Scandinavia is *not* off-side.' Lindemann spoke without rancour, with precision. 'It is the zone where NATO expects the first Soviet assault if they ever attack. That is why we have the big NATO nerve centre in the mountains just north of Oslo. My informants are most reliable. Balkan is very dangerous. He must be located, identified.'

'Bloody marvellous, isn't it?' Masterson rumbled in his public school accent. 'He waits till this meeting to tell us about what he calls their most dangerous agent. Christ! Are we working as a team, or are we not?'

Tweed kept quiet, watching the two men, who had never liked each other. He was trying to imagine any of the four grouped round the table wearing a beret. Lindemann was more than a match for Masterson's onslaught.

'The data about Balkan was too classified to transmit over the phone. Tweed has this information.'

'You have?' Masterson turned his aggressive personality on to his chief. 'Isn't that something we should all have been told as soon as you knew?'

'Lindemann has explained. I share his mistrust of the normal communications system. You know now. Why do you think you were brought back here so urgently?' Tweed ended tersely.

'I'd like to register a formal protest,' Grey broke in. 'And I want that registered in the minutes of this meeting. And who, I would like to know, is taking those minutes?'

'No one,' Tweed informed him.

'I would further like to register another protest. It is established procedure that minutes are taken of every meeting . . .'

'That procedure was just put on the shelf – for this particular meeting,' Tweed told him. 'No written reference to Balkan. Not without my express permission. Understood?'

'If you insist, I suppose so . . .'

'I beg your pardon?' Tweed's tone was icy.

'I withdraw that remark. Unreservedly.'

'Then perhaps you would like now to make your contribution?'

'All quiet on the western front,' Grey repeated. He was rather fond of the phrase. He beamed complacently. 'With important reservations,' he went on after a suitable pause. 'My contacts with the refugee organizations in Schleswig-Holstein lead me to expect action by the opposition imminent. The nature of that action is as yet unknown.' He glanced at Lindemann. 'Nor do I have any data on this so-called Balkan . . .'

'He is the top man – so difficult to detect,' Lindemann replied without looking up. He was using the red pencil to scribble notes. Red, Tweed presumed, must be Grey.

'Is this man among your refugee informants?' Tweed asked as he wrote a name on a sheet from his pad, folded it once and handed it to Grey. The name he had written was Ziggy Palewska.

Grey glanced at it, refolded the sheet and returned it to Tweed. 'I have never heard of the person.'

Which was astute, Tweed thought. Grey had concealed from everyone else even the gender of the informant. Tweed turned to Masterson who was twiddling a pencil between his large hands. Full of physical energy, not a committee man, Harry Masterson, unlike Grey, who revelled in long meetings.

'Harry, how goes it in the Balkans?'

'Damned frustrating. All known Soviet personnel and their hyenas have run for cover. I've sent certain men across the borders behind the penetration zones. Any day now someone

147

will let something slip. The Curtain has dropped with a clang – but as I have just said, I have people on the other side. Something's brewing. Take my word for it. I can't wait to get back . . .'

'I'm afraid you'll have to,' Tweed said, seizing on the opening, 'because I'm giving all of you one week's leave. In this country. No quick trips to Monte Carlo.' He looked quickly at Masterson as he said this, then he stood up.

'Inform your deputies to take charge in your absence.'

'But we've only been in our new posts six months,' Grey protested. 'We need more time to work ourselves in. Then maybe you will get more comprehensive reports . . .'

'One week's leave. In this country,' Tweed repeated. 'And I shall want a word with each of you separately before you start that leave.'

Monica waited until the end of the day before she tackled Tweed. He had spent the afternoon having brief interviews with each of his sector chiefs, meetings from which Monica had been excluded. 'I want them relaxed,' he had explained. 'They may think you are recording our conversations.'

He called Newman at the Hotel Jensen at five o'clock. As he had hoped, the reporter was just back from a day with Diana at Travemünde. His call was brief. He asked Newman to go to the Hauptbahnhof, to call him back from one of the public phone booths at the station. Within ten minutes the phone on his desk rang.

'Newman here. Don't worry about Diana – I can see her from this box. I brought her with me. What's up?'

'Do you know whether Dr Berlin has returned again to his place on Priwall Island?'

'You're in luck. I met Kuhlmann who is still prowling round Travemünde, mostly interviewing people at the marina. He told me Dr Berlin is still missing. Kuhlmann has men watching that mansion night and day . . .'

'Thank you. That's very interesting. Call me should he come back. I don't think he will. Everything all right?'

'A weird trivia. Diana has decided to take a secretarial course. Typing and shorthand. Now, don't fuss, I take her to

148

the school in Lübeck, leave her there. I know when she leaves and I'll be waiting for her.'

'Did she say why?'

'A sudden whim. I was surprised myself . . .'

'Shorthand and typing? In German?'

'At the school, yes. She has dug out some old training manuals for Pitman's in English. She's teaching herself in English. She has bought a small portable. Keeps it hidden away inside a locker aboard the *Südwind*. Apart from that, nothing new . . .'

'I should be with you in a week or so. Watch your back. Something is stirring in that part of the world.'

'Not much sign of it so far.'

'What about Kurt Franck?'

'Vanished into thin air . . .'

'Watch out for cripples,' Tweed said and put down the phone.

'Now!' Monica sat erect in her chair. 'Have you got five minutes? Good. What's going on? You've left Europe wide open – no sector chief on the continent. The deputies don't have the grip of the sector chiefs and you know it.'

'Strategy,' said Tweed. 'Europe wide open, as you say. And I would bet money Lysenko will know it within hours. It will encourage him to make a move. I'm sitting back to see what move he will make. The field will seem clear – I'm tempting him into taking advantage of that fact. When he does move I'll know what he's up to. Meantime I'm going to visit Masterson at his cottage down at Apfield near Chichester, Lindemann at his flat in town, and Dalby – presumably coping on his own at Woking now he's separated from his wife who has gone off to France.'

'You seem to put great hopes on seeing them in their homes . . .'

'They'll be more relaxed. Someone is going to make a mistake, give me the lead I'm seeking. And why do you think someone like Diana Chadwick would suddenly take up a secretarial course?'

'Because she expects soon to have to earn her own living.'

Tweed looked thunderstruck. He stood up and paced his office, hands clasped behind his back. Then he stood looking down at Monica.

149

'What would I do without you?'

'Did I say something?'

'Oh, nothing momentous. You just gave me another sign that a truly bizarre theory I've hesitated to take seriously could be the whole key to Balkan.'

Nineteen

'Diana Chadwick will be aboard Flight BA 737, departing Hamburg 18.20, arriving Heathrow 18.50, London time. Please have her met.'

Newman's voice was crisp, almost brusque. Tweed gripped the receiver tightly and took a deep breath.

'Bob, you can't do that . . .'

'Diana has agreed. I'll see her aboard the flight at this end myself. Today. I can't be handicapped by having to guard her . . .'

'What the devil do you think you're up to?' Tweed demanded.

'No arguments. I have a job I must do. On my own. I repeat – Diana will be aboard that flight . . .'

'I don't like it . . .'

'I didn't ask you to like it. You'll have her met?'

'I'll go myself – if I must . . .'

'You must.'

The connection was broken before Tweed could respond. He sat back in his chair and stared at Monica. She raised her eyebrows, cocked her head on one side like a bird.

'Newman has gone maverick again,' Tweed rasped. 'I have to go and collect Diana Chadwick off the Hamburg flight at 18.50 this evening. He's just put her aboard like a parcel . . .'

'Let's hope she doesn't have to travel cargo.'

'It almost sounded like that. He's freeing himself of the responsibility of guarding her so he can do his own thing. God knows what his game is – you know what he is when he's got the bit between his teeth.'

'Highly effective.'

150

'He takes too many risks for my liking.' Tweed stood up and walked over to the window, hands thrust inside his jacket pockets. 'On the other hand, with Diana being in England, she might just be the key I need to unlock the mystery of Balkan's identity . . .'

Peter Toll, an officer in the BND, arrived in Lübeck from his Pullach HQ near Münich, the day before Newman made his phone call to Tweed.

Toll, an old friend of Newman's, walked into the Hotel Jensen, found that Newman was in his room, and sent up his card inside a sealed envelope. The reporter was chatting with Diana over a glass of wine when the porter brought up the envelope. He opened it, then looked at Diana.

'Would you excuse me for a few minutes? I want to get rid of this chap quickly. He's a nuisance.'

'Who is he?'

'An informant I've used in the past. He's become unreliable. You'll stay here till I get back? Don't open the door to anyone except me. I'll rap like this . . .'

He beat a tattoo on the table, left the room, waited outside the closed door until he heard her turn the key, then took the lift to the lobby. Peter Toll was tall and lean, clean-shaven, in his early thirties, a man who smiled easily and was one of the most quick-witted men Newman had met. He wore rimless spectacles and moved agilely. They shook hands,

'Care for a stroll along the river?' Toll suggested.

'Why not?' Newman waited until they were outside and walking beyond where the tables with people drinking stood on the pavement. 'How did you know I was here? Where to find me?'

Toll pushed his glasses further up his long nose, a gesture Newman remembered. 'It's my job to know when suspicious foreigners arrive in the Federal Republic,' he joked.

'Come off it, Peter, you want something. You haven't travelled all the way from Pullach just to pass the time of day.'

'What a cynical chap you are,' Toll continued in English. 'I could be here checking a situation and decided to call in on an old friend . . .'

'Get to the point, I don't want to be away from the hotel too long.'

'Of course not, Diana Chadwick is a fascinating woman so they tell me.'

'*How* did you know I was here?' Newman repeated.

'Through Bonn . . .'

'Don't you mean Wiesbaden?'

'Kuhlmann would never inform me of your presence – not without pressure from the Chancellor. Kuhlmann is strictly concerned with the hideous killings of foreign girls. He's Criminal Police.'

'Now we're getting somewhere. What made Kuhlmann pick up the phone to Pullach?'

'Your continuing interest in Dr Berlin. Plus the arrival of Tweed.'

'And what is *your* interest in Dr Berlin?'

They had reached the point alongside the old town where an old hump-backed pedestrian bridge spanned the river. Toll led the way over the bridge and up a path between trees past a boathouse.

'Frankly, I wish I knew. Let's talk in German now.' Toll had switched to his native language.

'Vague answers don't interest me,' Newman replied in German. 'What's wrong with Dr Berlin?'

'On the surface nothing. He's got a world-wide reputation as a saint, a man dedicated to the welfare of the have-nots. But he keeps disappearing for long periods. Our best men have tried to keep track of his movements. He's a bloody conjuror – and plays the trick on himself. The vanishing trick. And he's so close to the border – it's at the end of the Mecklenburgerstrasse – the road he lives on . . .'

'I know. You have to have something more solid than that.'

'Leipzig. Twenty years ago he played the same vanishing trick in Africa. One morning he's in Kenya, the next he's disappeared. Reported dead in the jungle. Then he pops up in Leipzig. Treated for some obscure tropical disease. Hey presto! Eighteen months later another vanishing trick. He appears in the Federal Republic. First you see him, then you don't. People like that worry Pullach.'

152

'Still pretty vague. What do you want me for?'

'Your German is pretty good.'

They had emerged off the footpath on to a road and beyond that on to the highway leading to police HQ at Lübeck-Süd. Newman lit a cigarette and studied Toll who smiled back in the most innocent manner.

'Go on,' Newman snapped.

'You could still pass for a German. In the right clothes.'

'So my German is reasonable. Where does that get us?'

'Reports arriving at Pullach say Markus Wolf is running some major operation – from Leipzig.'

'What kind of an operation?' Newman asked.

'That's what we need to find out. The Russians are pulling the strings behind Wolf.'

'Par for the course. What do you want me to do?'

'Go behind the Iron Curtain . . .'

For several minutes Newman remained silent, and they walked together alongside the highway through the countryside. In the distance loomed the isolated complex of Lübeck-Süd. Behind them the green spires of Lübeck's churches speared up above the trees.

'Why me?' Newman asked eventually.

'Because, you see . . .' Toll was talking very fast. '. . . as I said, you can pass for a German. Because Wolf has arrested many of our agents in a sudden swoop. Communications across the border have been largely cut. That, I think, explains the strange lack of activity of the opposition's agents in the West. Some are lying low, some have been temporarily withdrawn. The information about our lost men seems to come from London. I am informing Tweed of that fact when I can contact him . . .'

'I don't know where Tweed is,' Newman said easily, 'but when you return to Pullach call London. You know Monica? Good. She may be able to get a message to him. And now, once again, why me?'

'I have one group underground inside East Germany Wolf knows nothing about. Led by a formidable man and a girl. *You* are not known in The Zone. It will be dangerous, but I think you could manage it.'

153

'Manage what?'

'Contact this group, find out direct from them – verbally – what is happening. I dare not use one of my own men who may be identified. And we are in the middle of reorganizing our radio communications system. The old one is blown.'

'You make it sound easy. How the devil could I ever hope to cross the border?'

'That I can arrange . . .'

'With what chance of success?'

'Guaranteed. I can only give details when you have agreed.'

'*If* I agree. I have to sleep on it.'

'Don't sleep too long . . .'

'And don't push it. I think we'll turn back now. I want to get back to the Jensen.'

'Of course, of course.' Toll was at his most amiable and went on speaking in the same light-hearted way, as though discussing a holiday. 'We do know that your old friend, General Lysenko, is in East Germany, peering over Wolf's shoulder . . .'

'You're sure Lysenko is involved?' Newman's tone sharpened.

'Quiet sure. So, he is the man you would be up against in the last analysis. Only fair to lay all the cards on the table. You know me . . .'

'I know you. Feed the dog the food he likes, get him in a good humour. Hold back the bits that might give him indigestion.'

'Now, Bob, when have I ever done that to you?'

A hurt tone in Toll's voice. His face expressed indignant disbelief. A good actor, Peter Toll.

'Just now,' Newman said as they turned down back towards the Trave and there was the distant sound of people laughing and talking. Another gloriously sunny day with glimpses through the trees of boats proceeding up and down the river.

'I don't understand,' Toll began.

'I won't even think about your offer unless you tell me exactly how I would cross the border. Where. How.'

'That is top secret information.' Toll paused, pushed up his glasses to the top of his nose. 'You go over straight through the minefield belt past a certain watchtower further south. The guards in that tower have been bribed. I have them in my pocket.'

154

'Oh, really? I do know something about the defences along the border. Each watchtower has three men on duty. *Three* men – not two. They worked out long ago that you might bribe two but the third man would always be the joker. He could pretend to agree, then report the other two to his superiors and gain promotion.'

'Correct,' Toll agreed. 'Let us go and sit on the grass by the river. No one can overhear us.' He waited until they were sat side by side. 'All three have been bribed – with gold. There is something about gold which draws out the avarice in men. They have been paid one-third of the agreed amount. They get the balance when they have safely passed you through – and back again on the return trip.'

'What about the watchtowers on either side?'

'They are some distance away, but they will be taken care of. One of the bribed guards will contrive a short-circuit. No one will be able to operate a searchlight . . .'

'And how do I choose a walk through the minefield?'

'The watchtower chosen overlooks a dummy section of the minefield. It is the route used by Wolf to infiltrate agents into the West. We know, but he doesn't know that we do know. We have taken the risk of letting his men through without intercepting them. Most important – we have not even followed his agents as they came through to avoid any of them becoming suspicious and reporting back. That was a very considerable sacrifice.'

'You have been more audacious than I anticipated. How many of your people at Pullach know about this open route?'

'Two. Myself and my chief. We have trusted no one. I would accompany you personally to the crossing point. At night, of course . . .'

'And supposing I did get through? How far do I have to travel to meet this underground unit?'

'Group Five, we call it.' Toll clasped his hands between his legs bent at the knees. 'The leader, a formidable man, as I have said, will be waiting for you just beyond the minefield belt. He will have an extra bicycle for you. Travelling at night through countryside you make no noise on a bike – also you hear any car coming a good way off. Plenty of time to hide away from

155

the road. I have given you all the data I am prepared to reveal until you decide – far more than I intended.'

'I also said where? I need to know the location.'

'Oh, my God! I suppose it's because you're a bloody reporter. You want every detail you can dig up. All this is confidential. Tweed must not know a word about it. We are working on the cell system . . .'

'Cell system?'

'No more than three members of a group know the identity of each other. The crossing point is near the ancient town of Goslar. And Group Five may have information on Dr Berlin. Satisfied?'

'Goslar? That's the Harz mountains area.'

'Which is difficult for the Vopos to control – or patrol. Now, what do you say? Incidentally, I am staying at the Movenpick Hotel. Under the name Allan Seeger. What do you say?'

'What I said before. I'll sleep on it.'

Newman didn't sleep on it. He lay awake most of the night. At least he had the satisfaction of knowing Diana was safe in her bedroom on the same floor. And that was the only satisfaction he did have.

Peter Toll had laid his bait with great skill. The crossing into East Germany might provide vital data on Dr Berlin. That fitted in neatly with what Tweed was trying to discover – the real role played by the elusive guardian of refugees. The reference to Lysenko was further temptation.

It seemed to provide a chance to deal a heavy blow against the Russian who had masterminded the murder of Newman's wife, Alexis, in Estonia further up the Baltic the previous year. If he was planning a major operation and it flopped that could be the end of General Vasili Lysenko. Gorbachev was not reputed to be a man who dealt kindly with subordinates who didn't deliver.

As he stirred beneath the sheets Newman was torn two ways. The idea of action appealed to him – he was feeling restless. But could he trust Peter Toll? *Guaranteed.* That was the word he had used about the border crossing. And by implication his safe return on the way back. Bollocks! No one could guarantee

156

he'd cross safely inside East Germany – let alone return un-detected.

The bland assurance of Toll worried Newman. He needed someone unknown to contact Group Five. But Newman *was* known to the GRU. Damnit, they had him on their bloody computer. All through the night he twisted and turned in bed, dripping with sweat from the humid atmosphere. Or was he sweating at the prospect of finding his way through that alleged dummy minefield? Was it still a dummy? Wolf had a habit of changing things round, never sticking to the same routine for too long. Cunning as a fox, Markus Wolf.

He fell into an uneasy sleep at 3.30. The dawn light coming in through the windows he had left uncurtained woke him. He got up, bathed, shaved, dressed, lit a cigarette and stared out on the deserted streets of Lübeck. The leaning towers with their witches' hats leered at him. He'd decide after an early breakfast.

'You're on your way to Heathrow. Aboard Flight BA 737, wearing a check suit very similar to the one you have on now . . .'

Newman had entered an empty compartment at Hamburg Hauptbahnhof on the train back to Lübeck after seeing Diana off. Aboard Flight BA 737. He had helped her check in her single case, had taken her to the entrance to Final Departures, where he had left her. He had returned to the station, boarded the train which had now left Hamburg behind, and Peter Toll had appeared, entered his compartment and made his statement as he sat down.

'What the hell do you mean?' he asked.

'One of our people who looks rather like you,' Toll explained and smiled. 'He's carrying a passport in your name. Officially you're now thirty thousand feet up and approaching London. That way the opposition forgets about you. They did have a man on your tail but we've arrested him. He'll be out of circulation until you get back over the border from the East. When they know he's gone missing – which will be soon because he won't report on your movements – they'll check with the contact inside Hamburg Airport. He'll go through the passenger manifests. Your name will come up as having left Germany.'

157

'Would you mind very much,' Newman asked sarcastically, 'telling me how long you've been planning this thing?'

'Over several weeks.' Toll smiled and waved a reassuring hand. 'We don't cobble up an operation like this overnight. Ever since I knew you were in Lübeck with Tweed.'

'On the bare-faced cheeky assumption I'd agree to your scheme?'

'I just hoped you would . . .'

'Like hell you did. Anything else I should know about?'

'A lot. A moving train is the best place for an intensive briefing. And when we get to Lübeck, I'll need a signed note from you authorizing me to collect your things. I can pack them . . .'

'They're already packed. One case,' Newman said in clipped tones.

'Good. That will save me time. You put on these dark glasses and this hat . . .' He produced from a plastic bag a Tyrolean hat with a tiny red feather in the hat-band. '. . . and collect the key for Room 104 at the Movenpick. You're registered as Thor Nickel. It's a busy hotel and you've been there two days. The man who looks like you occupied the room. All the loose ends are tied up once I get your case out of the Jensen and pay your bill. Here's a notebook for you to write them the instruction for me to deal on your behalf. We leave the train separately at Lübeck. You can walk to the Movenpick. Wait in Room 104 until I arrive. I think I've thought of just about everything.'

'Good for you.'

'Look, Bob. We're dealing with pro's. You have to disappear into thin air before you make the crossing . . .'

'You've really thought of everything? What if they enquire at the Jensen when you've cleaned up there? They could learn someone collected my case. Why would I fly to London and leave that?'

'I'll chat to the manager while I'm paying your bill. Gossip on about how the lady you were escorting to her flight was taken ill just before checking in. You decided to go with her – and sent me to collect your bag. OK?'

'That sounds fairly convincing,' Newman admitted. 'One other thing, I'm not carrying any weapons across . . .'

'Agreed.' Toll looked at Newman's hands. 'You're carrying

a deadly pair of weapons at the end of your arms. SAS trained.'

'If this thing goes right I shouldn't have to hurt anyone . . .'

'Which is exactly how we've planned it. Three days inside The Zone, the information is passed to you verbally, you come out with it inside your head. No problem.'

'People say that just before everything turns into a disaster area.'

'First night nerves?' Toll joked. 'Just before the opening performance on stage?'

'Just cynical.'

Toll left the compartment shortly after that, carrying a note Newman had written to the manager of the Jensen. They would disembark from the train separately at Lübeck.

Newman tried on the Tyrolean hat, checking his appearance in the mirror. It fitted perfectly. And that gave him an eerie feeling – the BND file on him at Pullach must be pretty detailed. The addition of the dark glasses altered his appearance entirely, gave him a detached, almost sinister, look.

Toll knew his job Newman thought as he sat down again. With the heatwave going on half the population were wearing tinted spectacles. At Lübeck he got out and saw Toll in the distance striding away. He had disappeared when Newman emerged from the station.

He walked the short distance to the Movenpick, and beyond the hotel the twin towers loomed. They looked more normal than they had when he had stared at them from his window early that morning after his almost sleepless night.

He turned left off the pavement, crossed the open space in front of the Movenpick and entered the lobby of the hotel. He was heading for the concierge to collect his room key in the name of Thor Nickel for 104 and the first person he saw was Kurt Franck.

Twenty

Tweed was waiting at Heathrow when Diana Chadwick carried her case out of the Customs exit. She spotted him immediately, rushed forward, dropped her case and hugged him.

159

'Oh, I'm so glad to see you. No, listen to me first,' she went on as he released her and before he could speak. 'There's a man on the same flight who looks terribly like Bob Newman. He's even wearing a similar suit – but it isn't Newman. Here he comes now.'

Tweed glanced at the exit. She was right. The resemblance was remarkable, but it was not Newman. Tweed stood by Diana, watching as the new arrival paused, looking round. He seemed in no haste to leave the airport. Then he put down his bag, felt inside his breast pocket and produced an airline folder which he examined. He checked his watch and put the folder back inside his pocket.

'Wait here,' Tweed said. 'I'll only be a moment, maybe a few minutes. But wait here,' he repeated.

Diana was one of those remarkable girls who never detained you by asking why. Tweed wandered round among the departing crowd, came up behind the look-alike and bumped into him.

'I do beg your pardon,' Tweed said quickly in German, 'I wasn't looking where I was going . . .'

'That's all right,' the man replied automatically in the same language.

Tweed moved fast. He went to the British Airways counter and chose an attractive-looking girl, getting in just ahead of a man who was approaching her.

'Can I use your phone, please? It's an emergency.' He showed her his Special Branch folder, a document carefully forged in the basement at Park Crescent. She reacted by passing him the phone and turned her attention to the man who was waiting. Tweed dialled a number, kept his voice down.

'Airport Security? Can I speak to Jim Corcoran? Oh, that's you, Jim. Tweed here. There's a man I want questioned – held. He's waiting outside the exit, just off a Hamburg flight. I'll be there to point him out. Hold him until I send someone from Park Crescent. Suspected drug dealer? That will do nicely.'

Tweed hurried back to the exit. Diana stood by her bag and kept looking at her watch, as though expecting someone to collect her. She'd make a very useful addition to my staff, Tweed thought, and was careful to keep away from her.

The man who looked like Newman was still standing in the same place. Tweed saw Corcoran, a tall man and heavily-built with sandy hair, walking fast. Behind him two other men hurried to keep up with him.

Another crowd of passengers from a flight was pouring out of the exit. Tweed positioned himself so the waiting man couldn't see him. Corcoran came straight up to him, his two companions staying discreetly a few feet back.

'That man in the check suit,' Tweed said. 'See the one I mean? He's just lit a small cheroot. I want to know who he is, why he is here, where he has come from . . .'

'Leave it to us,' said Corcoran and moved towards the target. Tweed waited only long enough to witness Corcoran and his two colleagues surround the man as Corcoran started talking to him. He walked quickly across to Diana and picked up her bag.

'I have a car outside. That chap can't follow you any more. I hope you approve,' he said as they walked to the outside world, 'but I don't trust a hotel. You'll be safer in Newman's flat in South Ken. It's quite a nice place.'

'Will Bob mind?' Diana asked as Tweed led the way into the lobby of Newman's flat and placed her case on top of a chest of drawers in a large bedroom at the back. 'Mind my being here?'

'Why should he?'

And to hell with him if he does, Tweed thought. He's dumped Diana in my lap without so much as a by-your-leave. Tweed had obtained the key to the flat from Monica before leaving for the airport: she had agreed to keep an eye on the place while Newman was in Germany.

He showed her the bathroom, the large sitting-room at the front with bay windows overlooking the street, the compact kitchen which was like a ship's galley set back inside an alcove with two steps leading up to it from the sitting-room.

Diana walked into the sitting-room and stopped. She gazed up at the high ceiling where the original cornices with a design of bunches of grapes and intertwined vine leaves had been left intact.

161

'What a lovely spacious room. This is like the England I used to know.'

'An old Victorian house converted into flats by a developer,' Tweed remarked. 'The value has soared since Newman bought the place two or three years ago. This year the value has gone up like a rocket. You'll be all right here?'

'I love the place. I'll be just a few minutes unpacking in the bedroom . . .'

Tweed used the opportunity of being on his own to call Park Crescent. He dialled his private number and Monica answered at once.

'Did you collect the package safely?' she asked.

'Yes. Good job I went myself. There's another package I want examining urgently. It's being held by Corcoran of Airport Security. Rush someone down there. Harry Butler or Pete Nield . . .'

'Harry is with me now. I'll send him at once. You'd like to speak to him?'

'Let's waste no time. I want the origin of the package, where it was despatched from. Who sent it. That's it. Expect me in an hour.'

He put down the phone, went into the kitchen and opened cupboards. Time for a chat with Diana over a cup of tea. It would have to be powdered milk, but he wanted to tell her where the local shops were, that he'd be back later to take her out for dinner, to settle her in. Over dinner he could explain how she could help him.

'Harry Butler has reported back,' Monica informed Tweed as he entered his office.

'That was quick.' Tweed sat in the swivel chair behind his desk and felt the tension drain out of his system. He had half-expected to find Diana was not aboard the flight. He was surprised to realize how much he had worried about her.

'Tell me,' he said.

'Harry waved the Official Secrets Act at the Newman look-alike, threatened him with God knows what. He's a German. One of ours. Walther Pröhl. Fully paid-up member of the BND from Pullach . . .'

162

'Oh, God!' Tweed doodled a German eagle on his pad. 'That I didn't expect. I thought he was opposition.'

'So the news is good . . .'

'No, it simply could be worse. How did the BND get in on the act?'

'Pröhl doesn't know too much. He was ordered to impersonate Newman and fly from Hamburg to Heathrow, wait there, then catch the next flight back. He's pukkah – he was carrying identification proving he is BND. But he travelled on a forged passport under the name Robert Newman, which means it appears on the passenger manifest.'

'That thought had already occurred to me. I don't like any of it. Did Pröhl give any clue as to why he was ordered to do this?'

'None at all. Harry is convinced he doesn't know. He received his instructions from Peter Toll . . .'

'This is getting worse.' Tweed took off his glasses and started polishing them as he continued. 'Toll is the youngest man ever to be promoted to Deputy Director – or the equivalent – of the BND. I rate him as A1 for detailed planning, but he's ambitious and that makes him reckless. He's a gambler for high stakes.'

'Not a man you'd choose as sector chief?'

'Only after a period of retraining – with emphasis on obedience to orders from me . . .'

'And in some way he's in touch with Newman?'

'Sounds horribly like it. That might explain . . .' Tweed stopped. 'Oh, never mind. What about the trace you put out on the mysterious Portman Paula Grey referred to in her diary?'

'You really shouldn't have done that,' Monica chided, 'read her personal diary . . .'

'Ethics I can dispense with when lives are at stake – when four girls have been horribly murdered. To say nothing of tracking down the odd man out who sat in at my conference this morning . . .'

'You really think there's a connection?'

'What about Portman?' Tweed repeated irritably.

'Samuel Portman, I think. Portman Private Investigations. He has a grotty little office in Dean Street, Soho. He's the only Portman known in the business. I checked with the Association.

Discreetly through a friend. The address and phone number are on that folded sheet of paper under your blotter.'

Tweed glanced at the sheet, refolded it and slipped it inside his wallet. 'I'll have to pay Mr Samuel Portman a visit in the near future.'

'Surely it's obvious what's bothering Paula?' Monica protested. 'She thinks Hugh is playing around with some other woman. Maybe she just wants to *know* – some women are like that . . .'

'You really think that sounds like Hugh Grey?'

'Not really. Now . . .' Her expression became dreamy. 'If it were Harry Masterson, I'd believe anything. He's capable of having three on the go at once – and concealing from each the existence of the others. But then his wife did walk away.'

'Which reminds me, where are they all now? Gone back to their burrows for their week's leave?'

'Harry is down at his country cottage near Apfield in Sussex. I don't think anyone is with him – he's painting. In oils. And playing classical records.' She paused with a puckish look, waiting for Tweed to ask her how she knew. He remained stolidly silent. 'I know that,' she said, a trifle piqued, 'because I phoned him with an excuse to check. I guessed you'd want to know where they all were.'

'I'm listening.'

'Guy Dalby is down at Woking in that Georgian estate house he lived in with Renée before she hopped it to France. He's painting, too – the walls of his house. That's two out of four whose wives walked,' she mused. 'The divorce rate is climbing. One out of three for the country in general, one out of two for service personnel . . .' She flushed suddenly. She had been thinking aloud. God! She'd clean forgotten for the moment that Tweed was separated, that his wife was living it up with some Greek millionaire in Rio. Unless by now she'd moved on. She began talking rapidly.

'Erich Lindemann is at his flat in Chelsea. Doing what, I've no idea. Not the communicative type. Did you notice he'd cut himself shaving? He had a bit of sticking plaster on his face – not like him to be careless. Last on the list, Hugh Grey. He's at his flat in Cheyne Walk . . .'

'I'd have expected him to have gone to that farmhouse in

Norfolk. Paula's out there most of the time – that pottery keeps her there . . .'

'He said he'd be going up there in a couple of days. He has work to catch up on. He is a workaholic. How is Diana Chadwick getting on?' she asked suddenly. 'You like her, don't you?'

'She's one of the pieces on a huge board. Try and get Peter Toll on the phone at Pullach for me.'

Monica realized as she dialled that Tweed had been engaging in a mental exercise most people found impossible. Conversing about one topic while his mind concentrated on something quite different. She spoke in German briefly, then put down the receiver.

'Peter Toll is not at Pullach. No information as to when he will return. Nothing.'

'And that,' Tweed said grimly, 'could be very bad news for Newman.'

Twenty-One

In response to Newman's call from Room 104 at the Movenpick, Kuhlmann arrived in ten minutes. He had driven like hell from Lübeck-Süd where Newman had caught him on the verge of leaving.

Newman hung a *Do Not Disturb* notice from the outside handle of the door after admitting the Federal policeman. He didn't want Peter Toll turning up while he was talking with Kuhlmann. He had also hidden his dark glasses and the Tyrolean hat.

'Why move to this place from the Jensen?' Kuhlmann asked as he sat down.

'I thought I was being followed. It's also more complicated. Diana Chadwick is no longer in Lübeck. She's in a safe place.'

'Don't tell me where.' Kuhlmann held up a warning hand. 'I am glad to hear of your action. I wish to God I could move all young attractive blonde girls out of the area . . .'

'And Kurt Franck?'

'I brought a team of men. They are searching the hotel. Do

165

you think he recognized you? He must have done, I imagine.'

'I'm not sure,' Newman replied candidly, without referring to his disguise. 'He was looking in a different direction.'

'Well, we will soon know.' Kuhlmann put a cigar between his thick lips without lighting it. He chewed on it for a moment. 'Where is Tweed? In another room here?'

'No. He has left Lübeck temporarily to check something . . .'

'If he is still in Germany I must know. I have strict orders from Bonn to keep an eye on him.'

'He is outside the Federal Republic, but I am certain he will be returning . . .'

He broke off as the phone rang, Kuhlmann said that would be for him and he stood listening, saying 'Ja', and 'Nein', several times. When he put down the phone he spread his hands.

'The bird has flown again. He checked out of his room about ten minutes ago. He must have recognized you. He left on a motor-bike. Road-blocks are being set up, but this is a complex area. I think we've lost him again.'

'At least he's on the run.'

Newman was appalled at the news. Unless Kuhlmann caught Kurt Franck he was pretty sure the blond German would report sighting him to the East. That was if, as he suspected, Franck was from The Zone.

'You say,' Kuhlmann remarked as he stood up to go, 'Tweed will be back. I predict that on his second coming all hell will break loose.'

'Why do you think that?'

'I know Tweed. On the surface mild and cautious. This time I sensed something different in him. A thrust of steel . . .'

'You cross the border tonight,' Toll announced when Newman had let him inside 104. 'Why hang out the *Do Not Disturb* notice? I came back twice before you'd removed the sign.'

'Kuhlmann was here . . .'

'Jesus! How did he find you?'

'I called him . . .'

Newman explained the sequence of events since his arrival at the Movenpick. Toll listened in silence, pushed his glasses up to the bridge of his nose and clasped his hands.

166

'Describe this Kurt Franck,' he said at last.

He listened again while Newman gave him a concise description. He showed no reaction when Newman finished. Then he shook his head after a brief pause.

'Doesn't ring any bells.'

'In that case, cancel the border crossing.'

Newman's tone was hard and tough. He stood up, lit a cigarette and walked to stare out of the window. Behind him Toll flexed his long fingers and frowned before speaking.

'What's gone wrong, Bob?'

'You have.' Newman swung round to face the BND man. 'There's no polite way to put this. I'm a reporter by profession. Lord knows how many people I've interviewed, but one thing I've learned – to spot when someone is lying. You're lying in your teeth when you say my description of Franck means nothing.'

'I can't be sure . . .'

'Be unsure then – or walk out of that door and don't come back.'

'Could be Erwin Munzel.'

'Who is?'

'Markus Wolf's top professional assassin. Specializes in making murder look like an accident.'

'Charming. How very encouraging.'

'I said I can't be sure,' Toll protested. 'How many blond Germans over six feet tall do you think there are?'

'Weight, height, age – I gave you them all, plus appearance – and manner. Manner identifies a man. His arrogant insolence with women. Does it sound like Munzel?'

'Yes, it does,' Toll admitted. 'Do you think he recognized you down in the lobby?'

'Looks like it. Otherwise, why run? How long do you think it will be before he reports my miraculous reappearance here to Wolf?'

'Quite several hours.' Toll was very positive. 'They've stopped using hidden radio transmitters for the moment. We have too many detector units flooding the area. We're pretty sure they communicate with the East by routing the message through several phone numbers over here. Then someone calls their contact inside West Berlin. The contact walks through one of the checkpoints and reports the signal verbally. That way it's untraceable. We just haven't found that West Berlin contact. Yet.'

'Several hours?'

The fact gave Newman an idea. He said he'd have to think over whether he'd go ahead with the crossing. Would Toll kindly push off and leave him alone while he did think? The German agreed reluctantly, gave a deadline of nine that night for a decision.

'I'll come back here and see you then,' he said and left.

Newman opened the door to make sure Toll had gone. The corridor was deserted. He closed and locked the door. Sitting down, he called Lübeck-Süd. Again he was lucky – Kuhlmann was at the police HQ.

'Otto, can you do me a favour? Without asking questions?'

'Name it.'

'Is it possible to put such pressure on our mutual associate, Franck, that he won't be able to make a call from a public phone box?'

'I will try.' Kuhlmann paused. 'Don't let your work take too great a toll on your energy.'

Breaking the connection, at Lübeck-Süd Kuhlmann dialled a number. His instructions were simple and given with vehemence. 'Karl, I want that manhunt stepped up. Call back everyone off duty. Flood Lübeck and Travemünde with men on foot and inside patrol cars. Show a very active presence. Check the identity of all blond men whether they conform to the description or not. Special target, public phone boxes. Don't overlook the railway stations. The whole district must know there's a big dragnet out. What? So, it upsets the tourists. Who gives a sod for them?'

After leaving the Movenpick Kurt Franck headed towards Travemünde on his motor-cycle. Outwardly he was a typical holidaymaker enjoying himself. But inwardly he was churning with anxiety.

He had three specific worries. The police could be looking for him again. After the abortive attempt to kill Tweed on the Kolk below the church, he had gone to earth. Normal procedure.

Catching a train from Lübeck for Copenhagen, he had left the train at Puttgarden. From there he caught the local bus to the tiny town of Burg on the remote island of Fehmarn. He had stayed for several weeks inside a small cottage on the outskirts of the town, a cottage owned by a Martin Vollmer of Altona.

Returning to Lübeck, he had again taken a room at the Movenpick, reasoning that this was the last place the police would look for him now. Again, routine procedure. Once the dogs have inspected a foxhole, they rarely revisit it.

He raced along the open road, keeping just inside the speed limit. The suburbs of Lübeck were now fading behind him and he was in open country. His second worry was Robert Newman. Had he really seen him entering the lobby of the Movenpick? Franck simply couldn't make up his mind.

He concentrated on the road ahead, staring through his goggles for the turn-off point, the track leading to the river. His third worry was reporting his possible sighting of Newman to Leipzig. He had to find a public call box so he could phone Vollmer.

He slowed down, glanced again in his wing mirror, saw the road behind was deserted and swung down the cinder track between the fields on either side. The track was overgrown with weeds, had been superseded by a metalled road further along the highway.

He switched off the engine, pushing the machine the last few metres to the water's edge. Here reeds grew high and there was no sign of human life. He still paused to listen. No sound except for the occasional cry of a sea-bird, the distant moan of a ship's siren arriving – or leaving – Skandinaviankai. Pushing the machine to the edge of the baked mud bank, he grasped the handles firmly and shoved with all his strength. The motor-cycle sailed forward, hit the water with a splash and sank out of sight. He waited until bubbles rising from the submerged machine had ceased to ripple the water's surface and set off to walk along the river's edge, carrying the case he had unstrapped from the rear of the motor-cycle when he had switched off the engine.

Franck had survived in the West by following his training and never taking a chance. In an emergency, always assume the

169

worst. It had been a favourite maxim of his Russian instructor. Franck was now in the process of changing his image before he re-entered a built-up area.

He reached the small power cruiser moored to the isolated landing stage, boarded the vessel. Once inside the tiny cabin, he opened his case, transferred the contents to a backpack he hauled out of a locker. The case was easily disposed of. He dropped a heavy length of chain inside it, snapped the catches shut and threw it overboard. Then he started the engine.

Half an hour later he moored the vessel to another quiet landing stage, hoisted the backpack on to his broad shoulders and started to hoof it along the nearby highway. Within ten minutes he was hiking into the outskirts of Travemünde near the ferry crossing to Priwall Island. He was looking for a public phone booth. He stopped suddenly, mingling with the evening crowd of holidaymakers.

Two uniformed policemen on foot had stopped a man with blond hair and were obviously asking for his papers. That shook him. The man was at least fifteen years older than Franck – but he had blond hair.

A patrol car cruised slowly along the front, the two policemen inside scanning the faces of the crowd. Franck forced himself to walk slowly away towards the waterfront. A phone booth stood empty on the far side of the road. He'd call Vollmer from there.

He was standing on the edge of the kerb, waiting for a gap in the traffic so he could cross, when he saw the uniformed policeman who had taken up a position a few metres from the booth. A dark-haired youth in jeans and a T-shirt entered the booth. The policeman's head turned, studied the youth, then looked away.

Franck swore to himself. Travemünde was crawling with police. And for some reason it looked as though they knew he might try to use a public phone. That worried him a lot. Had the police, even the BND, found out Wolf's system of communication via the contact in West Berlin?

Franck himself had no idea how the system worked beyond an agent eventually calling West Berlin. Markus Wolf had survived all this time by being ultra careful. Franck turned away and almost bumped into a tall handsome middle-aged brunette. He muttered an apology and walked on.

Behind him Ann Grayle frowned and stared at his back. Despite the humid warmth of the evening she was immaculately dressed in a white classic pleated skirt, a pale blue blouse with a high neck and a cameo at her throat.

As an ex-diplomat's wife she had an eye like the lens of a camera. She only had to see a face once and it was recorded for ever in that encyclopaedia she called her memory. Where had she seen that unpleasant-looking blond-haired giant? Then she remembered. Several weeks earlier he had boarded the *Südwind* when the Chadwick woman was entertaining Robert Newman, the good-looking foreign correspondent. She resumed her evening stroll.

As he plodded along the front Franck found he was sweating – and not from the heat. He had the feeling he had walked into a trap. That woman had seemed familiar. And he was known here. He had to get out of Travemünde fast – but first precautions must be taken.

He purchased the straw hat at a shop on the opposite side of the road; the pipe, tobacco and matches from another shop nearby. He stayed under cover of the second shop while he filled the pipe with tobacco and lit it. Franck never smoked a pipe – he was a 'wet' smoker.

Wearing the straw hat, the pipe clenched between his teeth, he emerged from the shop and made his way by the back streets to Travemünde Hafen station. Sitting on the platform, waiting for the next train to Lübeck, he felt hunted.

He struck a few more matches to light the dead pipe. He had noticed pipe-smokers spent most of their time relighting pipes – he wondered why they bothered. Aboard the train, he decided he'd try to phone from Lübeck Hauptbahnhof. At least he had covered his tracks.

At Lübeck Hauptbahnhof he approached the phone booth warily and was glad he'd done so. Another bloody uniformed policeman stood close by. That decided him. He bought a ticket for the next train due in which went to Copenhagen. He'd get off at Puttgarden before it moved aboard the ferry prior to crossing the Baltic.

At Puttgarden he'd buy a return ticket to Hamburg. Always

double back on your tracks. Another maxim hammered into him by his Russian instructor. God knew when he'd reach Hamburg where he'd find a safe phone to report to Vollmer in Altona. It could easily be midnight. But he felt a little better after getting some food and coffee at the restaurant at Lübeck Hauptbahnhof. As the train sped across the open flatlands towards Fehmarn Island he dropped off to sleep.

Inside the fifth floor office in the anonymous building in the centre of Leipzig another man from the East was thinking about food. Lysenko announced he was going out to get dinner.

'I'll stay at my desk,' Wolf replied. He had no desire for more of the Russian's company than was necessary. 'I can have something sent in. There could be a report from Munzel.'

'A lot of good Munzel is,' Lysenko growled. 'And now we know from our contact at Hamburg Airport that both Tweed and Newman have flown back to London. So Munzel has missed his opportunity to kill Tweed. All highly satisfactory. You're doing well,' he added with heavy sarcasm.

Wolf, a heavily-built man, his expression his normal graven image, jerked upright behind his desk. He stood quite still as Lysenko paused by the door.

'General, I would remind you I am not without friends in high places in Moscow. I have been at this game a long time. I have studied Tweed. He will be back. He never gives up. When he returns that will be his final encounter with me. Now, take as long as you like over your meal. I am in no hurry to see you again.'

He sat down, opened a file and began studying it as though he were alone. Lysenko fumed. No one talked to him like that. He opened his mouth to deliver a shattering reply, then closed it without speaking. What Wolf said was only too bloody true – he carried enormous clout in Moscow. Lysenko closed the door very quietly as he left, so quietly it made no sound. Wolf compressed his lips. He found Lysenko's reaction disturbing.

'Josef Falken is the name of the head of Group Five,' Peter Toll said as he drove the BMW south through the gathering dusk with Newman alongside him. 'He is the man who will meet you once you've crossed the border tonight.'

172

'Tonight? It's 10.30. That's pushing it a bit, isn't it?'

'I pulled forward the crossing date. Your seeing Erwin Munzel – if it was him – in the Movenpick lobby, calls for quick action.'

'In the hope that he won't get through to Leipzig before I make the crossing?'

'Not entirely.' Toll's tone was a trifle too assured. 'Josef shouldn't hang around near the border too long. I've succeeded so far by moving faster than Wolf . . .'

'So far? I find that reservation most encouraging. What does this Josef Falken look like?'

'Six feet tall, thin-faced with a great hooked nose, powerful jaw, blue eyes that look right through you. Forty-two years old. Official job, chief of bird preservation. That enables him to go almost where he likes, visiting bird sanctuaries. But not inside the border zones along the frontier and the Baltic. Married once. Didn't last. Away from home too much. Party member. That's all you need to know. Do you want to go over the mechanics of the crossing again?'

'Christ, no. Three times is enough . . .'

'So let's run through your identity once more. We're close to Goslar now . . .'

'The way you drive I'm not surprised.'

'Your identity,' Toll repeated.

'Albert Thorn. Senior plain-clothes officer in the River Police. Special security section. Main operational area the Elbe river. Born 1945 in Karlmarxstadt, still known then by its old name Chemnitz. At the moment on special assignment tracking drug ring suspected of dealing in heroin. I've got the rest. Do I have to go on?'

'No. Being a reporter, you have a photographic memory. I was impressed with the way you remembered all relevant details first time. You have the papers for the job. And, like Falken, you've a job which calls for widespread movement. But again, not inside the border areas.' Toll switched on the interior car light for a few moments and glanced at Newman. 'You look amazingly different.'

'Where did you learn to tint hair?'

Newman had been surprised at the skill Toll had shown inside a remote farmhouse south of Lübeck. He had shampooed his hair a darker shade, had used a small brush to deal with Newman's thick eyebrows. This had made the greatest change. His eyebrows now appeared even thicker, which gave him a grim, scowling look. He had asked why Toll had not used dye.

'Takes too long, can easily look artificial. Tinting is more effective, more realistic. Just don't wash your hair,' Toll had warned. 'And if it rains keep your hat on. How are the eyes?'

Inside the farmhouse Toll had produced a wooden case lined with green baize and divided into many compartments holding a variety of coloured contact lenses. Eventually, Newman had found a pair which fitted reasonably comfortably. His eyes, normally blue, were now brown. This also increased the impression of aggressiveness in his appearance.

'OK. But I wouldn't like to wear them too long.'

'Three days in and then you're out. And that was part of the extra training I insisted on at Pullach, along with other things. To learn to tint hair myself. That way only I know about you – I don't like extra technicians sharing the knowledge.'

This was one aspect of Toll which Newman found reassuring. His lone wolf character, his insistence on controlling an operation entirely by himself. It cut down the risk of leaks.

'Coming in to Goslar now,' Toll remarked as he slowed down.

An ancient town, dramatic in the night. By the street lights the silhouettes of old half-timbered buildings, many sporting turrets at the corners, loomed. Like something out of a Hans Andersen fairytale. Romantic and sinister at the same time. The streets were deserted and in the distance Newman could faintly make out evergreen forest – great stands of firs rising up shoulder to shoulder. They were moving into the Harz mountains.

'Getting closer,' said Toll, who seemed to find it necessary to keep up a flow of conversation. 'Come midnight you cross over. How are the clothes?'

Back at the farmhouse Newman had changed into a complete set of fresh clothes, down to his underwear. There had been a selection of sizes, all from East Germany. Over his suit he wore a lightweight raincoat. Inside his wallet – also from the German Democratic Republic – was a large sum of DDR currency.

'Comfortable,' Newman said as they left Goslar behind

174

and the car began climbing. 'Latest weather report?'

'A considerable drop in temperature in the Harz. Could be a mist. That will help – provided it arrives after you've made contact with Falken . . .'

'And if it comes earlier?'

'That's unlikely.'

Which means, Newman interpreted, he hopes to God it doesn't. They had left behind all signs of human habitation as they went on climbing between dark walls of solid fir forest. He could smell the aroma of pine coming in through the window and then the headlights played over a large copse of pine trees. Toll switched off the headlights, slowed even more, relying on only sidelights.

'Very close now,' he said. 'Don't forget the photos of yourself concealed in the soles of your shoes.'

'I asked you before – why do I need them?'

'And I told you,' Toll snapped. 'I don't know. Falken asked for them. Bloody well ask him when you meet.'

The temperature was dropping. Traces of condensation appeared on the windscreen and Toll switched on the wipers. The only sounds now were the purr of the engine, the whip-whap of the wipers. They hadn't passed another vehicle in over half an hour but the curving road had an excellent surface.

'How did you obtain my photos?' Newman asked. 'Like passport pictures. Blurred to hell . . .'

'Taken secretly by yours truly when you sat at one of the tables in front of the Jensen. I looked a little different myself when I snapped you. The blurring is deliberate. They were taken before we altered your appearance. I foresaw problems if the likeness was too good. I developed and printed myself. Another bit of training I requested at Pullach. Half those idiots back there are bloody amateurs. All senior personnel should be able to do what I can.'

It wasn't said in an arrogant way, Newman noted. A simple remark expressing a conviction. Again Toll's stock rose. His one weakness seemed to be impetuosity. This mad rush to the border. At such short notice. But maybe it had advantages. The least possible time for a mistake, a leak, a warning to the East.

'We walk the rest of the way,' Toll said. 'You won't mind? You won't have to.'

175

Newman sensed the suppressed tension in Toll as he stopped the car, turned off the sidelights and got out. He locked the doors and they moved uphill on foot. A heavy, menacing silence fell, the forest closed on them. Their rubber-soled shoes made no sound on the road. They moved like ghosts through the night. Newman checked his watch. The illuminated hands registered five minutes to midnight.

Inside the empty compartment of the train slowing to enter the Hauptbahnhof at Hamburg Kurt Franck checked his own watch. Almost midnight. He felt down the inside of his left sock. The broad-bladed hunting knife was safely tucked inside the sheath strapped to his leg. It was the only weapon he always carried.

The train stopped and he jumped on to the platform. Walking rapidly he climbed the staircase, checking over his shoulder. He half-ran over the bridge and hauled open the door of the phone booth. He wasted half a minute detaching the backpack so the door would close properly. Then he started dialling Martin Vollmer's number. His report would be rushed through to Markus Wolf. Including his fresh sighting of Robert Newman at the Movenpick.

Twenty-Two

Tweed sat facing Diana in a booth inside his favourite restaurant near Walton Street, South Ken. The service was discreet and efficient, the atmosphere intimate, the food among the best in London.

Tweed had once heard the proprietor remark in his upper crust voice, 'I set out to found a place where discriminating customers would appreciate good food at modest prices . . .' A bit poncey, but he'd achieved his object.

'Who are these people we are going to visit?' Diana asked. 'And this pheasant is delicious.'

'They do it rather well here. Who are we going to visit? Four different men, one of whom may be involved in a serious kidnapping case. I've explained the type of insurance General and Cumbria specialize in.'

'But why do you want me with you?'

'Because I have faith in feminine intuition. I know these people well. You'll look at them with a fresh eye. I want your impressions of them.'

'Sounds rather exciting . . .'

'We'll have to be careful,' Tweed warned.

'I'll be frightfully careful. I suppose I do know a bit about men by now,' she said reflectively and sipped her Chablis. 'Who am I supposed to be?'

A shrewd question, Tweed thought. 'I was just coming to that,' he said. 'You are an old friend of mine, over here on a visit from New York. Can you fake that? None of the four concerned have been to the States. They spend most of their business hours in Europe.'

'I have been to New York once, as I told you at Travemünde, but it was a long time ago. Can I fake it? I know I can. I'll just babble on, speaking a lot and really saying nothing. Haven't you noticed? Most people do that. It's rather like a game – I think I'm going to enjoy this. Who do we meet first?'

'Tomorrow we travel down into the country to meet Harry Masterson.' He looked up from his pheasant as he spoke the name to see her reaction. She stared back at him over the rim of her glass, her pale blue eyes steady behind her long lashes. 'He lives in Sussex in a typical old thatched cottage.'

'He's married?' she enquired.

'Divorced. He likes women and is very lively. Says the most outrageous things to see how you react . . .'

'Sounds fun. I'll play up to him a bit. Maybe he'll talk to me about himself. That type often does. Their favourite subject.'

'You're a cynic,' he teased.

'Just a realist. I'll tell you afterwards what I think of him. Doesn't sound like a villain.'

'This villain is dangerous because he's so clever at concealing his real character.'

'I'll get under his skin,' she said confidently. 'It will be lovely travelling round with you, Tweed. That crowd back at the marina can be such a crashing bore.' She raised her glass again. 'Here's to my spotting the odd man out . . .'

*

177

Tweed escorted Diana back to Newman's flat, refused her invitation to join her in a nightcap, used the waiting cab to take him on to Park Crescent. Monica was waiting for him when he entered his office.

'I kept on phoning Peter Toll at Pullach as you suggested,' she informed him. 'Three times at spaced-out intervals to keep up the pressure. He's still away.'

'I don't like it.' Tweed walked across to the wall-map he had put up earlier in the day, a map showing the whole of Northern Europe, including West and East Germany, the Baltic and Scandinavia.

'Harry Butler is still at Heathrow with that German, Walther Pröhl, the BND man who looks like Bob Newman,' she reminded him. 'Harry has reported in. First he starved Pröhl, who was famished. Gave him only strong black coffee to drink, which made Pröhl edgy. No new data from him. Then Harry had a meal sent in and Pröhl devoured everything, mopping up the gravy with his bread. That should have softened him up. Still nothing fresh. Harry says it looks as though he doesn't know anything more. What do you think Toll is up to?'

'Well, he's up to something.' Tweed turned away from studying the border between West Germany and The Zone. 'He sends a man who looks like Newman to Heathrow – which means what he is involved in concerns Newman. Pröhl has a return ticket to Hamburg and waits at the airport for the next flight back. Toll, therefore, was trying to convince someone Newman had left the Federal Republic. That someone, I'm pretty sure, is Markus Wolf, who probably has a man inside Hamburg Airport – someone who can check the passenger manifests.'

'I also called Samuel Portman, Paula Grey's private detective. You have an appointment with him tomorrow. His office at ten in the morning. He thinks you're a potential client. Is there something funny about Paula checking on her husband?'

'That,' Tweed told her, 'is what I'm going to find out. Lord, it must be late . . .'

'Nearly midnight,' Monica replied, glancing at her watch.

*

178

There was no wind, no sound, no light. The silence, the black fir forest, the dark sky were oppressive. Only seconds earlier the frontier zone ahead of Newman and Toll had been a blaze of lights from the distant watchtowers, beams of light moving slowly, like sinister eyes probing the forbidden area, search-lights from each individual tower. Toll had handed Newman night-glasses which he had raised to his eyes, focusing them on the watchtower immediately in front of them, seen through an avenue of grass and shrubs cut through the forest.

The watchtower was a concrete vertical column supporting a round cabin at the summit, a cabin with large windows and a shallow roof. The lenses brought the top of the tower so close Newman felt he could reach out and put a hand inside the open window.

Three men inside. One standing by a swivel-mounted machine-gun. A second operating his searchlight. The third fiddling with something which looked like a console equipped with switches. A beam swept slowly along the thirty-foot high wire fence which rose up about ten yards back from where they stood. At this point a gate was let into the fence.

'You go through the gate,' Toll whispered.

'I know.'

Newman, his hands clammy round the binoculars, studied the lie of the land beyond the gate. Tufts of grass. Stunted shrubs of gorse. Not cleared in the same ruthless way he had seen at other parts of the seven hundred-mile Iron Curtain stretching from the Baltic to Hungary, far to the south.

He heard a metallic clink. Toll had extracted his bunch of skeleton keys from his coat pocket. God knew how long it would take him to unlock that gate. Five minutes was the expected duration of the blackout to be organized by the crew in the tower he was gazing at, a blackout caused by deliberate shorting of the electricity.

'Best night for a month for crossing,' Toll hissed. 'No moon. Heavy overcast forecast. No wind. You'd hear trouble a kilo-metre off.'

'You said it before,' Newman whispered back.

And he had. Toll was repeating himself. Sign of nerves. He had good reason. God knew how many regulations he was breaking – a senior BND officer coming right up to the frontier.

179

Newman felt he should be grateful. All he could think of was the route he had to follow beyond that gate. When the lights went out. With luck the bloody lights wouldn't go out. That would abort the operation.

'Feeling nervous?' Toll asked.

'Just concentrating on the job.'

Newman handed back the glasses and his voice was ice-cold. That worried Toll. If they felt nervous they would have maximum alertness. Overconfident, they always took risks. Something he could do nothing about. Toll quenched his last-minute doubts.

Newman began to feel the cold seeping into him. They were standing behind a copse of trees, peering round the thick trunk of one giant fir sheering above them. No sign of mist. That was one thing to be thankful for. No mist, please. Not until I'm across – over the dummy minefield. *If* it was still a dummy. Markus Wolf had a habit of changing the defences without warning.

'Any minute now,' Toll said.

'They're late.'

Newman had checked his watch. Five minutes past midnight. What had gone wrong? His right hand felt the shaving kit inside the pocket of his raincoat. Minimum equipment. Ordinary razor, packet of East German blades – like the razor. Small brush. Piece of soap. Also manufactured in the Democratic Republic. Democratic. That was a laugh . . .

The lights went out.

Newman temporarily lost his night vision. He'd made the mistake of watching the lights too long. Toll reached out a hand, grasped his arm. He spoke so softly Newman only just caught what he'd said.

'Grab the back of my coat belt . . .'

They stumbled forwards to the gate, placing their feet carefully. Tufts of grass threatened to bring them down. Newman blinked several times. His night vision began to come back. They were at the gate. Toll raised the handle, prior to trying the first key. The gate opened, moved inward silently on well-oiled hinges. Toll was taken aback. He stood holding the handle, listening, and then he spoke.

'Gate unlocked. Something's wrong . . .'

'Get out of my way. I'm going through.'

It had been over four years ago. His training with the SAS unit. He hadn't thought about it until this moment. Everything came back in a flood, filling his mind. The sergeant who had drilled him unmercifully.

'Sometimes you'll get lucky. Grab it in both hands. The luck. You'll get one chance only. Don't hesitate. Not for a second. Do it, man . . .'

Newman had never known his name. He'd come from the Manchester area – judging from the way he spoke. Newman never knew where any of them came from. Bloody nightmare it had been. But a thorough bloody nightmare. 'Just call me Sarge . . .'

'You won't see it coming. The lucky break. When it comes see it. Grab it. Do it . . .'

Newman was through the gate and walking straight ahead, crouched low. Behind him Toll closed the gate, decided against trying to lock it, headed back for the parked car, long legs striding over the ground, downhill, fast. Once a man was through you left him to it. He was on his own. Just get well clear of the border – and hope and pray. He was too bloody confident, Toll said to himself and shrugged his shoulders.

Beyond the gate Newman was shit-scared.

The tower loomed up in the night like some alien, a Martian out of H. G. Wells. It was the guidepost. Walk straight ahead, pass the right-hand side of the tower, don't look up, keep moving at a steady pace. That much Toll had known.

Still crouched low, placing his feet flat, he thought he saw a shadow coming towards him. He blinked. Those damned contact lenses. Then he remembered Sarge again. 'Danger. Even a hint of it. Sight. Smell. Sound. Drop flat. Don't think. Drop fucking flat!'

Newman dropped flat, took the impact of the fall on his forearms, sprawled full-length behind a low patch of gorse, buried his head between his arms, head turned sideways. Then he began worrying. Had he done the right thing? Five minutes' duration of blackout, Toll had said. He was wasting precious time . . .

He heard the faint crackle, like the sound of a foot breaking

181

a twig. He lay motionless, listening. The shadow had been a man, a man walking stealthily towards him. He flexed his hands. Was he going to have to kill before he had even crossed the belt?

Another crackle, closer this time. Had he been seen? Was this an armed guard checking? He imagined the cold muzzle of a pistol pressed against his head. At least he was turned the right way. The cautious footsteps – they were now definite footsteps – were much closer. The stupid bastard might tread on him . . .

Newman blinked. He was staring at the side of a man's hiking boot, the type with spiked soles. The foot remained still. He knew, like himself, the unknown man was listening. Newman dug his elbows deeper into the hard earth, ready for springing to his feet.

Then he recalled something Toll had said. *This crossing is also used by the East Germans sending agents into the West. We always let them through, never follow them.* Something like that.

He was staring at the boot of an agent heading for the West. Hence the unlocked gate which had so worried Toll. By an extraordinary coincidence agents from each direction were passing at the same moment. Coincidence. He remembered something else Toll had said. Only a few minutes ago.

'Best night for a month for crossing. No moon. Heavy overcast forecast. No wind . . .'

That explained why Spiked Boot was coming out. The boot began moving again. Newman froze. The footsteps grew fainter. Heading for the gate. He couldn't waste another second. Very slowly Newman rose to his feet, glanced over his shoulder. The vague silhouette of the retreating shape had almost disappeared in the dark. Newman walked forward, aiming for the base of the huge watchtower rearing above him.

He paused by the side of the concrete circular pillar, looked up, saw the overhang of the cabin at the summit dimly protruding like a gigantic umbrella. From here he had to walk straight forward to the electronic fence where Falken should be waiting. He started walking, again crouching.

He stopped. Sweat streamed from his armpits. His right foot had trodden on something. He looked down, not moving the foot. It rested on a small mound shaped like an anthill. But this was no anthill. The sole of his shoe had felt unyielding metal beneath it. It rested on an anti-personnel mine.

The damned things detonated under pressure, the pressure of a man's foot. Was it a dummy? Toll had mentioned dummies. Or had the agent moving to the West known where the live mines were? He took a deep breath. Only one way to find out. Lift the foot with care, great care.

He used the heel, still resting on the ground, as a pivot, lifting the sole as though raising it from something live. Nothing happened. He walked on. Watch where you're putting your bloody feet. So much to watch. The tower. His rear. What might wait for him ahead.

On the East German side the minefield belt was lined with more fir forests, a solid black wall. He trod slowly among clusters of grass tufts, round stunted gorse bushes, watching for another of those hard-to-see mounds. He checked his watch. Seven minutes. He was late. The blackout was timed to last five minutes.

He kept moving. At any second the whole area might be flooded with light, those damned searchlights probing. He'd be a sitting duck for one of those swivel-mounted machine-guns. He saw a vague barrier, lower than the wire he had left behind. He had reached the electronic fence. *Don't touch!*

Where was the flaming gate? They were supposed to be opposite each other, the gates on either side. He had taken great care to walk in a straight line. Or so he thought. So easy in the dark to veer off course. He came up to the fence. No gate. To the left – or to the right? He had to guess correctly first time.

Newman glanced behind. He could just make out the tower. It was a little to the left. He moved along the fence to his right, keeping a distance of about a metre from it. He nearly walked past the gate, constructed of the same mesh as the fence. He checked his watch again. God! Ten minutes.

The gate opened away from him as though of its own volition. Startled, he paused. A tall figure stood holding the gate on the far side of the fence. Newman stiffened his right hand, ready to strike a blow with the side of his hand. The tall man called out, softly.

'Bismarck . . .'

'Rhine Falls,' Newman replied, completing the password Toll had given him.

'Hurry!' the voice whispered in German again.

Newman slipped through the gate. The tall man closed it and took Newman's arm, pulling him away from the fence. He must have had sixth sense. As they melted into the forest a glare of lights flooded the belt behind them. Searchlights began to probe, moving more swiftly, scanning the forbidden zone. He had made it by less than thirty seconds.

Fifteen minutes after midnight. Wolf looked up from his desk in surprise but his expression remained blank. Lysenko had entered the room and Wolf sensed he was still in a bad mood.

'Why have you come back?' he asked.

'Couldn't sleep,' the General growled. 'Any news?'

'Yes, there is. Contradictory reports. I don't like contradictions. The phone has been busy.'

'What has happened?' Lysenko lit a cigarette and stood with his hands in his trouser pockets.

'You know we heard the British reporter, Robert Newman, flew from Hamburg with Tweed to England?'

'Of course I remember that . . .'

'Kurt Franck has just reported he saw Newman at the Movenpick Hotel in Lübeck this afternoon. He was disguised – wearing dark glasses and a Tyrolean hat. That is, yesterday afternoon.'

'Franck could be mistaken.'

'Franck is never mistaken. He is one of my most reliable men. So now we have two Newmans – one in London, one in Germany. I'm wondering which is the real man.'

'What do you think is going on?'

'There has just been another report,' Wolf continued in the same monotone. 'From the Harz district. Someone short-circuited the electricity supply to the watchtowers. There was a blackout from midnight for exactly ten minutes.'

'Power failure?'

'With the system locked in to a back-up generator? I think not.'

Wolf stared at Lysenko without a trace of friendliness. The

184

Russian stared back at the eyes behind the horn-rimmed glasses. Lysenko often recalled a picture he had once seen of Mount Rushmore in the United States, the great cliff where the images of four American presidents had been carved out of rock. Wolf's graven image reminded him of one of those impassive rock faces.

'It is complex,' Wolf continued. 'We had an agent passing over to the West at that point. A blackout had been arranged for midnight . . .'

'Then surely that explains it,' Lysenko snapped.

'If you would be so kind as to let me finish my report without interruption? The blackout was arranged from midnight to precisely 12.05 hours. Seconds before my man operated a switch the whole system – including the back-up – was short-circuited. The black-out lasted *ten* minutes. Not five as planned. When my operative pressed the switch again to reactivate the system it didn't work. Five minutes later the system came back on for no apparent reason.'

'A technical hitch?' Lysenko persisted.

'I think not. The missing five minutes worry me.'

God, Lysenko was thinking, these bloody Germans, they have minds like Swiss watches. Probably that was why they almost defeated us during the Great Patriotic War. They aren't men – they're machines. He had come back to make his peace with Wolf, and here they were, at daggers drawn again. He decided to go on the offensive.

'Well, if you're so cocked up about it, what are you going to do?'

'I have already done it. The three men inside the watchtower facing the exit gate have been arrested. They are under interrogation. In any case, they will not return to that tower.'

'Wolf, tell me what you think really happened?'

'How do I know? The two reports – one from Franck, the other from Border Control – only came in a few minutes ago.'

'But you seem to link them. This so-called blackout and the mystery about Newman.'

'I phoned Moscow just before you came back on the special line. I held on while they checked Newman on the computer.' Wolf paused. 'He speaks fluent German. I have just issued a nationwide alert. Photos of him will be here by morning.'

185

Twenty-Three

The blurred glow of the border searchlights penetrated the darkness of the fir forest just enough for Newman to get a glimpse of Josef Falken before they had walked into pitch blackness. Tall and slim, he had a long face terminating in a pointed jaw. There was a hint of humour round the corners of the firm mouth, in his pale blue eyes. He spoke in a light-hearted way as though they were embarking on a leisurely hike in friendly territory.

'You ride a bicycle, so Toll informed me?'

'I can, yes. And after three days I will be crossing back over the same route?'

'Toll always plans ahead. The cycles are less than a kilometre from here. Your German is very good. You could pass for one. In fact, you may have to.'

Again the same buoyant note, an apparent total lack of stress. Newman decided he liked Falken. Then he stopped, reached out his hand and grasped the German's arm. He pointed into the forest to their left away from the narrow path they were following.

'Something – someone – moved up there . . .'

'Yes, my flank guard. Gerda is watching over us. You only need to know her first name. She is carrying an automatic weapon – and she can use it. First lesson for you, my friend,' Falken continued as they resumed walking along the uphill path winding through the forest. 'First lesson,' he repeated, 'this is wartime. We are the underground fighting an alien regime. We are Soviet-occupied territory – The Zone.'

There was silence for a few minutes as Newman digested this and they climbed higher. And now he knew why the searchlight glow had been a blur – the mist was rolling in, coils of white vapour sliding in between the trees.

To his left Gerda was no more than a faint shadow, flitting noiselessly through the forest along a course parallel to their own. It was not at all what Newman had expected. More like

186

being with a guerrilla group. He shivered as the chill of the mist penetrated his raincoat.

Falken wore a thigh-length leather jacket with large lapels which gave the garment a military cut. Corduroy trousers were tucked inside knee-length leather boots with rubber soles. The dense silence of the mist-bound forest was broken by no sound. Even their footware made no noise on the moss-covered ground.

'Here are the cycles,' Falken said, turning off the path and reaching under a clump of bracken. 'They gave me your height. I think this one should suit you.'

Toll's thoroughness again, Newman thought as he raised the cycle upright and perched on the saddle. It felt comfortable, just the right size. Falken hauled out a larger machine and looked at Newman.

'Make sure your lights are on – including the rear light. It is the regulation.'

'What about Gerda?'

'There is a third machine under the bracken with a basket for her weapon. She will follow us at a certain interval – in case of trouble I like a surprise rearguard . . .'

The path had ended at a tarred road and they began cycling alongside each other uphill. Falken pedalled slowly until he was sure Newman could handle his machine competently, then he increased the pace.

Falken cycled with his head bent forward. Newman realized he was listening carefully. He suspected the German had exceptional hearing – a man who looked after bird sanctuaries would be accustomed to picking up sounds other men might miss. They had reached the top of the hill and were cycling along a level stretch of road, the beams of their lights showing only a short way ahead in the oily mist when the headlights of a car parked off the road were switched on, catching them full in the face. A voice shouted the command.

'Halt! Border Police. Stand still. We have guns pointed at you . . .'

Tweed was still working at Park Crescent. He was an owl and his mind moved at full power late at night. He closed the last of the four files and pushed the stack away.

187

'Shall I try phoning Peter Toll again?' Monica asked. 'I've tried four times so far.'

Tweed checked his watch. 'One o'clock. That makes it 2 a.m. in Münich. Leave it till the morning . . .'

'Did you find anything in the files?'

'Nothing. Grey, Masterson, Lindemann and Dalby. Not a thing.' He leaned back in his chair and went on talking, thinking aloud. 'How did it all start? Ian Fergusson was murdered. That was the bait to lure me into Germany. Then Ziggy Palewska is killed. A second body to hold my interest. Lübeck. I'm attacked, probably by Kurt Franck. Misfire, thanks to Newman. The central fact of the whole mystery is only my four sector chiefs knew Fergusson was going to Hamburg. Let's call the odd man out Janus . . .'

'Why Janus?'

'Janus, the god who looks both ways – the man who looks both to East and West. Like January. Undoubtedly Wolf's – and therefore also Lysenko's – chief agent in the West . . .'

'But there appear to be two chief agents. Balkan also.'

'Balkan is somewhere in Germany for brief, maybe longish, periods. Probably controller of all Wolf's networks in Western Germany. Getting back to Lübeck, we have the strange figure of Dr Berlin. And Diana's shrewd comment – *maybe he wants you to see him*. Why would he want that?'

'Sounds an arrogant sod,' Monica commented.

'Lübeck still. Two horrible murders of attractive blonde girls. Three, if you add in Frankfurt six months ago.'

'You lack a connection – maybe several.'

'I have that feeling – that I am looking at different pieces of a huge jigsaw. I can't fit them together because I lack more pieces.'

'Maybe Newman has gone off to find some of your missing pieces. We know from my phone call that he checked out of the Jensen.'

'I just hope to God he hasn't crossed the border.' Tweed's gaze switched to the wall map. 'Peter Toll is brilliant but still impetuous.'

'Why use Newman? He has his own people . . .'

'Because he might need someone new. All four of our sector chiefs report a weird lack of activity by the opposition. Toll will have spotted that. So, he sends in someone fresh. Let's pray I'm wrong.'

'And why, may I ask,' Monica said tentatively, 'are you taking Diana Chadwick with you when you visit the famous four in their warrens?'

'Just to get a second opinion.'

'Oh, really? I don't think we're being frank any more. You have some other motive . . .'

Tweed stood up behind his desk, stretched his arms, suppressed a yawn. 'You go home now. Me too. I'll find you a cab. I have to visit that detective, Portman, tomorrow – no, today.'

Monica put the cover on her typewriter. 'And what about Harry Butler and that German he's interrogating at Heathrow?'

'We'll leave them there until I can get Toll. Harry can last out an incredible number of hours. Maybe the German can't.'

'I'll try Toll again in the morning.'

'Do that.' Tweed helped her on with her coat. 'I want news of what has happened to Newman.'

Newman stopped, braking his cycle, dropping his feet to the road, standing with legs splayed on either side of his machine. The crisis had come. He was ice-cold. Falken also stopped. Newman threw up one hand to shield his eyes from the glare of the car's headlights, holding the cycle with the other.

'Border Police!' the arrogant voice shouted again. 'Papers! Your papers!'

There were two of them, both clad in grey military greatcoats and rammed down over their heads were peaked caps with oblong-shaped cap badges. They had stepped forward into the lights, one of them held a carbine loosely in his right hand.

'Lay your cycles on the ground!'

Newman obeyed, stood up slowly, very erect. His left hand reached up slowly to his breast pocket. The guard with the carbine levelled his weapon, aiming it at Newman's chest.

'What are you doing?' his companion shouted.

'Getting out my papers. You asked for them. Kindly examine this folder.' Newman's tone was deceptively quiet. 'And tell that lout with you to lower his gun . . .'

189

'Lout?'

The talking man stepped forward, raised his clenched fist.

'Hit me and I'll see you spend the rest of your natural life behind bars!' Newman thundered. 'River Police. Special Security Section. Look at it, idiot!'

He thrust the opened folder under the man's nose, keeping a grip on the document. He held the folder at a slanting angle in the light from the car. The guard lowered his fist, took a step back. Newman took a step forward.

'Blundering fools!' he stormed. 'I'm a senior officer – on special assignment tracking down drug smugglers. You may have ruined the whole operation. Turn out those goddamn car lights. Give me a torch. Come on! Move, damn you!'

Psychological intimidation was not the only motive for raising his voice. Somewhere close behind Gerda was coming along the road, cycling in their rear. He was warning her.

'Go back and turn off the headlights,' the guard told the man with the carbine. 'I have a torch here,' he went on, producing the torch from the capacious pocket of his greatcoat. Newman snatched it from him, switched it on and beamed it straight into the man's eyes. He blinked and lifted his own hand. The cap badge of the Border Guards now showed clearly, the badge Toll had shown Newman at the farmhouse when he identified the different police forces in the DDR for Newman.

'Now you know what it's like,' Newman ranted on. 'To have a light shone at you point-blank. Only the mist may have stopped those headlights alerting the gang of bastards I'm after. Have you children?' he demanded. 'And what is your name?'

'Karl Schneider,' the guard said sullenly. 'And I have a boy and a girl . . .'

'You want the boy to grow up a drug addict? Hooked on heroin?' he shouted. 'Because that is what this anti-social gang of swine are peddling.' His voice dropped, became silky. 'Show *me* your identification. I may have to report this operation went wrong because of your crazy intervention . . .'

'We only do our duty.'

In a cowed tone, the words trailing off as Schneider gave Newman his folder. The Englishman checked it by the light of the torch, repeated the number three times as though impressing it on his memory, then shoved it back at the German.

'Your duty,' he sneered. 'Your fumbling incompetence, you mean.'

'Incompetence?' Schneider, indignant, perked up. 'And who is this man with you?'

'Josef Falken, Bird Sanctuary Conservation Service,' Newman rasped. 'Co-opted to assist me. He can move like a cat – which is more than you can do.' He raised his voice. 'I said incompetence. Instead of waiting by your car quietly, then waving us down with this torch, calling out in a normal voice, you have to illuminate half the Harz Mountains. And had we run for it your car is parked the wrong way – it would need a three-point turn before you could have come after us. By then we'd have disappeared into the mist. Perhaps,' he continued with a heavy sarcasm, 'you'd like to waste more time checking my companion's papers? That will look good on the report I may make. Especially if we miss our rendezvous with the gang of vipers we are hunting.'

'That will not be necessary,' Schneider replied. 'Please to proceed. And if you can see your way to overlooking this unfortunate incident. I have two children and a wife . . .'

'I will think over your request. Come, Falken, we have wasted too long already . . .'

They cycled off together past the parked car which now showed no headlights and pedalled through the fog-bound silence without speaking for several minutes.

'What about Gerda?' Newman asked eventually.

'She will have heard your voice, she will take to the forest, go round the Border Police, pushing her bike, then return to the road and catch us up. That is why we are moving slowly. You know, my friend . . .' Falken paused as though seeking the right words, '. . . that was a truly remarkable performance you put up. You are a natural actor. You overwhelmed them by the sheer force of your personality. I kept silent for fear of spoiling the show. Welcome to Group Five.'

'I know the type,' Newman said tersely. 'I've met them before. At the bottom of the heap, they bully any even further down. And they ass-crawl to their superiors. I loathe them.'

'You think that Schneider will report the incident?'

'It was a gamble,' Newman admitted. 'If Schneider thinks I will not submit a report he'll keep quiet. If he decides that I'm

191

likely to report him, he'll try to get in first. But I'd bet money he'll sleep on it. Then he may think it is too late. We can only hope.'

'My own estimate of the situation exactly.'

'May I ask where we are going? What information you will be providing for me to take back with me?'

'Why not?' Falken smiled. 'Soon we change our form of transport. We have a long way to go and cycling is too slow – but an excellent procedure near the border. First, however, I am intrigued how you knew we have a drug problem building up in the DDR.'

'I asked Toll what special job I might be assigned to as a member of the River Police. He told me about the heroin.'

'In some ways that man has no idea what conditions we have to work under. Which is why we take our own decisions. In other ways he often surprises me. He is only recently promoted – so naturally I wish to learn all I can about his ability. I have to think of the lives of the men and women I am responsible for. You may laugh, but they look up to me as a father-figure.'

'I'm not laughing. Talking about father-figures, what do you know about Dr Berlin?'

'My God!' Falken chuckled as he kept up his steady pedalling pace. 'You must be telepathic.'

'Why?'

'I asked Toll to send a reliable emissary so I could pass on verbally what we have learned about the august and much-venerated Dr Berlin . . .'

'You sound ironical . . .'

'I should. Your Dr Berlin is a fake.'

'You can prove that?'

'With the most solid evidence. Of course, if you were able to check the records at the Leipzig hospital where he went for treatment when he returned from Africa many years ago, you would find he was suffering from a rare tropical disease.'

'So what evidence do you have?'

'I want you to hear it for yourself. We shall transfer to a car shortly. Do you want a pee?'

'Yes. I'm all right for food – I ate well before I crossed over this evening . . .'

They dismounted and Falken pushed his cycle a few feet off the road, staying close enough so he would hear Gerda if she arrived. 'She has a squeaky rear tyre,' Falken explained as they relieved themselves. 'I told her not to fix it. You will like her – but she is very tough. Women can be more ruthless than men . . .'

They were remounting their cycles when Newman heard the squeaky rear wheel approaching through the mist. Falken commented on his acute hearing, took out a small torch and waved it slowly to one side and back again. A slim silhouette appeared out of the mist and braked.

Gerda would be in her late twenties as far as Newman could tell. Her hair was concealed beneath a head-scarf and she had a strong nose and a well-defined chin. She stared at Newman as she shook hands solemnly.

'I heard you dealing with the Border Police,' she commented. 'You have had much experience of this kind of work?'

'Not really, no. Just regard me as the new boy.'

'Gerda,' Falken broke in, 'has an Uzi machine-pistol concealed under that folded windcheater in her cycle basket. Can you use the weapon?'

'I was once trained to handle it, yes,' Newman replied, and left it at that. 'Now where are we going when we reach the car?'

'To let you interview someone about the real Dr Berlin. You are going to meet a witness . . .' He stopped speaking as Newman turned to look back the way they had come. 'What is it?'

'I can hear a car coming slowly. It could be Schneider and his sidekick, checking up on us . . .'

Gerda vanished off the road like a ghost, pushing her cycle at speed. Newman noticed she had swiftly turned off her lights. Falken chuckled again before he replied, taking the sting out of his remark.

'Mustn't get paranoid, Albert Thorn. They are probably simply returning to their police barracks at Wernigerode. At this game you suspect everything and everyone, I agree. But also remember you will meet many who are merely proceeding on their lawful occasions.'

The slow-moving car's headlights illuminated them from behind, then were dipped. As the vehicle passed them Schneider leaned out of the window, calling to them in a hoarse voice.

'Good hunting, Mr Thorn . . .'

The car moved faster and was gone, its engine sound muffled

almost immediately by the mist. Gerda rejoined them, jumped into her saddle and pedalled behind them.

'I thought there was a trace of irony in Schneider's voice,' Falken commented. 'And he made a point of letting you know he remembered your name . . .'

'Now who's getting paranoid?'

Falken shook with laughter. For a few seconds his cycle wobbled. Then Gerda overtook them, riding ahead. She gestured for them to halt, jumped nimbly from her machine and pushed it up a narrow track on the right-hand side of the road.

'We have reached the car,' Falken explained as they followed. 'It's a Chaika, a Russian car. It gives a certain authority to anyone riding in it. And if you think your recent experiences have been a little tense, they were nothing.'

'What's coming?' Newman asked.

They laid the machines on the ground and helped Gerda who was already using her gloved hands to haul away great clumps of loose undergrowth, exposing the hidden Chaika, swathed with a neutral-coloured blanket over the bonnet to protect the engine against the cold.

They next hid the three cycles, covering them thoroughly with the loose undergrowth. Gerda checked the finished product, walking all round the buried machines before she pronounced that she was satisfied. Under her arm she had tucked the windcheater concealing the stubby-nosed Uzi machine-pistol.

Falken settled himself behind the wheel of the Chaika, his long legs hunched. Newman, at his request, sat beside him and Gerda squeezed herself in behind them. The ignition fired at the sixth attempt.

'What's coming?' Newman repeated. 'Where are we going?'

'To visit the witness you will interview. Concerning gentle and shy Dr Berlin – who does not like his photograph being taken. Our destination, my friend? The centre of Leipzig – only the throw of a stone from the building containing Markus Wolf's headquarters. And at the moment he has a guest, a certain Soviet GRU general – military intelligence. Vasili Lysenko. He must be planning a major operation. Come on! Let's go!'

He swung the Chaika on to the track, turned on to the road and followed the direction Schneider had driven along.

Newman thought the chill of the forest night had increased enormously.

Twenty-Four

London's Soho had not improved, Tweed decided as he walked along the street. But at least he felt safe now. No longer any reason for keeping an eye open for cripples who might be skilled assassins. It was good to be back in peaceful Britain.

But soon, he thought, he would get restless again – restless to return into the field, to Germany. The human mind was a weird instrument. Always next, the spice of variety. *Portman Investigations* read the metal chrome plate attached to the side of the open doorway. *First Floor.*

He was surprised that the plate was shining and clean. He walked inside and started mounting the old bare wooden stair-case. He put a hand on the banister rail and hastily withdrew it. The rail was greasy to the touch.

The twin of the chrome plate outside was attached by the side of a closed door, minus the reference to the floor. He knocked, three hard raps. It was opened quickly and Tweed had another surprise. He was expecting something sleazy and shifty.

'Mr Portman?'

'Mr Tweed? You're prompt. More than most of my clients are. Come in, take a pew. Now, how can I help you along the twisted pathways of life in this vale of sorrows?'

A small, round-faced jolly-looking man in his mid-forties, Mr Samuel Portman. Plump-bodied, like a well-fed pheasant. Tweed wondered why he'd likened him to that fowl, then remembered what he'd dined off the previous evening with Diana. His blue, pin-striped suit wasn't Savile Row, but it was well-pressed and clean. Almost Pickwickian in appearance – without the spectacles. Tweed produced the folder and showed it.

'Special Branch . . .'

'Oh, really? Your girl who made the appointment didn't say.'

195

'We don't believe in the maxim it pays to advertise.' Tweed put the folder back in his pocket, his manner amiable. 'Paula Grey. One of your clients. Hawkswood Farmhouse, Norfolk. Why did she employ you?'

'I couldn't possibly disclose that. Confidential, our investigations. The keystone of our relationship . . .'

'You've tried, made the right noises, now stop wasting my time.' Tweed's tone had hardened. 'I can always take you back to headquarters. The investigation I'm conducting is very serious, may involve terrorists. Don't worry about Paula, she's no connection. Let's start again. When did you begin checking on Hugh Grey?'

'Well, since you're Special Branch, I suppose I must make an exception. I don't like it, mind you, don't like it at all . . .'

'We don't like terrorists. Get on with it, man.'

'Just over two years ago she came to see me. August it was. A very hot day. I couldn't really understand it. You see . . .' Portman hesitated. '. . . they weren't married then.'

'I know that. Get to the point.'

'She asked me to follow Hugh Grey, to report on his movements. She said she thought there was another woman. I haven't been able to find a trace of that. He goes abroad a lot. The number of times I've seen him off from Heathrow. Always to Germany. I couldn't follow him. The expense, you see.'

'And each time,' Tweed said casually, 'you found it easy – to follow this Hugh Grey?'

'No.' The little man admitted it reluctantly. 'Paula Brent – as she was before they married – phoned me the day before he was due to go off from Hawkswood. I'd drive out next day, wait for him near a crossroads out of sight, then pick him up. He knew I was on his track. He'd wait till he came to a traffic light near Much Hadham, slow down, then shoot across on the amber. I couldn't risk following through on the red. They might revoke my licence if the police caught me. They don't much like us – the police. And once *he* followed me here to Soho.'

'Tell me.'

'I lost him. Much Hadham again. Then I was driving through London and I picked him up in my rear view mirror. Couldn't believe it. Where would he pick up that skill? He's something in insurance. He was still with me when I arrived in Soho.'

'So he knows who you are? What you are?'

'Not bloody likely.' Portman perked up. 'I parked the car, then walked into a solicitor pal's office near here.'

'Surely he waited for you?'

'No. You see, I have an arrangement with the solicitor in question. He needs me from time to time. I foresaw I might have this problem one day. The plate outside the solicitor's office reads – I'm making up the other names – Blenkinsop, Mahoney and Portman. He thought I was a solicitor. It must have puzzled him.'

'How can you be so sure of that?'

'Blighter walked in to reception and asked the girl. *He* said he was Special Branch.' Portman stared at Tweed, watching his reaction.

'Cheeky sod,' Tweed replied immediately, expressing just the right amount of indignation. 'Give me your impression of Hugh Grey.'

'Full of confidence. But then these insurance chaps have to be – peddling the sort of stuff they do. I wondered if he was mixed up in drug smuggling, if his girl, later his wife, suspected the same thing.'

'Why?'

'Frequent trips abroad. The way he sometimes knew I was on his tail, the way he ditched me, and the way he enquired about me here in Soho. The skill,' Portman repeated, 'that's what I don't understand. Plus the cheek of the devil. Doesn't sound like insurance to me at all.'

'Must have cost his wife a fortune hiring you. Two years is a long time.' Tweed was probing, searching for he wasn't sure what. Portman clasped his hands behind his head, a gesture which reminded Tweed of Guy Dalby.

'It was spasmodic,' he explained. 'Only when he was leaving to go somewhere from Norfolk. Often I lost him, as I mentioned. I used to race direct to Heathrow, hoping to catch him there, but often he never turned up at Terminal Two – or I missed him.'

'Ever follow him anywhere else? Maybe to somewhere inside this country?' Tweed asked casually.

'Never once. Always Heathrow – or I lost him.'

That meant Grey had spotted Portman, eluded him, whenever he was bound for Park Crescent – or his *pied à terre* at Cheyne Walk for that matter. Grey certainly knew his job.

'How does Paula Grey pay you?' Tweed asked.

'Always in cash – no matter how large the fee. That's normal in such cases. Cheques can be traced. I gather she has her own business of some sort. In any case, a third of the population in Norfolk is part of the black economy . . .' He clapped a hand over his mouth. 'Now I've put my foot in it.' Portman frowned. 'You're a very persuasive chap – you get people to let down their guard.'

'I'm not interested in things like that. Last question. What is Paula Grey's attitude now?'

'She's still worried about something. Can we leave it at that?'

'Why not?' Tweed rose to go. So far Portman was intrigued with the novelty of his visitor. Soon he might begin to wonder about Tweed. 'One thing,' Tweed said as Portman accompanied him to the door, 'I've never been here. This interview never took place.'

'Official Secrets Act?'

'Well . . .' Tweed smiled, '. . . at least I never read it to you.'

'Did you find out anything from Portman?' Monica asked, all eager-beaver as Tweed closed his office door.

'I'm not sure. Only the absence of something.'

'That's right, go all cryptic on me. It means you have a definite lead but you're not telling. Want me to hang up your Burberry?'

'No, thank you. I have to collect Diana in a minute from Newman's flat, then we drive down to Harry Masterson's. He is at his cottage?'

'Yes, I called him as you asked. Said you might want to phone him. He said he'd be there all day – he's painting one of his portraits. What are you doing?'

Tweed had collected a pair of dividers from a cupboard and was standing in front of the wall-map. He placed one point on Vienna, then measured the road distance to Lübeck. He repeated the exercise with Bern and Frankfurt, again measuring the road distances to Lübeck. Then he stood back from the map and placed the dividers on a table.

'Any one of them could have managed it by road,' he said.

'I don't understand.'

'After the second blonde girl, Iris Hansen, was murdered out on the beach at Travemünde, I called all the sector chiefs. None of them were at home. And no one knew where they had gone.'

'Normal procedure if their security is tight – and it's pretty tight with this new lot you chose.'

'As you say. I'd better get off . . .'

'You're suggesting one of them could be a maniac killer? That would be terrible for the department.'

'It's not so good for the victims who were murdered,' Tweed replied and left the room.

'What a lovely cottage. The clematis is glorious.'

Diana walked with Tweed along the country lane to the gate of Harry Masterson's cottage near Apfield. Brilliant sunshine glowed out of a clear blue sky. In nearby trees birds chirrupped. Tweed had his hand on the gate, looking at the garden which was a mess, the lawn uncut, the rosebeds full of weeds, when he realized she had stopped, was standing like a frozen statue.

He looked up. Masterson had appeared in the doorway, his bulky figure filling it. Tweed glanced at Diana. Her face seemed even whiter than usual.

'What's wrong?' he asked.

'From here it's just like my mother's cottage in Devon. She was only forty-two when she died. I suppose the similarity gave me a shock.' Her normal exuberance returned. 'Come on, Tweedy, we mustn't keep him waiting . . .'

Masterson, his thick black hair gleaming in the sunlight, came down the scruffy footpath to meet them. Dressed in a pair of cream slacks and an open-necked white shirt, he held a paint-brush in his right hand which he transferred to the other hand.

'Welcome to Paradise Cottage, Tweed. And who is this delightful vision you've brought with you? Now the day is perfect . . .'

He shook hands with her and Tweed made introductions. He had warned her before what he would say.

'This is Diana Chadwick, niece of an old friend of mine. She's in London on holiday.'

'Niece, eh?' Masterson dug Tweed gently in the ribs. 'You can do better than that, Tweed.' He looked at her and grinned.

'If we take him at his word there's hope for me yet. Come on in, both of you. Care for a drink? And where the devil is your car? You can't have walked here.'

'I parked it up the lane. I wasn't sure I was on the right road,' Tweed lied. He'd wanted to surprise his host. Masterson hustled them inside, grasping Diana by the arm. He doesn't waste time, Tweed thought ruefully. He glanced up at the cascade of purple-flowering clematis flowing down either side of the doorway as he entered. Masterson glanced back, missing nothing.

'Damned good stuff, that creeper. Doesn't need a thing doing to it. Just grows and grows, like Topsy did. Can't stand gardening . . .'

'So I observed,' Tweed replied drily.

'I'll show Diana the cottage,' Masterson rambled on buoy-antly. 'You've seen the place, Tweed. Make yourself at home in the sitting-room. Help yourself to a drink. We'll be back soon . . .'

He winked at Tweed as Diana dropped her handbag on a settee in the cluttered living-room, the soft furniture covered with chintz designs. Cushions lay scattered at random, several on the floor.

Tweed waited until they had climbed the twisting, creaking steps of the staircase. He'd have good warning when they were coming back. His agile fingers picked up Diana's handbag, opened it, checked the contents quickly. No travellers' cheques, just a wad of folded banknotes. He counted them. £250. Mostly in twenties. When he'd met her at Heathrow she'd excused herself while she went to the Midland Bank exchange. He returned the notes to the zip pocket exactly as he found them and replaced the handbag on the settee.

Thrusting both hands in the pockets of his sports jacket, he wandered over to the bookshelves. The selection surprised him. A number of works by Jung and Freud, thrillers by popular authors, a large collection of travel books about Eastern Europe – the latter working material, he presumed.

He bent down to study Masterson's record collection, all LPs. Again an odd range of taste. Stravinsky, Beethoven, Chopin, Schubert and some music to dance to, mostly tangos. The hi-fi deck incorporated into the bookcase at eye-level was expensive. Hearing them at the top of the staircase, he grabbed a travel book and was sitting in an arm chair when they re-appeared deep in conversation, chattering and joking. Diana sat down on the settee next to her handbag. Masterson disappeared into the kitchen, Tweed heard the clunk of the fridge door and their host waltzed in holding a bottle aloft.

'Champagne for the troops! Come into the kitchen. Watch an expert at work!'

He was stripping off the foil as they followed him. Tweed took in the equipment at a glance. Modern laminated cupboards and worktops in dark blue. None of your rustic olde worlde equipment favoured by Hugh Grey who would always go for the new and the trendy. Harry Masterson wouldn't give a damn.

A collection of kitchen knives lay in the compartment of the wooden box next to the sink. So far as Tweed could see there was no sign of a chef's knife. Over the sink on the wall a brass plate (in need of cleaning) hung, rather like a medieval shield with a central boss.

'I'm going to hit that brass plate dead centre,' Masterson joked as he fiddled with the cork, aiming it at the plate. He aimed the bottle like a gun, the cork shot out and hit the boss.

'Bull's-eye!'

He held the bottle over an aluminium jug placed alongside three tulip glasses. The surplus champagne was caught inside the jug. Masterson was extraordinarily agile.

'That's some of mine,' he bubbled, filling the glasses, then handing them round.

'A toast! We must have a toast!'

'Well, what are we drinking to?' Tweed enquired.

'Damnation to our enemies!'

'What a funny toast,' Diana said after drinking. 'I can think of only one enemy I've got . . .'

'And who is that?' asked Masterson, wrapping an arm round her waist as he escorted her back to the living-room.

'A woman called Ann Grayle. Used to be a diplomat's wife,' she said as she sat down on the settee. Masterson perched his backside on the arm, next to her. 'I first knew her in Africa, Kenya – all of twenty years ago.'

'Kenya?' Masterson sounded intrigued. 'Twenty years ago it had just gained its independence . . .'

'In 1963. I was there before then in what Ann calls the good old days. They were, too. Lots of parties. Went on all hours. We saw the dawn come up over the bush. You know Kenya, Mr Masterson?'

'Harry. May I call you Diana? I'm going to anyway. And I've never been near Kenya in my life. Sounds just like my sort of place. Twenty-odd years ago. Don't you agree, Tweed?'

'Oh yes, you'd have played hell with the women, Harry.'

Tweed's tone was caustic. He was studying the two of them as he settled further back in a deep arm chair. Masterson's chin had a blued look. He had obviously shaved first thing but already he was showing a five o'clock shadow. He laid a large hand on Diana's exposed and shapely knee as she sat with her legs crossed.

'Why not make it a day in the country? I can rustle up something edible. For dinner we could all go to a super place not five miles away. The trout is out of this world.'

'I think we have to get back to London,' she said and lifted his hand from her knee, placing it back on his leg. 'Isn't that right, Tweed?'

'Yes, I'm afraid it is, but thanks for the invitation.'

Masterson jumped up, grabbed the bottle and refilled glasses. He looked at Tweed.

'Tell you what. I'll give you both a rare treat, show you some of my paintings. My studio's through that door. North facing light and all that. I don't show many people,' he went on as he led the way.

The studio was littered with oil paintings, some of them on the floor face up. Tweed followed Diana, holding his glass and stepping carefully over the pictures. A large old-fashioned wooden easel stood at an angle to the window, the painting Masterson was working on draped with a cloth so it was invisible.

'Sit down,' Masterson invited.

'Where?' asked Tweed.

'Sorry. Half a tick . . .'

He removed piles of sketch-books off two hard-backed,

rush-seated chairs. As they sat down Tweed was thinking all the furniture in the cottage had probably been handed down to Masterson from relatives – or picked up for a song in Portobello Road. The usual public school background – Masterson had gone to Winchester – which made a man totally unaware of his surroundings.

Like a matador, their host took hold of the cloth, paused and then whipped aside the cloth swirling it like a cape. Tweed stiffened, staring at the exposed portrait. A head with staring eyes hung in space. No head and shoulders, just the head, strangely alive. The eyes stared at Tweed with extraordinary intensity, a chilling coldness. Behind it a giant wave hovered, just before breaking, foam curling along its crest. It was a portrait of Hugh Grey.

'A poor thing, but mine own,' Masterson joked.

'I find it remarkable,' Tweed said in a subdued tone.

'Next one coming up . . .'

He whipped the unframed canvas off the easel, propped it up against a wall, collected another canvas, also draped with a cloth. He took trouble centring it and removed the cloth with his back to them so they couldn't see. Then he stepped aside.

This time Tweed was ready and sat with his hands relaxed in his lap. Guy Dalby. A three-quarter view, again the head only, suspended in a fog, the kind of fog Tweed associated with Norfolk. More like a ghost than a man, but still unmistakable a likeness. A devilishly clever likeness, but exaggerated, which made it even more life-like.

The hair was plastered down over the head and the expression was saturnine. Self-satisfaction oozed from every pore. *Devilish*. That was the word which sprang to mind. And the only visible eye, the left one, stared through Tweed.

'Is this really how you see your colleagues?' Tweed asked.

Masterson shrugged. 'I'm no Gauguin, as you must realize by now. It's a bit of fun. Next one coming up.'

He performed the same conjuring trick, standing with his back to them after he had substituted a third painting for Dalby's. Then he stood aside and picked up his champagne glass and drank the rest of the contents.

Tweed heard Diana stifle a gasp. Another head suspended alone in space, if you could use the term 'head'. A grinning

203

skull gazed at Tweed, ice-blue eyes embedded in the sockets. Against a background of a cloudless Scandinavian-type sky with extraordinary clarity of light. But it was Erich Lindemann. Stripped to the bones.

'A cold fish,' Masterson commented.

'Portrait painters,' Tweed remarked, 'always do a self-portrait. That I'd like to see.'

'It's not finished.'

Masterson, brash and abrasive, was abnormally defensive.

'I'd still like to see it,' Tweed insisted. He pointed to a canvas facing the wall.

'Don't miss a trick, do you? If I must . . .'

'You must.'

Masterson followed his previous pantomime, but hurriedly. He concealed the new canvas until it was perched on the easel, then stepped aside.

A fourth head, three-quarter view like Dalby's portrait, all seen against the background of a huge yellow sunburst. The single eye visible was cynical, mistrustful of the world. Beneath the strong nose the mouth curved in a sensual smile.

Tweed was reminded of a satyr. What impressed him most was the sheer brutal physical *energy* of the painting, emphasized by the sunburst radiating tremendous heat and drive.

'Pretty bloody awful,' Masterson commented.

'No association with the sea,' Tweed remarked.

'You noticed that? The wave behind Hugh Grey's picture – the sea mist background for Guy Dalby. Boaty types. They can keep it.'

'You're not attracted by messing about in boats?' Tweed suggested.

'God, no! The sea never keeps still. Give me dry land any time. Another drink?'

'Thank you, no. We'll have to be going soon.'

He looked at Diana who was staring round the cluttered studio. She frowned and shook her head slightly, a gesture Masterson caught. He grinned.

'Bit of a pigsty?'

'You need a good woman to look after you,' she told him.

'I'd sooner have a bad one.' He grinned again, wickedly. 'Do you qualify?'

204

'Not really. I'm a hopeless housewife,' she fended him off, picked up her handbag, accepted his offer to use the toilet so, for the first time, Tweed and Masterson were on their own. Their host sat down in a chair close to Tweed and dug him in the ribs. 'That's what you need to lighten your life. A bad woman. She's made to order.'

'Actually, she's pretty top drawer, Harry.'

'Better still.' Masterson smiled cynically. 'A niece you said. She's too old and you're too young. You'd make a good team. Think about it . . .'

When Diana returned Tweed said he'd also like to use the toilet. He left them alone for a few minutes, thinking about what he had seen. When he returned Diana was standing up, smoking a cigarette in her long ivory holder and pacing slowly round while Masterson sat on the settee.

'Don't forget what I said,' he reminded Tweed as he accompanied them to the garden gate and opened it. He was still standing by the gate a few minutes later when Tweed drove slowly past the cottage.

'Wrong way for London,' he shouted.

'Going to show Diana the creeks,' Tweed called back. 'See you . . .'

Diana glanced over her shoulder and waved through the window at the rear of the Cortina. Then she tapped ash from her cigarette in the tray and concentrated on the view ahead.

'That was funny,' she remarked.

'What was?'

'When I looked back he looked furious, a real grim expression. He made a pass at me while you were in the loo. I told him to grow up.'

'That's Harry,' Tweed replied and continued driving slowly, peering to his right. In a few minutes he slowed down even more, then stopped. They were heading for Bosham and through the trees he could see a forest of masts. Boating country. He released the brake and turned right along a well-defined track, stopping by a landing-stage at the edge of open water. A large power cruiser like the *Südwind* was moored to the side of the landing-stage. No one about. Tweed checked his watch. Precisely seven minutes from Masterson's cottage.

'Is he married?' Diana enquired.

'He was. Now he has a harem. One society beauty, one owner of a chain of hairdresser salons, one Sloane Ranger. They are girls . . .'

'I've heard of them. They have fun. That makes him a bit of a challenge.'

Tweed, to his surprise, felt a twinge of jealousy. It must have shown in his expression. She grasped his arm.

'Only joking. It's the champers – brings out the worst in me.'

Tweed stepped out of the car, jumped nimbly over the gap from landing-stage to power cruiser and began prowling around. He peered inside the wheelhouse. The craft had a brand new wheel from its appearance. He grunted, returned to the car. Painted on the hull of the cruiser was its name. *Nocturne.*

He backed the car down the track to the main road, then turned away from Masterson's cottage to return to London by a roundabout route. Through the trees the sun sparkled on the blue water.

'What was your impression of Masterson?'

'This is where I sing for my supper? A man for many women, as you said. But behind all that dazzle I sensed a ruthless personality. He'd let nothing stand in his way if he was after something. Which is probably what appeals to his girl friends. I thought his paintings quite horrible. Like the work of a madman.'

'And those are the other people you're going to meet . . .'

'One of them I'm not looking forward to.'

She didn't say which one.

Twenty-Five

Before he stepped across the gangplank on to Ann Grayle's sloop Kuhlmann dropped his cigar into the water. He wouldn't have done it for anyone else, but he'd gathered the imposing Englishwoman did not approve of his cigars.

She sat in her canvas chair on deck by the side of Ben Tolliver, the owner of a small cruiser who looked after the sloop. A man in his mid-sixties, sinewy and tall, his skin had a leathery look and he stared at the German from under white bushy eyebrows. Kuhlmann came aboard with a slim documents case tucked under his arm.

'Coffee, Mr Kuhlmann?' Grayle asked in her most upper crust voice. 'Black? No sugar?'

'That would be welcome,' he replied in English.

'Ben, please oblige.'

Tolliver heaved himself out of his chair and disappeared down the companionway leading to the living quarters. She patted the vacated chair and Kuhlmann sat down, glancing briefly at her crossed legs. An attractive woman. Was Tolliver, retired plantation owner from Ceylon – Sri Lanka these days – her lover? He doubted it. She could do better.

'You're sure that tall blond man you saw on Miss Chadwick's cruiser . . .'

'Dr Berlin's,' she corrected.

'As you say. Was that blond man the same as the hiker with the backpack you saw later on the waterfront here?'

'Quite certain.' Her tone had a whiplash quality. 'I don't make mistakes. I'm trained to remember people's faces, their names. In the Diplomatic Service you can't afford to forget. You do meet the most objectionable people and they're always the touchy ones. Have you got the Identikit picture from the description I gave your artist in the local police station?'

Kuhlmann produced a printed poster from the documents case and handed it to her. She stared at the picture, at the wording in German. *Kurt Franck. Wanted for questioning in connection with the murder of Iris Hansen.*

'It's better than the artist's sketch,' she decided.

'It's recognizable as Franck? That poster is now outside every police station in North Germany. Including the one here on the corner of the waterfront and St-Lorenz-strasse.'

'A perfect likeness.' She handed back the poster as Tolliver appeared with a tray containing a coffee pot and three cups and saucers, milk and sugar. The chinaware was Meissen. Only the best for Ann Grayle. Tolliver poured the coffee.

'The odd thing,' Kuhlmann commented as Tolliver dragged forward another chair and joined them, 'is the absence of more murders . . .'

207

'Then clearly the murderer is absent,' she told him. 'Find out who was here then and isn't here now. Make a list. The killer may be on it.'

'Very shrewd, but a long job. Any candidates?'

'You want me to play guessing games?'

'You know the waterfront visitors far better than I ever will,' Kuhlmann coaxed. 'And you're a very observant woman. You don't miss much.'

'Cream for the cat? And does it have to be a transient? One of the visitors?'

'But you'll think about it?'

'She's just told you she doesn't know,' barked Tolliver.

'I'll leave you to think,' Kuhlmann said, ignoring the other man, whom he disliked. A bully, the type who had spent years in Kenya bossing the natives. He was amused at the way Grayle had him eating out of her hand. Serve the old curmudgeon right.

'Ben!' Grayle's tone was commanding. 'Go and get me some of that nice German sausage for lunch. You know the type I like. No substitutes, mind you.'

'You mean now?'

'Of course I do. Surely you know I have early luncheon.' Tolliver climbed out of his chair, checked his wallet in his back pocket for money, walked off without a word.

'He shouldn't have been rude to you. Silly old sod.'

'He helps you crew this sloop – when you go south back to the Mediterranean?'

'No, he has his own scuttleboat, the engine's tied together with bits of wire. He has two sons. They help me crew. You'd be surprised, Mr Kuhlmann. I can practically sail this vessel myself. Need a bit of help with the sails sometimes to keep going. Now, I sent Ben off so we could talk.'

'While I remember, if we catch this Kurt Franck would you be willing to identify him?'

'Like a shot. He doesn't frighten me. I know the type. He probably lives off women. What we used to call a gigolo.'

'And I think there was something you wanted to say to me?'

'Yes. You said no more murders. I suggested the murderer was temporarily absent. Dr Berlin has vanished again.'

'So?'

208

'A vicious character. Arrogant, too. Not at all the philanthropist he pretends to be. I was once waiting at a road crossing over there. The lights were about to change in the traffic's favour. His Mercedes had pulled up. He had the rear window down and I saw those eyes of his, watching from behind his dark glasses, staring straight at me. I quite distinctly heard him say in German to his chauffeur, "Drive on." The swine damn near knocked me down.'

'Interesting.' Kuhlmann stood up. 'Thank you for the coffee. I must be going.'

He had reached the gangplank, was just about to walk across it, when she called out to him.

'Mr Kuhlmann, next time you come, do smoke a cigar if you feel like it.'

'Why do you say that? I thought you disliked them.'

'Because you're a gentleman. Not too many of them about these days.'

Kuhlmann made his way back along the landing-stage. He would never understand the English. Perhaps it was because they were surrounded by all that water.

'One of those three guards in that watchtower cracked,' Wolf informed Lysenko. 'Hoped to get off more lightly than his two fellow-conspirators, which is what my interrogators played on.'

'And?'

'They were bribed. With gold. No description of the enemy agent who did the job. He wore one of those ski-helmets. Tall and thin. They let one of the BND's agents through. Could have been Newman – his picture has been reprinted and circulated.'

'So, we have done all we can?'

'I haven't.' Wolf was going at full power, like a tracker dog which has picked up the scent. 'I've switched the interrogation team to the Border Police on duty in that area at night. Every man will be subjected to a very tough grilling.'

Karl Schneider of the Border Police, stationed at Wernigerode, was in a filthy temper. The object of his annoyance was his wife, Alma. She never stopped going on at him. He sat up in bed in the tiny flat housed in the huge concrete apartment block.

209

'Why wake me? I've been on duty all night, you cow . . .'

'Don't call me a cow. You should report meeting those two men in the forest at once. At once! Do you hear me?'

'How can I help it? They'll hear you the far side of the block. Now I'll never get back to sleep . . .'

He climbed out of bed, felt the stubble on his unshaven chin and started towards the toilet. She blocked his path, a scrawny-faced woman of forty with claw-like hands. He stopped, stared at her.

'You are not going to the lavatory until you've phoned and reported what happened.'

'My bladder is bursting.'

'Let it burst – for all the use it is to me. You have to get your report in first. Someone else may have already caught them.'

'What is there to catch? He was River Police. He showed me his folder . . .'

'River Police! There's no river for miles round that part of the border. Don't you ever think? You'll lose your pension, you will. And where shall I be – if you're knocked down by one of those big coaches? Penniless. You never think of me. Only of yourself. You'll report those two men now or make your own breakfast. And dinner. And supper. I . . .'

'All right. Get out of my way, woman.'

Karl Schneider took two decisions as he shuffled in his pyjamas to the phone in the cramped living-cum-dining-room-cum-kitchen. He would report the incident to his superior to shut up Alma – and at the first opportunity he'd respond to the advances made to him by that full-breasted, red-lipped typist in the barracks administrative block.

'Soon. Not yet, but soon . . .'

Erwin Munzel, alias Kurt Franck, spoke the words aloud although he was alone inside the loft of the barn on Fehmarn Island. He was gazing at his image in a hand mirror. The blond moustache he had grown covered his upper lip, flowed down to the corners of his mouth. The blond beard masked his jaw.

At the back of his head his hair draped his neck. He had almost the appearance of a hippie, but not quite. That would

210

be an error of judgement. The West German police did not look favourably on hippie types.

The steep-roofed barn stood in the fields, half a kilometre outside the hamlet of Burg, the largest collection of dwellings on the lonely island at the edge of the Baltic. Munzel had not gone near the cottage in Burg he had used during his earlier visit. The barn, also owned by Martin Vollmer as part of the small farm, was far more isolated. Even the inhabitants of Burg never came near the place.

During the two weeks Munzel had waited for his moustache and beard to grow, he had lived rough, feeding off canned meat and drinking coffee he boiled on a spirit kettle in the loft. The floor was covered with a thick layer of straw, he had a sleeping bag for nights, and the only access to the loft was a tall ladder he had hauled up behind him when he first entered his hiding-place.

Munzel had retreated to his refuge after making his phone call from Hamburg to Vollmer in Altona. Again he had followed the training of his instructor. *Double back on your tracks*. The police would never dream he would take a train from Hamburg back to Lübeck and on to Puttgarden.

Munzel was not at all sure they had his description. It all depended on whether Newman or Tweed had recognized him when he'd made his abortive attempt to kill Tweed in the Kolk. *Never take a chance on recognition*. He viewed himself from different angles in the mirror. Another few days and he'd be unrecognizable. Then he could move out into the open, call Vollmer for the latest news.

When he'd phoned Vollmer from Hamburg his Altona contact passed him a message from Wolf. 'The Captain will return. Then you can meet him again . . .'

The Captain was the codeword for Tweed. God knew why Wolf was so confident Tweed *would* return. But Wolf, Munzel knew, had made a special study of the Englishman, had built up a bulky file recording his appearance, his habits, his likes and dislikes. Some of the data had amazed Munzel when shown the file before crossing into the West. Almost as though Wolf had someone who saw Tweed frequently in London . . .

Munzel put the idea out of his mind. It was too dangerous even to contemplate. He put down the mirror, raised a hand to smooth down the long hair over the nape of his neck. Just a few more days . . .

'Now, as always, we assume the worst,' Falken announced.

'Why do you say that at this moment?' Newman asked.

Falken had driven him with Gerda to the strangest of places to rest up before they proceeded to Leipzig. They had covered a long distance in the Chaika, some of it in broad daylight. Then Falken had turned off a main elevated highway down a track leading alongside a small canal. They had stopped the car and got out at a lock-keeper's cottage, a square, ugly, brick-built building, one storey high and next to an ancient pair of lock-gates.

Beyond the old heavy wooden door, which Falken opened with a large key, a musty damp smell assailed Newman. They walked straight into the living-room which was sparsely furnished with cheap wooden chairs, a wooden table in the centre and framed pictures on the walls of various canals.

'We must conceal the car at once,' Gerda said. 'It is all right, Mr Thorn,' she remarked, addressing Newman. 'Josef and I will deal with it. Maybe you would light the fire?'

Then they were gone and he heard the car start up. Newman picked up a Leipzig newspaper thrown down on a couch which was losing its stuffing at one end. Dated a week ago he noted as he separated several sheets, screwed them up loosely and stuffed them under the pile of logs and twigs inside a smoke-blackened brick fireplace. He used the stubby lighter made in Karlmarxstadt, the place where he was supposed to have been born, to set light to the paper. He had to use a poker to coax the twigs to burst into flames and lick round the logs, and began a quick exploration.

Below the window the manually-operated lock-gates stood closed. The dark water was fresh, no sign of scum on its surface. There was an old-fashioned kitchen leading off the sitting-room, equipped with an ancient iron range for a cooker. All mod cons were conspicuous by their absence.

Through this window, partially obscured by condensation, he had a clear view across fields of some crop to the elevated highway in the distance. Another door led to a bedroom with a large double bed and a dark oak headboard. The place was depressing, but he noticed signs of recent habitation – the crushed stub of a cigar in an ash-smeared bowl.

He walked back into the sitting-room and Gerda was removing her head-scarf while Falken fiddled with the fire. Her hair was reddish-brown and soft, her blue eyes stared back at him with a hint of challenge. She wore no makeup but was more attractive than he had realized. They both moved very silently – he hadn't heard them return.

'Want to see how we've hidden the car, Mr Thorn? Come to the door . . .'

At the end of a track a few hundred metres from the cottage a great hump stood, a hump covered with an enormous sheet of canvas. Open at the end facing the highway, the front of a tractor was exposed.

'The Chaika is behind the tractor,' Gerda explained. 'Anyone spotting it from the highway will assume it is a large farm tractor.'

'Clever.'

'Mr Thorn, we have to be careful of everything – from the moment we wake until we sleep. And then only one sleeps – the other stays awake on guard. We can never relax. For this work you have to be strong. Up here.'

She tapped her well-shaped forehead and led the way back into the cottage. She was carrying the windcheater tucked under her arm. Newman gestured towards it.

'You have the Uzi with you.'

'Yes, see.'

She whipped the folded windcheater open and took hold of the automatic weapon, pointing the muzzle at the wall. He reached for the gun and she hesitated.

'You are familiar with the Uzi? It fires at a tremendous rate per second. You have to exert the most sensitive control.'

'I've trained with it.'

He balanced the weapon in his hands and she produced three metallic objects he recognized from the pockets of the windcheater. Spare magazines. He emptied the weapon he was holding, then rammed the magazine back into place, held the gun and aimed it at the wall.

'Yes,' she decided, 'you know it. That is good. You might have to use it. But only when there is no other option. We rely

213

on secrecy, on moving about without the Vopos realizing we exist . . .'

'Come here, my friend,' called out Falken who was sitting at the table. 'We have much to do.'

'I will make coffee and some food,' Gerda said, laying the Uzi wrapped inside the windcheater on the floor. She took an ancient cushion from the single arm chair and put it beside the windcheater.

'Isn't that dangerous – leaving the gun on the floor?' Newman asked.

'In an emergency,' she told him, 'it is the last place that intruders would expect to find a weapon.' She produced several packages from the capacious pockets of her green corduroy hunting jacket. 'Coffee,' she repeated, 'but we will have to make do with powdered milk. Liquids are tricky – they can leak.'

'Take the binoculars,' Falken said, handing her the pair he had unlooped from round his neck. 'Watch that road while you see to our stomachs.'

'Aren't field-glasses suspicious things to have if you're stopped?' Newman enquired as he joined Falken, sitting down at the table.

'Why! I am a member of the Bird Sanctuary Conservation Service. What is my job's first requirement? Binoculars – to observe birds and fowl from a distance.'

'Of course.'

'As I said earlier, we must assume the worst. Have you the extra photos of yourself Toll said he would supply?'

'In the sole of my right shoe . . .'

'Let me have it.'

'What is the worst we are assuming?' Newman asked as he handed him the shoe.

'That Schneider has reported encountering us in the forest last night. He may not have, but we cannot take the risk. If he has, they will be looking for Albert Thorn of the River Police. So! I am a magician.' He grinned engagingly. 'You now become Emil Clasen. Of the Border Police.'

'Border Police?' Newman's tone was incredulous.

'A double bluff. Whatever they expect you to be, it will not be a member of the Border Police. Also there is another reason which I will explain later.'

Falken had a chamois pouch he had unrolled, exposing its contents, a collection of delicate metal instruments. He held in one hand a pair of tweezers, in the other the shoe which he held up to the light. 'I think I see them. Very expertly concealed.'

He inserted the tweezers gently inside a slit in the thick sole of Newman's shoe, withdrew them holding the edges of three small photographs of Newman. He studied the photos.

'What are the tweezers for?' Newman asked.

'Part of my job. Essential equipment – like the field-glasses. I use them for extracting a thorn – any impediment – which may have lodged in the foot, say, of one of my sanctuary birds or fowl. I last used this on a rare goose.'

'And who does this cottage belong to?'

'The lock-keeper. Let us call him Norbert. An old man who is nearly seventy. He was anti-Nazi during the war. Afterwards he was anti-Communist. He says there is no difference. Both have their secret police. Both brain-wash the young, continue the process with youth movements. Both have concentration camps for non-believers. The Russians call it the Gulag. For some men the world is never right. Such a man is Norbert who looks after the lock.'

'Where is he now?'

'Probably in his flat in one of those monstrous blocks. This canal is still used occasionally for transporting coal aboard small barges. He has a schedule. He is here to open the lock-gates two days a week. We have forty-eight hours here and then we must leave – before Norbert returns. I have an arrangement with him . . .'

'This Norbert, he smokes cigars?'

'You have a keen eye. Yes, he does. Now, these photos. Taken I suspect before your appearance was altered?'

'Yes . . .'

'Do not tell me how your appearance *was* altered. In case I am caught and interrogated after you have left us and before you reach freedom.' He glanced at Newman, then back at the photos. 'It does not matter. These prints are blurred – deliberately, I suspect. They will pass for you. Too good a likeness is always something which draws attention to you under inspection.'

215

'What are they for?'

'This.' Falken produced a folder from his pocket. 'Border Police pass. And I have the correct glue ready – the glue used by those who prepare these passes.' He held up a small bottle on the table.

'How the devil did you get that? And the pass?'

'Let us say I have friends of friends inside a certain documentation centre.'

He had placed one of the photos over a ruled box in the folder, checking it for size. He marked the photo on the back with a pencil and used a small pair of very sharp scissors – again extracted from the chamois folder – to trim the print.

'I'm asking too many questions,' Newman suggested.

'Yes.' Falken smiled again without stopping work. 'And you may have observed I am not answering too many of them. But one thing I will tell you. The day after tomorrow we drive in to Leipzig. Prepare yourself.'

'We persist,' Wolf said to Lysenko, who sat opposite him on the other side of his desk. 'Now I need that chair. You can sit in my secretary's chair over there, behind her type-writer.'

'Why the hell should I?'

'Try to look like a member of my staff,' Wolf continued. 'I just heard on that phone call I took we have a visitor. A Karl Schneider, member of the Border Police. Just flown in to see me at my request.'

'So?'

'Your German is improving. Schneider reported to his superior he met two men in the forest close to the point where an agent from the West crossed the border.'

'That would be a long shot . . .'

'On the night the crossing was made? And Schneider met the two men close to one o'clock in the morning. The timing also is right. We will see what he has to say. I check every lead, however slim. Now, the chair . . .'

There was a timid rapping on the door. Lysenko jumped up, walked rapidly to the typist's chair and sat down. He opened a notebook on the desk and was glad he was wearing civilian clothes. Wolf called out, 'Come in.' He studied the visitor, wearing the uniform of the Border Police, peaked cap tucked under his arm.

'Please to sit down,' Wolf said amiably, gesturing towards the vacant chair.

He watched Schneider as the visitor walked nervously to the chair and seated himself. He put his cap in his lap and fiddled with it. Foxy eyes, Wolf noted. An ambitious man, he guessed. A cut above the average, but they selected personnel for the Border Police with care. Wolf nodded encouragingly and spoke softly.

'Tell me what happened. Please take your time. Any little detail may be important. I listen. You talk. You will find I am a good listener. Start at the very beginning and omit nothing. Relax, please. I am interested . . .'

Schneider sat silent for a short time, marshalling his thoughts. During the flight he had sweated over what lay before him. Now it was all so different. Wolf waited patiently. Lysenko was fascinated. This was a side of the German's character he had not seen. Wolf was treating the policeman like a good-humoured relative, a favourite uncle.

Schneider began to talk. Wolf listened without interrupting his flow of thought. A sturdily-built man, he was thinking, but the Border Police were subject to near-military discipline, a para-military force. He waited until Schneider had finished before asking a question.

'The other man who didn't speak. What was his name?'

'He told me, Comrade, but I've forgotten . . .'

'It doesn't matter. This Albert Thorn.' Wolf took one of the printed posters being distributed throughout the DDR out of a drawer in his desk. 'Is this the man?'

Schneider studied the poster of Newman, frowned, puckered his thick lips. He knew that what he said next might affect the whole outcome of this strange interview, maybe of his career.

'I'm not sure,' he said eventually. 'It could be him.'

'What colour were his eyes?'

'Brown,' Schneider replied promptly.

Wolf opened the file on Newman which had been flown in from Moscow. *Eyes: blue.*

'Schneider, come and look at this map with me. Show me where you stopped these two men on cycles.'

The map of the DDR was spread out over a large table. Schneider bent over it, took the pencil Wolf offered and marked the place with a cross. The phone rang, Wolf excused himself, picked up the receiver and carried on a brief conversation before ending it. He turned round, ignored Lysenko, looking at Schneider.

'A report from the daytime teams searching the woods in that area. Three bicycles have been discovered hidden beneath some undergrowth. Close to where you stopped those two men . . .'

'There were only two of them.'

'No matter. I hear you were once a farmer. Is that so?'

'For five years.'

'So you are an observant man. Farmers work the fields alone. They develop good powers of observation.' Wolf walked back to the map. 'Supposing I asked you to drive over this area – in civilian clothes – searching for these two men. Normally I'd send someone with you – but you will be less conspicuous without a guard. You would be willing to do that on your own?'

'Yes. But which area?'

'Here.' Wolf traced a route on the map with a pencil. 'From Wernigerode – where your barracks are – down to Aschersleben, on to Eisleben and to Halle . . .'

'I know the area. There is an elevated highway here.'

'We will supply a truck – equipped with a radio – and a suit of clothes, the kind worn by farmers. Also a gun. You patrol that route back and forth. See if you spot anything. Agreed?'

'Of course . . .'

'Go down to the next floor. Room 78. I will phone to tell them to expect you.' Wolf held out his hand. 'Good luck, Mr Schneider. This could mean promotion for you.'

'Oh, God, come quickly,' Gerda called out from the kitchen.

Falken jumped up, ran out of the room, followed by Newman. At the window Gerda pointed towards the elevated highway. An armoured car was slowly proceeding down the track leading to the cottage, just leaving the highway.

'Crew of two men, maybe three,' Falken said tersely. 'All armed. Plus the vehicle's machine-gun. We have a problem.'

Twenty-Six

'Did you get through to Peter Toll?' Tweed asked as he shut his office door. 'And I'm short of time. We've just got back from Masterson's place. I've left Diana at Newman's flat. We are going on to talk with Erich Lindemann.'

'I got through,' Monica said quietly. 'I think you'd better speak to him yourself. Shall I get him?'

'Do that. Please.'

He kept the folded Burberry over his arm as he wandered over to the wall map and again studied the border area. Monica's reply had an ominous ring.

'He's on the line,' she called out.

'Tweed here. Is that Peter Toll? At last. I've had a devil of a job reaching you. I want to know the whereabouts of the man who accompanied me to Germany. No names. Yes, I know we're on scrambler.'

'I have no idea . . .'

'Toll.' Tweed was at his most formal. 'Don't muck me about. I have Walther Pröhl under lock and key.'

'I wondered . . .'

'You wondered what had happened to him. Why he hadn't flown back to München. Now you know. And you know what I know. We could arrange an exchange possibly,' he went on sarcastically. 'My man for yours . . .'

'That's ridiculous. We cooperate . . .'

'Like you cooperated recently? You went ahead without saying a word to me. I want him back. Quickly.'

'Two weeks . . .'

'Like hell. Four days. Send out an alert. My next call is to your chief.'

'The situation is delicate. One week . . .'

'Four days,' Tweed repeated. 'No result by then, I call your chief.'

'There is no need to be hasty . . .' Toll sounded worried.

'I've said my last word on the matter. If anything should go

219

wrong I'll fly to München myself. You're on probation.'

'That's not for you to say . . .'

'I just said it. And, by God, I meant it. That's all.'

'What about Walther Pröhl?'

'He stays here until I get my man back.'

Tweed slammed down the phone, his expression grim. Again he glanced towards the wall map. Then he shook his head and folded the Burberry more tidily over his arm.

'You were pretty rough on him,' Monica observed. 'And I take it you were referring to Newman's disappearance.'

'Yes to both statements. I know now he has sent Bob into The Zone – without telling his chief. I'm worried stiff about it. Trouble is, Toll wants to do it all by himself, prove himself – because I happen to know he is on probation in his new post.'

'You do that yourself sometimes,' she reminded him gently. 'Do things without letting Howard know. You know the reason why you're so furious?'

'I suppose you'll tell me.'

'Peter Toll is a younger version of yourself.'

Tweed paused near the door. 'You could be right.'

'And what about Newman? Will he be all right?'

'I hope to God he will. He speaks fluent German. He will if he continues to think for himself. Now, time to go and have a friendly chat with Lindemann.'

'What was the verdict on Harry Masterson?'

'Inconclusive.'

'That's a bit of luck,' said Tweed and drove the Cortina into a vacant parking slot. 'That's where Lindemann lives,' he went on, pointing out to Diana who sat alongside him an old one-storey lodge at the entrance to a mews south of the Fulham Road.

'Looks cosy. He certainly takes care of the place,' she re-marked as she got out of the car.

Which was true, Tweed thought as he attended to the meter. The lodge had white stucco walls, freshly painted, as were the windows. The lower part was hidden by a privet hedge, neatly trimmed into a box shape. Beyond the wrought-iron gate was a tiny garden, no more than three feet wide. A garden mostly paved with small bricks broken by two round flower beds. The roses were in bloom, all the dead-heads carefully removed. Quite a contrast to Harry Masterson's unkempt wilderness.

Tweed raised the shining brass door knocker and rapped three times. The door had a fish-eye spyhole and when it was opened Erich Lindemann stood in the tiny hall beyond, clad in a pair of tennis flannels, velvet smoking jacket and a polka dot bow tie.

'Well, don't just stand there. Come in.'

The usual, direct-approach Erich. Tweed introduced Diana as a potential recruit to General and Cumbria Assurance. She shook hands stiffly, not smiling. Tweed wondered if she'd had the same shock as himself.

Those blasted paintings of Harry's. They distorted your view of people. Lindemann looked more skull-like than Tweed recalled. They went inside and Tweed smelt faintly the aroma of some scented disinfectant.

'Tea or coffee?' Lindemann offered as he led them into a small living-room with mullion windows overlooking the mews entrance.

'Coffee for me, please,' Diana replied.

'Me, too,' Tweed said.

They looked round the room as they sat together on a turquoise couch which had no cushions. The room was sparsely furnished. Against the opposite wall stood a dining-table, the long side pushed against the wall, its surface gleaming. Tweed could now smell furniture polish. In one corner stood a hoover still plugged into the wall socket. Lindemann had vanished inside the kitchen which had a swing door, now closed.

Sparse but immaculate. Tweed stood up, wandered over to a high cabinet. Bookshelves crammed with volumes behind glass doors at the top; at the bottom a flap closed, the key in the lock. He turned the key carefully. No sound. It was well-oiled. Lowering the flap, he peered inside.

At least a dozen bottles of Haig whisky stood in a row like soldiers standing at attention. Lindemann was a teetotaller – had never been known to take even a glass of wine. One bottle half empty. Behind it stood a tumbler half-full. Tweed sniffed at it. Whisky. He closed the flap, turned the key, went back to the couch. Diana leaned towards him, so near he caught a waft of perfume above the smell of table polish.

221

'Nosey, aren't we?'

He shushed her and the swing door opened. Lindemann beckoned to Tweed to join him. 'There are some *Economists* in the cupboard beside you,' he told Diana in his dry voice.

'Who is she?' he asked Tweed once inside the kitchen. There was coffee bubbling in a percolator, a dish of pastries neatly arranged on a plate.

'Diana Chadwick. I told you. Good background. Speaks German fluently. I'm not sure yet . . .'

The kitchen was little more than a galley. Tweed was reminded of the galley aboard the *Südwind*. He was standing close to Lindemann and a fresh aroma wafted into his nostrils, the aroma of peppermints. His host was sucking one.

'Was it wise to bring the Chadwick girl?' Lindemann asked.

'Why do you say that?'

'She doesn't know about Park Crescent?'

'No. Of course not. What is all this about, Erich?'

'I have seen her before. In Oslo.'

'When and where?' Tweed kept his voice down.

'I can't remember. I am simply sure it was her. That it was Oslo. Good strong coffee for you? What about Miss Chadwick?'

'The same.'

Lindemann had turned away to fetch a pile of crockery from the other side of the kitchen. Tweed lifted up a cloth carelessly thrown on the worktop. It seemed out of place with the rest of the well-organized kitchen. Under the cloth was an opened green tube of peppermints. He dropped the cloth back over them. Why conceal the tube?

'We are ready.'

Lindemann had arranged the tray. Cups, saucers, highly-polished silver spoons, plates, the pastries. Tweed took a last glance at the row of knives suspended over the sink, hanging from a magnetic strip of metal. No chef's knife.

'Danish pastries,' Lindemann said, offering the plate to Diana. 'Very bad for the figure.'

Behind his back Tweed stared. Lindemann had never before joked with an attractive girl in his experience. His tall form stooped over Diana, almost deferentially. She looked up and gave him her warmest smile as she thanked him. Tweed was about to sit beside her again when Lindemann took his place.

'The host's privilege,' he said to Tweed. 'You'll find that arm chair adequate, I'm sure.'

'These pastries are delicious,' Diana enthused. She turned to face her host, her blue eyes half-closed. 'You get them from a local delicatessen?'

'Actually, I make them myself.' Lindemann looked pleased. 'They are much better if you buy them from a shop in Copenhagen. Have you been there, Miss Chadwick?'

'Diana. Please. No, not so far. I would love to go there one day. You really are an excellent cook . . .'

'Living alone, one learns to look after oneself . . .'

Tweed remained silent while they chatted. They finished off the pastries and Diana asked could she see his kitchen. Lindemann jumped up.

'Of course.' He turned to Tweed. 'Make yourself comfortable in my study. You know where it is.'

The moment they had disappeared inside the kitchen Tweed went over to the bookcase, checking the volumes. Histories of the Scandinavian countries. The great sagas of legend. Biographies. Napoleon. Bismarck. Bernadotte, Napoleon's general who became King of Sweden. Laurence Olivier. Amateur theatricals.

He left the bookcase, crossed the room and opened the door to the bathroom, locking it behind him. An old-fashioned roll-top bath. Above the wash-basin a wooden cupboard. He opened it. Two shelves. Shaving kit on the top one. Bottles on the lower shelf. He picked up one which was half-empty and examined the label. *Hair Tint. Sable Colourant.* He placed it back on the shelf exactly as he had found it, flushed the lavatory, unlocked the door and emerged as Diana walked out of the kitchen, handbag under her arm, followed by Lindemann.

'I really think we ought to go,' Tweed said. 'Just thought we'd call in on you, make sure you were enjoying your leave.'

'I'll be glad to get back to work. There are a dozen policies I ought to attend to personally.'

'Excuse me just a second,' Tweed remarked suddenly. 'I think I left my Dunhill pen in your study.'

He opened the door and pushed it half-closed. The tiny room was empty. On Lindemann's desk a pad he had been making notes on was upside down, a glass paperweight perched on top.

Tweed lifted the weight, turned over the pad. Covered in figures in Lindemann's small handwriting, figures which looked like salary computations for his staff in Copenhagen. He replaced the pad, put back the paperweight and walked back into the sitting-room. There was no one else in the place. He had half-expected to find a hidden visitor.

Lindemann took Diana's arm, led her to the front door. She thanked him for his hospitality and they left. Tweed heard the door close behind them as he climbed into the car.

'And what did you think of him?' he asked as Diana arranged her skirt.

'A barrel of laughs.'

'Which means you didn't like him? He's a reputation for no interest in women . . .'

'That you'd better revise.'

'Really? Why?'

He had started the car but he paused in surprise. She took out her ivory holder, inserted a cigarette.

'He likes blondes. That I do know. A woman can always tell. In fact, I'd say he's interested in all types of attractive women. Don't let him fool you.'

'I thought maybe it was just you . . .'

'I never flatter myself. Tweedy, a woman always knows. He is interested in the opposite sex. Period. Did you find anything?'

'Maybe.'

'You don't even trust Diana, do you?' Monica asked as Tweed settled himself behind his desk.

'Why do you say that?'

'It's obvious. You have Pete Nield following her. Where is she now? Back in Newman's flat?'

'After leaving Lindemann's place I did drop her there. She said she was going window-shopping at Harrods. Nield managed to find a parking slot further down the street when we arrived at the lodge. And my main purpose in never leaving her alone is to *guard* her. She could be a key witness.'

'Witness to what?'

'That I'm not sure of yet . . .'

'All right, go secretive on me. Hugh Grey will be at his Norfolk farmhouse tomorrow. He's leaving his Cheyne Walk flat this evening to drive out there. And Guy Dalby will be home in Woking.'

'Then I'll drive Diana to Norfolk tomorrow. Get her impression of Grey.'

'Is that really the only reason you're travelling round with her to see the sector chiefs?'

'What other reason could there be?' Tweed enquired. 'We must stick to the point.' He stood up, began strolling round the office. 'There are two main threads running through this grim investigation. Who is the Janus man – the person responsible for Fergusson's murder? Because only four people knew he was on his way to Hamburg. The four sector chiefs. One of them has to be Janus.'

'And the second thread?'

'Who is Dr Berlin?'

'They all seem to be absent from Europe at the same time,' Monica remarked. 'I managed to contact Kuhlmann at Lübeck-Süd, as you requested. After four calls. He confirmed that Dr Berlin has still not returned to Priwall Island. What's the matter?'

'Something you just said . . .'

Tweed stood stock still, gazing through the heavy net curtains towards the trees in Regent's Park. They were in full foliage and the sun shone on them out of a clear blue sky. Tweed was not seeing any of this. His gaze was abstracted, like a man who has received a shock. He swung round.

'Read to me that report I dictated after my visit to Dr Generoso, the psychiatrist . . .'

'I typed it out. You can read it for yourself.'

'Read it aloud, woman. Please. I want to *hear* it.'

She extracted a folder from a drawer, took out a sheaf of typescript, began reading. Slowly. She'd had to do this before for him. He grasped it better listening.

' "A man leading a double life . . . One life here, the other on the continent . . . Now under great pressure . . . you propose to increase that pressure . . . you're treading on thin ice . . . Schizo . . . Kim Philby drank like a fish . . . a good example. The alcohol saved him. Release from all the tension he laboured under . . . murdering women at random . . . Very difficult to detect. The murderer might well appear perfectly normal most

225

of the time . . . likely to be obsessive in some direction . . . Maybe excessively neat. Fussy about small things . . . an over-weening self-confidence verging on arrogance . . . delight in fooling people . . . very like an actor, playing two roles . . . insufferable conceit, a feeling of great superiority over other human beings . . . Step up the pressure, you could step up the killings." And that is about it,' Monica concluded.

'I've been barking up the wrong tree!' Tweed snapped his fingers in his excitement. 'And something I repeated to you recently which Diana said was another pointer.'

'Really? Pointer in which direction?'

'Dr Berlin. Of course!'

Twenty-Seven

Through his field-glasses Falken watched the armoured car coming down the track off the highway. He held the lenses to his eyes for only a few seconds and then lowered the binoculars.

'I can see its wheels kicking up cinder off that track,' he commented. 'It's slithering all over the place.'

'If necessary it will slither down to the end of the slope and then drive on to here,' Gerda warned.

She ran out of the kitchen, followed by Falken. Newman stayed to one side of the window, watching through a patch of clear glass in the condensation. He didn't think they could fight the Army. And the retreat from the back of the cottage was across fields of ripening rye. They'd be spotted instantly.

He watched the ugly vehicle wrestling with the cinder track. Again he had gone ice-cold, as he had when they encountered the Schneider patrol back in the forest. Then he stiffened, his eyes narrowed. He waited a moment longer. To be sure.

'Come back here!' he shouted.

Gerda slipped into the room, holding the Uzi. Behind her Falken appeared, a Walther automatic pistol in his right hand. Newman gestured for them to keep away from the window.

'What is it?' Falken asked in a crisp voice.

'It's going away. They were simply using the track to turn

the armoured car so they could go back the way they came. They must have lost their way . . .'

'I do believe you're right,' Falken responded, peering out of the window from the other side. 'It is illegal to make a U-turn. They were worried a staff car might come along if they tried it.'

Newman watched the car proceeding eastwards along the elevated highway. Gerda stood beside him, he heard her let out her breath. Newman showed her his moist palms and wiped them dry on the back of his trousers.

'Feel my heart, Mr Thorn,' she said. 'Go on, feel it.'

He hesitated, then placed his hand over her left breast. He held it there and she smiled up at him, a Mona Lisa smile. Falken grinned and shoved the Walther inside his jacket pocket.

'Beating like a tom-tom,' she said. 'You feel it?'

'I feel it . . .'

She left the room again and Newman looked at Falken who still had a grin on his face. He came close to Newman, whispering the words.

'She likes you. If something happens to me, you do what she says. You obey her. Then you will be safe.'

'Nothing is going to happen to you.'

'In this game fate deals different cards. We just had a good card. Maybe the next one . . .' He broke off as Gerda returned and said the meal was ready. Newman left them to lay the table in the sitting-room. As he walked through it he noticed Gerda had put back the windcheater on the floor, presumably concealing the Uzi. From the canvas hold-all she had carried from the Chaika, Gerda produced black bread, cheese and some apples. He went outside to the back of the cottage to get some fresh air.

After they had eaten their simple meal and drunk black coffee, Falken took out the Border Police folder and the trimmed photo of Newman from the table drawer he had slipped them inside earlier.

'As I said, always assume the worst. We assume that Schneider reported the incident. So, they look for an impostor who carries a River Police folder . . .' He took the pot of glue out of the drawer and squeezed a very small amount in the centre of the back of the trimmed photo. Using his fingertips, he smeared the glue smoothly, removing any excess from the edges. He lifted the photo carefully, reversed it and placed it exactly inside the blank ruled rectangle in the new folder.

'Now we wait until it is dry, then we make it official.' He took a rubber stamp from his pocket together with an inking pad.

'Once I stamp the photograph with the official seal you are in business. The Border Police,' he repeated. 'Again in plain clothes, again on special assignment . . .'

'Tracking drug dealers again?'

'That would be excellent. Oddly enough, there has been much talk on our grapevine – which extends not only all over the DDR, but also beyond its frontiers to the East. Talk of the movement of a huge consignment of heroin. That you don't mention.'

'When we are on the move again you expect us to be stopped?'

'Inevitably. There are checkpoints everywhere. Constant patrols. And, I am a magician. I believe I told you before. You are no longer Albert Thorn. You have become Emil Clasen. Do not forget. And Gerda knows.'

'What about my River Police folder?'

'That I destroy. Burn to ashes in that fire . . .'

'That fire worries me,' Newman remarked, 'if you don't mind my saying so. The smoke from the chimney shows someone is here. I thought of that when I was watching the armoured car.'

Falken leaned forward and squeezed Newman's arm. 'I could use you in Group Five. But we have two choices – freeze to death or risk the fire. After all, Norbert has a fire all the time he is here. It is cold and damp by the canal. And no one can remember when Norbert is supposed to be here or back at his flat.'

'You seem to have thought of everything.'

'I wonder what I have not thought of? That is what always is haunting me.'

Karl Schneider drove back slowly along the road, his eyes switching from left to right and back again. Dressed in farmer's clothes, he wore a shabby peaked cap and under his left armpit

228

he felt the bulge of the 9-mm Walther tucked snugly inside its shoulder holster.

Schneider was driving a farm truck carrying a load of hay in the open back. He had been driving for two hours and the sun was high in a clear blue sky. The country fields spread out on either side and he felt he was back in the old days. They had been good times. Often a girl to take behind a hedge. They knew a thing or two, those country girls. That was before he had met Alma.

His expression grimaced at the thought. She was the one who had prodded him into joining the Border Police. 'You ought to better yourself, serve the State . . .' Screw the State. She was ambitious was Alma. For herself. Nagging cow.

He forced her out of his mind. Concentrate on the job. The reference to promotion was uppermost in Schneider's mind. If he had more money he'd get himself a girl on the side. Some nice willing girl to take his mind off Alma. He'd show her – where ambition led. To an intimate place.

He had driven over the elevated highway once without taking any notice of the lock-keeper's cottage, his attention distracted by a man on a motor-bike who overtook him. Not by the man actually. By the girl who rode pillion behind, trying to hold down her skirt which kept flying up, exposing a pair of slim legs. Stupid tart, wearing a skirt on a pillion. If he'd been the motor-bike rider he'd have shown her how stupid she was.

He came to the point where he'd completed his run, then turned back. This time when he approached the elevated section he was on the side of the highway nearest the cottage. He saw a curl of smoke rising from the chimney. Pretty warm day for a fire. Then he remembered the canal alongside the tumbledown building. That place would always be damp.

His eyes roved over the cottage, took in the little shed near the back. That would be the outside lavatory. In the middle of the field of rye rose a large canvas-covered hump. He slowed down, studying it curiously. The front of a farm tractor protruded from the open end of the huge sheet of canvas. He frowned, slowed further. No farm tractor was as big as that – as *long* as that.

Slyly, he kept on driving until he was well past the cottage. He came to where a cinder track led down into a hollow. At

229

the rear of the hollow was a pile of hay. He glanced in the rear-view mirror, saw the highway was deserted, turned down into the hollow and pulled up. Should he radio Leipzig? No. He'd check the cottage first: if he found the fugitives the credit would be his.

Schneider approached the rear of the covered tractor by a devious route, circling round the back where the ground sloped down, out of sight of the cottage. About a hundred metres from the hump he dropped to his knees and crawled slowly through the rye, now high enough to hide him completely.

Reaching the back of the hump, he stood up after listening for several minutes. He lifted the canvas and stared at the rear end of a Chaika. Something the man with glasses in Leipzig had said came back to him. Three bicycles found hidden beneath some undergrowth.

His mind worked slowly. They'd have needed other transport. They'd never have walked the long distance to the nearest village. They'd have needed a car. Maybe a Chaika?

The peasant cunning of Schneider, the foxy character Markus Wolf had immediately observed, told him he was on to something. He'd watch the cottage before he made a move. He had the high-powered field-glasses in his jacket pocket they'd given him in Room 78.

He found a small hillock surrounded with rye, lay down on it and focused his glasses on the tiny shed which was the lavatory. Whoever was inside had to come out to relieve themselves. That way he'd find out how many of them there were – who they were. It was only mid-afternoon. Plenty of time before dark.

An hour later a man walked out of the cottage and headed for the lavatory shed. Schneider focused his glasses. Thorn! Albert Thorn! That bastard River Police officer. And through the glasses he did look rather like the man whose picture he'd been shown on a poster in Leipzig.

Schneider rested the glasses on the ground, still lying full length amid the rye. Thorn had gone inside the shed, shut the door. Schneider hauled at the butt of the Walther and let go as his sweaty hand slipped. Cursing, he dragged a handkerchief from his pocket, wiped both hands.

230

Grasping the Walther again, he heaved it clear of the holster. Holding the weapon in his right hand, he flicked up the safety catch with his left thumb. The gun was ready to fire. He laid it beside the glasses which he raised again to his eyes.

Ten minutes later he watched a second, taller man emerge, walk to the shed. Looked like the swine who'd been with Thorn, the man who hadn't said a word. He was sure it was him. Schneider sweated some more, this time with excitement. He'd wait until dusk. Then he'd move in on them.

Newman and Gerda sat round the table in the living-room. It was Gerda's turn to watch the road and she was in the kitchen. She had made more coffee and the two men drank and talked.

'This witness you told me about,' Newman said. 'Can you tell me anything more about him?'

'It's a her. She was loyal to the regime until her son kicked over the traces. Some misdemeanour, insulting a Vopo when he was the worse for drink. They put him in a labour battalion. She's hated their guts ever since. She's sixty-something. I want you to hear her story from her own lips.'

'About Dr Berlin?'

'About Berlin, yes.'

'Afterwards I go back over the border past that watch-tower?'

'You go back over the border, yes.' Falken checked the time. 'Nearly dusk. Your turn to take over from Gerda. Stay on watch too long and your concentration goes. Like those people at airports who check the X-ray machines. Take your coffee with you.'

Newman walked into the kitchen, put down his cup of coffee on the iron range. Gerda was stifling a yawn as she stood by the window. It was almost dark inside the cramped kitchen.

'Your turn?' she asked and gave him a warm smile, handing the glasses over.

'Treacherous light this,' he said as he moved to the window. 'You imagine you see things.'

'So, stay alert. Don't let your imagination wander.'

She gave him a friendly punch on the forearm and disappeared into the living-room. He heard her say she was going out to the lavatory. There was a slam as the heavy front door closed. Then a sudden silence.

In the blue dusk he could see the headlights of cars moving along the highway. People going home from work. More traffic than there had been since they'd arrived. In the west the invisible sun had sunk behind a ridge of the distant Harz. Behind the ridge, sharp as a knife edge, the world seemed to be on fire.

He raised the glasses to his eyes, slowly scanned the fields between the highway and the cottage. The rye crop stood still in the windless evening. The blips of light continued moving along the highway, nearly all in an easterly direction, towards Halle. Fewer of them now. Rush hour was fading.

'Emil,' Falken called out from the next room, using Newman's new name, 'everything quiet?'

'Not a sign of life – except cars on the highway . . .'

'Come in here for a minute then. Something you need to know.'

Newman found the German sitting at the table, studying the new Border Police folder. He had already burnt the River Police document. Albert Thorn had ceased to exist, gone up in flames. Newman sat down. Behind him he heard Gerda unlocking the door, returning from the lavatory.

'Keep your hands on the table! Move and I'll blow your heads off . . .'

Newman stared at the open doorway where Gerda stood, key in her left hand, her face pale, grim. Behind her stood a man in farming clothes, peaked cap pulled down over his low forehead. For a moment he had difficulty in recognizing Karl Schneider. The German had no difficulty at all.

'Ah! Mr Albert Thorn! Of the River Police? And Mr What's-is-Name. Lay your bloody hands flat on the table! Both of you! Lean forward! You want a bullet in the guts?'

Gerda still stood frozen, as though with fright. Schneider used his left hand to give her a violent shove in the back. She nearly fell, but recovered her balance and turned to face him. His gun still covered Newman and Falken.

'Make the wrong move and they get it,' he told her. 'A third bullet for you, my pretty one . . .'

He stepped back, used his left elbow to slam the door

232

closed, then stepped forward again. Schneider was pleased with himself. It showed in the triumphant sneering grin on his pasty face. He had crawled through the rye patiently until he reached the rear of the shed which served as a lavatory. Now he knew there were only three of them. The girl didn't count. Two of them. He'd waited until she had left the shed, walked the few paces to the front door, inserted the key and opened it. Then he had rushed forward behind her. They'd be proud of him in Leipzig. He would get his promotion. He could smell treason inside this cottage.

Schneider flexed his left hand as the circulation returned. It had been cold out there in the dusk. Inside the cottage it was warm. He felt the warmth reacting on his chilled face, on both hands. They'd forgotten to provide gloves. But they'd hardly have foreseen this situation, the vigil he had kept on the hillock.

'Go and sit down at the table, you stupid cow,' he ordered Gerda. 'You've had your piss,' he added coarsely.

She released the key. It clanged on the flagstone floor. His eyes dropped, looked up quickly. 'Thought you could distract me, you fornicating bitch? I suppose they've both had some?'

He leered, then his eyes glanced at the open folder in front of Falken on the table. Newman sighed inwardly. If Schneider needed any proof of their guilt – and there had been a chance they could have talked their way out of the trap – the folder had ruined it. Gerda, still standing, spoke in a mocking tone.

'You want us to think you did all this by yourself? Where is the rest of your patrol?'

'By myself? Yes! No one else. Just me. I found you! By driving along the roads. By keeping my eyes open. You think you can fool a farmer by covering a tractor which has to be as big as a Russian tank?'

'I don't believe it,' Gerda jeered. 'A squalid little lout of a man like you? A peasant . . .'

Schneider levelled the gun midway between Newman and Falken with his right hand. His left hand bunched into a fist. He hit her a savage blow in the face. At the last moment she moved her head slightly, then fell back under the impact. She sprawled on the floor, sobbing.

There was a snap. Falken had closed the folder. Schneider

233

eyed the folder. 'Open that, you bastard,' he ordered. 'I want to see it – see the photograph . . .'

A rattle of gunfire reverberated. From Schneider's breast-bone downwards a row of bright red medallions seemed to sprout, as though stitched to his thin coarse jacket. Schneider was hurled back against the door as if pushed by a giant hand. His eyes bulged with astonishment. Newman felt himself jump with shock. The red splotches began to coalesce into one long streak as he slid down the door, sat on the floor, legs sprawled across the floor.

Newman glanced at Gerda as Falken leapt up. She lay propped on one elbow, the Uzi in her right hand, the inner lining of the windcheater showing where she had grabbed the weapon.

Falken bent down, checked Schneider's neck pulse. 'He's still alive. Amazing. Give me the gun . . .'

He took it from Gerda, walked back to Schneider, placed the muzzle against the side of the German's head after adjusting the Uzi's mechanism. He fired one shot. The head jerked, flopped sideways. Falken checked the pulse again. 'Now he's dead.'

'The blood!' Gerda scrambled to her feet. 'There must be no blood on the floor . . .'

Opening a cupboard, she hauled out two grey blankets. With Falken's aid she laid out the blankets on the floor, lifted the body on to them, wrapped it up like a parcel, tucking it in at head and foot.

Falken picked up the key from the floor, opened the front door, peered into the night, then disappeared. He returned almost immediately carrying a loop of rope. 'The mooring rope for barges,' he explained to Newman. 'Go to the kitchen and check the window . . .'

Newman ran into the next room, which was still in darkness, felt his way round the few pieces of furniture, stared through the window. His night vision came to him quickly, helped by the headlights of two cars driving along the highway. No sign of any movement in the fields.

'Nothing I can see,' he reported, going back into the living-room. 'I'd better check outside . . .'

'He must have come in from the fields at the back – he found

234

the Chaika,' Gerda said, bent down over the grisly bundle.

'You can use a Walther?' Falken asked. 'Good. Take this.'

Newman released the safety catch, opened the front door, stepped outside quickly and closed the door behind him. The cold of the night hit him after the warmth of the cottage. Holding the Walther in both hands, extended in front of him, he explored round the cottage, down the tow-path to the bank of the canal.

Then he took the more difficult route to where the canvas covered the tractor and the Chaika. At frequent intervals he paused and listened. The night was heavy with silence, the nerve-wracking silence you only experience after dark in the country. He resumed his walking, heading for the most likely hiding-place for the rest of a patrol. Behind the covered vehicles.

He was almost convinced Schneider had spoken the truth when he said he'd come alone. But it had to be checked. *Assume the worst.* An excellent maxim. He found no one behind the canvas hump. But, kneeling down, feeling the ground carefully, he detected flattened rye where Schneider must have waited and watched. For God knew how long. But he'd had the patience of a farmer.

Newman returned to the cottage.

The corpse lay on the flagstone floor. Wrapped in two grey Army blankets. Further wrapped in a sheet of canvas. And round two parts – the chest and the knees – the whole parcel was coiled with two heavy, rusting chains. Falken, who had opened the door, went back to the table where Gerda sat, shivering, small hands grasping a mug of steaming black coffee.

'No one out there,' Newman reported. 'He *was* on his own.'

'I knew that,' Gerda said in a cold voice, 'he boasted about it. But you were right to check. There is still coffee in the pot.'

Newman sagged in a chair opposite Falken. He suddenly felt unutterably weary, drained of energy. He drank some of the coffee Falken had poured, then looked again at the body.

'Where did you get the chains?'

'Snow chains. For Norbert's car in winter. We think the body must be weighted. To make it sink.'

'In the canal?'

'Out of the question.' Falken's tone was abrupt. 'It might be found. Then old Norbert would be in terrible trouble. We cannot risk that.'

'Bury it,' Newman suggested. 'During the night.'

'Impossible. The ground is too hard. We have to think of something else.'

'Such as?'

'I have no idea.' Falken sounded irritable. 'For God's sake let me think.'

'That was the first man I have ever killed,' Gerda suddenly remarked in a choked voice.

Newman laid a hand on hers. 'Try not to dwell on it. Remember, we'd probably all have ended up dead if you hadn't acted. I do understand how you must feel . . .'

'Leave her alone,' Falken broke in roughly. 'He was an enemy.'

'No need to get so tough about it,' Newman snapped back.

Gerda grasped his hand, squeezed it. 'You are a nice man, but he is right. Sympathy can undermine resolution. We have to be hard to survive . . .'

'And you,' Falken told Newman, 'may have to be hard before you cross the border again. I have decided we must leave this place early. Tonight, in fact. The people who sent Schneider may come looking for him. Your schedule is speeded up . . .'

'And what about the body?' Newman demanded.

'That is a problem. I am still trying to solve it . . .'

It was a novel problem for Newman. He'd never realized before just how difficult it was to dispose of a corpse so it would not be discovered.

Twenty-Eight

'Yes, what can I do for you, Mr Ted Smith?' asked Kuhlmann. 'I have got the name correct?' he went on in English.

He was sitting in the interrogation room on the tenth floor of the Lübeck-Süd police headquarters. Outside it was dusk, would soon be dark. Reception had called him. An Englishman, a tourist, had called at the building, wanted to see someone about the Kurt Franck poster he'd seen outside the local police station at Travemünde.

Ted Smith, in his late twenties, was dressed in hiking shorts, an open-necked shirt, trainer shoes, and when he'd entered the room he'd dumped an incredibly heavy-looking backpack on the floor at Kuhlmann's suggestion. If that was enjoyment, they'd better keep it.

Kuhlmann sensed the young man was nervous. He tried to put him at his ease by fiddling with his lighter, pretending he was having trouble lighting up the cigar.

'Yes, you have,' Smith replied. 'This may all be about nothing . . .'

'Tell me about it. We welcome information of any kind. On holiday?'

'Yes. Hitch-hiking. Then partly by train with a rail-pass. I came up from Hamburg three days ago. Decided to splash out a bit here. Took a room at the Movenpick.'

'Very nice, too.' The lighter flared. 'There, got it going.' Kuhlmann puffed at the cigar. 'Do you smoke?'

'The occasional cigarette. Four a day. Trying to give it up. Er, mind if I smoke too?'

'Go ahead.' Kuhlmann lit Smith's cigarette. 'Now what is this about Kurt Franck?'

'We . . . that is, I, saw him. About three weeks ago it would be. I went on by train to Copenhagen when I first arrived. Came back to Hamburg, then back again to here. I like Lübeck.'

'You saw Kurt Franck three weeks ago. Where exactly?'

'At the edge of a river on the way to Travemünde. He pushed a motor-bike into the river. We . . . I . . . thought that was a funny thing to do.'

'You keep saying "we". Is it a girl? No law against having a girl friend in Germany, you know.'

'Well, yes, it is. An American girl. Suzanne Templeton.'

'Where is she now?'

'Well, actually, she's waiting in the Volkswagen I hired – downstairs. Outside the police station. You see, we saw this poster in Travemünde and wondered whether we ought to do something about it. Then we were driving past here and we saw the *Polizei* sign. Sue told me to drive in.'

'Sensible girl. Let's have her up here. You don't mind? I find two pairs of eyes are better than one. She was with you when you saw Franck?'

'Actually, she was.' Smith hesitated. Fresh-faced, clearly his American girl friend was the one who had urged him to report what they had seen. Kuhlmann phoned reception, asked for the girl to be brought up, and sat puffing his cigar until a policewoman opened the door and showed a tall slim girl with a good figure into the room. Kuhlmann's eyes narrowed. She was blonde-haired.

Half an hour later Kuhlmann was driving his car along the road towards Travemünde which ran not so far from the river Trave. Sue Templeton, who sat beside him, had proved a great deal franker and more confident than Ted Smith. Yes, they had been making love in the deep grasses close to the river when they'd heard someone coming on their side of the river.

'He'd gotten this motor-cycle,' she'd explained in the interrogation room. 'I crouched on my knees, hoping he wouldn't see us as I peered over the grasses. A Suzuki, Ted said. He stopped the engine and pushed it the last few yards. He had a suitcase strapped on the back. He took that off and then pushed the machine into the river. We got dressed quickly . . .'

'We thought it was funny, you see,' Ted intervened. He looked uncomfortable and Kuhlmann guessed he wanted to skip over what they had been up to. 'Then he walked along the path at the edge of the river . . .'

Sue interrupted him. 'He was carrying the case. That might be important – because of what happened later.'

'What did happen?' Kuhlmann enquired.

'He walked about a mile along the footpath. We followed him at a distance – the path winds which made it easier and the tall grasses hid us from him until he reached this small power cruiser and went on board.'

'You didn't happen to notice the name of the cruiser?'

'The *Moorburg*,' she said promptly.

'Please describe him again.'

'Six foot tall. At least. Blond-haired. Early thirties and well-built. A tough-looking guy . . .'

That was when Kuhlmann asked them if they would accompany him in the car, try to find the place where the motor-cycle had been pushed into the water. Ted Smith had been reluctant, Sue had insisted it was their civic duty, as she had phrased it.

Kuhlmann drove slowly, giving her the best chance of locating the track they had wandered down to find some privacy. She was sure she could find it – even in the dark. Behind Kuhlmann a second police car followed, carrying the police team he had organized before they set out.

The American girl leaned forward in her seat, her breasts pushed against the safety belt as she stared along the headlight beams. An attractive young woman, she had the confidence and assured manner Kuhlmann had noticed before in many girls from the States.

'Slow down! Yes, it was here. Down this track!'

Kuhlmann swung the wheel, crawled along the track. In the headlights he could see the single wheel gulley impressed into the cinders by the motor-cycle. He pulled up a short distance from the river, took a torch from the glove compartment and they got out. He bent down as the second car halted behind them, examining the wheel mark. Too wide for a bicycle. Just right for a motor-bike. They walked on to the edge of the river, followed by two men in frogman's suits.

'Now, Sue,' Kuhlmann asked, 'from the marks it looks like this was where he pushed it in. Would you agree?'

'This is the place . . .'

They went back to the car and waited. Within five minutes the frogmen emerged, dripping water, hauling out a Suzuki motor-cycle in the beams of the headlights. Kuhlmann used the radio to call up reinforcements, left one man with the machine and then followed the other car as it backed to the highway.

'If there was a landing-stage where the *Moorburg* was moored,' he remarked as he drove on towards Travemünde, 'there will be a track leading to it. We just have to keep on trying. Any way you could identify that landing-stage where he

239

threw the suitcase into the river before taking off towards Travemünde?'

'Yes,' she said promptly again, 'it was in two sections – the one nearest the cruiser sagged, the end was under the water . . .'

God give me more witnesses like this one he thought as he drove on. Sue identified the first track they checked and the landing-stage at the end. Kuhlmann ordered the frogman who had travelled in the other car to dive in again. This time it took about ten minutes. The frogman emerged, holding a suitcase in both hands. Kuhlmann forced open the soggy object and stared at a length of chain.

'End of the line,' he said and stood up, gesturing for one of his men to collect the sodden case.

'No, it isn't,' Sue said. 'We saw him later . . .'

'It wasn't him,' Ted objected.

'I tell you it *was*! You weren't looking when he came out of the shop.'

'Which shop?' asked Kuhlmann.

'After the cruiser moved off we thought we'd lost him. We walked back to the highway and hitched a ride into Travemünde. We were walking along the front, looking for somewhere to eat, when I saw him. I know it was him,' she repeated. 'I'm studying law – that teaches you to be observant.'

'So far your powers of observation have amazed me. Go on.'

'He came out of a shop and he was putting on a straw hat. I saw his blond hair just before he put it on. One of those wide-brimmed hats. Ted went off to find a toilet so I followed the blond man. He went into another shop nearby and came out with a pipe in his mouth, one of those little curved things. It was the same man, I am certain. And he was dressed differently.'

'Let's get back inside the car. You are getting goose pimples on your arms . . .'

The night sky above them was clear, the Prussian blue studded with glittering stars. The balmy warmth of the evening was evaporating and a slight chill descended on the fields. Kuhlmann waited until they were settled inside the vehicle; Sue again sat beside him.

'Dressed differently, you said?'

'When we first saw him pushing the machine into the river he had on a dark blue windcheater, the same colour slacks tucked inside leather boots. Coming out of the shop in Travemünde he wore a light green T-shirt, khaki slacks, white sneakers and a large backpack – one with those chrome rods. He'd become a hiker.'

Kuhlmann sat chewing his unlit cigar. Sue Templeton's description of Franck corresponded exactly with that given to him by Ann Grayle, who had called at Travemünde police station and asked to see him.

Aboard the sloop she had told him how she had seen Franck when she was going for a walk, how Franck had almost bumped into her. That had been almost three weeks ago. At the time Kuhlmann had wondered whether Grayle had been mistaken. He looked up at Ted Smith in the rear view mirror.

'Will you be staying at the Movenpick a little longer?'

'Until the money gives out. Sue likes Lübeck . . .'

'Don't worry about money,' Sue interjected, 'I've got loads of travellers' cheques. And we're having such a good time. I like a good time.'

The remark jolted Kuhlmann. Shades of Diana Chadwick; the sort of remark she'd have made. Where was she now, he wondered.

'Money's no problem,' Sue went on. 'My father's a state senator.'

Kuhlmann received a second jolt. He looked at her, studying her sheen of blonde hair. In a way he wished they were leaving Germany at once. He looked at Ted again.

'I ought to warn you – in case you couldn't read the German on that poster . . .'

'We couldn't,' Sue told him.

'Then I must warn you, Mr Smith, that man you saw could be a mass murderer – his speciality is blondes. Three have been horribly killed already. Stick close to Sue. All the time.'

'I'll do that, and I'll buy a weapon.' Smith looked older and more serious than he had before.

'A weapon?' Kuhlmann queried.

'A heavy walking stick. I've seen them in the shops . . .'

'A good idea. And I'm taking you both to dinner at the Maritim Hotel in Travemünde. But first, I must make a report.'

241

He picked up the mike, called Lübeck-Süd, began detailing the new description of Kurt Franck. The only two points Ann Grayle had not mentioned were the straw hat and the pipe. He must have gone to the shops soon after she'd spotted him.

'Lübeck-Süd? Kuhlmann here. Kurt Franck. New description . . . *persona* of hitch-hiker . . .'

In the loft of the barn near Burg on Fehmarn Island he was now ready to move. For the third time Munzel checked his appearance in the hand mirror. Flourishing blond moustache and beard, more blond hair flowing down the back of his neck. Unrecognizable.

Dressed in a light green T-shirt, khaki slacks and a pair of white trainer shoes, he put down the mirror, hiding it with the spirit kettle under a pile of straw. He hoisted the backpack over his shoulders. It weighed like a hundred kilos, but he'd soon get used to it.

He looked round the loft, checking for traces of his using it as a refuge. There were none. He had cleared up carefully. Reaching down, he picked up the straw hat and rammed it over his head, then took the curved pipe from his pocket – already filled with tobacco – and clenched it between his teeth.

He descended the ladder slowly, arrived at the bottom and ran heavily to the open barn door. He peered out. No sign of life. He went back to the ladder – the only evidence that the loft existed – and hauled it down until he held it parallel to the straw-strewn floor.

His arm muscles felt the strain as he carried it outside and round the back of the barn. Very slowly he lowered it inside the grass-choked ditch which ran alongside the rear of the barn. He spent several minutes straightening the grasses until it disappeared from view, then he returned to the front and started along the track leading to the country road.

An hour later, having caught the bus from Burg, he sat on the platform at Puttgarden station. While he waited for the train to Lübeck he struck matches, lighting and relighting his pipe.

Franck was in a confident mood. With his changed appearance he'd be safe in Lübeck. He'd stay at the hotel opposite the

Hauptbahnhof – the International as far as he could remember. From there he would call Martin Vollmer in Altona for news of Tweed's movements.

Confident because the police hue and cry would be a thing of the past. Or at the worst they'd have him as a low priority. During his time on Fehmarn Island other crimes would have been committed. The police were like the press. Kurt Franck was yesterday's news.

Twenty-Nine

Newman drove the Chaika up the cinder track, the headlights swung in a wide arc as he turned east on to the highway. Behind them the lock-keeper's cottage was in darkness. Beside him sat Falken. Gerda had the dirty end of the stick – cramped in the back. Beside her was propped up the canvas-covered bundle which contained the corpse of Karl Schneider.

'The lake . . .'

It was Gerda who had thought of the place where they should deposit the motionless passenger. She had come running in from the kitchen with her suggestion. At first Falken shook his head.

'A long way off our route.'

'But you said we should leave here this evening,' she pressed. 'We can drive through the night, then go on to Radom's farm. We will be close to Leipzig for the morning. You can phone her to tell her we shall be early.'

'I suppose you could be right . . .'

'I know I am right. Aren't you always going on at me about we must be flexible in our plans, ready to change them at a moment's notice if the circumstances warrant it?'

'It will be dangerous . . .' Falken had glanced at the chained bundle lying on the floor. 'There are patrols out at night.'

'It may be even more dangerous to stay here. You said they'd probably send people out to find him – why he hadn't come back.'

'The lake it is, then . . .'

243

Newman had been impressed with the care they took to erase all traces of their stay in the cottage. Gerda used a dust-pan and brush to sweep black bread crumbs off the flagstones, had then used it to sweep the fading relics out of the fireplace. She had emptied her pan in the canal.

Falken had carried out a final inspection of every room. When they had gone out across the fields to collect the Chaika they left every window and the door open – to disperse all fumes from the fire, all warmth.

After backing the car, they re-covered the farm tractor exactly as they had found it. When they returned to the cottage the interior was cold and fume-free. They closed the windows, locked the door, left the key under the paving stone outside where Falken had found it.

'I'll drive,' Newman had said. 'You've both been without any sleep for Lord knows how long.'

'So have you, my friend,' Falken pointed out.

'Don't argue. I'm Emil Clasen – of the Border Police. If we are stopped they'll be more likely to accept me than you.'

'I'm supposed to be in charge of this unit and everyone tells me what to do,' Falken said good-humouredly.

'Nobody's ordering you about,' Newman said as he got in behind the wheel. 'Just do what I say and we'll all be happy.'

The moment he turned on to the highway Newman experienced the feeling of being a hunted man. It had been unnerving – easing the canvas bundle into the Chaika. At one second the body had seemed to move inside its mummified wrappings of its own accord. Gerda has gasped. Newman had told her it was just the weight of the chains as he finally heaved it inside.

Driving along the highway no one noticed Schneider's truck which was still parked in the hollow for storing hay. Newman was driving just inside the speed limit. Suddenly he realized both hands were clamped tightly to the wheel. Bad driving. He forced himself to relax, to hold the wheel with a lighter grip.

A police patrol car came towards them, its light flashing on the roof. Falken uttered a warning and Newman snapped his head off. 'Who's driving this bloody thing? Sorry,' he added after a moment. The patrol car was slowing down as they came closer.

It passed them as Newman maintained exactly the same pace. In his rear view mirror he saw the patrol car increase speed rapidly. Falken had glanced into his wing mirror.

'Why did they do that?' Newman asked.

'A test. Had you altered speed, showed signs of nerves, they might have stopped us. They are full of little tricks.'

'Bugger them.'

No one spoke for a long time after his pithy comment. Newman was aware of controlled tension inside the car. With the cargo they were carrying it was understandable. Everyone was frightened, edgy. Then they came to a side road.

'Turn here,' Gerda called out. 'We are close to the lake.'

Lysenko yawned, exposing a metallic filling in his teeth. He walked to the window and gazed down. Two o'clock in the morning. The fluorescent lamp standards threw an eerie light over deserted streets. He felt the stubble on his chin, turned to stare at the German.

Markus Wolf sat hunched like a Buddha behind his desk, studying a file. The man seemed to have inexhaustible reserves. He never stopped working. The green lampshade he had pulled down on the pulley suspended over his desk glowed on his impassive features. He looked up.

'Time I sent out patrols to look for Schneider. He should have reported back hours ago. I think something has happened to him.'

'What can you do?' snapped Lysenko.

'What I've just said. Send out armed patrols. Give them a description of the farm truck Schneider was driving. It can't have vanished into thin air. And we know the exact route that Schneider was following. I'm sending out a team of cars – all in radio contact with each other. They will also stop any vehicles they find travelling at this hour. On top of that the DDR is plastered with posters of Newman . . .'

'If it was Newman. You told me you'd had reports from your people at Hamburg Airport. No sign that the man who travelled under his name has returned. He could be in London.'

'He could be.' Wolf sounded unconvinced. 'But Tweed is a tricky man.'

He reached for the phone and gave a stream of orders, his voice a flat monotone.

The night was still, soundless, the air heavy. Beyond the man-high reeds and bulrushes the lake was a large expanse of black nothingness, like a vast parade ground of tar.

They had driven the Chaika as close as they could. Now Newman and Falken were heaving out the canvas-wrapped corpse. It seemed to have grown heavier, as though the body had already swollen up. Gerda stood on guard a hundred metres back, holding the Uzi, head cocked to one side as she listened.

'This is a bloody nightmare,' Newman said. 'I'll take the head and you handle the feet.' The bundle lay on the hard earth outside the car. They lifted it and the body sagged in the middle. Gerda had told them that at this point the lake went straight down, thirty metres deep.

They staggered under their burden. One of the links of the chains slipped, made a rasping noise like a death rattle. They nearly jumped out of their skins.

'Keep moving,' Newman gasped. He just wanted to get rid of the thing, to get back into the car. They reached the edge of the black water and Falken called out a warning. The ground had become slippery mud. They stood still and lowered the body to the ground, resting for a moment. They had to heave it as far out as possible. Falken was sceptical of Gerda's assertion that the lake sheered straight down at the edge.

'Ready?' Newman called out.

At her listening post Gerda frowned. She could hear traffic noises on the distant highway. One vehicle. An interval. Then a second. Another interval. A third. A strange time of night for traffic. Most people went to bed early. There was nothing to do, nowhere to go during the early hours in the DDR.

Newman and Falken began swinging the bundle back and forth as much as they could manage. Like a child's swing, gradually going higher. Their night vision was good now and they watched each other. Newman nodded. They'd drop it if they didn't do the job now. They let go.

The late Mr Schneider sailed out over the lake, dropped with a heavy splash into the water, then stayed there, only half-submerged. Something flew out of the reeds, slammed into Falken, almost knocking him down. There was a honking sound. Newman stared as Falken's arms moved with the agility of urgency. God, what was it?

Falken came forward. His right arm was coiled round the neck of a huge goose, his hand clasping it behind the nape of its neck. He stopped a few feet from Newman. It had a pink beak, pink webbed feet. It was honking like mad, making enough noise to wake half the district it seemed to Newman. Falken made odd sounds and Newman realized he was talking to the thing, quietening it.

'A grey lag,' Falken told him. 'In England they'd call it an Eastern Grey Lag. You have the Western variety. See the ring on its leg? It has escaped from one of the sanctuaries.'

'What the devil is happening?' Gerda had come running down the beaten pathway. 'What is it?' Falken repeated what he had told Newman.

'We will keep it,' he said. 'As long as I hold it like this, there is no danger of your being pecked while driving,' he assured Newman.

'Why take that with us?' Gerda demanded.

'Camouflage. If we are stopped. I do belong to the Conservation Service. In any case I would want to rescue it. One wing is slightly injured. It needs attention.'

'And why, therefore,' Gerda demanded, her voice pitched higher than normal, 'are we hanging about?'

'Because of that,' Newman replied, pointing to the lake.

The goose had quietened down. On the surface of the lake the canvas-wrapped body floated, still only half-submerged. Gerda stared in horror. God, was it going to stay like that? The same thought was in the mind of the two men as they stood and gazed at the floating hump.

It was suddenly terribly silent. The goose remained still in Falken's grip. Then the hump rolled away from them, sliding slowly below the surface. There was a ripple – no more – marking where it had descended to the depths. The ripple also vanished and the black water was again smooth as a sheet of oil.

Gerda gasped with relief. 'Let's go. Now. Get away from all this . . .'

*

'We shall soon be at Radom's farm,' Gerda called out from the back of the car. 'And I've just remembered – they have geese. Won't there be a problem with Pinky?'

Pinky was the nickname she had given to the grey lag. Newman was behind the wheel as they drove on along the deserted highway through the night. Falken, sitting beside him, still held the goose in the same manner, its beak turned away from Newman. It seemed quite happy with Falken and hadn't honked once since they'd got back inside the Chaika.

Newman guided the car round a long bend. Beyond it was a long straight stretch. Red lights, winking, stood in the highway about half a kilometre ahead. He reduced speed, staring at the lights. Three cars, nose to bumper, were parked across the full width of the highway.

'Trouble,' Newman said as the red lights came closer.

'Road block,' Falken commented. 'Checkpoint. Who are they looking for, I wonder?'

Thirty

Munzel was feeling pleased with himself. He had provided himself with good cover. Just by keeping his eyes open, by taking the opportunity when it presented itself. Now he felt safe. In Lübeck. In Travemünde. He thought about the police. Up yours!

Boarding the train at Puttgarden, he had wandered slowly along the corridor, looking for an empty compartment. He had passed one with only a girl inside when the idea came to him. From her way of dressing he could tell she was German. And a brunette. Not a blonde.

As he'd glanced in she'd looked up. She'd more than looked – she'd held his stare, then looked slowly away. One knapsack on the rack above her pretty head. He went back, opened the door.

'Do you mind if I sit in here?' he had asked at his most polite, giving her an engaging smile.

'Please do. I'm only going to Lübeck. Then you can have the compartment to yourself.'

'But I'm going to Lübeck too . . .'

Heaving his backpack on to a corridor seat, he'd sat opposite her. He put himself out to be amusing, to make her laugh. She liked the look of him, he could tell.

'I'm a trainee for hotel management at a place in Hamburg,' she told him. 'I've just come down from Copenhagen. It is so nice there – but the last week I thought I'd like some German food . . .'

She was small and slim with a good figure and a fine pair of legs. She wore jeans and a flowered blouse. A red windcheater lay on the seat beside her.

Ten minutes before they reached Lübeck he had persuaded her to team up with him. She had laid down conditions. A room of her own. Naturally, he had agreed. His mind churned. That presented a problem when he registered at a hotel. He wanted the best possible cover, re-entering Lübeck. Then he had his brainwave.

Alighting at the Hauptbahnhof, he asked Lydia Fischer if she would watch his backpack while he phoned his parents. There were no police in the entrance hall as he went inside a booth and dialled Martin Vollmer's number. Vollmer immediately asked where he had been. 'I took a vacation,' Munzel snapped. Code terminology for going into hiding. 'Any news of Tweed?' he'd continued. 'I'm back in Lübeck.' Vollmer had said no, and would Munzel call in daily at noon?

Munzel chose the nearest hotel, the International, across the street from the station. Inside the reception hall he left Lydia with his backpack in a chair and walked to the reception counter. The night clerk looked sleepy and bored.

He registered as Mr and Mrs Claus Kramer, explained he had just caught a dose of the flu which he didn't want to pass on to his wife, so he booked two rooms – a double for himself, a single for his wife. When he'd got beyond the infectious stage they'd both occupy the double. The clerk showed no interest in his explanation and reached for two keys.

They had eaten in the hotel dining-room. The place wasn't cheap but Munzel had wads of money, mostly 100-DM notes. No travellers' cheques. After the meal Lydia had said she was tired and she had gone straight to bed. Munzel had a drink in the bar and went to bed himself.

Now, lying in bed, he couldn't sleep. He felt exhilarated, an arrogant pleasure in his own cleverness. About three weeks earlier clean-shaven Kurt Franck – with a trim haircut – had stayed at the Movenpick by himself. Who would associate the bearded man with the golden locks and the hiker's outfit with Franck? Especially as he had become a couple. Mr and Mrs Kramer – and staying at the International, a mere couple of hundred metres from the Movenpick further up the street? A nice bluff, he congratulated himself. Now all he had to do was phone Vollmer each day. Vollmer had told him they were confident Tweed would be coming back.

He stretched his long thick legs under the duvet, then sat up, swung his feet on to the floor and unstrapped the sheath containing the broad-bladed knife from his leg. This was what had been keeping him awake. He slipped the sheath with the knife inside under his pillow, stretched out again and was asleep in a few minutes.

Inside the room they shared at the Movenpick, Sue Templeton stood naked under the shower, shampooing her blonde hair. She bathed daily and revelled in the hot jets of water spiking her skin. They were stimulating her.

'Ted!' she called out. 'Fetch me a towel. I forgot it . . .'

'You'll forget your pantyhose one of these mornings.' Handing her the towel, he felt her grasp him by the forearm and just had time to slide off his dressing gown before she hauled him inside with her. 'Stupid cow,' he told her. 'But I could get to like it . . .'

'And who didn't want to report that killer to the police?' she teased him. 'I like that too . . .'

'You don't know he's a killer. They just want to question him. Bet you wouldn't recognize him if you ever saw him a second time.'

'Oh, yes I would. Even if he'd grown a beard and wore a false moustache.'

'Stupid cow. Why would he grow his beard and stick on a false moustache?'

250

'I don't know. Men do funny things. You're doing a funny thing now.'

'Serves you right. You shouldn't have pulled me in here.'

'Vopos. People's Police,' Falken said as Newman stopped the car.

Jackets buttoned to the neck, breeches tucked inside leather jackboots, Sam Browne belts which dangled truncheons, holsters sheathing automatic pistols, Newman noted. He felt chilled to the bone – and not with the night air. A fat policeman swaggered towards them, saw Falken holding the goose and stared.

Falken lowered the window with his left hand. The policeman came close to the window and stared inside. Falken released his grip on the goose's neck.

'Papers!' snapped the policeman.

He reached out a pudgy hand. The goose's neck shot out of the window, its mouth open and pecked viciously. The policeman snatched his hand away, took two steps back. Falken coiled his arm round the neck, withdrew the goose inside the car. He smiled.

'Take them out of my left breast pocket,' he invited. 'You can see I can't risk trying to get them.'

'What the hell is it? Why are you carrying that about this time in the morning?'

'Conservation Service. This is a rare grey lag. Escaped from one of my sanctuaries. You can see the ring on its leg. The Minister was very disturbed when he heard we'd lost it. I thought I knew where I might find it. I got lucky. Go on – my left breast pocket . . .'

The policeman wandered round the front of the car. Behind his back some of the half-a-dozen police were grinning. One chuckled aloud. The fat Vopo turned round, glared at them, hoisted his Sam Browne belt higher and unbuttoned the holster flap. He came up on Newman's side.

'Papers,' he snapped again.

'Border Police. Special assignment unit. And we're in a hurry.' He held the folder in his right hand inside the car. The Vopo extended his left hand cautiously. The goose's neck whipped like a cobra past Newman and pecked the Vopo's

251

hand. He yelped, stared at the hand and tucked it under his right armpit. His plump face was suffused with fury. His right hand dropped to his holster, grasped the butt of the automatic.

'I'll shoot that fucking bird . . .'

Falken's manner changed as he again coiled his arm round the goose's neck. His voice was commanding, hectoring. 'Do that and say goodbye to your pension. The Minister can with equanimity replace you – replacing a grey lag is a different matter. I told you! This fowl – it's not a bird – is a very rare specimen. And I warned you. And you'd better get that hand attended to – it could turn septic.'

'Also,' Newman began, 'you're holding me up.' He checked his watch. 'Almost five minutes so far. Do you think I'd be out this time of night if my mission wasn't urgent? Any more delay and I'll take your name, report you. You've seen my folder, you brainless clot!'

The other policemen stood close by, arms folded, grinning. The fat Vopo hesitated. Newman switched on the ignition and waited, his expression bleak. He looked at his watch again, stared at the Vopo.

'These people have been helping me,' he ranted on. 'They know the district. So I help them. Which delayed me. Any more delay and I miss my rendezvous . . .'

The Vopo swore to himself, heard the laughter behind him, swung round in a fury. 'Let them through, you bastards. I want nothing more to do with this lot.'

The driver behind the wheel of the central car blocking the highway moved, leaving clear passage. Newman roared on through the gap, watching his rear view mirror. One of the policemen was walking towards the fat Vopo carrying something. A first aid kit, he guessed. His hands were slippery on the wheel and as he drove he wiped each hand on his trouser leg.

'Oh, thank God for that,' Gerda called out from the back. 'I am trembling all over. Nice grey lag.'

'Camouflage. I told you,' Falken said. 'How far is it now to Radom's place?'

'About ten kilometres from here. Up a side turning to the right. I'll warn you as we approach it.'

'Step on it,' Falken advised Newman. 'Forget the limit. Risk it. Then if they have second thoughts and come after us we'll be off this highway. We'll get a little sleep at Radom's. Then in the morning it's Leipzig. And there we have to be careful.'

'What the blazes do you think we've had to be so far?' Newman responded and put his foot down.

The road-block they had left behind had been re-established, the three cars forming a barrier across the highway. The fat Vopo's injured hand had been sterilized and bandaged by one of his men.

'There, Gustav, now there is no danger of infection.'

'Thank you,' Gustav growled. 'Now take up your position.'

Gustav was fuming. His left hand looked as though he wore a small white boxing glove. And he was well aware that he was unpopular with his men, that they were secretly laughing at him.

He stood by the radio car, wondering whether he should report the incident. He was very reluctant to do so. That blasted goose had made him look such a fool. He could well imagine how they would react back at headquarters if the story of his mishap reached them. He'd be a laughing stock for weeks.

And he was fed up anyway. Like his men he had been got out of bed to carry out this screwy patrol. All of them were still half-asleep, tired and unenthusiastic as he was. The goose had given them something to joke about. Before they went off duty he'd warn them to keep their mouths shut – otherwise they'd find themselves doing a lot more night duty. He moved away from the radio car. No, he wouldn't send in any report.

'Gustav, another car is coming,' called out the Vopo who had attended to his hand.

From the same direction as the goose car. Gustav felt in his pocket with his right hand. His fingers closed round a wad of forged notes he'd taken off a shopkeeper. He watched the headlights come closer, slowing down. If this was nobody important, he'd plant the notes on him and 'find' them, then arrest the driver. *That* he would report – which would drive out of his men's heads the goose car incident. Releasing the notes, taking his hand out of his pocket, he adjusted his peaked cap. Gustav, member of the People's Police, protector of the proletariat, knew how to take care of himself.

*

253

The Chaika was parked in the side road. Gerda had left Newman and Falken with the vehicle while she walked to the farm to warn Radom they were coming. She approached the heavy five-barred gate which was closed and the only entrance between a high hedge.

The first light of dawn was streaking the eastern sky, shafts of fiery and unseen sun. The honking started before she reached the gate despite the lightness of her tread. More and more honking murdered the quiet. She paused by the gate as the geese kept up their chorus. A stooped, wide-shouldered figure holding a shotgun appeared.

'Ulrich,' she called out, 'it's Gerda. That is you?'

'Who else would it be?' Radom replied in a deep voice. 'Come in. The geese are penned up.'

'Falken is waiting down the road. With a friend. A friend who has no name. We have a car, a Chaika.'

'Lousy Russian car. Bring them in. Drive the car into the yard close to the house. Hildegarde is up. You need food?'

'I think so. I will fetch them . . .'

The gate was open when Newman drove the car inside. In the dark a stooping figure closed the gate as soon as he had taken it into the yard. Gerda guided him to an old single-storey farmhouse with a roof angled like a ski-slide. Radom came up to the car, said something to Gerda so rapidly in German that Newman couldn't get the gist.

'Follow him. You have to drive round the back.'

Newman crawled after the stooped figure, hobbling along at a surprising pace. He passed an ancient and monster-sized farm tractor with a high seat. Radom led them round the back of the long farmhouse, along a track across a field and into a hollow surrounded with trees.

'You leave it here,' Gerda whispered.

It was the dark making her talk so softly. The honking of the geese ceased the moment he switched off the engine. In Falken's arms the grey lag was alert and watchful, switching its pink bill from side to side.

'He can sense the other geese,' Falken said as they alighted. 'We sleep here until mid-morning,' he told Newman. 'We must be as fresh and alert as possible when we enter Leipzig.'

254

Inside the low-roofed farmhouse Newman blinked in the strong light. He was amazed to see that Radom had to be at least eighty years old, a powerfully-built man with a grizzled chin and sharp eyes. A slightly younger woman, dressed in a long apron with a mass of grey hair and hawk-like features stood cooking something which had a cheesy aroma on an old-fashioned stove. She was introduced as Hildegarde by Gerda while Radom disappeared back into the yard. A few moments later there was a grinding roar.

'What the devil is that?' Newman asked as Falken settled himself in a basket chair with the grey lag.

'Radom starting up the tractor. He will drive it over any of the wheel tracks the Chaika made. They will disappear. In case the Vopos come to search for us here. That horrible fat one may report our presence. He had a radio car.'

The room was very long, oblong in shape with a large wooden table in the centre, a table large enough to serve twenty people, a table with its surface scrubbed spotless. They were seated together by an open fireplace where birch logs burned and crackled. Hildegarde was cooking her cheese dish at the other end of the room, out of earshot.

'I don't like this,' Newman told Falken firmly. 'I don't like it at all . . .'

'Don't like what, my friend?'

'Staying here for even a short time – endangering the lives of this old couple. It's not right. I want to move on. Now!'

'For many hours we have had no sleep, no food, nothing to drink. It is essential we have these things,' Falken snapped. 'Sleep, after food and drink . . .'

'You don't give a damn, do you? If they were younger it would be different. Someone has to run the underground. I understand that. But,' Newman continued vehemently, 'I refuse to be a party to risking this old couple. I want to leave. Now!'

'You don't understand at all . . .'

'Explain it – if you can.'

'We are all very fatigued . . .'

'Stick to the bloody point,' Newman rasped, keeping his voice down.

'Of all the people I work with, Ulrich Radom is the

255

most reliable, the cleverest. Look how he is using the tractor to . . .'

'I know about that. All right, he's very careful. Good for him. Now *you* be careful – get us out of here . . .'

'If you will just keep quiet and let me finish my explanation you may see it differently . . .'

'Then get on with your explanation. But make it quick.'

Falken's lips tightened. He opened his mouth to speak, to hit back, his eyes furious, when Gerda leaned forward and laid her hand on his knee.

'Emil,' she said quietly, using Newman's new identity, 'is entitled to his explanation. Calm down. Tell him . . .'

'Another thing,' Newman interjected, 'supposing the Vopos do arrive in force. We can't get away from here.'

'But we can,' Falken contradicted. 'Why do you think the car is parked in that hollow? Because there is another way out from the farm – across the fields by a sunken road leading to another side lane. From the lane we drive back down to the highway.'

'And you think the Vopos won't hear the Chaika being driven away!'

For the first time since they had met he began to doubt Falken's judgement. The German was near the end of his resources. He was losing his sense of perspective.

'The Vopos will not hear the Chaika,' Falken said. 'If – and I hope it does not happen – they arrive, you will see. And when we sleep we all sleep in our clothes and with our shoes on. Ready for instant departure.'

'Fine! Just dandy.' Newman's tone dripped sarcasm. 'What is to prevent these Vopos bursting in on us before we have a chance to reach the Chaika? Tell me that.'

'The geese,' Falken replied.

'It could be someone else. Not Vopos. One of his neighbours.'

'He has none. No neighbours. No friends. He has deliberately cultivated the reputation of being a man who hates and distrusts everyone. When people did call he met them with a shotgun. That soon discouraged idle visitors. If the geese honk, the Vopos are coming. And they will hear them a long way off. Time enough for us to leave. Now, maybe you will use your mouth for eating the excellent meal I see Hildegarde has laid for us? Yes?'

Newman sat at the table, still not completely convinced. Radom had finished using his tractor and came in to sit with them. His wife sat in a basket chair and watched them, hands clasped placidly in her lap.

'Cheese soup,' said Gerda.

'It's wonderful,' Newman replied, spooning more of the liquid out of the bowl. His stomach reacted to the warmth, the tension gradually faded. Gerda watched him.

'Try your drink,' she suggested with an impish smile.

'What is it?'

'Try it.'

He picked up his glass, swallowed a mouthful, then choked and waved his mouth. His mouth, throat, stomach felt to be in flames. Gerda poured him water. He drank a large portion, set down the second glass.

'What the hell is that stuff?'

She giggled. He made a playful gesture of punching her. She giggled again. He took a more cautious sip. It was very good, again relaxing his insides, once he got it down.

'Schierker Feuerstein,' she said. 'Fire water. From the Harz mountains. Like the cheese soup. Once the Radoms lived in the Harz. The drink is good? Yes? No?'

'Fire water is the word for the stuff.'

'After this meal you will feel a different man. You will wish you had a willing girl . . .'

'Gerda!' Falken frowned, indicating Hildegarde with his eyes.

'It is good that we now all talk in a more friendly manner,' she remarked. 'Emil will sleep like a dog – providing he drinks all his fire water.'

'I'm beginning to fall asleep now,' said Newman, pushing away the huge bowl. 'No, thank you,' he said to Hildegarde. 'I am full. I couldn't take any more. It was marvellous.'

She had hurried to the table to serve more; now she replaced the spoon inside the soup tureen and covered it with the lid. Before Falken had started his meal Radom had collected the grey lag and taken it away.

'He's putting it in a separate coop, away from his own geese,'

257

Falken had explained. 'I will collect it later. Never use the same stratagem twice. The fat Vopo may have reported that there was a goose in the car. Now, to bed. Mid-morning we have to be up, on our way.'

Newman shared a small room which had two single beds with Falken. First, they shaved to make themselves presentable. 'There may be no time later,' Falken warned. 'And don't even take off your shoes.'

Lying under the duvet in the darkened room which faced west, Newman listened to Falken's even breathing in the other bed. The German had fallen fast asleep. Newman tossed restlessly, uncomfortable in his clothes and shoes. He'd have given anything for a bath. His stomach felt a great deal happier – the huge quantity of soup he had consumed had driven the chill from his bones.

He sank into a troubled doze, feeling now the full pressure of being a hunted man, a man deep inside the DDR and Lord knew how many kilometres from the Western border. Images floated into his disturbed mind.

Crossing the minefield belt . . . meeting the East German agent coming from the opposite direction . . . the mist drifting through the dark forest after he'd met Falken . . . headlights glaring . . . the first encounter with Schneider . . . the damp lock-keeper's cottage . . . the nerve-chilling moment when Gerda re-entered the cottage followed by Schneider aiming his Walther . . . the killing of the German . . . the body which obstinately refused to sink beneath the dark silent lake . . . the honking of geese.

'Get up, Emil! Quick! The Vopos are coming.'

Falken was shaking him roughly by the shoulder. Newman blinked. The honking of the geese was for real. Broad daylight was flooding through the windows. We are trapped was his first reaction . . .

Three hours earlier Wolf had been surprised to see Lysenko arriving in his office. Freshly-shaven, below his bushy eyebrows his eyes were alert, there was a spring in his step as he threw his outer coat over a chair. He stared at the trestle bed pushed against one wall, the blankets neatly folded back.

258

'What is that for?' he asked.

'I've had a nap. In an emergency I sleep on the job.' Wolf gave a wintry smile. 'Oddly enough, I understand Tweed in London does the same thing at a time of crisis. I know that man's habits as well as my own.'

'Fresh developments? I see you've put up a wall map.'

'Yes. Come and look at it . . .'

It was a large-scale map of both West and East Germany, extending to the Baltic in the north. Pins with red-coloured plastic heads had been pressed into the map. A red crayon had been used to circle a certain area.

'Why the pins?' Lysenko asked crisply, scratching his chin.

'They identify the points where incidents have occurred since the traitors in that watchtower short-circuited the electricity. This pin is the watchtower, this one where Schneider stopped two men on bicycles. This one where a patrol discovered Schneider's abandoned truck in a hollow by the side of the highway.'

'When did you learn this?'

'The report came in over two hours ago. A pattern is forming, a route . . .'

'And the red circle?'

'The area where I have sent out fresh patrols to search every building – every cottage, farmhouse, isolated barn. Anywhere fugitives might spend the night. I did not spend long in bed,' he went on. 'A report has also come in from Erwin Munzel. He has surfaced. In Lübeck. He is waiting there for Tweed to come back.'

'You seem confident he will do that . . .'

'I know Tweed. He never gives up. As soon as he is on his way I shall know. From Balkan at Park Crescent.'

'And that route you said the fugitives were following. Where does it lead to?'

'Here. Leipzig. I am sure of it. Look at the pins again. They must have killed Schneider – he would have reported in long before now. That is the most positive evidence of all. And I have flooded Leipzig with patrols, many in plain clothes. We are going to catch these people on our own doorstep!'

*

The honking of the geese was a deafening chorus which went on and on. Newman followed Falken into the living-room as Hildegarde slipped past them into the bedroom. 'She is making up our beds,' Falken said quickly.

Newman paused in the large living-room, glancing round for any sign of their visit. On the metal worktop beside the old-fashioned stoneware sink stood two dirty soup bowls and two glass tumblers. *Two*, not three. The relics of the Radoms' breakfast, apparently. Hildegarde had washed up Gerda's bowl and glass. The three glasses which had contained Harz fire-water had also disappeared.

'Come on!' Falken called out as Gerda appeared. 'Move. Out the back way . . .'

They followed Falken who led them through a doorway at the rear of the farm, running along the track over which Newman had driven the Chaika. Gerda was close behind, clutching the windcheater, concealing the Uzi machine-pistol.

The sky was cloudless, the sun shone down and the August heat was building up. Newman found he was sweating as he ran, with effort or fear, he wasn't sure which. They reached the Chaika in the hollow and Falken climbed behind the wheel, Gerda slipped into the back and Newman sat alongside Falken who remained still, making no effort to start the engine. In the distance the honking of the geese reached new heights of indignation.

'What the hell are you waiting for?' Newman demanded.

'Radom's diversion.'

'Which is?'

'Listen . . .'

He had hardly spoken when from the far side of the farm-house came a roar, the explosive bursts of an exhaust pipe, the wild throbbing of an engine which sounded as though it was on the verge of bursting out of its casing. Falken smiled, started his own motor and drove forward up the gentle incline out of the hollow and down the other side into a sunken lane.

In the front yard Radom was perched on the high seat of his monster of a farm tractor, clashing the gears, revving up the motor as three cars appeared. The first vehicle drove straight through the closed gate, hurling it into the yard, followed by the other two cars. The motorcade stopped, doors were flung open, Vopos spilled into the yard, several heading for an old barn, others running inside the farmhouse.

The leader of the patrol ran up to the tractor, shouted up to Radom, who waved one hand helplessly. The engine sound increased as he clashed gears. The machine jerked backwards. The Vopo waved his hand, gesturing behind the tractor which was backing at speed towards one of the parked cars. Radom moved more levers, the tractor stopped with a back-breaking jerk, inches away from the car, then surged forward. The Vopo swore, jumped back out of its way.

'*Kaput!* Out of control! Can't stop it,' Radom shouted down at the Vopo.

The Vopo moved to the rear, searching for a way to climb on to the tractor. The rear exhaust belched a jet of fumes into his face. He backed off, choking, eyes watering, grabbed for his handkerchief as the tractor began to move in a circle and Radom moved the levers again. The honking of the geese was completely drowned by the appalling roar and thunder.

Falken had driven the Chaika almost to the end of the sunken lane. He turned right on to the deserted country road leading back to the highway. Then he accelerated, slowing only at the bends.

'You see,' he said to Newman, 'why I say Radom is one of my most reliable allies? The Vopos will never have heard this car leaving above the sound of that racket. And I tell you something else. Radom and his wife will make the lives of the Vopos a misery. They will be glad to clear out.'

'How? Apart from that deafening row?'

'The Vopos may well be thirsty – it is a hot day. They'll get nothing to drink. Hildegarde will see to that.'

'Again, how?'

'As soon as she'd made up the three beds – which would take her no time at all – she'll have turned off the water at the main. Very hard to find, the mains tap. She'll tell them something's gone wrong with the water supply. No milk. The cows haven't been milked – they drank what there was for their breakfast. No Harz fire water. That is locked away in a concealed cupboard. No nothing . . .'

'But something for us,' Gerda called out. 'Bless her, the old saint.'

'What's that?' Newman called over his shoulder.

'A basket with a cloth over it. Black bread. Canned food and fruit. A thermos of coffee. She must have prepared this and brought it out to the car while we slept. We can survive for another day without going near a shop. There's even a large bottle of mineral water, some paper cups.'

'A remarkable couple,' Newman said. 'But I worry about them. If they play up those Vopos they could turn rough, wreck the farm.'

'Then they will get the surprise of their lives,' Falken commented. 'Radom won't tell them, but he has influence in high places. His farm should have been merged long ago with a collective. His protector stopped that.'

'And who is this benefactor?'

'A man called Markus Wolf.' Falken chuckled. 'Wolf has one weakness. His stomach. He likes good country food – fresh eggs, butter, fowl. Radom provides it. Those Vopos make the wrong move and they end up working in a labour battalion.'

'Pull up,' Newman said suddenly. 'Isn't that the highway?'

'Yes.' Falken had stopped the car. 'Why?'

'Because I'm taking over the wheel. I'm Border Police. And you're both risking your necks for me. But before we change places, I want to know what's waiting for me. This witness – who is she?'

'We are close enough now to tell you. She was the nursing sister at the hospital for tropical diseases where Dr Berlin arrived twenty-odd years ago when he returned from Africa – because he was afflicted with a rare tropical disease, they said.'

'Go on.'

'Karen Piper – that is her name – was attached to the private ward Dr Berlin occupied. Eventually she became what you would call in England the matron. What she will tell you will come as a great shock. Now, if you insist, we change places.'

They had turned on to the broad highway when Falken made his remark. 'I have a feeling we are going to be lucky in Leipzig.'

'Why then,' asked Gerda, 'does my woman's intuition tell me we are driving into terrible danger?'

Thirty-One

No way could they approach Hawkswood Farm stealthily, parking the Cortina some distance from it and walking the last few hundred yards, as they had with Masterson's Clematis Cottage. The flatlands of the Wash spread away from it in all directions.

'Where is the sea?' Diana asked as Tweed stopped the car by the picket gate.

'Over there, beyond the dyke.'

At ten o'clock in the morning the great bank shimmered in the haze. The sun was high in a vault of cloudless blue. It was going to be another hot day but the air was fresh with a tang of salt from the invisible Wash. The funnel and superstructure of a small cargo vessel appeared, seemed to glide along the top of the dyke.

'Heading for King's Lynn,' Tweed said as he opened the door and alighted at the same moment as Hugh Grey appeared round the side of the farmhouse, a Labrador panting at his heels with its tongue out. Wearing an immaculate check sports jacket, powder blue slacks, a striped shirt and a plain matching powder blue tie, he looked extremely fit.

'Welcome to World's End,' he called out to Tweed, looking at Diana with interest.

Tweed made brief introductions as the raven-haired Paula opened the front door and stood very still. Grey took Diana by the arm as though she might stumble and Tweed saw Paula's mouth tighten. She shook hands with Diana with an expressionless face and led the way into the farmhouse. Oh Lord, Tweed thought, she's taken agin her already. Grey made no pretence of concealing that the reverse was the case with him.

'I was just taking Charles for walkies,' he announced, pink-faced like a cherub. 'Fancy a breath of fresh air, Diana? We can have coffee when we get back . . .'

'That would be nice.' Diana clutched her handbag under her arm and smiled warmly.

'We'll expect you in a couple of hours then,' Paula remarked, her face still blank.

'Oh, we shan't be that long, darling. Just taking Charles for a short trot.'

It would be Charles, Tweed thought as he settled himself in the same arm chair he'd occupied on his previous visit. The name somehow went with any dog Grey would own.

'Expect you when we see you,' Paula replied. She was pouring coffee from a brown earthenware pot. The front door banged shut as she went on. 'This is fresh coffee, Mr Tweed. You just happened to arrive when I'd made it.'

'It smells very good . . .'

'And who is the *femme fatale* you brought with you this time?'

The coffee cup wobbled in the saucer as she handed it to Tweed. She nearly spilt some but he took it from her in time. She was trembling. Whether with fear or fury he couldn't decide. Had their arrival coincided with the mother and father of a row?

He didn't think so. Grey was good at concealing his emotions, but he'd seemed perfectly normal when he appeared. None of the little signs Tweed could have detected if there had been trouble. Puzzled, Tweed sipped his coffee, working out his reply. The ploy that Diana might be coming to work for them didn't seem tactful, considering Paula's reaction of instant dislike.

'She's the sister of a friend,' he said. 'She's got a bit of holiday and has never seen this part of the world. You like sporting prints, I see.' He glanced at the framed pictures on the walls.

'I hate the bloody things. Makes the place look like a pub. Hugh says they go with the farmhouse, give the place the sort of atmosphere visitors will expect.'

She spoke as though Hugh had arranged the whole farmhouse like a stage set. Decorated with the right props. Tweed recalled he'd lived here with his first wife. Perhaps Paula had tried to effect some changes and he'd resisted her ideas. He found the theory unconvincing. But she'd given him the opening he was looking for.

'Somebody – can't remember now who it was – referred to that party you held here about two years ago. The date July 14 sticks in my mind . . .'

Over the rim of her cup her face froze. She stared back at him, her eyes very still. 'You do have a good memory, Tweed. I suppose you need it in your job. It was Hugh's birthday. We had some of his colleagues here. Harry Masterson, Guy Dalby and The Professor – Erich Lindemann. It was quite an evening. Broke up in a quarrel. They'd had far too much to drink. And they all drove home afterwards. Lucky none of them were stopped by the police. Except for Lindemann, of course.'

'Why Lindemann?'

'Didn't you know? He's teetotal. Never drinks anything but fruit juice and coffee. Bit of a dry stick. Doesn't drink, doesn't smoke. Hasn't any interest in women.'

'You mentioned a quarrel,' Tweed probed gently.

'Oh, yes. I'd better set the stage for you. Harry Masterson drank half a bottle of whisky, then went on to wine and liqueurs. Guy – Dalby – sat quietly consuming a large quantity of white wine. Frankly, Hugh was well away, too. They left very late – we have nowhere to put people up. I did suggest they could kip down in the sitting-room here, but they refused. Near the end of the meal Hugh – he's ambitious, you know – started asking his guests what they expected out of life. Fishing for information. We weren't married then, just living together. Harry got very aggressive, Guy was argumentative. I went to bed and left them to it.'

'When did they eventually leave?'

'Between about one and two in the morning. All separately. You seem very interested in a two-year-old party . . .'

'It was the quarrel which intrigued me.'

She jumped up. 'God, I've forgotten the cakes. What a rotten hostess I am. No. You must try them. Please. Home-made. I'd like your opinion. New recipe . . .'

She disappeared beyond the door into the kitchen. He sat holding his cup while she was gone. What was the girl's name? The one Inspector Cresswell at King's Lynn police station had told him had been brutally murdered. In the early hours of the morning of July 14. Carole Langley. That was it.

He looked up as Paula came back with a plate of macaroons

and offered them. He took one to be polite and she sat down again.

'As you see, they're macaroons, not cakes. I'm not with it this morning. I nearly burnt myself making those.'

'Very good. I like the flavour. Oh, you referred to my companion as a *femme fatale* . . .'

'Which was very rude of me. The point is I drove up to town yesterday afternoon to meet Hugh. We were in Knightsbridge about fourish and saw someone just like her. Hugh said, "I do believe that's Diana Chadwick." When I asked who she was he said she was a friend of one of his staff at the Frankfurt office.'

And you didn't believe him, Tweed thought. All part of your hiring Portman to investigate your husband. He understood now Paula's hostility. *Bringing that woman into my home, taking her out for a walk on your own as soon as she sets foot over the threshold.*

She offered another macaroon and he took one.

'These are really excellent. Stick to your new recipe. We were talking about your party. I'll bet you didn't get a lot of sleep that night.'

'You're right. I lay in bed tossing and turning, listening to them going at it hammer and tongs. Again, except for Lindemann. He never said a word . . .'

'How did it break up then? You said they left separately.'

'Harry Masterson must have driven off about one, as far as I can remember. Shortly afterwards Lindemann went. I'd got up to go to the bathroom and I watched from the window. Just because I couldn't sleep. Dalby drove off at 1.30 a.m. I do know that because I looked at my watch. Then I flopped into bed and slept and slept.' She stared at the front door, made a warning gesture. 'Shush! They're coming back . . .'

Tweed was surprised. She had even more acute hearing than his own. Probably the familiar creak of a gate. The door opened, Diana came in, and immediately Tweed knew something was wrong. Her normally white face had a flush of anger. Grey was beaming, casual and assured as always. Tweed stood up.

'Hugh, could you stand another breath of fresh air? I've had no exercise since I got up.'

'Be my guest.' He grinned. 'Come to think of it, you are!'

Charles sprawled on a rug, mouth open, panting. They left

him behind as Grey led the way, opening the gate and turning left.

'Fancy a walk to the dyke? A look-see at the Wash?'

'Suits me. Hugh, there's something I wanted to talk to you about . . .'

'Guessed as much. You never leave business behind, do you? You ought to learn to relax, have some fun.' He looked sideways at Tweed. 'Or maybe at long last you are having fun – with Diana. Dishy. Just what the doctor ordered for you . . .'

'Did you,' Tweed persisted, 'or did you not have me followed while I was in Germany?'

'As a matter of fact, I did. Put two of my best men on the job. I thought you needed some protection. I didn't know you had Newman escorting you. They tracked you to Lübeck and Travemünde. After all,' he went on defensively, 'you were in my sector. I felt responsible. And you were near Dr Berlin. The BND people are worried about him.'

'Why?'

They continued walking along the smooth-surfaced tarred road elevated above the surrounding fields while Grey considered his reply. Arriving at a small track, they turned off the road to the left, heading towards the distant dyke.

'They have him under surveillance because he came from Leipzig. Nothing definite to go on. About half the time they lose him. He simply vanishes into thin air. My men were aboard that ferry you took to Priwall Island to attend his party. They got no further than the gate. No invitation cards.'

'You have been a busy little bee . . .'

'I repeat, you were in my sector. If it had been Howard I would have done the same thing. You're right on the edge of the border there, you know.'

'I know.'

Tweed said nothing more as they strolled on under the blazing sun. They came to the end of the track. To their right stood a lonely farmhouse, smaller than Grey's. No sign of life. Grey led the way up a rise and down the other side. The track narrowed to a small uneven path strewn with humps of grass.

The dyke loomed closer. They walked in single file, Grey in the lead, the path was so narrow, dropping into a ditch on either side. Grey suddenly broke into a run, leaping up the steep landward side of the dyke. Standing on the top his hair was blown by a breeze offshore. Tweed joined him at a more leisurely pace.

'Most people never see this.' Grey was at his most buoyant, waving both arms wide to embrace the view. 'The peace of it all is truly magnificent. World's end . . .'

Below them a steep path descended to an area of mud-flats and snaking creeks, winding in and out of the marshland. An ancient landing-stage had been reinforced with fresh timbers. Beyond, the vast expanse of the Wash stretched away to the horizon, a blue sea which went on and on until it reached the continent.

It was very calm, water without a ripple. The breeze no longer blew. Not a vessel in sight. The surface was smooth as a lake of oil. It looked as though you could safely walk across it. Grey took in a deep breath, spread his arms again.

'The freshest air on the planet.'

'Hugh,' Tweed said quietly.

'Yes?'

'If I return to Hamburg you will under no circumstances put any of your streetwalkers on my track.'

Streetwalkers was Park Crescent jargon for shadows, trackers. Grey dropped his arms, stiffened with resentment. Then he lifted his hands in a theatrical gesture of resignation.

'If you say so.'

'I do. Now, we'd better get back.'

Grey ran down the side of the dyke. Tweed glanced back before he followed. Along the edges of the creeks were areas of murky soft mud mingling with sand. Sinister islets of green sedge peered above the mud. Quicksands.

All the way back to Hawkswood Farm neither man exchanged one word with the other. If anything Grey's face was even pinker than normal, flushed with annoyance at Tweed's rebuke.

Diana and Paula were engaged in the over-polite conversation adopted by two women who disliked each other. Tweed heard a snatch as they entered the farmhouse and Grey said he had to go to the bathroom and would be back in a minute.

'So you don't really like England as it is today?' Paula was saying. 'May I ask why?'

'I read an article once by Jimmy Goldsmith, I think it was, and he said it all. The trouble with Britain today is the breakdown of the caste system. No one knows where they are any more.'

'And that was how life was in Kenya?' Paula enquired sweetly. 'A nice cosy caste system? The natives knew their place?'

'They did before 1963. Then came independence and the rot set in . . .'

'How perfectly rotten,' Paula commented, sipping more coffee.

'Indeed, yes.' Diana gave her warmest smile. 'Massacre everywhere. Mugabe in Rhodesia, Idi Amin in Uganda. You name it.' She looked up. 'Enjoy your constitutional, Tweedy?'

'Is that what it was?' Tweed broke the surface tension with a rueful smile, sagging into his arm chair. He raised his hands in mock horror, including Paula. 'Fresh air. Smells most odd. If you don't mind we'll have to push off soon.'

'Nothing doing!' Hugh returned from the bathroom full of joy and bounce. 'You're staying to lunch. Paula can rustle up a bit of a meal. Can't you, darling?'

'I love the way men talk of rustling up a meal,' Diana said archly. 'Just as though we snap our fingers. Hey presto! A meal appears as though by magic.'

'You're welcome to stay,' Paula responded without great enthusiasm. 'And since this is my shopping day and I haven't done any yet, Hugh can take us to The Duke's Head in King's Lynn. Can't you, dear?'

Tweed stood up, shook his head. 'Very kind. But we have an appointment in London. Thank you both. And the macaroons were a delight.'

'Wave you off then,' Grey suggested. 'Next time we'll lay on a feast.' Tweed noticed that as they were leaving he did not take Diana's arm, was careful not to touch her after she'd thanked Paula.

They settled themselves inside the car while Hugh and Paula stood apart at the gate. As Tweed began to drive away he saw in the rear view mirror Hugh still standing there, both hands clasped above his head in a boxer's salute. The soul of self-

269

assurance to the end. Paula had gone back inside the farmhouse.

'Were you in the vicinity of Knightsbridge yesterday afternoon?' Tweed asked as he drove away from the Wash towards King's Lynn.

'Yes. I told you I was going to Harrods . . .'

'Any idea what time?'

'About four o'clock. Why?'

'Hugh and Paula saw you. That is, Hugh saw you and pointed you out to Paula.'

'But how on earth would he know who I was?'

'From a photo. Now, be a good girl, don't ask any more questions.'

She made a moue, asked if she could switch on the radio, did so when Tweed nodded. She lapsed into unaccustomed silence as Tweed thought. He guessed what had happened. The two men Grey had used to follow him – he'd noticed them on the Priwall ferry – had secretly taken photos. Including some of Diana. Normal procedure when a subject – himself this time – was under surveillance.

He also knew why Grey had taken this course of action. For his protection! Cobblers! Grey was ambitious, had wanted to grab as much of the credit as he could if Tweed had pulled off some coup. Monica had been right – Hugh Grey was after his job. At least he was efficient. And he'd owned up to having Tweed followed. That was a plus for Grey. It was the sector chief who tried to win the game by concealing information from his superiors who was a menace.

Later he'd omitted to inform Tweed about the taking of photos after he'd been ticked off on the dyke. Again understandable. Why add further blots to his copybook? Tweed realized Diana had not said a word recently. He stopped the car. 'Like to take a last look at it before we drive back to what passes for civilization.'

He lowered the window and the salty air was blown into the car by a breeze. He scanned the vast flatlands, the few dwellings dotted along the roadsides, separated from each other by miles. The great dyke edged the skyline. Now he'd switched off the engine the only sound was that of the whispering grasses, bending in the slight wind.

270

'You're very quiet,' he remarked.

Sensing his mood, that he wanted to drink in the atmosphere, she had switched off the radio when he stopped. It had been playing tango music.

'Hugh Grey made a pass at me while we were talking. He took me down a gulley leading towards the dyke. I told him to go to hell. He wasn't pleased.'

'Hence your flushed face when you arrived back?'

'I tried to conceal it – because of his wife. Paula and I didn't take to each other. Now I think I know why. He chases women and she knows it. We were like a couple of cats, circling round each other while you were out with Grey.'

'I'm sorry. On both counts. I'd hoped you'd enjoy the trip.'

'Don't get into a fuss.' She laid a hand on his arm. 'I've enjoyed the scenery.'

'What did you think of Grey? If you can stand back and forget his outrageous behaviour?'

'Full of his own self-importance, but that could be me just being catty. Very able at his job, I'd guess. Good at operating on his own, capable of taking responsibility. Perhaps a bit impulsive at taking too many initiatives. Ambitious. In a few years he may quieten down. He apologized all the way back to me. I think he was frightened I'd give the game away to his wife. When do we eat?'

'As soon as we can. Somewhere on the way back.' He started the engine and drove off. 'Do switch on the radio again.'

She turned the knob. They were playing another tango. Diana leaned back against the head-rest, half-closed her eyes, began humming the tune softly. Tweed came to the end of the winding country road, turned left on the A17 leading to King's Lynn. He had a call he wanted to make.

'What is that music?' he asked.

'*Jealousy*. A tango that goes back to the twenties as far as I know. Paula's theme tune,' she added wickedly. 'We played it a lot back in the old Kenya days at parties. Don't mind me. I'm indulging in a bout of nostalgia. And you're looking very thoughtful.'

'Paula said something significant to me. A chance remark and I'm damned if I can recall it. Do you mind waiting in the car at King's Lynn?'

271

'Of course not. Looking for somewhere to eat?'

'No. I'm calling at the police station. I have to make an urgent call to the office.'

'Open all hours,' Inspector Cresswell said with a wry smile as Tweed sat opposite him. 'Last time you came I was on night duty. What can I do for you now?'

The short, dark-haired inspector didn't appear to have moved since Tweed last saw him. Except that this time he was smoking a briar pipe. It went with his stolid careful personality.

'Have you got any further with your enquiries into the murder of that girl Carole Langley?'

'You have a good memory for names. I expect it's your job. No fresh developments is the short answer. The file continues to gather dust. What about you?'

'Same answer. No fresh murders, thank God. By the way, when you were investigating the case when it was fresh, did you call on a friend of mine? A Hugh Grey at Hawkswood Farm. Gedney Drove End area – roughly.'

'I know the place.' Cresswell sucked noisily at his pipe. A wet smoker. 'As a matter of fact, I did. Called personally. Had a girl staying with him. They've married since. But you'll know all this.'

'Of course. Any joy?'

'Not a thing. They'd gone to bed early.' Cresswell chuckled but it was not a dirty laugh. 'They're inclined to do that in the early days. Neither of them had heard a sound. No cars passing their place in the early hours. Of course, if by then they were asleep . . .'

'So, no lead there.'

'Or anywhere else.' Cresswell watched Tweed over his pipe. 'It's stretching things a bit, isn't it – to try and link up a murder in East Anglia with yours across the water?'

'It's stretching things a lot,' Tweed agreed as he stood up. 'I'd better be getting on. Thought I'd just call in on you as I was in the area.'

'Very good of you. Maybe we'll see you again.'

'Always possible. Thank you. And goodbye. For now.'

Tweed was relieved as he left the station and climbed behind the wheel. Despite his exuberant bonhomie, Grey had a careful discretion. Obviously he'd not said a word to Cresswell about the party, about the identity of his guests – and persuaded Paula to go along with him. That was important. A murder investigation leading to the heart of the SIS at Park Crescent would have been embarrassing, even dangerous.

'I asked a passer-by,' Diana said, 'if there was a good place to eat here. She suggested The Duke's Head.'

'The Inspector told me the food was awful there,' Tweed lied. There was always the chance one of the staff would remember his last visit to Paula, something he wanted kept secret.

'There's a place at Woburn Abbey on the way back,' he said as he started the motor. 'And, if we can manage it, we'll pay a call on Master Guy Dalby this evening.' He frowned as he drove round the town, following the one-way system, which tripled the distance. 'I do wish I could remember what Paula said. It was a bit odd. . . .'

Thirty-Two

Tweed had left Diana at Newman's flat for a few hours, driving on to Park Crescent. He entered his office, closed the door and stood quite still. Monica sat behind her desk, her head stooped over a file. In Tweed's favourite arm chair Howard lounged, one leg propped on the arm.

'I've waited for you,' he said, which struck Tweed as the unnecessary remark of the year.

As always, Howard was faultlessly dressed. He wore a new navy pinstripe suit, inevitably Chester Barrie from Harrods. His spotless white shirt was bisected by his blue club tie. The cuffs were shot well clear of the sleeves. Gold chased cuff links shaped like slim barrels dangled from the cuffs. The black shoe at the end of his propped leg, which was swinging gently, gleamed as though made of glass.

'Is there a problem?' Tweed enquired as he sat behind his desk.

'Oh, nothing much. Just the fact that one of our four European sector chiefs has to be a rotten egg. Probably in the pocket of Moscow for years. A man you promoted, a man I brought into the Service originally.'

Tweed's expression showed nothing of his astonishment at this statement of co-responsibility. Monica's head shot up in sheer disbelief, then bent over the file again.

'Do you propose to return to Germany again?' Howard asked.

'Possibly. Depends on how things develop.'

'Come to ask you a favour, Tweed. To extract a promise from you.'

'What promise?'

'That when you return you take back-up.' Howard adjusted the plain navy blue display handkerchief in his breast pocket, swung his leg on to the floor and leaned forward. 'I suggest Harry Butler and Pete Nield. Both speak German. Both are good men to have in a tight corner.' He waved a large pink hand in a sweeping gesture. 'Don't care how you handle it. Take 'em with you. Send them on ahead. Up to you. As a favour to me,' he repeated. 'We're right in the shit on this one, aren't we?' He glanced towards Monica. 'Excuse my language.'

'I would say that sums it up, yes,' Tweed agreed, searching for a trap, finding none.

'Position is this. Correct me if I get it wrong. Fergusson went to Hamburg. I was taking a well-earned leave in France.' He smiled in a deprecating manner. 'Only five people knew Fergusson was going. Grey, Masterson, Lindemann, Dalby – and yourself. Fergusson gets the chop soon after arriving. One of our most experienced and cautious men. So they had to know he was coming. Which brings us back to the Frightful Four, one of them at any rate. Isn't that it?'

'That's it.'

'Of course, someone could have read the minute you recorded of the meeting . . .'

'Except that I deliberately made no mention of Fergusson's mission in it . . .'

'Highly irregular.' Howard smiled thinly. 'But the fact that you didn't proves someone's guilt up to the hilt. Pity is we've no idea who that someone is. And by the way, if you don't mind talking about it . . .' Howard sounded utterly weary and

274

he paused, obviously expecting an objection from Tweed. He raised his thick eyebrows when none came and went on. 'I gather you've seen Masterson, Lindemann and Grey so far on home ground, so to speak. Any luck?'

'Too early to say.' Tweed noticed Howard's look of resignation, so he explained. 'When you visit three men in little more than twenty-four hours – in their homes, as you said – the mind takes in a vast number of impressions. It's only after thinking about it later, sorting wheat from chaff, that you know whether you heard – spotted – anything significant. I need longer,' he ended firmly.

'Fair do's.' Howard stood up, brushed a speck of dust from his sleeve, straightened his tie. He paused at the door before he opened it. 'And Butler and Nield will be in attendance?'

'Agreed.'

Monica waited until they were alone, then threw down her pencil with such force the point broke. She sat very erect, tucking in her blouse.

'All the years I've been here, I've never seen him like that.'

'He's worried.'

'Of course he's worried! He knows the PM wants to get shot of him. You refused to take over his job after the Procane business. When this thing breaks – when *you* find who it is – she'll boot him out . . .'

She stopped talking when the door reopened, Howard came in again, closed the door. His manner was apologetic.

'When you find the weevil in the granary I suppose there's no way we can keep it from the press?'

'Let's see what happens,' Tweed replied in his most soothing manner.

'Leave it all to you. Let me know if I can help.'

'There!' Monica burst out when they were alone again. 'What did I tell you? He's sweating out his own position. And why did you agree to Butler and Nield joining you when you return to the continent?'

'Because I may genuinely need them. This thing is getting bigger all the time. And poor Bob Newman may be lost forever.'

'If he's behind the Iron Curtain . . .'

'He's there, all right,' Tweed said grimly. 'I must go now and collect Diana. Time to beard the Dalby in his den. Down in deepest suburbia.'

'You think it's wise to take this Diana Chadwick everywhere?'

'I'm taking her on trust . . .'

'Do that with a woman and you could be in dead trouble. I know my own sex.'

'The thought had already crossed my mind,' Tweed replied and left the office.

Diana walked into the sitting-room of Newman's flat from the bedroom. Tweed was looking at her shorthand notebooks spread out on the elegant dining table.

'I see you're studying English as well as German shorthand. Pitman's,' he remarked.

'I'm getting on very well. I take it down from radio talks. It's not all that difficult. Learning typing is the bore – I've got a portable I hired in the smaller bedroom. I'm thirty words to the minute – typing. With shorthand I'm up to ninety.'

'That's very good. Now, we'd better go. After interviewing Dalby we have to drive back here, then get dinner.'

'How do I look?'

He studied her. She wore a powder-blue dress nipped in round her slim waist and with a mandarin collar. Pale blue stockings and gold shoes. He blinked. She twirled round to give him the full treatment.

'Out of this world,' he pronounced.

She came very close. He caught a whiff of perfume. 'Can we go to the same place for dinner? The one with cubicles just off Walton Street? I'd love the pheasant again.'

'We'll see. If we get moving now we'll just miss rush hour and get down into Surrey before the armadillo cavalcades block the highways.'

'A lot of people living round here,' Diana remarked, waving her ivory cigarette holder.

'Swarms. Commuter country,' Tweed said. 'They all troop to Woking station for their daily ordeal. Best commuter service up to town round London.'

The main road from West Byfleet was tree-lined. Side roads led off. Battalions of newish houses marched into the distance. All to the same pattern. Neo-Georgian. They had open fronts, gardens leading to the sidewalk edge, American-style. They drove on.

'There he is. Dalby.' Tweed pointed with one finger as he turned a corner into a side road. It was the first house. A large porch supported a brace of twin pillars. 'King's Cross Station,' he commented as he pulled into the kerb.

In the middle of a sweep of neat green lawn Dalby was pushing a petrol-driven mower. The lawn was decorated with islands of tidy shrubs, rhododendrons and evergreens. Several of them were specimen shrubs, standing at attention like exclamation marks. Dalby switched off his machine briefly to shout.

'Welcome to Cornerways.' He made a quick gesture towards the open front door. 'Go inside, sitting-room is at the end of the hall. Be with you in a minute. Downstairs loo if you want it. Must finish this bit . . .'

The catlick dropped over his forehead from well-brushed hair. His garden clothes were a pair of grey flannels, the creases razor-edged, striped shirt and fire-red tie. The machine burst into a roar as he switched on again, his nimble figure pushing the mower again at speed.

There was a smell of fresh-mown grass in the balmy evening air as Tweed and Diana walked up the crazy-paved path. It was like Hampton Court, Tweed was thinking. On either side of the front door stood two expensive-looking pots. Inside each a hydrangea was in bloom. They'd been freshly watered.

'I don't know how he keeps the place like this – with his wife gone,' Diana whispered, standing in the hall.

The floor was woodblocks, highly polished, scattered with rugs placed exactly parallel to the walls. Tweed led the way into a large sitting-room running the full width of the house. Through the French windows at the rear more Hampton Court spread away, a candidate for an illustration out of *Better Homes and Gardens*.

Diana sat down in a blue-upholstered arm chair to one side of an Adam-style fireplace, crossing her legs. Tweed walked to the front windows and watched Dalby switching off the mower. He was wearing a pair of dark glasses. He came bustling in, legs moving like a marathon walker.

Tweed made the introductions. Dalby shook hands with

Diana. Unlike Masterson and Grey he never gave her displayed legs a glance. He offered drinks and they both chose a glass of white wine.

'Splendid! I have a bottle of '83 Chablis in the fridge. You smoke?' he asked Diana. 'Light up then. No inhibitions here. Back in a minute . . .'

He returned with a silver tray supporting three elegant glasses. Sitting down opposite Tweed, he stared at him through his dark spectacles. Tweed had the oddest feeling he'd lived through this scene before.

'Cheers!' Dalby sipped, put down his glass, removed the spectacles. 'The light out there is incredibly strong. Where do you come from, Miss Chadwick?'

'Diana . . .'

'She's the sister of a friend of mine,' Tweed intervened, keeping to the story he'd used at Hawkswood Farm. 'On holiday from a job abroad. How are you getting on, Guy, on your own – if I may ask?'

'Why should I mind?' He turned to Diana. 'My wife, Renée, has gone back to France. Didn't like England. I didn't like her cooking. Garlic. With everything. Upsets my stomach.' He patted it. 'We're much happier now.'

'You have some . . . help?' Diana enquired.

'The Doukhobor lady. Absolute treasure. Comes in daily. When I'm here she cooks as well as cleans. No garlic.'

'Still, it must have been a traumatic experience,' Diana ventured, her tone sympathetic. 'I'm sorry.'

'Sorrow doesn't come into it.' Dalby held his glass up to look through it. 'You get these little local difficulties. Like losing a member of your staff. You just reorganize. Cheers!'

He spoke as though a shop had stopped stocking his normal cornflakes for breakfast. You simply changed to another brand.

'Your back garden looks really glorious,' she went on, staring out of the French windows.

'Come and have a look.' Dalby jumped up. 'If you find one weed you get a bottle of champagne. Tweed, know you're not interested in gardens. Pile of *Country Life*s over there. Have a look at the house if you like. Biggish place. Four beds, three recep., my study, two bathrooms. Back soon!'

Diana followed him into the hall, clutching her handbag

under her arm. Tweed could hear their conversation as they walked along the hall.

'What is a Doukhobor lady?'

'My nick-name for her. Very fat. Arms like tree trunks. Always wears a head-scarf. Looks like a Doukhobor. A Russian religious sect. Fled from Russia to places like Canada before the Second World War. Escaping religious persecution . . .'

The voices faded. Tweed stood up, walked quietly into the hall. He peered into the dining-room which overlooked the back garden, walked on. Dalby's study was at the end near the front door. He gently pushed open the half-shut door.

A small, square room, the single sash window overlooking the front porch and masked with a heavy net curtain. Tweed glanced at the piles of papers, the files, neatly arranged. Insurance policies and proposals, all headed General & Cumbria Assurance Co. Ltd. Excellent camouflage.

He turned to the bookcase placed against the inner end wall. Histories and travel books – Switzerland, Italy and Spain. Dalby's sector. But none on Libya or the Middle East – the forward penetration zones. More of the same on Scandinavia, Canada and the US. Nothing to do with his sector. More camouflage.

Leaving the study, pulling the door half-shut again, he went into a large rectangular-shaped kitchen looking out over the back garden. Modern equipment – dark blue formica cupboards and worktops. Eye-level cooker.

On the worktop next to the sink was a wooden chopping-block. An array of French beans, neatly chopped, lay under a wire-mesh cage. Tweed stared round, seeking a chef's knife. A magnetic knife rack was attached to the wall above the sink supporting a row of various knives. No chef's knife.

Through the windows, between two tall evergreen trees he saw Diana talking with Dalby. He was now wearing a smart grey jacket which matched his trousers. Tweed wandered back into the sitting-room. Compared with Masterson, Lindemann and Grey, Guy Dalby at home was exactly the same as he was at work. Normal was the word which sprang into his mind as he sat down again after collecting a *Country Life* at random. Completely normal.

'Freshen up your glass?'

279

Dalby skipped into the room, followed by Diana, who now had a single rose projecting from between her breasts. She had a dreamy look as she sank into her arm chair.

'Not for me, thank you. I'm driving,' Tweed replied. 'Find a weed?' he asked Diana as Dalby replenished her glass.

'Nary one. And I looked!'

'No champagne then,' Dalby said crisply. 'Thought that I was safe.' He refilled his own glass, sat down and gestured towards the French windows. 'We could have gone out that way, but it would have taken an hour to deal with the security locks.'

'Your Doukhobor lady is coming back?' Tweed enquired. 'I saw signs of a meal being prepared in the kitchen.'

'That was me. It's her day off, blast the woman. I hate cooking.' He smiled briefly. 'Never do anything in life if you can get someone else to do it for you. The road to achievement. And may I ask when can we all get back to our respective headquarters, get on with something worthwhile?'

He was the only one of the four who had asked that question. A sign of his impatience. Again, par for the course with Dalby.

'Soon,' Tweed replied. 'I'll be in touch.'

'Are the natives friendly round here?' Diana asked.

'Not if I can help it. Bunch of robots. Don't know why those little yen men have to invent mechanical versions. I'm surrounded with them.'

'Robots? I don't believe I understand,' Diana queried.

'See the keep-fit merchants walking past that window at the front every weekday. And it's quite a hike to Woking station. All dressed alike. Regulation uniform. Brief-case at the ready. Executives they call themselves. Work for one of the big corporations up in town. A lot in oil, as they say. At a party they even talk alike, use the same jargon. Like a code language only the initiated understand. Robots. Maybe they manufacture them on some huge conveyor belt at a secret factory.'

'What an absolutely lovely description. But it must be lonesome for you,' she suggested.

'I'm hardly ever here. The Doukhobor has a key. Keeps the place up to scratch while I insure the world against imaginary perils.'

'Imaginary?'

280

'Guy is a cynic,' Tweed explained. 'And I think we'd better get back. We have a dinner date. With a couple of pheasants.'

'Then I'm ready!' Diana jumped up out of her chair. 'You must excuse my manners,' she said to Dalby and smiled with her eyes half-closed. 'It's just that I adore pheasant.'

'Mustn't keep the gentleman waiting then.' Dalby stood up. 'Bathroom before you go?'

'Yes, please. No! Don't show me. I saw it. Off the hall by the front door . . .'

There was a brief silence between the two men as they waited. Dalby walked over to the French windows, right hand thrust into his jacket pocket, thumb protruding. It reminded Tweed of pictures he'd seen of Hitler. The drooping catlick served to heighten the impression.

'I'll be glad to get back to Bern,' Dalby said quietly. He turned suddenly, grunted with pain and grabbed at his right kneecap, stooping over. Then he straightened up and shook his head.

'Touch of arthritis. Catches you when you least expect it. Ah, here is your lady . . .'

He escorted them to their car, shook hands formally with Diana and opened the door for her. He said 'Goodbye,' left it at that as she swung her legs inside and made sure her dress had come in with her. Tweed nodded, got behind the wheel and turned into the drive beyond the house leading to a double garage, backing out again into the road.

Dalby stood quite still, then turned on his heel, went back inside the house and closed the door as Tweed drove off. They had passed through West Byfleet, heading back to London, when Diana made her remark.

'He was very quiet when we left.'

'That's Dalby. He'd said "Goodbye", observed the courtesies, so there was nothing to add. Very sparing with words, our Guy. What did you think of him?'

'Very balanced, very normal . . . What's the matter?'

Tweed had swerved slightly on a deserted stretch of straight road. *Normal*. The very word he had himself applied to Dalby. He glanced at the rose at her breast.

'Nothing. Go on.'

'Oh, it's the rose!' She was amused. 'It doesn't mean a thing.

281

I made a big fuss about his roses. He asked me in his clipped way whether I'd like one to take back. I said yes. He went into a shed he's got right at the end of the garden, came out with a pair of garden gloves and secateurs. He snipped off a rose, used his gloves to break off the thorns and handed it to me. Then he went off back to the shed to leave the gloves and clippers. He couldn't have been more matter-of-fact.'

'What is his attitude to women?'

'Indifference. He's polite, courteous, but his main interest in life is his job. Women come a poor second. I think that's all I can say about him. There were moments when I thought he was playing a part – the part of a man with iron self-discipline. Just normal. Very normal.'

They came to a three-way roundabout. Tweed swung the wheel and took the second turn-off. 'I think this time we'll avoid Weybridge, go a different way back. Along the Portsmouth Road. Hope you're a good sailor.'

'Why?'

'A section called the Seven Hills ahead. Regular switchback. Here we go.'

'Can we call at the flat before we have dinner? I'd like to change into something devastating.'

'Can't wait . . .'

In the large sitting-room inside Newman's flat Tweed found himself humming a tune. Diana was changing in the bedroom. What the devil was the tune he thought as he picked up off a couch her handbag? That blasted tango. *Jealousy.*

He rifled through the handbag quickly with expert hands – careful to disturb nothing. Under her suede cosmetic sac he found a thick bundle of twenty-pound notes. He counted them quickly. Six hundred and fifty pounds. Since he'd previously checked she'd acquired from somewhere another four hundred pounds. He closed the bag, replaced it exactly as he'd found it on the couch. She came into the room thirty seconds later.

'Is my handbag somewhere here? Yes, there it is.' She was wearing a flimsy dressing gown. She tucked the bag under her arm. 'Give me five minutes and I'll devastate you.'

282

Thirty-Three

They again dined at Tweed's favourite restaurant, and again occupied the same booth for four people, sitting by the wall and facing each other. Diana looked round as she sipped at her aperitif, Cinzano. Tweed had contented himself with a glass of the white house wine.

'I love this place,' Diana enthused. 'And not just the food. The atmosphere too. I'm not sure how they've done it.'

'The pink table cloths and napkins, the intimate layout, the attentive service,' Tweed diagnosed. 'Spend a fortune in Harrods?' he enquired jocularly.

'Not one penny! I'm saving up.' She smiled. 'Being so very strong-willed.'

'How are you off for money? Still some travellers' cheques left?'

'Don't use them.' She drank the rest of the Cinzano. 'You will chide me, but I only carry cash. That's why I always carry my handbag with me. No, I haven't a banking account in London. Years since I've been here. Ooh! Here's the pheasant. You spoil me, Tweedy.'

She waited until they were served before asking the question.

'When do we fly back to Germany? You were a bit vague when Dalby asked. Dedicated man. Obviously champing at the bit to get back to Bern. And you will be coming back with me, won't you?'

'Eat your pheasant before it gets cold.'

'I chatter too much, don't I? It's just that I'm enjoying myself so much.'

'First answer. We fly back to Hamburg soon. I'll try to come with you – but don't hold me to it. And, yes. Dedicated is the word for Dalby. I see you left behind the rose he gave to you.'

'Plonked it in a vase of water in the bedroom.' Tweed had ordered a bottle of Montrachet. She watched him over her glass. 'I might have worn it if you'd given it to me.'

'Finish your pheasant. The desserts here are good . . .'

283

He drove her back to the flat, she invited him in for a nightcap, he refused, saying he had notes to make, promised to phone her in the morning and drove on to Park Crescent.

Monica, whom he had phoned from the flat while Diana was changing for dinner, was waiting for him behind her desk. He sighed as he put his raincoat on a hanger, went behind his own desk.

'I don't know why you work for me. The awful hours I ask you to keep. Any sensible woman would have thrown the job in my face years ago.'

'And how would I have spent my days back at the flat down in Pimlico? Talking to Jonathan the cat? I find his conversation rather limited. Can I report now on what you asked me to do?'

'I'm all ears.'

The building was very quiet at 11.30 at night. Everyone had gone home except the security guard on the front door. The curtains were drawn across the windows and there was no sound of any traffic. A time of night Tweed liked, when his brain was at its most active.

'I called Peter Toll at Pullach. Very defensive. Nothing on Newman. Peter pleaded for two more days . . .'

'That's all he's got.' Tweed's expression was grim. 'Then I lower the boom on him, contact his chief. Bob is somewhere out there behind the Iron Curtain.' He glanced at the wall map. 'I feel it in my bones. Now, what does that remind me of? Something Guy Dalby said. No matter. Go on.'

'We still have Harry Butler holding Walther Pröhl, Toll's man, at Heathrow. The security chief was getting restless, so Harry invoked the Official Secrets Act. Is Pröhl still on hold?'

'Definitely, but transfer him to Wisbech from Heathrow.'

'To keep up the pressure on Toll?'

'No. It's an attempt to protect Newman. It will have been reported to Markus Wolf that a man looking like Newman – and travelling under his name – flew out of Germany. It may just confuse my old opponent. Next?'

'I phoned Kuhlmann again. He reports Dr Berlin has still not reappeared at his home on Priwall Island. They're searching but can't get even a whisper of where he's gone.'

'Bad news. It looks more and more as if I'm right. Don't ask me anything. I just hoped to God I was wrong. Any more murders of young blonde girls?'

'No.'

'Which again confirms the pattern I'm building up. Pretty horrific – for us.'

'Be mysterious. Now you and Diana have seen all four sector chiefs on home ground, have you found anything out?'

'Yes and no.' Tweed leaned back in his swivel chair. 'And I need that wall map changed tomorrow. Replaced by one of the whole of Western Europe – including Britain and Scandinavia. A much larger stage is involved than I suspected at first.'

'That reminds me. Do you know a Chief Inspector Bernard Carson? Scotland Yard. Central Drug Squad . . .'

'Yes, when he was with the CID. A tough customer. Why?'

'He wants to come and see you urgently tomorrow. I made an appointment – provisional, subject to my confirming early in the morning. At ten o'clock.'

'Confirm.' Tweed wrinkled his forehad. 'I wonder what he can possibly want?'

'You'll find out when you see him. Should I make myself scarce?'

'Wait till he arrives. So that's it?'

'No. You were going to tell me about your visits with the glamorous Diana . . .'

'Glamorous? Why do you say that? You haven't even seen her.'

'Just the way you talk about her.' Monica smiled cynically.

'Well, for starters, during one of those visits she acquired another £400. In cash. Twenty-pound notes. I told you that I'd checked her handbag . . .'

'You haven't pried again!'

'I have. Earlier this evening at Newman's flat when we'd got back from seeing Dalby. Over dinner she confirmed she has no bank account here, that she doesn't use travellers' cheques. She had £250 when I first checked. Now, out of the blue she has another £400. So who gave it to her?'

'I think you're downright unethical. A woman's handbag is sacred . . .'

'Nothing's sacred when I'm tracking treachery, maybe even a mass murderer.'

'All right. Now, you have total recall. She carried this hand-bag on each visit? Good. Did she keep it with her during each visit? Who of the four had the opportunity to slip her money?'

She waited, placing a pencil between her teeth, lightly holding the stem. Tweed closed his eyes and concentrated. His visual memory was phenomenal. He started talking, eyes still closed.

'Harry Masterson was first. Clematis Cottage. He took her off to show her the upstairs, but she left her handbag on a settee. That was when I first checked to see how much money she had. At no time did she have it with her when she was alone with Harry.'

'Not conclusive. Women have places on their person where they can conceal twenty banknotes. Inside her tights is one place.'

'The next one we visited was Lindemann,' Tweed said as he saw in his mind their entering the lodge at the corner of the mews. 'Don't think there was anything there . . .'

'Except dusty tomes,' Monica commented caustically.

'Just a minute! Don't say anything. There was something. I remember Diana suggested she'd like to see his kitchen. They went in together and were alone for quite several minutes. When Diana came out she had that handbag tucked under her arm. That money could have been handed to her then.'

'What about Hugh Grey?'

Eyes still closed tightly, Tweed moved in his mind to Hawks-wood Farm. Hugh bustling down the weed-strewn garden path to greet them, Paula staying at the door. The big sitting-room, the dyke rising up in the distance.

'Grey took her for a walk. Quite a long one while I chatted with Paula. He could easily have handed her the wad while they were outside.'

'That leaves Dalby . . .'

'Who took her outside to look at the back garden while I stayed inside. Another opportunity.'

'So any of them could have handed her the dibs. Back to square one. What was Diana's impression of them? Like some coffee? I made some just before you came in. It's in the thermos.'

'Yes, please.'

He went on talking while Monica opened the top drawer of

one of the steel filing cabinets, took out two brown mugs, the thermos and a carton of milk.

'She loved Harry, thought he was great fun . . .'

'She has good taste.'

'She even liked Lindemann, which surprised me. Hugh Grey she didn't like at all. The idiot made a pass at her while they were out walking . . .'

'Should have been Harry. That's his prerogative.' She put a paper place mat on Tweed's desk, perched the mug on top. 'There you are. Black as sin. That leaves Dalby.'

'She admired him. Said he was dedicated. As for his attitude to women, she thought it was take-them-or-leave-them. Work came first.'

'She's shrewd as well as a man-eater. Don't like the sound of her at all.'

'Why a man-eater?'

'From what you've said she had them all dancing round her at the end of a string. A man's woman. Other women probably hate her guts. Which means they wish they had her power over men. Why is she so important? You've watched over her like a mistress ever since she arrived . . .'

'Because she's a witness.' Tweed suddenly jumped up from behind his desk. 'God! What a fool I've been. I've shown her to all of them – and one of them is Janus. She needs round-the-clock protection. Get Pete Nield on the phone for me . . .'

'At this hour? He'll be asleep in his flat at Highgate . . .'

'I said get him on the phone! Tell him to drive down here the moment he's dressed. I'll be waiting for him.'

'Anything you say. My, she really is something, this Diana . . .'

Tweed was agitated. Monica watched him as she made the call to Nield. He prowled restlessly round the office. He pulled the flaps out of his jacket pocket, straightened them. He clapped the palms of his hands against his backside. He fiddled with his tie. Couldn't keep still.

She finished the brief call, put down the phone and tried to calm him by talking.

'Nield is on his way. Expects to be here inside thirty minutes. No traffic on the roads at this hour. Now, did you notice

287

anything significant during your visits? You wanted to see them on their home ground.'

'Yes, I did. A landing-stage projecting into The Wash. It had recently been reinforced with fresh timber. Then Clematis Cottage. Masterson loathes the sea. I went to the lavatory, opened the window. Leaning against a shed with other rubbish was a ship's wheel. Not ten minutes' drive away I found a large power cruiser called *Nocturne*. Chopin composed nocturnes . . .'

'I do know that . . .'

'No one was about. I climbed aboard, peered inside the wheelhouse. The vessel had what looked like a brand new wheel. In Lindemann's bathroom I opened a wall cupboard. There was a bottle of sable hair colourant. He doesn't drink. In a cupboard in his sitting-room I found half a glass of Scotch. At Dalby's place I found nothing . . .'

'Thank God for that. My head's spinning . . .'

'Except in the kitchen. Dalby had been slicing French beans. No sign of the knife. That's it.'

'My, we have been a busy little bee. Might I enquire how all those different things link up?'

'I've no idea . . .'

'So I might not enquire. Drink your coffee. Nield will roll in soon now.'

'You asked how these things link up. That's the point. I'm convinced there's a link missing.'

'Wouldn't it be strange if Bob Newman supplied the missing link?'

Part 2

Death Cargo

Thirty-Four

It was 1 a.m. Moscow time. Inside his large office in the four-storey building visitors to the Kremlin never see, Mikhail Gorbachev stood staring at General Vasili Lysenko. He wore a smart grey two-piece suit, a white shirt, a red tie.

His large thick-fingered hands rested splayed on the conference table which separated him from his visitor who stood stiff as an automaton. Gorbachev's large rounded head was stooped, his lips pouched. A distant bell chimed once.

'I had you flown here at short notice from Leipzig,' Gorbachev began in his quick, choppy way of speaking, 'because the consignment of heroin for England has now reached Leningrad. Ready for shipment. The largest amount of heroin ever transported as one consignment my advisers tell me. Five hundred kilos.'

'It is enormous . . .'

'Like your responsibility for seeing it arrives safely. This will do more to demoralize the population of that island than a dozen atom bombs. You understand the weight of your task?'

'Yes, General Secretary . . .'

'The English are now alert to the heroin peril. Any attempt to move this massive consignment through the normal channels would fail. They watch the airports, the seaports. So, we use the entirely novel route you have devised.'

'Balkan will not fail us . . .'

'He had better not fail *you!*' Gorbachev corrected.

As he spoke he hammered his clenched fist on the polished surface of the table, then began moving about the room, his right hand stressing his words with hard chopping movements.

Lysenko listened with a sense of fear mingled with awe. The General Secretary was an overpowering mixture of physical and mental dynamism. He exuded sense of purpose, supremely certain of the direction in which he was moving.

'While I talk peace the demoralization of the West must be

291

accelerated. Heroin is the main weapon, England the main target.' Gorbachev swung his bulky figure through a half-circle, suddenly facing the other man. He gave a broad smile, throwing his visitor off balance. 'Of course, you have my full confidence, Lysenko.'

'Thank you . . .'

'Of course we know at the moment the London Central Drug Squad is concentrating on Holland, the chief continental point of departure for drugs from South America bound for England.'

'That is true.'

Lysenko was again startled by Gorbachev's grasp of details. As soon as this new sun had risen over the Kremlin Lysenko had realized the way to deal with him was tell the truth. It was this realization which had kept him in his present post as a general in the GRU, Soviet Military Intelligence, when many of his old colleagues had been shoved into the waste bin of history.

'So,' Gorbachev continued, his expression now grim, 'they will not be expecting the consignment by the new route. And not a word about it to Markus Wolf.'

'Really? He would resent it if he found he was being excluded . . .'

'Exclude him. Wolf is a monument now. Almost thirty years at his present task. He may be Deputy Minister for State Security in the DDR. Who cares? A monument,' he repeated. 'I've had to shift them all over the Motherland. Men who have grown slack and comfortable, who thought they were indispensable. I dispensed with them.'

'I understand.' Lysenko still stood stiffly to attention.

'Relax, Comrade. I'm not going to eat you. Yet! One thing worries me. *Tweed*. I told you I read his file. He is the one man who might sniff out this immense heroin consignment.'

'He is still in London. Balkan has confirmed that. He says he is certain Tweed will return to Germany. Tweed never gives up . . .'

'That is why I worry. You know the tremendous effort put into transporting the consignment secretly to Leningrad. Munzel has failed once. Normally he wouldn't get a second chance. He only has this fresh chance because you say he is the

292

best. And it must be done by an East German. No risk of egg on our face.'

'Wolf does know about the other consignment which will be moving shortly – the shipment of arms from Czechoslovakia via the DDR to Cuba for Nicaragua.'

'Doesn't matter. That is a little local affair compared with the heroin. Down to you, Lysenko. Supervising the transport of the heroin into England. That's all.'

Gorbachev stared at Lysenko from under his thick eyebrows. He had almost more hair in the brows than on the rest of his balding head. He waited until his visitor reached the door before he gave a last instruction.

'Lysenko! No communication, no reference to the heroin by the normal channels. Telephone, teleprinter or computer. The Americans have developed sophisticated equipment to penetrate our communications system. The problem has not been solved. If you have to contact me, use the phone – but refer to it as "the cargo". Just that phrase. Your plane is waiting. Get back to Leipzig . . .'

General Vasili Lysenko had a lot to think about on the flight to Leipzig. At Moscow he had boarded the Tupolev 134 as the first passenger, bypassing the normal formalities and security checks. They had given him his own section of the aircraft closest to the air crew's cabin, curtained off from the rest of the plane.

He was always relieved to leave Gorbachev's presence still holding his present rank. You just never knew which way the General Secretary was going to jump next. He was turning the Soviet Union upside down. No one who didn't come up to scratch was safe, regardless of position or track record.

Dawn was a bar of lurid light on the distant horizon. Lysenko was unaware of it as he thought of what he had been told. And he'd noticed Gorbachev had not even assigned a code-name to the heroin. Just 'the cargo'. An additional precaution. Code-names could leak, people speculated what they might mean.

'The cargo' was Gorbachev's pet project. And, as he had said, the effort which had gone into transporting the huge haul had indeed been prodigious. First the endless camel train carrying it out of Pakistan, starting its long journey weeks ago.

293

It had travelled by a dangerous route. A small section of the route had crossed the eastern 'tongue' of Afghanistan bordered by Pakistan, India, even China – at its most eastern tip – and, to the north, Soviet Russia. They had sent a young Russian general to launch an offensive in the Afghan area against the rebels.

His directive had been to destroy the rebel forces, to occupy the 'tongue'. The Soviet High Command who had sent him had known his task was impossible. It had been a diversion – to keep the Afghan rebels busy while the camel train proceeded across the Pamirs by a pass, then down into the Turanian Plain.

At Khokand the cargo had been put aboard a six-coach armoured train. Only a portion of one coach was needed to store the heroin. A further precaution. The heroin habit was growing inside Russia. The rumour had been spread that the train was transporting armaments.

It had made the long journey to Moscow. There the heroin coach had been uncoupled, attached at dead of night to an express bound for Leningrad. Gorbachev himself had supervised the details of the fabulous journey. Now it would be transhipped by sea to its ultimate destination. By a most devious route. With the aid of Balkan.

Chief Inspector Bernard Carson of the Central Drug Squad was a tall, lanky man in his late fifties and with curly brown hair. His manner was always calm, even off-handed, no matter how great the crisis which faced him. He sat in Tweed's arm chair while Tweed stood by the window. At his request, Monica had left them alone.

'What I've come to see you about doesn't really concern you at all,' Carson explained. 'But I'm a bit bothered.'

'You are?'

Tweed was surprised. He couldn't remember Carson ever admitting to even being ruffled before.

'Word is out on the street that the biggest consignment of heroin ever moved is on its way to this country.'

'May I ask what are your sources of information?'

'Oh, we have a whole underground network of dealers and pushers who – for a consideration – tell us things. They're all keyed up to distribute fast this huge consignment. That's the key to their success. Never hold on to the stuff. Offload it. Fast! Spread it over a small army of pushers. Lose it. Here in London. The Midlands. This poison is spreading through the whole country. I have no doubt the rumour is true.'

'So why come to me?' Tweed asked.

'Because you have your own networks across the whole of Europe. I'd hoped you might hear something. It's the *route* I want . . .'

Carson said it with unaccustomed vehemence. He drank some of the coffee Monica had brought in earlier.

'It's Holland at the moment, isn't it?'

'That's the gospel according to St John. All my colleagues agree with it. Their eyes – and those of the Customs boys – are glued to Holland.'

'And your view?'

Carson shrugged. 'I just get a funny feeling about this one – that it's different. Never known such activity, anticipation, on the streets. The bastards are practically salivating. It could be that somehow they're bringing in an unprecedented amount – maybe even a hundred kilos. Gambling on getting in the big haul at one throw of the dice. If so, God knows how they hope to do it.'

'Bernard,' Tweed said abruptly, 'I can't help you.'

'How come?' Carson looked bewildered.

'Because I'm convinced you know something you haven't told me. You've given me nothing concrete to go on. Forget it.'

Carson stirred uncomfortably in the chair. 'I should have realized you'd sense it. OK. But this is highly confidential . . .'

'Tell me. If you're going to.'

'We had a man on the spot in Pakistan, a very good man. He was based at Peshawar. The base the Yanks are using to ship guns and ammo to the Afghan rebels, bless their cotton socks . . .'

'I know where Peshawar is.'

'This is the really confidential bit. Our chap had a contact inside the Soviet Embassy at Islamabad. Bought and paid for. Our chap reported rumours of a large heroin consignment bound for the West. The Soviets must have got on to our man. Pathans were used to carve him up . . .'

295

'That's rather horrible. I'm sorry.'

'Goes with the territory. Our man knew that. But some of our back-up people arrived, caught the Pathans in the act.'

'What happened to them?'

Carson cocked his right hand like a pistol, made a motion of pulling a trigger. 'Sympathy, the liberal option, doesn't figure in our business. Our chap was still alive – only just. He said one word before he closed his eyes. Sounded like *Hansa*.'

'You're sure it was Hansa?' Tweed pressed.

'Nearest our people could get to it.' Carson stifled a yawn. 'Sorry, I'm twenty-four hours without sleep. Word doesn't mean a damned thing to me.'

'Hansa,' Tweed repeated. 'The Hanseatic League. A federation of major shipping ports banded together to protect their trade interests. Formed in 1241. Founder members Hamburg and Lübeck. Para-military, too. They had armed groups to accompany caravans of goods moving in Europe against roving bandits.'

'History was my worst subject,' said Carson. 'I don't see the connection . . .'

'Neither do I. Yet.'

Tweed walked over to the new wall map of Western Europe Monica had put up. He took a wooden pointer from a drawer to reach the higher sections. As he spoke, the pointer located the towns.

'Tallinn in Estonia, Stralsund and Rostock in East Germany, then Lübeck, Hamburg and Bremen – to name just a few. There were ninety towns in the League at the height of its power.' He turned away from the map. 'And the funny thing is one of my people also used the same word – Hansa.'

Carson uncrossed his ankles, straightened up, suddenly alert. 'So maybe your man could tell us something?'

'He's also dead. Murdered in Hamburg. By the Soviets – or their proxies, the East Germans . . .'

'Looks as though I came to the right place after all. That is stretching coincidence too far – literally. My man is killed in Peshawar, yours in Hamburg – and in both cases the last word they said was Hansa. It couldn't be . . .'

'Yes, it could.' Tweed replaced the pointer in the drawer, pushed it shut. 'Bernard, I want you to promise me something.

Not one word about this outside this room. Confidential, you said. Now I'm holding you to it. I want your solemn promise.'

'Reluctantly, yes. But I could check the records . . .'

'Don't! Take no action. I think I may have underestimated my man who died in Hamburg. Incidentally, if you do lay your hands on a consignment the size of one hundred kilos, what precautions do you take?'

'Every precaution possible. It doesn't always work. With the potential profit that amount could bring in you can't trust anyone. Not even inside the Drug Squad, between you and me.'

'How long ago since your chap in Peshawar was killed?'

'Eight weeks ago. To the day. About four weeks ago we began to get reports of the excitement building up in the streets . . .'

'So we may not have much time left. I'm up against an unknown deadline.'

Thirty-Five

'Better that the nursing sister who attended Dr Berlin thinks you are a German newspaper reporter,' Falken said as he drove along the highway towards Leipzig. 'You remember her name?'

'Karen Piper.'

'Good. You are still alert . . .'

'Why shouldn't I be?'

'My friend, you are not the only outsider I have escorted in the DDR. Pullach used to send other people – couriers – who had not been here before. Within twenty-four hours we realized they were suffering from battle fatigue. To put it bluntly, under the pressure of being inside enemy territory, their nerve cracked. They became a menace, a danger to Group Five.'

'How did you handle them?'

'Slipped them back across the border immediately. If possible.'

'And if not possible?'

'Our lives were at stake. We had no alternative. Let us leave it at that.'

My God, Newman thought, they had to shoot them, bury them somewhere. He could feel the tension building up inside his stomach. Tight muscles. A slight queasiness. He concentrated on the road ahead.

The modern four-lane highway extended into the distance through open countryside. To left and right there were fields and woods. The sun shone down out of an almost clear sky, but some miles ahead clouds were building up like a storm gathering. The air was humid, oppressive.

The traffic was heavier than Falken had expected. Huge six- and eight-wheel diesel trucks roared past them, belching fumes. Falken kept well under the speed limit, seemed to be in no hurry. On a main highway the limit was 100 kph. Falken was moving at 60 kph. Hence the convoys of heavy stuff thundering past.

'You're playing it safe,' Newman observed. He nodded towards the speedometer. It was the only sign of tension he showed.

'We're early for the appointment with Karen Piper. Mind you, I shall arrive early – to check out the lie of the land.'

'Who does the talking if we're stopped by a patrol car?'

'I was just coming to that. You do. Border Police. That gives you clout. You use it pretty well.'

'But we're so far from any border here . . .'

'You wouldn't believe the powers that document in your pocket gives you. Special Assignment Unit. In plain clothes. You can go anywhere in the DDR. And you don't have to explain what you're doing. Unless East German Intelligence stops us. One of Wolf's men. Then anything can happen.'

'I'll bluff our way through. But, just supposing I don't?'

'We shoot our way out. No messing. And this is where I turn off this highway, take a roundabout route along country roads before I head back for the highway closer to Leipzig.'

He glanced in his rear view mirror again. He was an excellent driver. Newman had noticed his eyes constantly flickering to that mirror for a fraction of a second. He signalled, swung off the highway on to a hedge-lined, winding lane.

Newman found his stomach muscles relaxing now they were

away from the highway. He'd been screwed up, watching all the time in the wing mirror, through the windscreen, for the approach of a patrol car. There was a limit to the number of times you could bluff your way through a road-block, the Vopos in a patrol car. Falken went on talking in his quiet, easy manner.

'We're meeting the Piper woman in a camper parked underneath a complex of main roads. We call it the zig-zag. A smaller version of that freeway complex in Los Angeles we see on TV – Spaghetti Junction.'

'You see things like that on TV?'

'You'd be surprised how many homes have colour television – and their favourite programmes are those from the West. We're not supposed to watch them, but no one cares any more.'

'Sounds a bit public – this camper rendezvous . . .'

'Chosen with care. It provides plenty of escape routes. Use a place out here and where do you run if the Martians arrive? Piper approved – for the same reason. You'll see.'

'And what happens after I've interviewed her?'

'You head straight for freedom. Under Gerda's control. We've been over that. I won't be coming with you. I have another job needing urgent attention. Also a man and a girl attract less notice.' They were climbing a steep hill, the view blocked by the crest. 'If we are stopped,' Falken continued, 'you'd better know Gerda is travelling on papers in the name Gerda Nowak. She is a secretary at Markus Wolf's headquarters in Leipzig. Normally he operates out of East Berlin, but he's been at his second base for some time. I think I'll leave you to make up your own story about her – should it ever come to that. A spontaneous explanation is often more convincing.'

They drove over the crest and the road dropped down a steep hill. Driving towards them from the other direction was a green car with two men in the front. The car stopped at the bottom of the hill, on the level, blocking the road.

'I must be telepathic,' Falken commented with a bleak look. 'Trouble ahead. I can smell it . . .'

'Intelligence.'

The taller of the two men in civilian clothes flashed a folder by the window Newman had lowered. Newman nodded, grasped the handle, opened the door and alighted as the tall Intelligence officer stepped back. Both men in their forties, clad in grey lightweight raincoats, hatless, poker-faced.

Newman left the door wide open, took several paces to one side, which gave Gerda a clear field of fire with her machine-pistol. He hitched up his slacks, glanced beyond the gateway leading to a field. Half a kilometre away an abandoned stone quarry reared, a rusting bulldozer standing amid the pile of rocks at its base. A good place to hide bodies. God, he was becoming as hard as Falken. A few more weeks inside the DDR and he'd become even harder. He spoke calmly as he reached for his folder, one equal talking to another.

'Border Police. And may I see your folder again? Once I was nearly mugged by a bogus Intelligence officer. Thank you . . .'

They had the look of hardbitten businessmen, out for the last penny. The taller man had a scar down his right eyebrow. The smaller one shuffled his feet impatiently, giving the impression he was a subordinate who left his colleague to do the talking.

'Looks OK to me,' Newman said, handing back the folder as he checked his watch, steel-plated, made in East Germany. 'I am in a hurry. Special assignment. Drugs . . .'

'Drugs? You did say drugs?'

'Heroin.'

He saw the two men exchange a quick glance. I've said the wrong thing, he thought. He stood quite still as the folder was handed back. He pushed it a bit further.

'I have a rendezvous to keep. My informant won't wait.'

'Who is the girl?' the tall one asked, his expression giving nothing away.

'Gerda. That's enough identification. She's the go-between. She knows the informant. I don't. The man behind the wheel is the fastest driver in the Democratic Republic. That I need. I also need to make up for lost time.'

'Martin, move the car for Mr Clasen,' the tall man ordered.

'One more thing,' Newman called out after he'd got back into the Chaika, closed the door. 'If you see a blue Lada driven by a man wearing a Russian fur hat, don't stop him.'

'A fur hat? In this weather?'

'Status symbol, I suppose.'

'Stupid, strutting Russkies,' the tall man sneered.

Falken drove on. Newman neither waved to nor glanced at the two Intelligence men as they left. He still maintained the same placid confident pose he'd assumed while talking to them. They rounded a bend and Falken spoke with a hint of amusement.

'A very different performance from that you put on for the late unlamented Schneider.'

'You don't shout at East German Intelligence. Something funny about that conversation. I seemed to say exactly the right thing. Drugs seems to be a kind of password.'

'Just so long as they're not mulling it over back there and deciding there was something funny about us.'

'You see, Martin,' the Intelligence officer was saying to his driver as they approached the highway, 'there is substance to the rumour about the movement of heroin on a large scale. That Border Police chap is involved in it, I'm sure.'

'Maybe it's better for us if we forget we ever met him.'

'Met who?'

The rumours were rife at Intelligence headquarters in Leipzig among senior officers. Discussed in whispers behind closed doors. Gorbachev had overlooked one thing. The operation had no code-name. This had aroused curiosity. Markus Wolf himself knew the Russians were up to something they were concealing.

He kept his own counsel. Never asked one question. He had guessed this was the real purpose of Lysenko's temporary residence in Leipzig. Let them get on with whatever they were playing at. They'd make a balls of it. Then call on him to get them out of the shit. After all, it had happened before.

They were back on the highway, caught up once more in the roar and exhaust fumes from the trailer trucks. Falken drove just inside the speed limit, looking all round as they approached the road complex. No sign of patrol cars. He swung off down a slip road, then turned into a lay-by and switched off the engine.

The traffic thundered overhead. They were parked underneath the intersection of two massive concrete bridges. Surrounded by the concrete supports holding up the whole edifice. Newman closed the window and the decibels of the traffic roar were reduced.

'There is the camper,' Falken said, pointing to his right.

'Looks conspicuous,' Newman commented.

The large vehicle, perched on its high chassis, had an empty look. Net curtains were drawn over the windows. Double doors at the rear. A step to make for easy entry. Parked on waste ground, beaten earth with a track leading to it. Overhead one of the bridges sloped down across its roof, leaving a space of maybe twelve feet.

'It's permitted,' Falken said. 'Camping is one of the main ways of taking a holiday in the DDR. And this is the right time of the year. Now, some instructions for you. So listen carefully. At some stage I leave you with Gerda, as I have said. Until you are safely in the West, do not touch alcohol. The laws against drinking and driving are most strict. You are seen leaving a bar, you have had nothing to drink, the Vopos see you. You may be arrested. At best, they will fine you on the spot. Never have a bottle in any vehicle you travel in. You have not touched it. The bottle is sealed. But if they find it, again – you may be arrested. Above all, obey Gerda . . .'

'For God's sake,' Gerda called from the back, 'stop lecturing him. He's saved us twice. First, Schneider in the fog when he'd just crossed the border. Then the Intelligence men. He knows what he is doing . . .'

'You are right,' Falken conceded. He smiled at Newman. 'I've wondered at times who is the boss of this outfit. I don't like the waiting. I admit it.'

'How much longer?'

'Piper should be here at noon. We give her eight minutes to be late, then we go . . .'

'Without my talking to her? After I have come all this way!'

'There are security rules we never break.'

'And we wait here?'

'For a short while longer, yes.'

Newman tightened his mouth, decided to argue no more. Falken was obviously feeling the strain. Little wonder. He

302

looked at the camper again. It had been freshly painted, the net curtains were clean, the chrome gleaming. It was the location which was so depressing.

Rank weeds surrounded it, clumps of something which could be sorrel. In the distance, beyond it, a track pitted with clumps of grass ran ruler-straight along a deep gulch below the fields on either side. He asked Falken what it was.

'One of our escape routes. An old railway track, disused for years. They took away the rails. The sleepers are now no more than powder. Driving along that in the camper you cannot be seen from the fields alongside it. Now, we will go and inspect. I go first, you wait here. Get behind the wheel. Just in case.'

'In case of what?'

'In case someone is waiting for us inside the camper. When I wave my arm, you come.'

He opened the door and the thunder of heavy traffic invaded the car again, beating against Newman's ear-drums. How the hell he was going to hear a word Karen Piper said he had no idea. He slid behind the wheel. Without looking round he sensed Gerda's tension as they watched Falken wander casually across to the camper.

He walked all round the vehicle, rapped on the window of the driver's cab, waited, hands on his hips. Inside the Chaika the temperature was rising rapidly. It was going to be a record day for heat. Newman took out his handkerchief, wiped the back of his neck, his forehead, the palms of his hands. Thank God they had all had a pee before they left the country road.

'It's all right!' Gerda said.

Falken had unlocked the door, climbed inside the camper. Now he was back at the door, waving to them. Newman glanced at his watch. Five minutes to noon. He climbed out and Gerda called to him.

'Take this for me, please, Emil.'

It was the cloth-covered basket of food and coffee and mineral water Hildegarde Radom had prepared for them. He realized Gerda needed both hands to carry the Uzi concealed inside the windcheater. He locked the Chaika after she had jumped down and started running to the camper. The traffic roar seemed worse as he followed her; over the fields a heat haze shimmered and made him feel hotter, more tired. He'd have to get himself into an alert mental state for questioning the Piper woman. He foresaw it would be no easy interview.

The interior of the camper was more spacious than he'd expected. Two couches which could be used as beds ran down each wall. Falken was erecting a fold-out table between them while Gerda stood on guard by the window facing the Chaika. Newman stood by Gerda, wondering why he felt he had walked into a trap.

'You sit here when you interview Piper,' Falken said, patting the end of one of the couches. 'Then you can see the clock up there on the wall which will be behind her. Watch that clock.'

'There's a time limit?'

'Eight minutes from the moment you start talking . . .'

'That's bloody ridiculous. Obviously you've never inter-viewed anyone. You need time to get them to relax, to gain their trust, to get them to confide in you.'

'Eight minutes.'

'Stuff you! I've come all this way for this one interview.'

'Eight minutes. There are . . .'

'I know! Security rules you never break! Well, you listen to me for once. If I can do it in eight minutes I will. But it takes as long as it takes.'

'This place is not safe . . .'

'Why choose it then?' blazed Newman.

'No place is safe . . .'

'You should have chosen somewhere which would have given me more time. We stayed long enough at the lock-keeper's cottage. Norbert, wasn't it?'

'We have to sleep somewhere . . .'

'We didn't bloody sleep there. We slept at Radom's. You have two bosses now, Falken. Gerda. And me. What is it?' he asked Gerda, who had left the window and was walking to the rear doors. It was surprisingly quiet inside the camper. When Newman asked Falken why, the German explained the windows were double-glazed, the vehicle was well-insulated. 'The win-ters here are grim,' the German remarked. 'And this is the most up-to-date camper you can buy.'

The quiet was shattered as Gerda opened the right-hand rear door. A pounding roar filled the interior. Gerda stood listening, then closed the door. When she turned round she held the Uzi ready for action.

'I can hear a police siren, a patrol car approaching at speed.'

Thirty-Six

'What was it you wanted to see me about, Hecht?' Wolf asked the tall Intelligence officer. He was alone in his office for an hour or so, thank God. Lysenko had gone to lunch.

'We met and stopped these three people in a Chaika on a side road off the highway. The man in charge was an Emil Clasen of the Border Police . . .' Hecht hesitated.

'Continue. You have my full attention.'

Wolf never bullied his subordinates. He demanded efficiency but treated them with courtesy. And it was well known that if an agent was caught in the West he would do everything in his power to arrange an exchange – to save his own man.

'I haven't told Martin I was coming to see you. I understand there are rumours about the movement of a large consignment of heroin.'

'Go on,' encouraged Wolf, careful not to comment.

'This member of the Border Police was on special assignment. I checked his identity. He mentioned drugs. I thought you should know.'

'Thank you.' Wolf stared at the officer through his square-shaped glasses with thin hornrims. 'But so far you have given me nothing unusual. There are a number of Border Police who are on special assignment – searching for drugs rings.'

'It was just as they were driving away that Clasen made his remark. I can quote his exact words. "If you see a blue Lada driven by a man wearing a Russian fur hat, don't stop him." '

Wolf pulled a notepad in front of him, produced a pen. 'You said three people. Who were the other two?'

'A girl he called Gerda, late twenties, attractive, wearing a head scarf. The driver was about forty, tall, lean. I can remember the registration number . . .'

305

Wolf scribbled down the details. He put down his pen, folded his arms and looked at the officer.

'Thank you for reporting this, Hecht. Not a word to anyone else. All right? You have shown initiative. I shall not forget.'

He waited until Hecht had gone. Nothing in his expression betrayed the anger he felt. Were the Russians – Lysenko – using one of his own units in some secret operation without informing him? That he would not put up with. It was the reference to the man with the Russian fur hat which had alerted him. He lifted the phone, dialled an internal number.

'Organize a dragnet. Target a Chaika. Here are the details . . .'

When he'd finished he called back Hecht, recalling a detail he'd overlooked. He took Hecht over to the wall map, asked him to show him exactly where they had stopped the Chaika. Thanking him, he waited until he was alone again, then pressed another pin on to the map.

Falken had opened a window. The three of them stood close to it like frozen statues, listening to the siren growing louder, nearer and nearer. Newman found the tension almost unbearable. It's the heat, he told himself as he felt sweat dribbling under his armpits. Despite the roominess of the camper he felt hemmed in, claustrophobic, was aware of the bridge just above them pressing down. Beyond the window two massive concrete supports reared up, increasing the trapped feeling. Falken looked at his watch.

'We can't wait for her much longer . . .'

'We'll wait till she comes,' Newman rapped back.

'I decide when we leave . . .'

'Not on this occasion. This is my ball game – interviewing Piper.'

'When I say we go, we go . . .'

'Shut up, both of you,' Gerda snapped. 'You're like two squabbling schoolboys. Listen.'

The siren was overhead, passing along the road above them. It faded into the distance. Falken used his handkerchief to wipe beads of sweat off his forehead. He again looked at his watch and Newman could have hit him.

'Here she is!' Gerda called out.

Newman peered through the curtains, scarcely able to credit what he saw. A motor-cyclist, features concealed under a crash helmet, had pulled up close to the Chaika. The rider swung a leg off the machine, kicked the support strut into position, left it standing erect and took off the helmet.

A woman in her late sixties, dark hair tied in an old-fashioned bun at the back, clad in a leather jacket, trousers tucked into leather boots. Falken opened the rear door and she hurried forward, climbing nimbly inside. The German slammed the door shut, ushered her forward. As he had been instructed earlier, Newman was wearing dark glasses. Gerda also wore a pair of tinted spectacles and her head scarf. 'No point in her being able to identify you,' Falken had said. 'Then if she should be picked up by the police, questioned, she won't be able to describe you accurately. She knows me anyway . . .'

Newman sat on the couch, facing the clock on the wall behind where Falken had sat Karen Piper, studying her. A hawk-like nose, sharp eyes, a thin mouth, a firm jaw. Just the type to rise to become a matron. He was aware she, in her turn, was studying him. He opened the conversation.

'You are Karen Piper?'

'Er, yes . . .'

Newman noted the brief hesitation. Falken's security was total. He had not even given him her real name. Probably at the woman's request. She kept fluffing up her hair where the helmet had pressed it down. Underneath the leather jacket he could see a lace-edged blouse, high at the neck, an enamel brooch with the painting of a lady dressed in clothes of the nineteenth century. Karen Piper had questions of her own, her eyes never leaving his.

'Where are you from? I must know before I speak.'

A throaty voice, harsh and commanding in earlier days.

'West Germany . . .'

'Which part?'

'That I am not telling you . . .'

'Your profession?'

'Newspaper reporter . . .'

'Which paper?'

'*Der Spiegel.*'

'Oh, I see.' For the first time she was impressed. Newman

307

was watching the clock, as was Falken. He jumped in before she could continue her interrogation.

'I'm short of time. So are you. The longer you stay here, the greater the danger. Let's get on with it. What have you to tell me about Dr Berlin?'

'He's dead.'

'No, he isn't. He's living in the Federal Republic. Near the border. On Priwall Island, Travemünde.'

'He died over twenty years ago. Your Dr Berlin is a fake. I can prove it.'

'Please do so,' Newman requested.

'In 1963 I was a sister employed at the Hospital for Tropical Diseases in Leipzig. The date was December 15. I was working on the private wards – reserved for Government bigwigs and the Party members. They brought in their so-called Dr Berlin on a stretcher. His face was completely bandaged . . .'

'You saw this yourself?'

'I was there when they carried him out of the ambulance. I accompanied him to the ward. The doctor in charge wouldn't let me take his temperature. That was what first aroused my suspicions. He was supposed to be suffering from a high fever. Later I saw the temperature chart. It registered four degrees above normal. I was told to keep away from that ward. Another sister was put in charge. The daughter of a Party member.'

Her lips curled at the recollection. She continued staring at Newman as she went on with her story.

'The matron at that time was a fool. She was supposed to organize a roster of three sisters. On duty round the clock. There was a muddle. I was put on duty two days after the patient had arrived. I looked through the watch window. I could hardly believe my eyes. The patient was walking round the ward, smoking a cigarette. He had stubble on his chin, but no beard.'

'That was significant?'

'Ever since I had known him as a *youth* he had a black beard.'

Newman leaned forward. 'You mean you knew him earlier?'

'Before he left to set up his mission station in Africa. My family was friendly with his. The man I saw through the watch window was not Dr Berlin . . .'

'Without his beard,' Newman began.

308

'I knew him before he first grew his beard. When he was clean shaven. The man I saw was not Dr Berlin,' she repeated. 'Like him, yes. And he was smoking English cigarettes . . .'

'How do you know that?'

'When one of the favoured sisters . . .' Again her lips curled in a sneer. '. . . brought out the waste bin I offered to empty it. I found English cigarette stubs. And when I saw him walking round the ward I thought he looked English. Anglo-Saxon, certainly. Maybe Scandinavian.'

'Could you please describe him?'

'After all these years? God in heaven, I was frightened – the security was so tight. No, I can't remember what he looked like. It was only a glimpse I got. But enough to know he was not Dr Berlin,' she repeated firmly.

'The security was tight, you said. What kind of security?'

'It was controlled by a Russian colonel. He always wore civilian clothes. A man in his middle forties. His name was Lysenko . . .'

'How do you know that?'

'The doctor in charge always referred to him as The Colonel when talking to the other sisters. Once I heard him use his name. Only once, but it stuck in my mind.'

'Can you describe him?'

'Short, heavily-built. A brutal-looking man. He had bushy, bristly eyebrows. Clean-shaven otherwise.'

'Earlier,' Newman reminded her, 'you said there was a muddle, that you were put on duty in that ward for two days. You must have seen him close up then?'

'After seeing him through the window I didn't know what to do. I went to the canteen for half an hour. When I got back he was lying in bed, his face covered with the bandages again. I checked his temperature. Normal. The chart showed a high temperature. I felt his pulse. Normal. I checked his blood pressure. Normal. Whoever he was, that so-called patient was perfectly fit. I marked the chart four degrees higher – to fit in with the previous reading. The doctor was appalled when he found I was in attendance. He changed the roster, then he took me into his private office. He said he had deleted my name from the roster, that I must never let anyone know about the mistake.'

'Why was he so considerate?' Newman asked sceptically, probing for inconsistencies.

'He once made a very bad error treating a patient. I was the only one who noticed. The patient died. He knew I'd seen his blunder. I never said a word.'

'A form of gentle blackmail on your part?'

'Nothing of the sort!' She reared up. 'He was simply a nice man who repaid a debt.'

'Excuse me,' Newman soothed her down, 'I misunderstood. Was that the last time you saw the bogus Dr Berlin?'

'No. I am a bird-watcher.' She glanced back at Falken. 'I have received much help in my hobby from my friend here. So I always carry a small pair of binoculars. Two weeks after this patient arrived I saw him in the distance, walking in the park round the hospital. I used the binoculars. He had grown the black beard. He looked very like the real Dr Berlin, but I could tell the difference. The following night he left and I never saw him again.'

'Left the hospital, you mean?' Behind her he saw Falken gesturing at the clock. Ten minutes. The interview had to end quickly.

'In the middle of the night. They said he had to meet someone.' She snorted. 'Who ever heard of a patient leaving at that hour?'

'Why are you telling me all this?'

'Because of what they did to my son.' Her voice was vehement. Her eyes flashed malice. 'He is a good boy. Maybe a bit headstrong, but they ruined him. All over a bottle of vodka they found in his car. He answered back the policeman who stopped him. He quarrelled with the judge. A bit headstrong. But now he is breaking rocks to help rebuild the autobahn near Plauen. He was training to be an accountant . . .'

'I'm so sorry,' Newman interrupted. 'That really is terrible.'

'Mrs Piper,' Falken said quietly, 'you must leave now. Your safety is at risk.'

'So soon?' She stood up, followed Falken to the rear door, talking over her shoulder to Newman. 'You will not identify me in your article as a sister at that hospital? They couldn't trace me from what you write?'

Newman had a flash of inspiration. 'Don't worry. I shall call my informant Dr Z. That will protect you completely . . .'

He saw that Gerda was carrying the windcheater but had forgotten the food basket which was nowhere in sight. She sensed what he was going to say and shook her head. Falken locked the rear door when they had left the camper. Karen Piper hurried to her motor-cycle. She was putting on her crash helmet when they climbed back inside the Chaika.

'Now we wait for her to go,' Falken said. 'And I've twisted my ankle crossing that rough ground. I think you'll have to drive the camper, Emil.'

'The camper?'

'Time to switch vehicles. We should have done that earlier, but there was no opportunity. I'll leave the key in the ignition here. It will make it look as though we're coming back if it's discovered. That's why Gerda left the food basket in the camper.'

Piper started her machine, never gave a glance in their direction and rode off up the slip road. They were walking back to the camper, Falken was now leaning on Newman for support, when they heard the chorus of sirens. Screaming like banshees. Coming from all directions, so it seemed to Newman.

'Hurry!' Falken gasped. 'They'll block all the exits.'

Thirty-Seven

The sense of being hemmed in by concrete increased as Newman walked slowly to the camper, held up by helping Falken whose ankle was obviously hurting him badly. The heat, the humidity was trapped by the overhang. And the sirens were almost deafening now.

Gerda had run ahead, had unlocked the door on the driver's side, then ran round to unlock the rear doors. She vanished inside and reappeared inside the driving cab.

'Had to fool Piper,' Falken said, talking in short bursts. 'Make her think we're still using the Chaika . . . If they catch her, break her down under interrogation . . . she can't tell them we've switched to the camper . . .'

Newman helped him up the step, Falken flopped on the couch as Newman slammed the rear door closed and ran to the front. Gerda was sitting in the passenger seat, nursing the Uzi inside the windcheater.

'I'll guide you,' she said as she handed him the key and he slipped it into the ignition, turned it. The engine fired first time. The petrol gauge showed 'full'. He played with the gears briefly to get the hang of the mechanism.

'I'm ready. Which way? Guide me . . .'

'That way. Keep under the span of the bridge. Then turn on to the old rail track. Drive down inside the gulch. If we make that they won't see us.'

He drove over the wasteland after lowering his window a few inches. The siren had merged into one endless wail as though they were all meeting at the zigzag. She told him where to turn. He moved on to the rail track. They were no longer protected by the overhang of the bridge. If someone peered over the wall they'd be seen.

The track descended steadily inside the gulch, the banks rose higher on both sides, above them were glimpses of the dense mass of rye crops growing. He accelerated. Falken had said the wooden sleepers had crumbled to powder. Not all of them. Newman had to grip the wheel tight as the vehicle bumped over still intact sleepers concealed beneath the growth of weeds.

'You're all right now?' Gerda said. 'Just stay inside the gulch . . .'

'Not much choice, have I?'

'I'm going back to check through the rear windows, see what is happening.'

'Have fun.'

Newman's mood had changed. The nervousness had gone. He was ice cold. The action filled his mind. Now he had something to do, to concentrate on. Ahead the track disappeared round a bend. He pressed his foot down further. If he could reach that bend, get round it, he guessed they'd be out of sight of the zigzag. Which was exactly what had sent Gerda running back to the rear windows.

Falken was holding on tight to the end of the couch, his leg with the sprained ankle sprawled along it. He was being bounced all over the place. He gritted his teeth, managed to smile at Gerda as she passed him.

She peered through the right-hand window. The track ran away into the distance. The huge massif of the zigzag reared up where the track ended. No one was peering over the wall yet. Hurry! The camper swayed from side to side, rocking like a ship at sea, putting maximum strain on the springs. Then she felt the vehicle turning slowly, following the curve of the track. She stood very still, holding on to the door handle, gazing at the zigzag. Don't look yet! Please, God, don't let them look yet . . .

The camper continued moving round the curve. The zigzag was disappearing. Then it was gone. She let out her breath. Her hand gripped the handle so tightly she had trouble unflexing her fingers. She went back to Falken who again smiled. She could tell he was in considerable pain. She sat beside him, gently pulled down his sock. His ankle was swelling, turning blue.

'I'll get the first aid kit, fix that for you . . .'

'Later. Get back to Emil. He's doing well but a little moral support will help.'

'Back soon.'

She flopped into the passenger seat, glanced at Newman who was staring ahead where the track ran dead straight inside the gulch for about a kilometre. He hit more of the intact sleepers, the bouncing started worse than ever.

'We're out of sight of the zigzag,' she told him. 'Now no one can see us.'

'I'd like to slow down. I'm shaking this thing to pieces.'

'Good idea. Want one of your nasty East German cigarettes? I can get the packet out of your pocket.'

'No thanks. Never smoke when I'm driving. You can drop a lighted cigarette in your lap at the wrong moment, get smoke in your eyes. Only fools and addicts smoke and drive. Tell me, is the roof of this camper well below the level of the gulch?'

'Well below. I told you, we can't be seen now we're round that curve.'

'And where are we heading for?'

'Leipzig still. By our own private route. The rail track.'

'You've used it before?'

'Once. So I know what lies ahead, where we have to leave it

at what used to be a level crossing. That's a distance yet. Then we move back on to the highway into Leipzig.'

'Look,' he protested, 'I'm going the wrong way for the border. We're heading due east.'

'You're thinking of the way you came in – past the watch-tower. You don't go out that route . . .'

'But I was told . . .'

'Pullach can be naïve. Falken's always cursing them. Never once has he passed a guest back across the border the way he came in. You don't get twice lucky in our world. It's my responsibility to put you on a different escape route.'

'Via Czechoslovakia?'

'No.' She hesitated. 'We never tell an outsider too much in advance. You understand?'

'Too bleeding right I do. In case I'm caught. Then, like the Piper woman, I can't tell them much under interrogation.'

'The system works. It's a question of survival. I will tell you that you're going out via the Baltic. But not how. Yet.'

'The Baltic! That's one hell of a way north. Practically across the full depth of the DDR.'

'That's the way it has to be. And now I'd better go and attend to Falken's ankle. Be back soon.' She smiled as he glanced at her. 'You really are doing very well. We trust you more than most we've had sent to us.'

Newman felt relieved and anxious at the same time. Relieved that the camper roof couldn't be seen above the gulch, anxious about this new escape route to the Baltic. He'd never dreamt they'd try to send him out via the extreme north. That meant driving a vast distance before he even came in sight of safety. And he'd had enough experience now to realize the highways were the danger points. Patrol cars, road-blocks, God new what else. He forced his fears out of his mind. Concentrate on the present. He looked ahead and frowned.

Little more than a kilometre away the gulch was spanned by an old hulk of an arched stone bridge. Presumably – as Gerda had said they'd used this route before – the bridge was wide enough for a vehicle. Trains had once passed under it regularly. But the camper was an exceptionally high-roofed vehicle. Had they travelled in a camper last time?

He stopped, left the engine ticking over and made his way

back inside the camper. Gerda had just finished bandaging Falken's ankle, was pulling up his sock gently. They both looked up with a surprised expression.

'What is it?' Falken asked sharply.

'An old road bridge ahead. Were you in a camper when you used this route before? I'm thinking of roof clearance.'

'No. We travelled in a car. And this was a narrow gauge railway, smaller coaches than the average.'

'We'll have to hope we get through. And, since I've stopped I'm going to climb the gulch bank, take a look-see . . .'

'I'll come with you,' Gerda said.

They used the rear door, stepping down into ankle-deep weeds sprouting from the old track. Together they scrambled up the steep side of the gulch, pushing their way through thistles and grasses. Here and there an outcrop of limestone protruded, embedded deeply into the embankment. They slowed down as they neared the top. Cautiously they raised their heads above the level of the rye growing to the verge of where the embankment fell away. Looped round her neck Gerda had brought with her binoculars Falken used in his conservation work. He kept a pair in the camper.

'Oh, my God, no!' she cried.

'See what you mean,' Newman replied tersely.

Away across the rye field the ground sloped up to a hill. A road leading to the bridge ran along the mid-slopes. And two patrol cars were moving along it, heading for the bridge.

Gerda raised the binoculars to her eyes, focused them. She groaned. Newman reached out with his hand and gently pulled the binoculars downwards over her breasts.

'The sun could flash off the lenses, alert them.'

'Emil! There are four men in each car. That's most unusual. They must be looking for someone . . .'

'Us, probably. We'd better move. Mind your feet on those rocks. We don't want two people with damaged ankles on this trip.'

They scrambled their way down through the mess of thistles and reached the bottom together. Gerda almost tripped but Newman grabbed her arm, steadied her. They ran back inside the camper and Newman slammed the door shut. Falken looked up and raised his eyebrows.

315

'Trouble?'

'Plenty,' Newman told him. 'Two patrol cars heading for the bridge, crammed to the gunwales with Vopos. Eight to be exact. I have to race them to that bridge, hope we can shelter underneath it. Hold on tight. They're bound to see us if we're in the open when they cross it . . .'

He ran back to the cab, thanking God he'd left the engine running. Gerda followed, sagging into the passenger seat as Newman released the brake. Again he rammed his foot down. The vehicle leapt forward, felt like a plane lifting off, crashing up and down over solid sleepers. Gerda, her facial muscles taut, stared ahead through the windscreen. She left him for a moment, returned holding the Uzi.

'There are eight of them, you said,' he warned. 'They'll be armed. Our only hope is to hide . . .'

'If we get there in time,' she reminded him, staring again fixedly through the windscreen.

And if the damned camper will go under that bridge, Newman thought. And if the bridge is wide enough to conceal us so neither end of this bloody great thing doesn't stick out in full view.

The camper jounced, wobbled, rocked as Newman kept his foot down hard on the accelerator. The arched bridge seemed an incredibly long way off. It *crawled* towards them. Beyond the bridge the sky was black as battalions of storm clouds massed. The heat inside the cab was appalling. They were partitioned off from the main part of the camper by a flimsy door, presumably to give privacy when people slept while the camper was driven through the night.

Newman's hands were sticky on the wheel. The left front tyre hit an obstacle. The wheel slipped out of his grip. He fought to control it as the camper swerved towards the embankment. Just in time he swung it back on course. He wiped each hand separately on his trousers as Gerda glanced at him.

'One of those bloody rocks. Must have rolled down on to the track. I could do without a repeat performance.'

'You'll make it . . .'

'We have to.'

His eyes were glued to the stone balustrade at the top of the bridge, the point where some policeman in one of those two cars would glance over the parapet and see the camper. Unless

316

they could get under that bridge first. He was gambling with dice he couldn't see. The cars had been moving fast.

He risked a shade more speed. The moment he'd applied the extra pressure the wheels met more solid sleepers. His backside was lifted clear off the seat. Gerda's shoulder bumped against his. She apologized, still staring forward. Would they never reach the goddamn thing?

A grey veil of rain was slanting down beyond the bridge. Thunderheads were building up. Maybe that was why it was so boiling hot inside the cab. They were close enough now for Newman to see the parapet was no higher than an average man's thighs. In the old days – when the trains still ran – schoolboys must have leant their elbows on that parapet, watching a train pass beneath them. No sign of the two cars crossing. Yet. They had to arrive at any second. There'd be no escape from the gulch. The Vopos would hold the high ground.

He rammed his foot down further. One final spurt. They couldn't lose now. Yes they could. The arch looked too low to permit passage for the camper. It was going to be a matter of inches. Maybe he'd take the roof off. Through his open window he thought he could hear sirens. On a lonely country road? Yes, because it would wind. Sirens wailing to warn any traffic concealed round a bend. Definitely sirens.

'Push the door open!' he told Gerda.

She reached behind her, pushed the door back, held it open.

'Hold tight, Falken! Emergency stop!'

He jammed on the brakes, nearly catapulted himself through the windscreen. They were under the bridge. Suddenly it was dark. Out of the blazing sunlight. He pushed Gerda's shoulder.

'Jump out! Check the front. Make sure it's under the arch. I'll check the back . . .'

As she slipped out he was running back the full length of the camper. Falken had both arms stretched out, holding on to the end of the couch, to the back. His expression was wary as Newman rushed past him. He turned the handle of the rear door, leapt down on to the step, on to the track, looking up.

The rear end of the camper was at least three feet inside the overhang of the crumbling stone arch. He ran to one side and between the camper and the curved wall. Gerda ran from the

317

other direction towards him. God, it was sticking out at the front. She was panting as she reached him.

'It's well inside at the front. How's the back?'

'Well inside. Listen . . .'

The sirens had stopped. They could hear the cars coming, slowing down. To take the hump-backed bridge slowly? Newman looked up at the vaulted arch. The cars reached the bridge, stopped. Engines switched off. They had parked above them.

Thirty-Eight

'A Chaika, you said. Under the highway complex? Yes,' Wolf agreed, speaking on the phone, 'tell your men to wait, watch for their return. They should keep well out of sight.'

He put down the receiver, stood up and walked to the wall map, talking to Lysenko as he inserted a fresh pin, locating the road complex.

'I understand from Balkan in London that Tweed often adopts the same method – uses a wall map, marks incidents with pins. In some ways he and I are alike. Strange . . .'

'And do you mind telling me what has happened?' Lysenko enquired.

'Remember my man, Hecht, stopped three people in a car on a country road here? A Chaika. A patrol has just found a Chaika empty underneath the road complex here. They are still heading for Leipzig – observe the route the pins follow.'

'Search the surrounding countryside?' Lysenko suggested.

'No, that might frighten them off. The key was left in the ignition. I think they will be coming back – if it is the same trio.'

'Oh, I understand now.' Lysenko smirked. 'Two men and also an *attractive* girl, Hecht told you. I know that area – there are rye fields everywhere. We can imagine what they are doing, can't we?' He smiled lecherously. 'One girl with two men – she must be lively.'

Wolf did not smile. An austere man, he did not appreciate the dirty mind Lysenko was displaying, revelling in his vision of what was taking place. And so odd, he thought as he returned to his desk. The Russian had a brilliant mind for espionage. Yet where sex was concerned he was a common lecher.

'I am putting more men on the streets of Leipzig,' he decided. 'Everyone possible will have their identities thoroughly checked. If there is something wrong with those three suspects they will walk into a trap.'

'What are you basing your suspicions on?'

'The continued disappearance of Schneider of the Border Police. The fact that his farm truck was discovered in that hollow by the highway. I think he has been killed. And now I must check on the imminent movement of those armaments from Skoda in Czechoslovakia bound for Rostock and shipment to Cuba.'

Newman pressed himself against the stone wall of the bridge. Behind him Gerda did the same thing, holding the Uzi. Down in the quiet of the gulch they could hear voices above them. Some of the Vopos had left their vehicles to stretch their legs.

'Good place for a pee,' a voice suggested. 'I'll clamber down under the bridge in case someone comes along . . .'

'Think I'll join you.' A second voice.

Newman glanced at Gerda, then froze. He could hear scrambling feet on the rocky, weed-strewn slope by the side of the bridge. A small rock came loose, rolled down and settled in the middle of the track. More loose stones followed it. He heard a curse.

'Let's relieve ourselves here, Günter. You'll break your bloody leg. There are some big rocks under this mess.'

There was the faint sound of water gushing against the wall of the bridge. Silence for a few seconds. Followed by the receding scramble of feet carefully picking their way back up the bank. Newman glanced at Gerda, who shook her head with relief.

Now there were voices talking above them, the two men leaning on the parapet as far as he could tell. They went on for several minutes before the lighted cigarette stub dropped just beyond the archway. It landed amid a clump of tinder-dry grass. There had been no rain for weeks from the arid state of the parched gulch. The clump began to smoulder, ignited.

'Günter, you stupid sod, you've started a fire. Better get

down there and put it out. There have been enough warnings on TV . . .'

Newman knew he had seconds to decide. Was someone still looking down over the parapet? He pointed to the clump for Gerda's benefit. Moving carefully, watching where he put his feet, he peered out from under the arch, looking up, sideways. No one. He put his foot firmly on the burning grass, pressed down, held his foot there, removed it, slid back under the arch. He waited, sweat streaming down his forehead.

'Hey, Günter! Don't bother. It's gone out. Just watch it in future . . .'

A clap of thunder like the boom of a siege gun muffled the rest of his sentence. It was suddenly very dark. Large spots of rain began falling. The cloudburst came without warning. Rain hammered down into the gulch, turned to hail. Doors slammed above them. Hailstones the size of large peas came down. They heard them pounding the roofs of the two cars parked on the bridge. Then solid sheets of rain. Newman retreated further away from the arch, alongside the camper. The sound of car engines starting up, driving off.

'Gerda, I want a word with Falken. Do you mind staying for a few minutes. It needs someone outside to hear another car coming.'

'Go talk with Falken.'

Newman climbed into the cab, walked into the living quarters. He sat opposite Falken, told him quickly what had happened. Through the rear windows he would see the rain falling, blotting out his view down the gulch after a few yards.

'Falken, a word about this Dr Berlin business. All right, he's a fake. The Piper woman convinced me. But what is he really up to? Why take all this trouble to establish him in the West? I have a friend in the British SIS. High up. And *he* needs to know all you can give me.'

'We think he's Balkan, the code-name for the controller of the vast Soviet spy network in the Federal Republic. When I say Soviet, I mean by proxy. Markus Wolf is his immediate controller, but the Russians pull the strings.'

'And how on earth do you know all this?'

The scepticism was obvious in Newman's tone. Falken hesitated, eased his leg into a more comfortable position along the

320

couch. Beyond the rear windows the rain had become a solid wall of water pounding down.

'My friend simply won't believe you,' Newman pressed. 'Not without background details. Would you? In his place?'

'No. This is highly confidential. Somewhere in the DDR I know a senior officer in Intelligence. He wants to clear out to the West when his father dies. The father is eighty-nine. He'll need my help to cross the border. He's building up his credit balance with me by passing on information. He heard about Balkan. By accident. Is that enough for your friend? It has to be.'

'That will do nicely . . .'

'I was going to tell you about Balkan later – just before I left you with Gerda. But not my source.' Falken smiled. 'You reporters are very persuasive chaps. You have to be, I suppose.'

'And when do I start the journey along the escape route? Soon, I hope. For your sake as well as mine. You can do without having me on your back. I reckon our luck is due to run out pretty soon now . . .'

He stopped speaking as Gerda pushed open the door separating the cab from the living area. She squelched in her shoes. Taking them off, she took out a fresh pair from a cupboard, used a cloth to partially dry her feet before putting them on.

'You'd better come and see what's happening, Emil. I think we have trouble.'

Falken heaved himself up on one elbow, opened the flap of one of the cupboards above the couch. Newman asked him what he was looking for.

'Walking stick. I'm coming with you . . .'

Newman found the stick, a heavy briar with a curved handle. Falken took it from him, planted his legs on the floor and stood up. He grinned as he tested his damaged ankle.

'That's better. Now Gerda has bandaged the ankle I have support. Let's see what's wrong.'

Newman followed Gerda beyond the flap door, holding it open for Falken, and stared through the windscreen. The gulch had turned into a river, inundating the track. Water sluiced down the banks, the level was rising as they watched it. Weeds

321

torn away by the force of the deluge floated on the surface. The curtain of rain reduced visibility to only a few yards.

'Is this camper amphibious?' Newman asked grimly.

'I wonder whether we can make it,' Falken mused aloud. 'The camper has a high chassis. Even so. The drains, the soakaways have got blocked over the years.'

'I say we start now,' Newman said. 'It can only get worse.'

'We were just going to eat,' Gerda protested. 'I'm hungry.'

'Always eat, sleep and pee when you can. The first two will have to wait. I suggest we deal with the third while we're still under the arch . . .'

'There's an elsan lavatory at the back,' Gerda reminded him.

'We may want to leave no trace that we've occupied this vehicle,' Falken said as he opened a door. 'No, Emil, don't help me. I must learn to get as mobile as I can. Gerda, get out the other side of the camper.'

Newman stood alongside Falken as they relieved themselves. The German went on talking, his stick hooked over one arm. The noise of the rain was like flails beating the ground. Both men stood on a stone ledge projecting from the stonework, just above the water level.

'You drive, of course,' Falken said. 'Gerda can feed you – so we accomplish two tasks at the same time. The danger is the water will flood the engine . . .'

'I know. I've had to cope with that before.' He glanced beyond the arch. 'The one advantage is we're hardly likely to be seen while this lasts.'

'Especially from the air.'

'The air?'

'A traffic helicopter. One of Wolf's machines. They'll all be grounded. This rain may save us.'

Newman drove out from under the arch cautiously. He'd had to switch the ignition on six times before the engine started. Not a good omen. The windscreen wipers gave him no vision. They'd lost the battle with the downpour before they started swishing.

He drove slowly beyond the bridge, just able to see the banks on either side, steering a course midway between them. It was pure hell. Then he felt the track descending down an incline.

Jesus! They were moving into deeper water. The rain hammered the roof above the cab. Rivulets of water poured down the windscreen. He bumped over something unyielding. Another of those bloody sleepers. Just so long as he didn't hit another rock. The speedometer registered 10 kph. The engine felt sluggish. He leaned forward, hardly able to believe his eyes. Ahead of the camper a wave was travelling over the surface away from him, a wave built up by the high bumper of the vehicle. God, no wonder the engine was protesting. Gerda sat in the passenger seat beside him, holding a sandwich made of rye bread and cheese. He was ferociously hungry. He shook his head. 'Not now, thanks. I need both hands for the wheel.'

'So, I feed you, like a bear at the zoo. Bite off what you'd like.'

She held the sandwich close to his mouth. He took a bite and chewed. Between eating four large sandwiches he risked taking one hand off the wheel, took the cardboard cup of hot coffee and drank. Sensibly, she only half-filled the cup each time. The world became a different place.

Falken stood behind them, leaning against the door with one shoulder, supporting himself with the stick. He kept checking his watch, leaning forward, looking for landmarks. He watched the odometer. The rain slashed down as heavily as ever. Newman glanced out of the side window. The camper seemed to be floating. They had reached a level stretch. The engine started coughing. It was flooding. Here we go, he thought.

His knuckles were white with gripping the wheel. Then he felt the angle of the track changing, climbing. He kept to the same speed, resisting the temptation to press his foot down a little. The engine was still coughing. Hold out, just a few more yards. Please!

'Now you eat, Falken,' Gerda said.

She had a cloth spread out on her lap. It held a pile of the sandwiches she'd made back in the living area. She held one up to him.

'Help yourself, Gerda . . .'

'No! The cook eats last. Take it!'

He took it, devoured it, swallowed some of the coffee she had poured into the cup from the thermos. Only when he had eaten four sandwiches did she start helping herself. The rain still sluiced down, but the camper was moving through shallower water. Newman increased speed gradually – to shake the water out as much as to move faster.

'How far to that level crossing?' he asked.

'About a kilometre, I guess,' Falken said. 'And I am guessing. If I could see ahead I could tell more accurately.'

'No danger of driving past it?'

'None at all. The gulch disappears. Just don't drive any faster.'

'You're joking, I take it?'

The rain began to ease off. They could see further ahead. Newman noticed they were climbing, the banks of the gulch were dropping. He ate another sandwich, drank more coffee. Eat when you can. Gerda folded the empty cloth, picked up the thermos and went back inside the camper. Newman took advantage of her absence to ask the question.

'When does Gerda take over from you?'

'In Leipzig. I may have to leave you quickly. Don't look so worried – I can manage with this stick. That's partly why I've been standing here, to test my ankle. When we do reach the level crossing and head for the highway, drive fast. Inside the speed limit, but fast. We're behind schedule. For you. Gerda simply has to get you to the rendezvous for the last stage of your journey.'

'Last stage? Sounds like a bloody long one.'

'It is. And it could be the worst – the very worst. You won't be able to relax for a second. No sleep for you all night. Think you can stand it?'

'I have a choice?' Newman enquired.

'None at all.'

Thirty-Nine

The traffic jam on the main highway leading into Leipzig went on for ever. The camper was stationary. Concrete multi-storey apartment blocks of a Leipzig suburb rose on either side.

Newman rested his arms on the wheel, trying to control his impatience.

The next vehicle ahead was a Volvo. Behind him a big diesel truck shut out the view. He was glad it wasn't the other way round. At least he could see what was happening ahead, could watch the Vopos trying to sort out the mess, waving on cars in the opposite direction. Single-line traffic. That is all I need, Newman thought as Falken hobbled into the cab, sagging into the passenger seat.

'We are very late,' Falken observed.

'You have a rendezvous with someone?'

'No, but you and Gerda have. With someone who cannot wait. I'll be glad when you're on your way. We don't care who gets Dr Berlin – as long as someone does. I've lost valuable men because of that swine.'

'Any other information I can pass on for you?'

'Yes. That is what I came to see you about. Tell Peter Toll at Pullach Markus Wolf has broken the code for our radio transmissions. That is why they have ceased. Tell him switch to the Weimar system. Weimar the town. He'll know what to do.'

'I feel hemmed in here – more so than back at the zigzag. What happens if I'm challenged?'

'You bluff your way through. You've done it before . . .'

'And supposing I don't pull it off? Where do we go?'

'You have to carry off a bluff. Look around you – there is nowhere to run, to hide. It's that damned storm. It must have flooded stretches of the road. Now, listen to me. You have to get out to pass on the information inside your head. You think only of yourself. In Leipzig, if Gerda gets into trouble and you can slip away, you do so. No heroics. We have expended too much effort to have you caught.'

'You mean I just leave her in the lurch?'

'You leave her to cope on her own. She will expect it. That is an order. And now I will get back inside, lie down on the couch on this side with a travelling rug thrown carelessly over my legs. Gerda is huddled up behind you. Three become one.'

'I don't follow that . . .'

'We were stopped at the road-block just before we reached

325

the Radom farm. The patrol saw two men and a girl. We were stopped again by those two Intelligence men on the country road. They also saw two men and a girl. Either may have reported us to Leipzig. Now we try to look just like one man on his own. If they come up to us they're likely to arrive on the driver's side – at your window. Do the best you can.' Falken paused as he prepared to lift himself up. 'And if Pullach really wants to help us, they will send you to join us as a member of Group Five.'

Newman was left alone. He pursed his lips. Falken had just paid him the highest compliment. He had little time to dwell on the subject. A Vopo, very fat with a beer belly, was walking down the line of stationary traffic, glancing at each vehicle.

Let me have men about me that are fat. The quotation flashed into Newman's mind. Shakespeare. *Julius Caesar?* He wasn't sure. He lowered the window. The portly Vopo hitched up his Sam Browne belt, peered in Newman's window.

'And where are you off to?'

'Supposed to be a holiday. I don't know whether she'll come now. Camping out in this weather?'

'If she likes you enough, Comrade. Make her like you enough.' The Vopo's jowls shook with amusement. 'You'll keep her warm enough inside there. Just the two of you?'

'Why would I need her mother?'

The jowls shook again. Newman thought he was probably the first driver who had not grumbled at the hold-up.

'How long before we start moving?' Newman asked. 'You have a difficult job, I know. But if I'm late her mother will get back before we leave.'

'We can't have that, can we?'

The Vopo walked back the way he had come to the traffic control point. He disappeared but within two minutes the traffic flowing in the opposite direction stopped. The traffic ahead of the camper began moving forward. As he passed the control point Newman waved thank you to the fat Vopo who personally waved him on, giving a significant wink. All boys together . . .

Which one of you is Janus? Tweed asked himself the question as he looked round the four sector chiefs on either side of the conference table at Park Crescent.

326

Harry Masterson, his chin showing traces of another five o'clock shadow, drummed his fingers quietly on the polished surface. Hugh Grey, seated on Tweed's right, had his usual eager-beaver look, ready for anything. Erich Lindemann to the left, waited, pad and four coloured pencils arranged neatly in front of him. Guy Dalby sat perfectly still, his eyes never leaving Tweed, who cleared his throat.

'Gentlemen, I've summoned you to this rather early morning meeting to save time. You can all return to your respective European headquarters at the first opportunity. By now your people may have come up with some theories about the lack of opposition activity. It worries me. It signals some major operation. But what? I hope you find out quickly. I have a feeling we're short of time.'

'And what will you be doing?' Dalby asked in his brusque, businesslike manner. 'Where can we contact you?'

'I return to Hamburg.' Tweed paused, his eyes scanning the four men, searching for the smallest reaction. 'I fly back there within the next forty-eight hours . . .'

'Maybe some protection this time? Discreetly, of course,' Grey suggested.

'No!' Tweed was emphatic. 'I go alone. I work better that way. As to contact,' he addressed Dalby, 'call Monica. Talk to her as though you're talking to me. I'll be keeping her posted.'

Masterson grinned, smoothed down his jet black hair with one hand. 'Can't keep away from the field, can you? Itchy feet – that's your problem.'

'I especially expect results from the Balkan sector,' Tweed rapped back. 'That's where the hornet's nest is.' He switched his gaze. 'Any comment, Erich?'

Lindemann was scribbling away on his pad with the red pencil. Which one was that? Tweed was too far away to see. Lindemann laid down the pencil, folded his hands.

'Nothing I can think of.'

Typical, Tweed thought. Dry as dust. No wonder he'd earned the nickname of The Professor. While they all waited he removed his glasses, deliberately took his time cleaning them on his handkerchief. At a side table Monica sat taking notes for the minutes she'd type later. Now she also watched Tweed with

327

a puzzled expression. Not like him to prolong a conference. He regarded most meetings as a waste of time, to be got over with as soon as possible. Pressure, Tweed was thinking. That was what the psychiatrist, Dr Generoso, had said would drive a man leading a double life to panic eventually. He was putting on the pressure now. The silence became oppressive. Someone shuffled their feet. He glanced round the table again.

Grey sat with a smile of anticipation on his pink face. He was expecting another pronouncement. Masterson smoothed his gleaming hair again while Tweed went on polishing his glasses. Dalby sat with his arms folded, quite motionless as he stared at his chief. Iron self-control. Lindemann was scribbling on his pad, this time with the green pencil. Did he change the colours for each sector chief? Nutty way of going on. Tweed replaced his glasses, spoke suddenly, watching them closely.

'Dr Berlin.' Another loaded pause. 'Any information any of you can get on him. Supposed to be the Light of the World, the guardian of refugees, the protector of the helpless everywhere.' His tone was heavy with irony. 'I just wonder.' He held up a hand to silence Grey who had opened his mouth, anxious to make a contribution. 'No comments, please. Just dig. Deep as you can go into his background.'

Tweed clasped his hands on the table, studying each man in turn. Janus was here, at this very meeting, concealing himself behind a mask. The man who looked both East and West. And possibly a mass murderer. Unless I've got it all wrong.

No, I'm damned if I have. One of these faces sent Fergusson to his death. That's for certain. And they were all in Frankfurt, attending the meeting I held just after promoting them. The night the Dutch girl was slaughtered. And they were all in Europe – whereabouts unknown – when Helena Andersen, the blonde Swedish girl had been cut to pieces on Priwall Island. As was the case when Iris Hansen, the girl, again a blonde, from Copenhagen had met the same grisly fate.

But most telling by far was the two-year-old unsolved killing of Carole Langley in East Anglia on the night of July 14. The four men he was looking at had attended Hugh Grey's birthday party at Hawkswood Farm. Too much coincidence. It gave him an eerie feeling to be sitting with these four men. They all looked so normal. Dr Generoso again. He'd said such a person might well appear completely normal for long periods. Tweed stood up.

'Meeting ended.'

'Tweed is coming back . . . flying to Hamburg . . . within forty-eight hours . . .'

The caller, using German, was speaking from a phone booth in the Post Office near Leicester Square. Martin Vollmer, in his apartment in Altona, took the message, thanked the caller, but already the connection was broken.

Vollmer cradled the receiver, waited a few seconds, lifted it again and dialled a number. He had to wait for the phone to ring five times before it was answered by the girl he was calling.

'Tweed is coming back . . .'

For the second time the wires were humming across West Germany. Always the same message, couched in exactly the same words. Until it reached the office of a lawyer in West Berlin. He took the call, put down the phone, told his secretary he had to go out, and walked the short distance to Checkpoint Charlie where he crossed into East Berlin.

'What's happened? Why are you looking so smug?' demanded Lysenko as Wolf put down the phone. He had just entered the room.

'As I predicted, Tweed is coming back. Flying in to Hamburg. I predict something else. He will make straight for Lübeck. I have arranged for Munzel to be informed. You don't look so smug yourself . . .'

'The timing!' Lysenko barked. 'It's going to be close. We have a major operation under way.'

'What major operation? Or does it, by chance, not concern me?'

'It does not. You have enough on your plate. The timing? How many times do I have to ask you a question? I don't like this at all. Tweed is a menace.'

'I probably know more about Tweed than you do,' Wolf commented. 'As to timing, he's expected in Hamburg about two days from now according to the report from Balkan.'

'Then Tweed has to be eliminated quickly . . .'

329

'I have already sent a message to Munzel – who is waiting for his arrival in Lübeck.'

'We can't be sure he'll go back to Lübeck,' Lysenko snapped.

'Which is why I've also alerted our man at Hamburg Airport – Tweed will be followed from the moment he comes through Customs.'

'Munzel made a hash of the job before. This time he must do the job. And fast.'

'He will deal with the problem as soon as he can. More than that I cannot guarantee. How much time would you say he has?'

'A week. Two at the outside.'

'I think you can sleep well tonight.'

Inside his hotel room at the International, facing Lübeck's main station, Erwin Munzel sprawled in bed as Lydia Fischer, the German girl he had picked up on the train from Puttgarden, took a shower. He was finding her very satisfactory – and not only as a cover. He reached for the phone as it began ringing.

'Vollmer speaking . . .'

The voice paused. Munzel had to think of the code word after his recent enjoyable experience with Lydia.

'Sylt is the place I've booked for the holiday,' he said.

'Listen. Tweed is coming back. Flying in to Hamburg within the next two days. Call me at noon as usual. You have three days to complete the deal after the customer arrives.'

'I don't work to time schedules . . .'

'You do on this one. Or lose your job.'

Vollmer had gone off the line before Munzel could protest. He lay staring at the ceiling for several minutes. When Lydia came out of the shower he went into the bathroom and took a quick shower himself. He dressed quickly, talking as he did so.

'You wanted to do some shopping on your own. How about doing it now? I have some business calls to make.'

He waited until she had left the room, then packed half his clothes in the suitcase he had recently purchased. Leaving the International, he walked in blazing sunlight past the Movenpick and continued on over the bridge on to the island.

He paused outside the entrance to the Hotel Jensen, peered

330

in, saw there was only a girl on reception – not the manager – and walked in. He booked himself a room in the first name that came into his head. Hugo Schmidt from Osnabrück. Ascending in the lift, he unlocked the door of a room at the back.

It took him only a few minutes to put his clothes inside the wardrobe and a couple of drawers. He left toothbrush, paste and shaving kit in the bathroom. Then he went back down in the lift and walked out of the hotel, the key of the room still inside his pocket.

He was second-guessing Tweed, gambling that if he did turn up in Lübeck he'd go back to the Jensen. The English were conservative, habit-ridden. Now all he had to do was to wait for Vollmer to warn him Tweed was on the way.

Forty

They were in the middle of Leipzig and Gerda sat alongside Newman. He needed her to guide him. He drove slowly along the Gerberstrasse at eight o'clock in the evening. Peering through the windscreen, he twisted his head to look up. An immense modern slab-like building soared into the sky.

'What's that place?' he asked. 'Must be thirty storeys high.'

'The Hotel Merkur. The best place to stay for miles around. It has three restaurants.'

He drove on, following her directions. Falken was sprawled along one of the couch seats in the living area. They came to an intersection just as the lights turned against them. Newman braked. There was the slam of a door behind them.

'What was that?' Newman enquired.

'Falken has just left. Look, there he is . . .'

The tall German was hobbling along the pavement past the camper with the aid of his stick. He continued for a few metres and stopped. Two men in civilian clothes had blocked his path, were talking to him.

'Oh, my God,' Newman said. 'Plain clothes police.'

'I think so, yes,' Gerda replied, watching.

Falken had produced his folder, making a performance of

balancing himself on his stick. Now he was waving his arms, flapping his hands like a bird. The two men started grinning. After examining the folder it was handed back to him. Falken went on conversing with them.

'He's diverting their attention from us,' Gerda said. Newman sensed the strain in her voice. 'I think he was talking about the grey lag when he flapped his arms. He's waiting for us to drive on.'

Falken had glanced briefly over his shoulder as he gesticulated. Newman fumed. Why didn't the bloody light change? It seemed obstinately stuck on red. The longer Falken had to talk the greater the danger one of the two policemen would ask the wrong question.

'When the lights change don't speed up,' Gerda warned, sensing his frustration. 'Falken will cope . . .'

The lights changed. As instructed, Newman turned left slowly. In his wing mirror he saw Falken hobbling away, the two plain clothes men strolling in the opposite direction. Oddly, Newman felt lost. Falken, the friend he had shared the past few days with, had gone out of his life as swiftly as he had entered it. Again Gerda sensed his reaction.

'No goodbyes. Just till the next time. Concentrate on your driving. We're in Leipzig. And it's crawling with the wolf-pack.'

'Wolf-pack?'

'Markus Wolf's men. I've seen them all over the place. You keep straight ahead here . . .'

Newman swallowed. He had a lump in his throat. For Falken. Ridiculous sentimentality. Keep your eye on the road. Gerda placed a hand gently on his wrist. She had very small hands.

'Emil, listen carefully. We shall soon leave the camper and kill some time in a café. You are going out tonight. A very tough young man called Stahl will drive you overnight to Rostock, the Baltic port. You will travel inside a big armoured truck carrying arms to Cuba. We think they are bound for Nicaragua. It will not be comfortable – you will be sealed inside the truck for many hours.'

'Who is this Stahl?'

'You should know – in case the truck is stopped, but that is most unlikely. He is a Party member . . .'

'You have to be joking, I hope.'

332

'He is a Party member,' she repeated. 'Which is why he has been entrusted with the task of driving this vital consignment. We knew him when he was a youth. Very intelligent. He hated the system, wanted to escape to the West. Falken persuaded him to go the route – do all the right things in the hope he would be selected as a Party member. It worked. Aboard that truck he will take you into the dock area. From there you travel by sea to the West.'

'Aboard what kind of ship? Bound for where?'

'I have no idea. One important thing not to forget – when you talk with him. He knows only Falken and myself. He must not know about Radom. We use the cell system – taking a leaf out of the Soviets' book. Turn left here, follow the one-way system.'

It seemed to Newman they were driving in a large circle as they moved into the suburbs. They passed shopping parades. Many had signs, Volks-this, Volks-that. The people's-this, the people's-that. All State-controlled. One shop window was full of colour TV sets.

The pedestrians were well-dressed, looked well nourished. A great contrast to his stay in East Berlin as foreign correspondent several years before. One thing had not changed compared with the West. The men and women had a stolid appearance. No one seemed to be enjoying themselves. They trudged along with their plastic shopping bags, drab as their surroundings. A grey, dull and dreary atmosphere – even by the light of the setting sun.

'Drive in to this camp site,' Gerda instructed. 'Park it under those trees over there – away from the other campers. Then wait while I pay the fee.'

He turned in off the highway along an asphalt track, swung off the track over rough grass. He had hardly stopped when Gerda opened the door, dropped to the ground and disappeared.

The suburbs had ended abruptly. The camp-site was on the edge of open country. Fields of grass stretched away into the distance. Very few people were about. He checked his watch. 8.30 p.m. Soon it would be dark. Where would they link up with Stahl?

Newman had to wait fifteen minutes before Gerda returned

and she was carrying a large string bag in either hand full of cans of food, a loaf of bread and cartons of fruit juice. He looked round quickly. Still no one about. He opened the door, took the bags off her and she climbed into the cab.

'Let's be quick,' she said. 'Put away all this stuff inside the cupboards above the washing-up sink. I'll lay the table for two.'

'We're going to eat here?'

'We're leaving here as fast as we can. But if the police do find this camper they'll think we're coming back. With the table laid for a meal and food in the cupboards . . .'

He remembered Falken's instruction. *Obey Gerda* . . . While she laid the table he put away the contents of the bags. She went on explaining.

'And someone on the camp site may have seen us. Just before we go I'll pull back one of the curtains. Anyone peering inside will see this table laid. Everything has to look quite normal.'

'We do need to eat soon,' Newman told her. 'If we can.'

'And we're going to. But we must get away from here. Emil, you do have your shaving things?'

He patted the pocket of his raincoat where he carried the small hold-all containing shaving equipment, soap and a comb. She opened the cupboards he had stacked, took out a small bottle of mineral water and a collapsible plastic cup.

'Put these in your other pocket. The water is for drinking and shaving. You'll be sealed inside the truck for hours. It is important you have shaved by tomorrow morning. The police may think you are a drug addict unless you look normal. Now, we leave.'

Newman noticed how tidy the camp site was. No paper bags thrown down on the short-cropped grass, no mess of used cans and bottles. Near the exit on to the road they passed a family, a couple with two small children, returning. Gerda said 'Good night', and then they walked along the pavement.

It gave Newman an odd feeling of nakedness to leave the camper. They had travelled inside their cocoon for only a few hours but it had sheltered them from a hostile world. Now, as they walked side by side towards a built-up area he felt terribly exposed.

'Where were all the people on the camp site?' he asked.

'Out doing what we're going to do. Getting something to eat. They're on holiday. Often the woman cooks lunch, but to give her a break the husband takes her out for the evening meal.'

'We have the time? I'm thinking of meeting Stahl . . .'

'I've made the time – I want to get some hot food inside you before you board the truck. And we meet him after dark – out in the country. You'll see. We're going in here.'

They had reached a modern shopping parade of two-storey buildings. The shops were closed but a restaurant standing on its own was open. Gerda, clutching her windcheater, carefully wrapped round the Uzi, led the way inside.

It was an old place, looked as though it had been there since before the Second World War. The walls were lined with dark oak panelling, the ceiling supported with heavy oak beams. Gerda ensconced them in a booth alongside one wall so they sat facing each other with the heavy table between them.

A waiter wearing a green apron took their order. He hardly glanced at Newman as Gerda ordered for both of them. Newman had beer to drink, a heavy dark beer in a large tankard. Gerda sipped a glass of white wine. Newman felt a sense of strain – Falken had slipped out of his life in a matter of seconds and soon it would be, 'Goodbye, Gerda . . .' He wasn't looking forward to that.

'This place seems pretty old,' he remarked.

Gerda watched him as she replied, ran a hand through her chestnut-coloured hair. 'I heard Leipzig and the suburbs were badly bombed during the war. This place survived. One of those flukes.'

They talked quietly, but there were few other customers and no one close. I don't know a damned thing about her, Newman was thinking, and I can't ask. If I'm caught, put under pressure, I mustn't be able to give them anything which would identify her.

They dined off fish, well-cooked by a dry method, and *kartoffel*, the soft tasty German potato, and a plate of rye bread. Newman devoured the enormous portion and Gerda watched with approval.

'They give you plenty here,' he remarked.

'I don't think you heard – but I ordered a double portion. I want you full up before your trip.'

335

'How much longer have we got?'

'We've time for coffee. The mocha is good here. Then we must leave.'

She had checked her watch. Outside it was dark now and street lamps threw a pallid glow over the deserted street. They drank their coffee in silence, Gerda watching Newman again. He felt much better, and much worse – he really would have liked to get to know this girl much more closely.

'What about that machine pistol?' he whispered after he had paid the bill.

'I'm dumping it when I can. It would have been dangerous to leave it inside the camper.'

Her words were prophetic. As they walked back past the camp site on the opposite side of the road they saw a patrol car parked at the entrance. Vopos, flashing torches, were moving among the campers. They walked on, careful not to hurry.

'We cycle to the highway where we meet Stahl,' Gerda told him, again checking her watch. 'And we are in good time.'

'Where do we find cycles?'

'You will soon see.'

She took his arm and they walked like a couple who had known each other for a long time. Half a mile beyond the camp site an area of allotments spread out to one side of the road. She led him down a cinder pathway, stopped by one of the small huts which presumably was for storing tools – spades, rakes and other equipment.

He held the windcheater masking the Uzi while she took out a key from her handbag, inserted it in a large padlock and turned it. She disappeared inside, reappeared wheeling out a cycle, propped it against the shed, vanished again and brought out the second machine.

There was a chill in the air now. She took the windcheater from Newman, extracted the Uzi and rammed it inside her saddle bag. Putting on the windcheater, she watched Newman adjusting the height of his saddle, testing the brakes. He looked at her.

'Ready when you are . . .'

'I'll just close the padlock, then I'd better lead the way.'

She pushed her cycle along the cinder track, only mounting

her machine when they reached the road. She turned right, away from the suburb and the camp site and he pulled alongside her, then told her to stop.

'What's the matter?'

'Lights. Falken said the police would stop cyclists without lights.'

'You're so right. I must be losing my grip.'

They switched on their lights at front and rear and resumed cycling. There was no other traffic on the road and they had to cycle warily – after no rain for weeks the storm had made the road surface greasy. Beyond the grass verges on either side were deep ditches and beyond them open fields with, here and there, islands of tree clumps blurred in the gloom. Overhead the sky was a sea of clouds and the chilly breeze was raw as they cycled together.

'Now I want us to stop for a minute,' Gerda said.

They had been careful to use the toilets at the restaurant so Newman was puzzled for a moment. He watched while she took her handbag out of the saddle bag, took out a handkerchief, hauled out the Uzi and wiped it clean of fingerprints. Then she stepped on to the grass verge, using her handkerchief as a glove and threw the machine pistol into the ditch. It sank out of sight with a splash followed by a brief gurgle. They cycled on.

Shortly after she had dumped the weapon they reached an intersection where the country road they'd cycled along met a main highway. Gerda turned left on to the highway and pulled over on to the verge about a hundred metres from the intersection.

'We meet Stahl here. He'll come from that direction.'

She pointed the way they had come, checked her watch, took a small pair of field glasses out of her handbag. Leaning the cycle against her thighs, she raised the binoculars to her eyes and focused them, looking back down the highway.

'What's the idea?' Newman asked.

'Night glasses. I know the registration number of the truck Stahl will be driving. I have a small torch. I have to signal before he gets here. I want to be sure it's the right vehicle before I start flashing a torch about.'

'You really are well organized.' Newman hesitated. 'Is this where we say Goodbye?'

'No – till we meet again . . .'

'I'd like to thank you for all . . .' he began.

She placed an index finger over his mouth. 'It's the other way round. Why don't we just say it was good knowing one another? That we make a good team. And if a car or the wrong truck comes along we're conspicuous – so we pretend to be lovers.'

'We'd better practise then.'

He laid both cycles on the verge, took her in his arms, one hand behind the nape of her neck and kissed her full on the lips. She stiffened for a few seconds, then wrapped her arms round him and pressed her breasts against his chest. She kissed him ravenously, her whole body merged against his.

'Oh, damnit,' he said, looking over her right shoulder.

She released him, breathing heavily, turned to look in the same direction, the field glasses dangling from their strap round her wrist. In the distance two headlights like great eyes were coming down the highway. She pressed the lenses to her eyes. Newman kept his fingers crossed. This couldn't be Stahl. Not yet.

'It's him,' she said.

Newman glanced all round. No other traffic in sight. Behind the headlights the huge truck lumbered closer. Gerda flashed her torch on and off. Two short flashes, one long one. The truck passed the intersection, slowed, pulled up alongside them. A big job. An eight-wheeler. The cab attached – part of – the vehicle. A Mercedes. The driver kept his engine running, peered out of the window and Gerda called up to him. Something Newman didn't catch. A heavily-built young man with thick brown hair descended to the roadway and Gerda made swift introductions.

'Stahl, this is Emil Clasen . . .'

'Come with me,' Stahl said to Newman, then noticed the cycles lying on the verge. 'You'll only need one of these now,' he said to Gerda. He picked up Newman's machine, hoisted it above his head and hurled it clear across the ditch. It landed deep inside the field of rye, disappeared. 'Back of the truck,' he said to Newman. 'Hurry . . .'

Using a deadlock key, he opened one of the two rear

338

doors, handed Newman a torch he'd hauled out of his trouser pocket and pointed inside the dark cavern. Newman turned to say something to Gerda but Stahl took his arm in a strong grip and urged him up inside the truck. Gerda thrust the field-glasses into his hand. 'Take these. They might be useful.'

'Seat for you at the far end,' Stahl called up. 'Use that torch – or break a kneecap. We'll talk later. We're too near Leipzig here. The porthole windows in these doors are one-way armoured glass . . .'

The door slammed shut and Newman was in pitch darkness. He switched on the torch as he heard Stahl locking the door. The porthole windows had circular flaps shutting him off from the outside world. He swivelled one flap upwards, switched off the torch.

Gerda appeared on her machine, cycling back towards Leipzig as Stahl released the air-brakes and the huge truck started lumbering forward. In the brief moment he'd had the torch on he'd seen a hanging strap attached to the wall of the truck. He held on to it with his left hand, watching Gerda's rear red light receding. The truck picked up speed. Then he froze.

A patrol car, travelling very fast, was approaching the inter-section. He doubted whether they had seen the truck stop. Moving at that speed they'd have been inside the suburbs. He raised the night-glasses and pressed them against his eyes. The road surface along the highway was good, the truck was so heavy it hardly swayed.

The patrol car swung out of the intersection on to the high-way, passed Gerda cycling, stopped, perfomed an illegal U-turn, drew up alongside Gerda. Two Vopos stepped out, halted her. Then he realized she was showing them her papers. One of the Vopos shook his head, opened the rear door, bundled her inside and followed. The other man climbed behind the wheel. Oh, God! And the bastards had left her cycle lying on the verge. He couldn't do anything. He was trapped inside the truck. The patrol car drove off, turning back towards Leipzig. Newman felt sick as a dog.

Forty-One

Inside the moving truck Newman swivelled the torch slowly round, getting his bearings before he looked for the seat at the front. There was a narrow central corridor which ran straight to the driver's cab. Along either side of the corridor long heavy wooden boxes were piled on top of each other from floor to roof.

They reminded him of ammunition boxes. Each had a handle at the end made of rope thick as a ship's hawser. They were held in position by leather straps which pinioned them to the walls. He checked for stencil markings which might indicate the contents. Nothing.

He made his way cautiously along the corridor. The walls of the truck puzzled him. From the outside the vehicle had the appearance of a refrigerated truck. There had been some lettering along the side of the vehicle but Stahl had hustled him aboard so quickly he hadn't read it.

At the front end the driver's cab was closed off from the main body of the truck. In his torch beam he saw a sliding panel and guessed that gave access to the driving cab. He found a small space just behind the cab beyond where the last boxes were piled up. To the left a leather padded seat was screwed to the floor. Opposite was an enamel bucket with a lid; toilet facilities, he guessed.

He sank into the seat, still wearing his raincoat, suddenly exhausted. It had been constant tension ever since they'd left Radom's farm. First the camper underneath the zig-zag. His concentrated interview with Karen Piper. Their flight along the old rail track. Hiding under the arched bridge as the Vopos stayed parked overhead. Then the storm, driving the camper along the flooded gulch.

Above all, what hit him now was seeing Gerda taken away by that bloody patrol car. Would she bluff her way through? He had no idea. Probably he'd never know her fate. He switched off the torch to save the battery, then stood up and knocked on

340

the panel to let Stahl know where he was. The panel opened briefly. Stahl called out over his shoulder.

'Comfortable in there?' An ironic note.

'I'm all right . . .'

'Talk to you soon. When we can safely stop. Things you should know . . .'

The panel was shut in his face. Newman had caught a brief glimpse of the highway stretching ahead into the night. The powerful headlight beams showing a deserted road. More trees now, some lining the edge of the highway. He kept on his raincoat. It was cold inside the truck.

He didn't expect to sleep, but sagged on the chair he dropped into an uneasy doze. The vehicle was moving faster, the huge tyres carrying it on and on. He wished he had a compass to check in which direction they were moving. He blinked his eyes open. The truck had stopped.

Stahl opened the rear door and Newman jumped down on to the highway. His night vision was good – he'd deliberately felt his way back along the corridor without using the torch. The truck was parked in a lay-by, dense fir forest crowded to the edge of the highway on both sides.

'Get into the passenger seat in the cab. Join you in half a minute.'

Stahl was closing the door, locking it as Newman strolled along the highway past the truck, stretching the ache out of his legs. The night was heavy with silence, the air fresh and invigorating. As he reached the cab Newman saw Stahl had parked on the crest of a hill, giving a view of many kilometres in both directions. Not a pair of headlights in sight.

He climbed up into the high cab, closed the door and Stahl nimbly mounted the other side, shutting his own door. He offered Newman a thermos and a package wrapped in grease-proof paper.

'Sandwiches and coffee, Comrade.'

The 'Comrade' startled Newman for a moment, then he realized it was a reflex greeting on the part of Stahl. After all, he was a Party member.

'The coffee's welcome,' Newman said, unscrewing the top which served as a cup. 'The sandwiches I'll eat later.'

341

'Good idea. We have five minutes, then I have to get moving. You go back inside the truck. You've got identity papers? Let me have a look. And we're parked here because we can see anything coming for kilometres.' He whistled as he checked Newman's folder by the overhead light.

'Something wrong?' Newman asked.

Stahl shrugged his broad shoulders and grinned. 'No. Something's right. Border Police. Special assignment. Couldn't be better. If we're stopped – but especially when we arrive in Rostock.'

'Why?'

'Most people in the West know about the minefield belt along the landward side of the border between the DDR and the outside world. Not so many know there's a similar forbidden zone along the Baltic coast. Minefield, patrols, dogs – the lot. You're Border Police so you're permitted entry. We're not likely to be stopped,' he went on in his confident way, 'because of what we're carrying. If we are, you're in the guard's seat. And you're the boss. Special assignment? Escorting the stuff I'm carrying.'

'Which is? Or shouldn't I ask?'

'You found the bucket? Your own private toilet? Well, when you go back, open the box behind the bucket. They forgot to padlock that one. Arms for Cuba, as you probably know. They come from the Skoda works in Czechoslovakia.' He handed back the folder. 'Be ready to show that. Kick up hell if we are stopped. Boot them up the ass. Thanks.' He took back the thermos.

'When do you expect to reach Rostock?'

'About dawn. The way I'll drive between cities. With a bit of luck it will still be dark. Easier to smuggle you aboard a ship bound for the West. We'll stop again later and I'll tell you more.'

'I thought this was an armoured truck . . .'

'It is.' Stahl grinned again, swallowed some coffee. 'Tap the side gently when you get back. This is quite a vehicle they designed, the bastards. On the outside it looks like a refrigerated truck. Camouflage. It's armoured, all right.'

'Why all the secrecy?' Newman asked. 'Inside the DDR?'

'Because they're clever. It's never broadcast to the West –

for obvious reasons – but there is a resistance movement here. Small but powerful, well armed. They know someone like Falken would love to get his hands on what you're travelling with, that he can muster a large number of men. So they send me through like any ordinary truck.'

'You said earlier we shouldn't be stopped . . .'

'The chiefs of police along the route we're taking are given my registration number. They spread the word it's a consignment for the Party. Let it through. But, we shall be stopped at certain points,' Stahl warned. 'You pay tolls to use certain highways. I just pay and move on. So don't worry if I stop and you hear voices. Just keep quiet.'

'Thanks for the tip. My nerves will rest easier.'

'That special assignment folder you're carrying. Can I ask if you've had to use it? What you said? Sheer curiosity. I find it lonely sitting hour after hour in this cab.'

'Drugs. I was chasing a drug ring.'

'Funny that,' Stahl commented, 'that you should use drugs. After what I heard.'

'Why?'

Newman was only casually interested. He drank the rest of his coffee, thinking how much warmer it was inside the cab.

'Because we heard something – maybe information you should pass on to the BND when you get back. We have a man at Leipzig Airport. Won't tell you what he does. Recently a Tupolev landed from Moscow. Quite a fuss about the passenger. Colonel in the GRU. He came off the aircraft dead drunk. Vodka. Could hardly get down the mobile staircase. Got into a waiting car and started to drive off. Our chap went on board. Guess what he found.'

'You tell me.'

'This stupid colonel's brief-case. Let's call our man Karl – not his real name. Karl carries a lock-pick. He used it on the locked brief-case, glanced through the papers inside a file. One of them – Karl understands Russian – was a report about a cargo of heroin bound for England. Five hundred kilos . . .'

'How much?' Newman was suddenly alert. 'That's enormous.'

'So we thought. Then Karl saw the car coming back. He put the file back, locked the brief-case, slipped it back under the

343

seat and hid in the crew's cabin until they'd collected it and gone.'

'Any indication as to the method of transport?'

'Yes. By sea. Aboard a Polish freighter. The *Wroclaw*. It was routed to call in at Rostock shortly . . .'

'Which British port was it heading for?'

'The report didn't say. Or maybe Karl didn't get that far. I think we ought to get moving soon now. Funny about that brief-case. The Russkies aren't as bright as they'd like the world to think. Thank God. I'm going to have a pee before we start.'

'I'll join you. By the way, can I ask which route we're taking to Rostock?'

'Why not. Magdeburg, Stendal, Tangermünde – then due north through Pritzwalk, the lake district, Güstrow and on to Rostock.'

He made it sound like a morning's outing to Brighton. As they relieved themselves at the edge of the forest Newman's head was spinning with what Stahl had just told him. They were walking to the rear of the truck when he asked his question.

'Do you really think Karl got it right – five hundred kilos?'

'Karl never gets anything wrong.'

It was nearly midnight at Park Crescent. Everyone had left the building long ago – except Tweed, Monica and the two men seated in his office. Which was why Tweed had chosen this late hour.

'I'm taking you with me to Hamburg for protection,' he opened the conversation. 'Normally I wouldn't dream of travelling in this way, as you know.' He paused and threw out his hands in a gesture of resignation. 'But the PM insists. Last time I flew there I took Bob Newman with me – but he's disappeared.'

'Sounds as though the PM knows what she's doing then,' Harry Butler commented.

Tweed studied the two men. Both spoke fluent German, so that made sense. Harry Butler was the taller, more heavily-built of the pair; also the older and more experienced. He had a wary look, a relaxed manner and moved as though treading through a minefield.

Pete Nield was dark-haired, had dark, quick-moving eyes and was a man for a tight corner. Slimmer, he took trouble over his dress and was wearing a smart navy blue business suit with a carnation in his buttonhole.

The two men were a great contrast in personality but together they worked well. There was a famous occasion when they had acted as streetwalkers, tailing a Markus Wolf agent for a whole week before he made the contact they were seeking. During all those long seven days the experienced German agent had never once suspected their presence.

'Any suggestions as to how we go about it?' Tweed asked.

'First,' Butler began in his deliberate tone, 'we'll both be happy to work on this one. Ian Fergusson was killed in Hamburg. Maybe we'll get lucky, meet up with the character who did the job.'

'Weapons,' said Nield. 'We can't take them with us. But can we get some at the other end?'

It was a typical Nield question. Tweed looked dubious, caught Butler's eye, who nodded his agreement with the suggestion.

'I suppose we could obtain you something from Kuhlmann,' Tweed replied.

'Kuhlmann?' Nield said. 'He's a toughie. I met him once. He never wastes a word – or a moment. Is he involved?'

'Yes and no. We can talk about that later.'

'The method,' Butler questioned, again typically. 'We travel with you on the aircraft? Good. The most effective technique is we travel separately. Pete takes a seat across the gangway from you. I'll be further back. What about arrival in Hamburg?'

'I'm staying for one night at the Four Seasons.' Tweed pulled a wry face. 'Cost us a bomb, but the PM has put no limit on the budget this time. Both of you stay there, too . . .'

'But arrive separately,' Butler said firmly. 'Pete takes the first cab. You take the next one. I follow behind. That way we'll know if we're being followed – if *you* are being tailed. Could there be a leak? About your flying to Germany?'

Tweed hesitated, caught Monica's eye. 'There is a leak, I know that. And what I've just said is totally confidential.'

'Then what I've just outlined is a good plan,' Butler stated. 'No chances. Not this time.'

Forty-Two

The truck was moving at high speed through the night as Stahl headed non-stop for Rostock. Newman placed the grease-proof-wrapped package of sandwiches on his seat, then swung the torch beam on to the single wooden box jammed in against the wall behind the enamel bucket.

The padlock through the two ring-bolts was loose. He took it off and raised the heavy lid. By the light of the torch, steadying himself with one hand pressed against the rear of the cab, he stared down at the contents. Row upon row of Skorpion machine pistols neatly stacked. His light reflected off grease on the working parts. And Stahl had said other boxes contained ammo – the magazines for the weapons. He was travelling with a medium-sized armoury, enough to fuel a small war.

He closed the lid, carefully replaced the loose padlock, picked up his sandwiches and sat on the seat, opening the packet. Doorsteps of rye bread with sausage between them. He began to eat ravenously.

He felt a pang of nostalgia when he took from his raincoat pocket the bottle of mineral water Gerda had given him. He unscrewed the top and drank greedily. Unremitting tension made you thirsty. His mind was a muddle of thoughts as the truck thundered on.

Gerda being bundled inside that patrol car, caught at the last minute. Of all the lousy luck. Five hundred kilos of heroin bound for Britain. The Soviets – Gorbachev – would use any filthy method to demoralize their strongest opponent in Europe. What was the name of that Polish freighter? The *Wroclaw*, that was it.

Newman's nerves were twanging. He had to get out of the DDR. Get back and tell Tweed about Dr Berlin, about the heroin. Two separate and vital pieces of information. He just *had* to slip out of Rostock. He ate all the sandwiches, dropped the greaseproof paper into the bucket.

The truck was swaying now. Stahl was keeping his foot down.

The motion, the emotional fatigue, sent him into a deep doze. At some place during the night he was woken by the sound of voices. The truck had stopped. He tensed, suddenly alert. Then he heard Stahl making a joke. Of course, he was paying one of the tolls. The truck started moving again.

Newman didn't expect to get any more sleep. He was cramped and aching from sitting in the chair. I'd better walk up and down the corridor, get limbered up, he told himself. Before he could stand up he drifted off again. He was vaguely aware of two more stops, more voices from the direction of the cab, but he ignored them.

He woke suddenly, stiff as a board, checked his watch by the illuminated dial. 4 a.m. Another hour or so. This time he made himself stand up. Switching on the torch, he walked down the corridor to the rear, turned round, paced back, turned again, using one hand to keep his balance by pressing it against the walls of boxes.

He was limbering up now. He scratched his chin, felt the stubble. Somewhere before arriving at Rostock he had to shave. That was something he couldn't achieve while the truck was in motion. He began to feel claustrophobic, hemmed in. Reaching the front, he used his clenched knuckles to tap the wall above the bucket. It felt like solid steel. The window panel slid back suddenly. Stahl called over his shoulder.

'You awake in there, Emil?'

'Fresh as paint. I need a shave . . .'

'Last stop before Rostock coming up. Five, ten minutes from now. Don't go to sleep.'

The panel closed, shutting off the outside world. Again Newman had caught a glimpse. Still pitch black. Headlights coming towards them. Open country. A big lake over to the right, black water still as ice, lights reflecting in it from lamps alongside a landing-stage. Boats moored in a marina-like area. Reminded him of Lübeck. Diana Chadwick. The upper-crust Ann Grayle and her sloop. Dr Berlin's two power cruisers. What were they called. *Südwind* and *Nordsee*. That was it. He remained standing so he couldn't fall asleep, waiting. For the last stop before Rostock.

*

347

The call from Moscow came through to Lysenko just after four in the morning. He took it in the apartment they had allocated him, less than a kilometre from Markus Wolf's Leipzig head-quarters.

Lysenko was fuming. He'd had to arrange for a scrambler phone to be installed. Now Wolf had arranged to sleep on the trestle bed in his office there was no privacy there. He recog-nized the deep, decisive voice immediately. Gorbachev himself.

'The despatch of the cargo had to be delayed. I've had reports that it is expected at its destination.'

'It would have to be delayed for two weeks in any case,' Lysenko pointed out.

'I know. But I suggest the transhipment goes ahead. It will be safer that way.'

'Under their noses,' Lysenko agreed. 'I have already ar-ranged for just that. And Balkan is now back in Europe.'

'So the timing is perfect.' Gorbachev's tone reflected his satisfaction. He added a rider. 'But do not assume everything is all right until delivery has been made.'

There was a click. Gorbachev had broken the connection. Lysenko went back into the bathroom to continue his shave. He also felt satisfied. His greatest worry had solved itself. Balkan was back . . .

'Couldn't you have had them followed?' Monica asked Tweed as he prepared to leave for his flat in Chelsea. 'The four sector chiefs, I mean – when they flew back to Europe yesterday.'

'I thought of it, then decided against it. Masterson, Grey, Lindemann and Dalby – every one of them trained men. They'd have spotted streetwalkers within hours. Whoever is Janus, is then alerted. I couldn't risk it. Give him enough rope and he will hang himself. I hope.'

'And you still have no lead?' she persisted. 'As to Janus' identity – not even after thinking over your visits with Diana to their homes?'

'I have too many.' Tweed smiled ruefully. 'I can't get out of my head the idea that the key is what method Janus uses as his release from the enormous tension of leading a double life. Dr Generoso laid some emphasis on that.'

'So?'

348

'Alcohol is the usual one. Philby used it. Grey drinks – in moderation. Harry Masterson can knock back any quantity and still know exactly what someone is saying. Lindemann is teetotal – but I found that Scotch hidden away in a cupboard. That leaves Dalby, a bit of a wine buff. Come to think of it, I didn't see any sign of even a single bottle at his place. He probably keeps it under lock and key . . .'

'I mentioned Diana a moment ago. I've got her ticket for your flight tomorrow . . . today, I mean,' she said, checking her watch, '. . . but you didn't mention to Butler and Nield that she'd be coming with you.'

'It will be a nice surprise for them.' Tweed looked at his own watch. 'God, it's four in the morning. I am sorry – I should have sent you home hours ago.'

'Why? You know I'm an insomniac – especially when we're up to our necks in a mission. But you're not going to have much sleep.'

'A nap is all I need. And I can't wait to get back into the field. My real anxiety is Newman. What's the latest from Peter Toll at Pullach?'

'A big nothing. And I think Peter is getting worried.'

'He'll have something to worry about when I meet him.'

'Next stop the frontier zone,' said Stahl, 'then on to Rostock. There we have a problem – finding a ship to take you out.'

The statement stunned Newman. The truck was parked alongside a small lake, quite deserted. No marinas, no landing-stages. It was still dark. Ahead the highway stretched for miles. As he'd jumped down from the rear of the truck Newman noted the same view behind them – a long stretch of highway. Again Stahl had chosen a place to park where they'd receive plenty of warning of the approach of another vehicle.

Seated behind the wheel Stahl was smoking a cigarette, waiting for his passenger's reaction. Newman couldn't help thinking that Falken would have had the next move planned out. He had to decide this one for himself, but Stahl was much younger than Falken.

'You have a suggestion?' he asked.

'The obvious way out is for you to slip aboard the *Wroclaw*.'

349

'Which you said was bound for Cuba with your consignment of Skorpions?'

'The Polish master is a Captain Anders. He hates the Germans. He was born in Breslau, as it used to be called when it was a part of The Reich in Hitler's time. Now it is part of Poland – and its new name is the same as Anders' ship, Wroclaw.'

'Go on, there has to be more.'

'I am a friend of Anders. He knows I am hostile to the regime, but nothing of my real work. I know he has carried dissident Poles to Sweden in the past. It all depends what he thinks of you – whether he would agree to smuggle you aboard.'

'What kind of a man is he? Describe him in a few words.'

'Very tough. Makes up his own mind. Once he's done that you can't shift him.'

'I don't want to end up in Havana,' Newman objected. 'What is the alternative?'

'I leave you in Rostock – inside the port area. You find your own ship. You are Border Police. Those papers will take you anywhere inside the forbidden zone.'

'And what, may I ask, was the original plan? The one Falken approved?'

Stahl was taking quick, nervous puffs at his cigarette. He's windy, Newman thought. I shouldn't have expected another Falken-Gerda team. And he's known about this problem ever since I came aboard his truck. All the way from Leipzig he's been trying to think of a solution – and come up with zero.

'There was a ship due from Denmark,' Stahl admitted. 'Just before I left the depot I phoned my contact in Rostock. He told me the Danish ship has been delayed in Gedser. Something to do with engine repairs. Normally it's a regular ferry run between Gedser and Warnemünde – that's the ferry terminal on the Baltic coast. Rostock is a short distance up the river Warnow. It's up to you. I can't decide for you, Clasen.'

Thanks a lot, Newman thought. Just abandon me in the middle of the protected frontier zone. But get rid of me, soon as you can. I'll have to take over control, he decided.

'This Captain Anders. How do I communicate with him? I don't speak Polish . . .'

'You don't have to. He speaks German. Your problem with him is you are a German . . .'

350

Which was the first time Newman realized he had passed for a German even with Stahl. He was careful not to disillusion him. A decision had to be taken.

'Can you arrange for me to have a few private words with this Anders? I mean for certain.'

'That I can do.' Stahl took out his pack, lit a fresh cigarette from the stub of the old one. 'For certain. And now you had better get back to your seat.'

'I'm not going back inside the truck. I'm staying here – beside you. All the way from now on.'

'You can't do that. I'm supposed to be alone.'

'Who knows that – in Rostock?'

'Well . . . no one. But if they phone Leipzig.'

'They won't. You said my papers authorized me to move about anywhere inside the frontier zone. You have papers for the consignment you're carrying?'

'Yes. I show them at the port entry gates.'

'Give them to me. Come on, Stahl – no bloody arguments. I also want you to go back inside the truck and fetch me one of those Skorpions. Plus one magazine. You can get that?'

'Yes. They're packed under the guns in that box opposite your seat. But I don't like it. You're not going to use the gun?'

'No, you idiot! It's for show. Get moving. You said that we had to get on to Rostock. Do as I tell you.'

His sudden air of brusque authority intimidated Stahl, who left the cab, returning in a few minutes with the weapon and the magazine. Newman, familiar with the weapon, inserted the magazine, then looked at Stahl.

'Leave me to do the talking. Your job is to take this truck to the *Wroclaw*.' He waited until Stahl had started the engine, was pulling out on to the highway, before he made his final comment.

'And don't smoke a cigarette when we get there.'

Half an hour later as the first cold shafts of dawn light spread across the eastern sky, Stahl slowed down. Ahead a row of red lights lined the side road they had turned on to. A high wire fence stretched away on either side. A closed gate confronted them as two armed guards strolled out of the hut on their left. They had reached the frontier zone.

Forty-Three

Erwin Munzel had an alarm clock inside his head. He'd 'set' it for 4 a.m. He woke, immediately alert, climbed carefully out of bed without disturbing Lydia Fischer, his German girl friend.

He washed and dressed in the bathroom with the door closed. Using one of the hotel pads, he wrote Lydia a note. *Couldn't sleep. Have gone for a walk. Wait for me for breakfast. Love.* He left it tucked under her bedside lamp, collected the room key off the dressing table and went down to the lobby, using the stairs.

'Four hours' sleep does me,' he told the International's night porter as he unlocked the front entrance door. 'I'll be back for breakfast.'

Not that the stupid old cretin gives a damn, Munzel thought as he turned right and walked towards the centre of Lübeck. It was cold at that hour. He was glad he'd put on his thick corduroy trousers and a heavyweight sports jacket. On the opposite side of the street there was no activity inside the Hauptbahnhof. It was still dark and in the distance street lamps threw a weird light on the Holstentor; its ancient twin towers with their witches' hat summits looking menacing in the shadows.

He crossed the deserted bridge over the Trave and a breeze blew his long blond hair. As he'd expected, the door to the Hotel Jensen, where he'd booked another room, was closed. He pressed the bell and a girl opened it cautiously on the chain. Recognizing his blond beard, she let him in.

'Time for bed, wouldn't you agree?'

Munzel gave her his most engaging grin, pressed the elevator button and went up to his room. He had the room key he'd taken with him in his hand and once inside he locked it again and began moving fast.

First he kicked off his shoes, rumpled the bedclothes and pillow, then got into the bed, pulled up the duvet and wriggled around, rolling from side to side. Throwing back the duvet, he got out again. Munzel was nothing if not thorough. He knew

352

chambermaids could tell whether a bed had been slept in or not.

He went into the bathroom where he'd left his spare set of equipment on the glass shelf over the wash-basin. He cleaned his teeth, put the brush back inside the glass after spilling paste on the shelf. He turned on the tap again, lathered his shaving brush, ran it over the palm of his hand, then cleaned it off, leaving it damp and in a different position on the shelf.

Taking one of the bath towels, he held it for a few seconds under the bath tap, squeezed it out, and hung it up. He used the tablet of soap, wetting it under the tap, then rubbed it vigorously round the bottom of the bath. He washed out the bath by leaving the tap running briefly, went back into the bedroom and sat in a chair with a table lamp on while he read a paperback.

He went downstairs to breakfast in the back room as soon as he knew it was open. The cold night air had given him a good appetite. He ate three rolls, drank three cups of coffee and was leaving as a couple came into the room.

With the room key in his pocket he walked out, noting that a man was now on reception. He arrived back at the International to find the doors open and by now it was broad daylight. A clear sky promised yet another hot day.

Lydia was in the bathroom when he re-entered the bedroom. She called out that she wouldn't be long. He told her not to hurry and sagged into a chair. He was successfully keeping up acceptance of his residence at both hotels. Tweed was coming back, so Vollmer had said. He'd phone the Altona number at noon from the station to get the latest news. Munzel was convinced that when Tweed did return he'd go back to the Jensen. And Erwin Munzel would be waiting for him.

Day had not yet broken when Tweed returned to his office at Park Crescent, carrying his suitcase. Reaching the first floor, he stopped. There was a light under his door. George, on duty downstairs, had not said anyone else was in the building.

Taking a firmer grip on the case in his right hand, he used his other hand to turn the handle slowly, keeping close to the wall of the corridor. He threw the door open, swinging his case

353

backwards, ready to hurl it forward into the room. Behind her desk Monica looked up, startled.

'Sorry.' Tweed let out his breath. 'George didn't say you were here. And why are you still here?'

'I knew I wouldn't sleep if I did go home. So I had a bath upstairs. And I thought Toll might call from Pullach with news about Bob Newman. I switched the phone through to the bathroom extension while I wallowed.'

Which is the real reason why you stayed, Tweed thought. Monica had a soft spot for Bob Newman. He took off his coat and settled himself behind his own desk.

'A pretty short nap,' Monica observed.

'An hour. It was enough. I'll get in a good night's rest at the Four Seasons tonight. The flight leaves at 10.35. I can get breakfast round the corner.'

'Flight LH 041,' Monica confirmed from memory. 'Arrives at Hamburg 12.55. Local time.' She played with her pencil. 'I've been wondering about Diana Chadwick. You're sticking pretty close to her.'

'I've told you. She could be the vital witness.'

'Witness to what?'

'Not yet. I'm not sure I'm right.'

'I've been wondering about something else. I like the office when no one else is here – gives me a chance to ruminate. And don't say all cows do that . . .'

'Did I say a word?' Tweed threw up his hands in mock horror.

'Dr Berlin. Why did you throw that into the pot when you had the sector chiefs at that meeting? You said you were flying back to Hamburg – knowing one of them is Janus. Then near the end of the meeting you mention Dr Berlin. I know you. If you've something you want to stick in people's minds, you hold it back until the end of a meeting or conversation.'

'To put even more pressure on Janus.'

'You've lost me again.'

'Because, as before, I'm not sure yet.' Tweed sat up erect in his chair. 'Monica, all the threads are coming together. I can vaguely discern a pattern forming. Isolated facts which I didn't connect up are slipping into place. The trigger which will detonate the climax – which may be very close – is my return to Germany.'

354

'Why?'

'I'm convinced now some very big Russian operation is planned, will soon be activated. That's why everything went all quiet – not only on the western front but right across Europe. Janus is up to his neck in whatever the operation might be.'

'So it could be very dangerous. Thank God you're taking the heavy mob with you.'

'I agree.' There was a look of eager anticipation in Tweed's expression. 'And when that climax comes I intend to be there.'

At the wheel of his black Porsche Harry Masterson was driving through the night as though all the fiends of hell were at his heels. Vienna was already far behind. He had crossed the border into West Germany at Salzburg – and there he had joined the autobahn.

Salzburg . . . München . . . Bypass Augsburg . . . Bypass Ulm . . . Bypass Stuttgart . . . Karlsruhe . . . Mannheim . . . Frankfurt . . . then due north via Hanover to his ultimate destination. Hamburg.

He was already approaching Mannheim. Driving non-stop all night he'd be in Hamburg by morning. In the high-speed lane he overtook great eight-wheel trucks lumbering through the night, belching great exhausts of diesel fumes.

In the glow from the dashboard his black hair gleamed. His chin was unshaven, a thick dark stubble which was the beginnings of a beard. A Mercedes drew alongside him. He glanced to his left. The driver, a blonde-haired girl, gave him a superior look as she flashed ahead. He signalled that he was turning back into the fast lane.

His foot pressed down hard on the accelerator, way over the speed limit. He moved like the wind, overtaking the Merc at the moment it was also about to pull out to pass a truck. As he passed her he glanced at the girl. She looked furious. He grinned, then her headlights were fading into the distance as he kept up the pace. Macho Masterson. No one overtook him. Certainly not some blonde tart who undoubtedly put it about if the mood took her.

It had started the moment he had arrived at headquarters in Vienna. Pat Lancing, his deputy, had the message. Strictly for Masterson only. A phone number. And one word. *Candlestick*.

He'd closed the door of his private office, dialled the number. His top agent working under cover behind The Curtain. The Candlestick Man. They called him that because he was thin as a celery stalk, very stiff and erect. Based in East Germany.

Which was poaching on Hugh Grey's territory. The DDR was his penetration zone. Harry didn't give a toss. Just get the info. The phone conversation had been brief. Urgent – would Harry meet him outside the Opera House in thirty minutes? Harry had said yes, slammed down the phone, left the building, climbed inside the Audi held for his use.

He'd driven slowly along the Opern Ring, spotted Candlestick, pulled into the kerb and Candle had dived into the front passenger seat almost before Harry opened the door. While he listened, Harry drove round the whole Ring system at a sedate pace.

'I've just come out of the DDR,' Candle had said. 'I think I'm being followed . . .'

'Great. That's all I need.'

Candle had hardly heard him as he rabbited on in German. 'I came from Leipzig through Czecho, crossed the border at Gmünd. I thought you should know quickly . . .'

'Know what?'

Candle was wearing a rumpled brown raincoat and a cap. He'd never looked anything much, which was part of the secret of his success. He didn't look clever enough to worry about. His face looked more bony than ever, his thin nose longer, his spaniel eyes more mournful.

'That Dr Berlin has just returned to the Federal Republic – from London.'

'How the hell do you know that?'

Harry's technique was always the same dealing with agents who worked for money. Aggressive manner, short bursts of invective. Put them on the defensive. Make them feel important and they'd ask for more money.

'I got it from a contact in Markus Wolf's headquarters in Leipzig . . .'

'Wolf works out of East Berlin. Every schoolboy knows that.'

'He has a secret HQ in Leipzig. My contact is on his staff. He listened in on a conversation from someone in East Berlin.'

'And who was this person in East Berlin talking to?'

'Markus Wolf himself. They use the code-name Balkan for Dr Berlin . . .'

'Balkan? Dr Berlin? What is this goulash you call information?'

'My informant knows about the code-name. He is high up in Wolf's organization. An Intelligence officer, if you must know.'

'I need to know everything if I'm to believe anything.'

'It took all the money you gave me to obtain this – the fact that Dr Berlin is someone in London . . .'

'All the money?' Masterson sounded incredulous. 'That should have lasted you for months. It was a small fortune.'

'What I've given you is worth a small fortune,' Candle insisted. 'Someone in London,' he repeated.

'Sounds like a bloody fairytale to me,' Masterson snapped.

'Check it with London. But be careful – Dr Berlin could be someone high up. My informant said he was . . .'

'So, give me a name.'

'Oh, he didn't know that . . .'

'Sweet Jesus! You throw my money around like confetti. You don't expect more, I hope?'

'If I'm to go back there, find out more, I need funds.'

'Take this.'

Masterson opened the glove compartment, handed Candle an envelope stuffed with deutschmarks. He drove on while Candle carefully counted the amount. He slipped it inside his pocket, looking more mournful than ever.

'It's not what I expected . . .'

'It's all you're getting. Anything else? No. Right. Where do I drop you?'

'In front of the Opera House. I'm staying at the Astoria – it's only a short walk from there. I don't want to be on the streets a moment longer than I can help. I was followed.'

'You said that before. Shake them, for God's sake. I'll be seeing you.'

He'd dropped Candle back in front of the Opera House, driven on to his office, told Lancing to take control until he got back. His Porsche was parked in a secret garage some distance from headquarters – no one on his staff knew it existed.

Masterson recalled all these recent events as he sped along

357

the autobahn through the night. He had to reach Hamburg by morning. The information Candle had given was disturbing – to him personally. He could have flown, but he needed mobility.

Hugh Grey flew direct to Frankfurt International, took a cab from the airport to his headquarters – housed in a concrete slab of a building near the Intercontinental Hotel where he frequently entertained visiting members of the Bundestag from Bonn.

'Keeping my finger on the pulse,' was one of his favourite phrases.

He spent the rest of the day reading carefully typed reports prepared by what he called his 2-ic. If it was down in writing no one could later say he'd misunderstood them. Grey was notorious for his use of files.

It was late evening when he called in his deputy, Norman Powell, told him to take charge again. 'I have to check on something which has just cropped up,' he explained. 'And – taken by and large – you've done quite well. Keep up the good work . . .'

Grey had chosen Powell for the job for two reasons. First, he was good at admin. Second, a plodding man, Powell posed no threat to his own job. Grey had a leisurely dinner by himself at the Intercontinental's *Rotisserie*, ordering only a half-bottle of Chablis.

After the meal he collected the office Volvo from a nearby underground garage and drove north out of Frankfurt, moving quickly on to the autobahn. He didn't realize it, but Masterson was coming up behind him, still driving like a maniac between Mannheim and Frankfurt. Grey drove carefully, keeping within the speed limit. His destination – Hamburg.

Guy Dalby, characteristically, moved faster than any of his colleagues. He could have flown from Gatwick direct to Belp, the small airport outside Bern. Instead he flew to Geneva. He'd phoned his deputy before leaving London and Joel Kent was waiting for him at Cointrin Airport.

They had dinner together at the *Au Ciel* restaurant with huge picture windows looking out on to the nearby Jura Mountains.

358

Dalby listened while Kent, in his late thirties and very bright, talked. They drank a Montrachet '83 with their meal which Dalby selected after careful study of the wine list.

'I have to go on somewhere else,' Dalby informed Kent over the coffee, checking his watch. 'Keep things humming over . . .'

This decision did not surprise Kent in the least. Dalby was a man who believed in visiting his agents in the field to hear direct from them what was happening. The meal over, Kent left Dalby in the restaurant. He had no idea what Dalby's destination might be, nor would he have dreamt of asking. Dalby was a lone wolf.

Erich Lindemann landed at Kastrup, the airport for Copenhagen, waited at the carousel, collected his case, walked through Passport Control and Customs, and made for the bar in the exit hall. He chose a table with its back to the wall, ordered coffee, drank it slowly.

All the time he watched the entrance to the bar, searching for a familiar face. On board the flight from Heathrow he'd made one trip to the toilet at the rear of the aircraft. He had walked slowly down the central gangway, a dreamy look on his face. He was studying every single passenger and his photographic memory recorded them all. At Cambridge he had been a brilliant student; he only had to read a page once and all the relevant data was recorded in his mind.

Now, as he sipped his coffee, he checked to see if one of the passengers followed him into the bar. None of them did. Tweed had not, as he'd suspected he might have done, sent a streetwalker to tail him.

Wearing an old pair of grey flannels and a sports jacket with leather elbow patches, he carried his case back into the entrance hall, paused to glance round like a man unsure of his bearings, checking again, then went out and climbed inside a cab.

'Hotel d'Angleterre, please,' he said in English, his precise voice carrying through the open window where several people stood with luggage, presumably waiting for the airport bus.

Half-way along the fifteen-minute drive into the city past a pleasant suburb with neat houses, trim lawns, trees and shrubs, he tapped on the partition window. The driver slid the glass panel back.

359

'I've just realized the time,' Lindemann said. 'Drop me instead in the Rådhuspladsen.'

He paid off the driver in the bustling Rådhuspladsen – the Town Hall Square – and walked the last few metres to his HQ inside an old building. The chrome plate at the entrance to the staircase read *Export-Import Services North*. Inside his office he placed his case against the wall and sat behind his desk as his deputy, Miss Browne ('with an "e", please') came in with an armful of files.

An ex-senior Civil Servant, Miss Browne was in her fifties, a tall severe-looking woman with grey hair and the nose of a golden eagle. There were no greetings. He sat back, steepled his hands and listened while she reported.

'Any further news from Nils Omdal about Balkan?' he asked.

'Not a word.'

'Then I'll be catching the shuttle to Oslo.'

They called it the shuttle because the fifty-minute non-stop flights from Copenhagen to the Norwegian capital were so frequent. Lindemann picked up his case, glanced at his desk. It was a model of tidiness. The two phones, his slide rule, notepads and pen set neatly lined up.

'A most competent report,' he told Miss Browne, who was now standing. 'Keep the wheels turning while I'm away. Not sure how long.'

'Any means of contacting you?'

'None at all . . .'

He crossed the Rådhuspladsen as though seeking a taxi. He gave the Rådhuset, with its steep roof and old tiles, an approving glance. One of the many things he liked about Copenhagen. Only two high-rise buildings anywhere near the city centre – the Royal Hotel and the SAS place you passed on your way in from Kastrup.

He walked on past a cab rank and continued on foot until he crossed the wide Vesterbrogade and hurried inside the main railway station. He was in good time to catch the express – the train bound for Rødby. There it would be shunted aboard the huge ferry for transportation across the Baltic – to Puttgarden, Lübeck and Hamburg.

Forty-Four

Newman was grimly aware this was the most dangerous hurdle – entering the fortified coastal zone. Stahl had stopped the truck in front of the closed wire gate. 'No!' Newman whispered. 'Don't switch off the engine.'

The warning lights threw a red glow over the bonnet. The two guards walked towards him as he lowered his window. He studied them as they came towards him, trudging on leaden feet, holding their machine pistols slackly in one hand, their faces haggard with fatigue. They'd been on duty all night, probably due to be relieved shortly. That might just help.

The man closest to the cab was tall and thin, his companion was short and squat. Newman said nothing at all as the thin man stood beneath his window. He simply handed out the document he'd taken from Stahl, his expression bleak as he checked his watch.

'What's this?' the guard demanded, snatching the sheet of paper.

'Read it. You can read, I presume? And we're late. If we miss the ship at Rostock, God help you . . .'

'Don't talk to me like that . . .'

'I said read it! You can recognize a movement order when you see one, can't you? And you might look at the crest at the top. Then perhaps we can get moving.'

'We've had no notification about this vehicle. I want to see inside it . . .'

'Absolutely forbidden! Read the bloody thing.'

The squat man had joined his comrade, was peering over his shoulder as the thin one examined it in the headlights. Newman heard the squat man mutter, 'Be careful. That's Intelligence . . .'

'I still want this truck opened up,' the thin man insisted.

Newman turned down the handle of his door, half-opened it, but he remained inside the cab. The two men looked up at the sound. Newman gestured towards the guard hut.

361

'I'm not hanging about here any longer. Is there a phone in that thing? I'm calling Markus Wolf. He'll be pleased to be woken up, I'm sure. And I'll need your names. That information he *will* want. Look at the signature at the bottom.'

'God,' he heard the short guard say, 'it is Wolf's signature. Like I said, be careful . . .'

Newman pressed home his advantage, his tone terse and clipped. 'It also says,' he quoted from memory, 'that this is a sealed consignment which must be permitted free and uninterrupted passage inside the Rostock port area. *You* . . .' He paused, 'are interrupting its passage.'

'I've read it.' The thin guard handed the document back to Newman, saw the Skorpion Newman held casually across his lap, carefully pointed away from the open door. 'What the hell is that for? Who are you?'

Again Newman said nothing. He produced his folder, handed it to the guard, checked his watch again and looked at Stahl with an expression of extreme impatience. The German had begun to sweat, beads of perspiration appearing on his forehead.

'Wipe your forehead,' he whispered. 'Use the back of your hand.'

'Border Police,' the thin guard said. 'Special assignment, too. Why didn't you say so earlier?'

'Because,' Newman said with cutting emphasis, 'the movement order is explicit, should have been sufficient. And this gun is to protect the consignment. I have orders to shoot anyone who attempts to look inside this truck. Now, open the bloody gate.'

'We have to check . . .' the guard began, handing back the folder. 'Let them through,' he told his companion. 'Just doing our duty, Comrade,' he maundered on as the gate swung inward automatically. The three red lights moved with it, which gave a weird effect, and Newman realized for the first time they were attached to it.

'Drive on, for God's sake,' he snapped at Stahl.

The vehicle lumbered forward, picked up speed. In his wing mirror Newman saw the gate closing behind them. They were inside the fortified zone.

*

362

About three kilometres beyond the guard post they were passing through a wooded area as the dawn light grew stronger. Newman told Stahl to pull over as they came up to a lay-by.

'Why?'

'So I can get a quick shave. I have a feeling Captain Anders is a man impressed by personal appearances. And you'd better shave, too. You can borrow my kit afterwards . . .'

'I've got my own stuff.'

'Use it then.'

Newman unwrapped the hold-all containing his shaving materials, propped a small mirror against the windscreen, turned on the overhead light and made the best job he could of it. He'd forced his companion to follow suit hoping it would lift his morale. He'd sensed Stahl had been badly shaken by the episode at the guard gate.

Freshly-shaven, they drove off out of the wooded area. Soon Newman could make out against the pale glow of the lightening sky the silhouettes of great mobile cranes, the type of cranes you see alongside a dock area.

And there was more traffic about. Wheeled and on foot. Workers trudging along for early shifts, trucks coming out from the port area laden with cargo. Huge standards of timber. Brought in from Sweden. Tankers – undoubtedly laden with oil from the Soviet Union.

A strange glow hung over the docks. The Martian-like cranes stood out against the glow of fluorescent lights mingled with the growing dawn. Then it began to rain, a heavy downpour. Stahl switched on the wipers and Newman's view bleared as rivulets streamed down the windscreen. Still clasping the Skorpion, he slipped into a doze, unable to keep his eyelids open.

He was woken by Stahl shaking his arm. He blinked, realized he felt much fresher, more alert. It was still raining heavily, pounding on the cab's roof with a steady staccato. Ahead were the dock gates.

'I'll leave the talking to you,' Stahl said.

No talking was called for. The gates opened inward. A man in oilskins beckoned the truck to proceed. 'Leipzig must have phoned through our registration number,' said Stahl and drove on. The truck bumped over rails set in concrete. It was daylight, if that description could be applied to the grey murk which shrouded the docks.

'The rain could help you,' Stahl commented. 'Everyone will be keeping their heads down.'

He'd recovered his nerve. They passed a giant mobile crane standing on rails. Newman lowered his window a little, peered up. At the top of the crane a light was on inside the cabin. The smell peculiar to ports all over the world drifted in through the window – a compound of resin, oil, tar and the salt air coming off the Baltic.

'Leave the Skorpion with me,' Stahl continued. He reached under his seat with one hand, pulling out a bundle which he handed Newman. 'Oilskins, you'll need them. I have to take the truck immediately to the *Wroclaw* for loading of the guns. I'll send Captain Anders to see you. Then you're on your own. There's a small hut where you can shelter.'

'How quickly will he come? The longer I hang around the greater the risk . . .'

'No idea. Up to him. You can't hurry Anders.'

'Thank you for getting me so far,' Newman said as he struggled into the oilskin. It had a hood which he pulled over his head.

The truck rumbled past great storage sheds, their roofs gleaming in the rain. Seamen dressed in oilskins and rubber boots hurried across the truck's headlight beams which Stahl still had on. The vehicle was crawling. A huddle of ships, moored prow to stern, their funnels poking up into the murk, told Newman he was close to the wharves. Stahl confirmed the thought.

'There's the hut where I'm leaving you. Just wait. You left nothing back in the truck?'

'Not a thing. I was careful. A screwed-up piece of greaseproof paper in the urine bucket. That's it.'

'You get off here. Good luck. You'll need it . . .'

With this encouraging farewell Newman stepped down off the stationary truck, slammed the door shut as the rain hit him, and the truck was moving out of sight round a corner. He'd no doubt Stahl was glad to see the last of him. He pushed open the door of the single-storey shanty-like structure, listened and stepped inside, leaving the door half-open.

Half an hour later, still standing – there was nowhere to sit – he was joined by a German seaman who rushed in out of the downpour. He produced a pack of cigarettes, offered one to Newman, who shook his head, and lit it for himself.

'Waiting to catch a ship, mate?' the German asked.

'I hope so.'

He wanted to get rid of the man. Anders might arrive at any moment. The seaman went on puffing at his cigarette, stamping his feet. His boots squelched water.

'Not as bad as it looks,' the German commented. 'Heard the met forecast. Out there beyond Warnemünde the East Sea's as smooth as a millpond. No wind. Overcast all day. I'd better be off. My bosun's a bastard . . .'

Anders arrived half an hour later. A short stocky man with broad shoulders, he wore a navy blue duffel jacket and a peaked cap. He took off the cap and shook water from it out of the door. In his late fifties, Newman estimated. A weatherbeaten square face, a jaw like the prow of an icebreaker, piercing blue eyes. He stood there like a rock, hands thrust into the pockets of his jacket.

'I'm Anders. Who are you?'

'Emil Clasen. I need passage aboard the *Wroclaw*. I want to get out to the West. Anywhere convenient to you will do.'

'I'm not taking you.'

It was like a blow in the face to Newman. He'd come so far. To be pipped at the post now, abandoned inside the DDR. Newman stared back at the Pole. He had to say the right thing first time. There'd be no second chance. What the hell was the right thing?

Then he remembered. Stahl had said Anders didn't like the Germans. Stahl had said that he – Newman – passed for a German. He took a deep breath. He had to gamble everything on one throw, pray that his assessment of the Pole was correct.

'I'm not a German, you know. I'm English.'

'I look stupid?'

'I said I was English and I am. I desperately need passage out of here to the West.'

He'd said these words in his own language. Anders studied his clothes, looked back at his face. His expression showed extreme doubt.

'They have language laboratories in Moscow to teach you to speak perfect English,' he replied in German. 'So, you say you're English? I haven't much time to waste on you. Where were you born?'

'Hampstead, London.'

'I know that place. A solid wall of houses. Kilometres away from open country . . .'

'No it isn't. There's Hampstead Heath where you can walk along endless paths between grass and trees.'

'You know where King's Lynn is?'

'Norfolk, East Anglia.'

'It's on the coast. I've docked there. What river is it on?'

'The Ouse. And it isn't on the coast. It's several miles inland – up the Ouse. Very flat country.'

'What's your job?' Anders demanded.

'Newspaper reporter. Foreign correspondent. I came over the border a few days ago after a story. Illegally.'

'You're a bloody crazy idiot, that's for sure.'

That was when Newman realized he'd been accepted. He kept the relief out of his expression. Anders shrugged. Looking outside, he peered into the rain, then spoke in his brusque manner.

'I got everything ready – in case I decided to take you. We go aboard slowly. No one will question you – not when you're with me. I have a reputation. For tearing people's balls off if they try to interfere with me. I've prepared a cable locker on deck. You travel inside that. You stay there till I come for you. I'll put something heavy on the top after you get inside. That will discourage anyone from looking inside. We're not sailing for some time. You'll just have to put up with it. Come on. No point in hanging about. And I'm the only man aboard who will know you're on the *Wroclaw*. Just keep quiet inside that locker.'

For Anders, Newman guessed, this was a major speech as he walked with the Pole past another huge storage shed. Inside open doors he saw agricultural machinery, painted a bright orange and arranged in neat rows. The rain had slackened –

was now a heavy drizzle. Overhead the clouds were stationary, the colour of molten lead.

Anders moved with a heavy deliberate tread, staring straight ahead, saying nothing. Beyond the shed Newman saw a freighter moored to the dock, its single smoke-stack carrying the Polish emblem. Aft it had a high bridge and the ship was equipped with a small forest of radar and other sophisticated devices.

It struck him it had the appearance of a spy ship. Forward an immense hold was open as loading proceeded. Suspended from a crane inside nets he recognized the long wooden boxes he had travelled with all the way from Leipzig. Stahl's truck, backed to near the edge of the wharf, was being unloaded by men stacking the boxes out in the open. Another team heaved them inside another of the huge carrying nets. The Skorpions for Cuba were going on board.

'Don't slip on the gangplank,' Anders warned.

It was the first remark he'd made since leaving the hut. At the foot of the gangway – it had a hand-rail on either side – stood a burly seaman. He saluted Anders, who merely nodded. The captain then ran up the incline like a two-year-old. Newman followed more cautiously.

He gripped the rail with his right hand and its surface was greasy, as it was underfoot. Anders waited for him, then led the way to the starboard side, out of sight of the loading. He stopped amidships, looked round, saw no one was about, lifted the lid of a huge wooden box screwed down to the deck. The cable locker.

'Get in. Move!' he growled.

Newman swung himself over the side and dropped into the box. He landed on something soft which gave under his weight. Anders reached forward a large hand, pressed him down by the top of his shoulder. The lid was swung closed on its hinges and Newman was crouched in darkness.

Hauling out of the pocket of his oilskins the torch he had been given by Stahl, he switched it on and examined his new quarters. The soft thing he'd landed on was a rubber dinghy equipped with a small outboard motor.

Thud! Newman nearly jumped out of his skin. Then he realized something heavy had been dropped on the lid, some object Anders had dumped to discourage anyone from exploring inside the locker. He went on with his examination. There was a lot to discover.

A long length of thick rope was coiled inside the dinghy, rope knotted at intervals. He found one end was attached with a reef knot to a metal ring at the rear of the dinghy near the outboard. It puzzled him, but he went on with his exploration.

Unwrapping two packets wrapped in a Polish newspaper he found one contained a bottle of mineral water and a bottle of vodka. Inside the other was a loaf of rye bread, a hunk of cheese and a knife for slicing the bread. Bread and some cheese – at least he was keeping to a regular diet.

Tucked into a pocket in the side of the dinghy he found a torch, a marlinspike and, inside tissue paper, a compass. 'I got everything ready,' Anders had said. A methodical man, Captain Anders. A practical man. But already he had reminded Newman of a British captain in the Merchant Marine he'd once known. The men who commanded ships all over the world were of a similar breed, irrespective of the political system they happened to live under. They were either very good or very bad. In Newman's opinion Anders came top of the poll in the former category.

Newman took only a small nip of the vodka. He followed it with a larger gulp of the mineral water. Immediately he'd swallowed the water he cursed his folly. There was a little matter of the inevitable call of nature. Then he remembered Anders and continued his search. He found the enamel jug with the tight-fitting top tucked under the outboard. Now all he had to do was to sit it out. Literally.

Forty-Five

He woke up aching, cramped and with a crick in his neck. Newman was lying in a foetal position, curled up inside the dinghy. His first thought was that the *Wroclaw* was moving, its engines ticking over with a steady hum. The sea had to be very calm – the vessel seemed to glide over the surface.

His second thought was the time. He checked his watch by the illuminated hands. 7 p.m. It couldn't be. He switched on the torch resting against his hand. It was 7 p.m. He recalled that the last thing he'd done before he must have dropped off into deep sleep was to wind up the watch. Then it had registered 7 a.m. He had slept for twelve hours.

That worried him – until he realized he was ravenously hungry. He made himself sandwiches with the rye bread and the cheese. As he ate, pausing occasionally to drink some mineral water, he tried to think what to do next, to work out the likely position of the *Wroclaw*. He realized very quickly it was impossible – he'd no idea when it had sailed from Rostock.

His next problem was to decide whether to eat all the food or whether to keep some in reserve. Instinct told him to curb his appetite. Then he remembered what Falken had said. Eat, sleep, pee – when you can. Something like that. He devoured all the bread and cheese, but drank only half the water. He didn't touch the vodka. It might dull his senses, make him light-headed.

Finishing his meal, he found the enamel jug, crouched to relieve himself, then put back the lid firmly. It had a rubber ring which made it practically watertight. Just as well – in case of spillage. He began to feel quite normal, but he ached in every limb.

Despite his confined space, he managed to do some exercises, stretching his arms, his legs, flexing and unflexing his fingers. Then, kneeling, he reached up and gently pushed at the lid of the cable locker. It wouldn't move, solid as concrete. This gave him a claustrophobic feeling and he recalled experiencing the same sensation in milder form when he was travelling inside Stahl's truck. God, he was going to be glad to get out in the open, to be able to move around again.

The vessel continued steadily on course, moving incredibly smoothly. The seaman who had shared the hut with him inside Rostock docks had been right in his forecast. *Smooth as a millpond*. The Baltic, from what he had heard, was rarely like this. That was, if he was still in the Baltic. Could the vessel have turned north, passed Copenhagen, and moved up into the Kattegat between Denmark and Sweden?

There was no way he could calculate his present location. He

369

had no data to work on. The time of departure from Rostock. The speed of the vessel. He began to feel disorientated. No idea where he was. Trapped inside this box. He took a deep breath as he had a moment of panic. That was when he heard someone moving the heavy object off the lid.

He did two things instinctively. Switched off the torch. Grasped the marlinspike, which he now realized Anders had left him as a weapon. He crouched, ready to spring, staring up. The lid was lifted.

The evening sky was a brilliant azure. Silhouetted against it was the wide-shouldered Anders. He dropped a folded sheet into the locker. He spoke quickly, his voice low.

'The ship will be stopping shortly – to make a transhipment. I don't know what it is – something to do with the bloody Russkies. Keep very quiet. I've arranged with my Chief Engineer to fake engine trouble when they've finished their business. That's when you leave. I'll be back . . .'

'Where the hell are we?'

'In the Bight of Lübeck. In DDR coastal waters. Be ready to move fast when I come back. I must go . . .'

The lid was swung closed on its hinges. Very quietly. Newman waited for the *thud!* of the heavy object being replaced. Nothing. Anders had either forgotten (unlikely) or someone had appeared and the Pole had not wished to draw attention to the cable locker.

Newman experienced a curious mix of sensations. The claustrophobic feeling disappeared – now he knew he was no longer entombed inside the locker. But he felt trapped, in great danger. That reference to the Russkies. Anyone could lift the lid, discover him.

From the brief words Anders had spoken Newman gathered *they* were in charge of this secret transhipment operation, whatever that might be. He had little doubt that, if caught, he'd be treated as a spy and shot – to keep his mouth closed.

To take his mind off his new fear he switched on the torch and examined the sheet of paper Anders had dropped inside the locker. His palms were moist. He wiped them on his trousers and studied the sheet.

It was a section of a chart. He'd been astounded, perplexed,

370

when Anders told him they were in the Bight of Lübeck. Geography had always been one of his good subjects. He'd felt sure that the direct route from Rostock to the Kattegat and across the Atlantic to Cuba was a course which would have taken them north of Fehmarn Island. The map confirmed his deduction.

Emerging from Rostock into the Baltic, the *Wroclaw* had sailed west and then south-west – instead of *north*-west – into the Bight, the great bay, of Lübeck. Why? Could the consignment of Skorpions be due to be landed secretly in West Germany – near Lübeck? It didn't make sense.

It was 9 p.m. by his watch when the *Wroclaw*, moving slowly, reduced speed even more, then – at precisely 9.30 – stopped. It was suddenly very quiet without the vibration of the engines. He heard feet clumping along the deck past the locker. Voices in the distance. He looked up and round three sides of the lid was a thin bar of light. That had kept the air inside the locker fresh. He eased himself up into a crouching position.

He raised the lid slowly, barely three or four centimetres. Five seamen, standing at the ship's rail with their backs to him, stared out across the sea. Now the *Wroclaw* was stationary it was rolling slightly. A sky like porridge, dense with grey clouds, had replaced the azure blue.

As the vessel rolled, Newman had glimpses of the Baltic. A large white power cruiser which seemed familiar was heading full speed for the *Wroclaw*, leaving behind a white wake. It was about half a mile away. Newman used his knuckles to hold up the heavy lid.

The ship continued its gentle roll, giving Newman further glimpses of the approaching cruiser. It reduced speed as it came close. Behind the glass of the wheelhouse Newman could just make out the head and shoulders of the man steering the cruiser. He wore a balaclava helmet, reminding Newman of his days training with the SAS. He lowered the lid carefully, sat down on the edge of the dinghy, which provided a cushion for his aching backside, and rubbed his sore knuckles.

The activity on deck soon increased. Feet clumping quickly. Orders shouted. Muffled by the locker walls, Newman couldn't be sure, but he thought they were talking in Russian. He waited half an hour before he risked lifting the lid again. He was very

371

puzzled – that power cruiser, big as it was, could never take on board the Skorpion load Stahl had brought from Leipzig.

The cruiser was lashed to the side of the *Wroclaw*. Loading was well under way. But it wasn't the Skorpion boxes they were transhipping to the cruiser. He watched as seamen, organized in a chain, transferred small sacks to the cruiser.

More seamen were now aboard the cruiser, taking the sacks handed down to them from the freighter. Newman couldn't see inside the cruiser, but he had the impression the sacks were being carried below decks. No sign of Anders. No sign of the man in the balaclava helmet. And it was impossible to see the name of the power cruiser. He lowered the lid carefully and sat down again. What the hell was going on?

Newman drank more mineral water, ignored the vodka. He was scared again. One of those seamen might take it into his head to peer inside the locker. Life was like that. You relaxed, thinking the worst was over – and the worst was to come. It just needed one of those Russian-speaking seamen to find him and he was dead. He shivered with the cold.

The events of recent days passed through his mind like film shots. Crossing the border under the watchtower after he'd left Peter Toll. The first confrontation with Schneider inside the mist-bound forest. Cycling with Falken – with Gerda behind them. The lock-keeper's cottage. Schneider bursting in on them. Gerda shooting him with a short burst from the Uzi . . . The road-block . . . Radom's farm . . . The zigzag . . . Karen Piper . . . Hiding inside the camper under the bridge . . . Driving the camper through the water-filled gulch . . . His last sight of Falken diverting the Intelligence men . . . of Gerda bundled into the patrol car. Not now, dear God. Not now.

He switched on the torch and double-checked the chart. A cross showed the position of the *Wroclaw* – with the vessel's name neatly printed. The position where it was stopped now, presumably. A line showed the south-westerly course he must follow . . .

He stopped looking at the chart. He could hear the engine of the power cruiser starting up, fading rapidly away. He realized the clumping of feet, the sound of voices, had stopped. He checked his watch. 10.30 p.m.

He hurriedly stowed everything away inside the dinghy –

including the enamel jug. He stuffed the folded chart inside his belt. He'd just finished doing these things when the lid was lifted. He tensed, looked up. Anders stared down. It was night.

'Time to go,' Anders said.

'I'm ready . . .'

'Get out then. This side . . .'

The starboard side of the deck was deserted. In the dark the freighter's lights glowed, bow and stern and on the bridge. Anders hauled out the dinghy, coiled the rope, lowered the dinghy down the side of the hull. The heavy outboard touched the calm water first, then the rest of the dinghy settled.

Newman was glad he'd stowed away everything inside the compartments lining the interior. The dinghy bobbed up and down against the hull as Anders held on to the other end of the rope.

'You understood the chart?' he asked.

'Perfectly. And I know Lübeck . . .'

'Listen carefully. I've posted lookouts forward but not aft. You found the paddle? Good. You're going down this rope into the dinghy. I'll hold on until you're inside and then drop the rope. Coil it inside the dinghy. Wait! You must wait – until the *Wroclaw* starts moving. There's a risk.' His voice was grim. 'But it's the only way you can leave unseen by a lookout. The moment the ship starts moving push yourself away from it with the paddle. Then paddle like hell away from us – the risk is you'll get caught up in the screws. You'll end up as mincemeat if that happens. The outboard would get you clear in good time – but you can't start that until we are well away. The motor would be heard. If it wasn't, you'd be seen. Do you understand?'

'Perfectly. I'd better go . . .'

'You say you know Lübeck?'

'Yes . . .'

'Then you might make it.'

Newman swung himself over the rail, grasped the rope, began the descent. He understood now why Anders had knotted the rope at intervals. He grasped the rope just above each knot. Without the knots he could have slid, endured agonizing rope burn. He used his feet like a mountaineer, bouncing out from

373

the hull with each phase, then planting the flat of his shoes against the hull. It seemed to go on forever. His arms were weak from hours of enforced confinement inside the truck and then cooped up in the locker. He felt at any moment he'd let go. Then he remembered Anders, taking the whole brunt of his weight. The Pole had the strength of a lion. He gritted his teeth, kept moving. If Anders could stick it, so could he.

When he was least expecting it, his feet landed in the dinghy, which rocked all over the sea. He paused, still holding the rope, then gingerly lowered himself inside the dinghy. He looked up for the first time since he'd come over the side. Anders, feeling the rope slacken, was peering down. He dropped the rope, disappeared.

Newman began hauling in the rope which had dropped into the sea. A loose rope was dangerous – just the thing which could get tangled up with the ship's screws. He worked fast, coiling the rope. Then began the nerve-wracking search for the paddle, the one thing he'd missed when examining everything inside the locker. He couldn't locate it. Anders must have arranged some signal with a crewman on the bridge – he'd had no time to return to it. The crewman had contacted the chief engineer. In a frighteningly short period of time the *Wroclaw*'s engines came to life, throbbing with increasing power. Where the devil was the bloody paddle?

He found it seconds before the *Wroclaw*'s hull began sliding past him, bringing the screws at the stern closer every moment. It was strapped to the starboard side of the dinghy. He pulled it free, took a firm grip on the handle and pushed against the hull with all his strength. The dinghy drifted a few feet away. Not far enough. He paddled furiously, dipping into the water, now choppy from the forward movement of the freighter. The dinghy bobbed, fell, bobbed, fell again over the waves. He seemed to be as close to the freighter as before.

Now he could see – hear above the beat of the engines – the churning wash of the great screws slicing through the water, a powerful gushing sound as the Baltic was threshed into a foaming wake. The undertow! If he wasn't clear of the vessel, the undertow swept up by the revolving screws would sweep him back, take him straight into the mincing machine Anders had warned him against, chopping him to pieces.

He thought of the blonde girls who'd been savaged by some maniac in Travemünde, the horror Kuhlmann had described. They'd been scratched compared with what would happen to him if those screws sucked him in.

The hull continued to slide past. He forced his weary arms to continue paddling. With fearful slowness the dinghy seemed to drift away from the *Wroclaw*. With fearful speed the stern came closer, the thrashing roar of the screws grew louder. He glanced over his shoulder.

The stern was abreast of him. The maelstrom curdled round the dinghy. He could *feel* the insidious pull of the undertow, dragging the dinghy to destruction. He paddled madly in the frothing sea. The dinghy rocked furiously, almost tipping him overboard. Water slopped inside it. He could no longer tell what was happening. He looked quickly over his shoulder again, stared.

The stern of the *Wroclaw* was receding. The water was less choppy. The ship sailed on, turning due north for the Fehmarn Belt, the stretch of the Baltic dividing Denmark from West Germany. Newman stopped paddling. He collapsed, leant forward, utterly exhausted.

Forty-Six

His first landmark was the flashing light at the top of the Hotel Maritim in Travemünde Strand. The sea was still lake calm and he sped towards it at full speed.

'Thank God,' he said to himself. 'I'll make the western channel.'

Which was rather important. The eastern channel on the other side of Priwall Island was inside the DDR. He'd waited awhile to gather the strength to start up the outboard. It had responded to the third pull. He was soaked to the skin. He'd used the enamel jug – after emptying it – to bale out the dinghy.

He felt he'd been away five years as the lights on shore came closer. It was after midnight. There was no other seaborne traffic. He had the Baltic to himself as he guided the dinghy up the channel, past the Maritim, past the old tall brick-built edifice which had served as a lighthouse before they transferred the lamp to the summit of the multi-storey hotel.

Back from the dead. That was his thought as he cruised deep inside the channel. He saw the *Südwind* moored to its landing stage and hardly gave it a thought. He was cold, miserable, relieved at the same time. All he wanted was a hot bath and a change of clothes.

Afterwards, he could never work out why, but he guided the dinghy to a certain landing-stage, his speed now reduced to a modest pace. After midnight, but there were lights aboard the sloop. He cut the engine and the dinghy drifted the last few yards under its own momentum.

Ann Grayle came out on deck, holding a glass, wearing white slacks and a blouse. The sky had cleared on his way in and it was a balmy night. She stood very erect, staring down at him.

'Good God! It's Bob Newman. You look wet through. Come on board and we'll sort you out. Ben!' she called. 'Put on the kettle. Hot coffee.' She stared again at Newman. 'What you reporters will do just for a story . . .'

Lysenko made the call to Moscow the following morning. Again he used the phone in his apartment so he wouldn't be overheard by Markus Wolf. Gorbachev came on the line immediately.

'The cargo was safely transhipped yesterday evening. Balkan arrived back from London just in time to take it over . . .'

'No codewords over the phone,' Gorbachev reprimanded him. 'I heard you use two. Watch it.'

Lysenko swore inwardly. The General Secretary was referring to his slip in naming London. He'd better be more careful.

'There will be a delay of two or three weeks,' he continued. 'That is, before it moves on to its ultimate destination. For the time being the cargo is safely under cover.'

'Any news of Tweed?' Gorbachev enquired.

'Arrival imminent . . .'

'That problem must be solved. Quickly. Keep me informed.'

The connection was broken. Lysenko slammed down the receiver, rubbed the stubble of his unshaven jaw, stared at the rumpled bedclothes. Helene, the German girl he'd met, had been good – very good. Make the most of it while you're away from the wife, he told himself. But bedtime romps and vodka didn't seem to go together too well any more. Maybe he was getting too old for it; hence that stupid slip on the phone. As he ambled to the bathroom he decided he'd give it up – not Helene, just mixing her with vodka.

Tweed disembarked from Flight LH 041 with Diana at Hamburg. Ahead of him Pete Nield was going through Passport Control. Behind him Harry Butler strolled, carrying his suitcase, his eyes studying the other passengers. Who, he was asking himself, was Tweed's glamorous blonde companion?

The foxy devil hadn't mentioned her. And from what Butler had observed during the flight they knew each other pretty well. Still, it was good cover – a couple attracted less attention than a single man alighting from an aircraft on his own.

Outside the exit hall Nield was getting inside a taxi when Tweed emerged with Diana. A man wearing a shabby raincoat and standing by a bookstall, pretending to look at a paperback, watched them. Martin Vollmer shoved the book back on to the rack of the revolver and hurried after them.

Butler, who never missed a trick, had just come out of the Customs and saw Vollmer's reaction. He followed him. Tweed was helping Diana into the rear of a cab, got inside himself and told the driver, 'Four Seasons Hotel, please . . .'

Butler watched Vollmer take the next waiting cab. Inside it the German gave his directions. 'Follow that cab. Don't lose it. That man owes me money.'

'And he'll go on owing. They always do. Anything you say.'

The convoy proceeded along the boulevard-like highway leading to the city. Nield first. Then Tweed and Diana. Behind them followed Vollmer's cab. And two vehicles behind Vollmer, Butler brought up the rear. His instructions to his driver had been explicit as he handed him a ten-deutschmark note.

'That's your tip,' he said in German. 'The fare's separate. That cab the thin man in the brown raincoat got inside. Tab him. I want to find out where he's going.'

Inside the city the convoy crossed the highway bridge which divides the two lakes – with the Binnenalster on the left. On the far side it turned down the Neuer Jungfernstieg, moving down the western shore of the lake. The fussy little water buses were scuttering across the smooth surface. The sky had a few clouds which seemed to hang motionless in a sea of blue as the sun blazed down.

Nield was inside the hotel when Tweed's cab pulled up at the entrance. A hundred or so metres back Butler watched as Vollmer's cab slowed to cruising pace. He saw the occupant peer out of the window as Tweed and Diana disappeared inside the hotel. Vollmer's cab then picked up speed and Butler settled back against his seat. Sooner or later he'd track down Brown Raincoat's destination.

At reception Tweed registered both himself and Diana in their real names. The two rooms Monica had reserved were ready and he paused to show her the luxurious reception hall and the dining-room, feeling glad to be back.

'It's a marvellous place,' she enthused. 'Simply divine.'

'Possibly the best hotel in all Germany.' He led her away from the reception counter, lowering his voice. 'I have some phone calls to make. The plane was on time – 12.55. Can you wait a little longer for lunch?'

'I have to unpack. I'll stay in my room until you come for me . . .'

Tweed had asked for – and been given – the same double room he'd occupied on his previous visit to Hamburg when he had identified the body of Ian Fergusson. Number 412. He tipped the porter who brought up his case and then, alone, stood for a moment gazing out of the window at the view. The foliage was still on the trees below him and beyond stretched the placid waters of the Binnenalster.

It was still holiday time. Crowds stood on the landing stage area at the end of the lake, not so far from where the police had discovered Fergusson's floating body by the lock-gates in the early hours. There was a queue for ice cream cones. He was thinking of poor Ian Fergusson. He shook his head, went to the phone, asked for the room number Nield was occupying, a detail he'd noticed in the hotel register. He asked Nield to come up and see him.

Tweed was standing in the middle of the living-room when Nield entered. The moment he arrived Nield knew something was going to happen. Tweed stood very erect, his voice was crisp, decisive.

'We're leaving here this evening after dinner. We're heading straight for Lübeck by train. After you've had lunch get a cab to the Hauptbahnhof, buy four single first-class tickets for Lübeck.'

'That's quick . . .'

'I'm going to surprise the opposition by moving faster than they'll expect. After you've bought the rail tickets, phone the Hotel Jensen in Lübeck and book three rooms. Myself, Harry and one in the name of Diana Chadwick. Then call the Movenpick in Lübeck and book yourself a room there. You're back-up – out of sight.'

'Anything else?'

'Not at the moment.'

'Then I'd better get downstairs and grab a bite to eat.'

The phone began ringing almost as soon as Nield had left the room. Tweed picked up the receiver.

'Who is it?' he asked cautiously.

'Harry. Harry Butler. I tracked him. It's Altona . . .'

'Get back here as fast as you can.'

In Lübeck Munzel had made his daily call to Vollmer at the usual time. Noon. He'd got the ringing tone from the flat in Altona but no reply. Swearing to himself, he left the station and walked back across the street to the International Hotel. He had no way of knowing that at that moment Vollmer was waiting at Hamburg Airport, checking arrivals from London. His man who normally carried out this assignment had gone down with an attack of gastritis.

Munzel took Lydia Fischer to the Movenpick for lunch. He felt he needed a change of surroundings, of menu. As they talked and ate their grilled sole and chipped potatoes Munzel was unaware he was being watched by Sue Templeton, the American girl friend of Ted Smith – the couple who had shown Kuhlmann where Munzel had thrown his motor-cycle into the river Trave.

'I'd recognize that man again if he'd grown a beard,' she had said jokingly to her English boy friend.

Now, as she ate her lunch with Ted, she kept glancing across

379

the room at the blond-bearded man with the long golden hair. She really wasn't sure. She said nothing to Ted, who had only one topic in mind. An hour in bed with Sue to start the afternoon off.

Sue lingered over her coffee for some time when Ted had signed the bill. Then she suddenly grabbed her shoulder bag.

'I think I'm going back to that shop where I spotted a dress.'

'I'm going upstairs to get into my pyjamas . . .'

'And you'll still be in them when I get back. See you.'

She followed Munzel and the girl he was with out of the restaurant, still uncertain. Her walk was shorter than she'd expected. She saw them go inside the International, hovered as she checked her lipstick, then walked in after them. She went up to the concierge, gave him her warmest smile.

'That man with the blond beard who just came in with a girl. Is he staying here? He looks exactly like a friend I knew in New York.'

'He is staying here, yes.'

The concierge was discreet. He gave no name. Sue thanked him and went back to the Movenpick. Five minutes later Munzel came out of the lift and walked across to the station. Again he dialled Altona. This time Vollmer answered the phone.

'Tweed has arrived in Hamburg. Had a blonde girl with him. He's staying at the same place as last time – the Four Seasons. Call me tomorrow. Normal time . . .'

Munzel stepped out of the phone booth with a feeling of immense satisfaction. He was quite sure that within the next few days Tweed would turn up in Lübeck. That gave him time to work out how he was going to do it.

Tweed had lunch with Diana in the dining-room, the same room used for breakfast. He preferred the grill room but that was closed. They were both dining off *paillard de veau* and a selection of fresh vegetables which Diana raved about.

'I've never tasted such wonderful vegetables, Tweedy. And look at the variety – broccoli, French beans, *mange tout* and the most gorgeous cauliflower. I simply love this hotel.'

'Yes, it is out of the ordinary.'

Tweed looked round. The only thing he found off-putting

were the cherubs. Perched on plinths round the central dining area were sculptures of life-like naked cherubs. Very fat cherubs. He could do without staring at plump buttocks while he was eating, thank you very much.

'How long are we staying?' Diana asked over the dessert as she attacked a huge sundae in a tall glass.

'Hard to say.'

After lunch they wandered round the spacious ground floor. The walls were decorated with tapestries depicting men hunting on horseback. Diana revelled in everything, which, reflected Tweed, was one of her many attractions. He told her he had a few more phone calls to make and she said she'd rest in her room until he came for her.

Seated in a chair by the windows in the reception hall Harry Butler waited, reading a German newspaper. He was still clad in grey slacks, sports jacket, a white shirt and a Paisley tie. Tweed went up in the elevator with Diana, let her out on her floor, went up to his own, then walked down the staircase to the last landing and gestured to Butler to join him.

Inside Room 412 Butler slumped into an arm chair. Tweed sat behind the writing desk and listened.

'You were followed,' he told Tweed. 'He saw you come here, then went on in the same cab to his place in an apartment block close to the U-bahn station at Altona. It overlooks a small park. Apartment 28. There's the address.' He handed Tweed a sheet of paper torn off his pocket notepad.

'How did you find the exact apartment?'

'He went up in the elevator. I watched the numbers over the elevator bank, saw the floor where he stopped, ran like hell up the staircase. Got there just in time to see him disappearing inside 28.'

'He could have seen you?'

'Absolutely not.'

'We might just have the start of the communication line from here into East Germany. We'll leave him for the moment.'

'He knows where you are,' Butler pointed out. 'That could be dangerous.'

'I'm sure it is. But that's my strategy. And we're leaving for Lübeck late this evening. After dinner. I want to get there before they expect me . . .'

'That could be even more dangerous,' Butler insisted. 'For you. The last time you were in Lübeck you said you were attacked. This time they may pull it off.'

'It's your job – and Nield's – to see they don't. Harry, I am stepping up the pressure on Lysenko. I'm convinced he's about to launch a major operation – that he wants me out of the way first. For some reason he thinks I may detect the nature of the operation. I haven't. Yet. But I do think in some way it centres on Lübeck. I'm going to stir up the pot like mad. Someone on the other side is going to make a mistake – and when they make it I want to be there.'

'It's your hide . . .'

'It's my decision. And you have another job. That girl who came with me – Diana Chadwick is her name. Your other job is to protect her life. She could be a key witness. Don't ask me to what. I haven't worked it all out yet. I think it goes back years into the past. Just make sure nothing happens to Diana. And she doesn't know either you or Nield exist.'

'You are playing this one close to the chest. Suggests to me you don't know who you can trust . . .'

'I can't trust any of them.' Tweed became businesslike. 'I need that notepad for a moment.'

Tweed took a small sheet of plastic from his wallet, slipped it under the first sheet, began writing on it. He wrote only a few words, then handed the notepad back.

'That's where we're staying in Lübeck. There's a room booked in your name. When we get off the train – we travel separately, of course – Nield leaves first. He's staying at a hotel called the Movenpick. Only a few hundred yards' walk from the station. You and I take separate cabs to the Jensen, register like strangers to each other. I'll be travelling with Diana. And I'll give you her room number at the Jensen at the first opportunity. Any questions? If not, I'll get room service to send us up some coffee. Wait in the bathroom when it arrives.'

'No questions,' Butler said laconically.

He was studying Tweed. He'd known him a long time. There always came a time like this. First there was the waiting – the period when Tweed sniffed the air, trod cautiously, merged into the background, feeling his way forward carefully. Then, without warning, came the big change.

Tweed went over on to the offensive, using all his guile to smoke out the opposition, taking risks, even setting himself up as a target – which was exactly what he was doing now. Butler noticed another change. Tweed's tone of voice when he referred to Diana. He'd never heard him talk about another woman in this way – not since Tweed's wife (Roedean and all that) walked off with a Greek shipping tycoon, for God's sake. His musings were interrupted when Tweed gave him Diana's room number, then checked his watch. Tweed rubbed his hands in anticipation.

'Only another few hours – then Lübeck . . .'

Munzel made his second phone call to Vollmer from the station brief. Vollmer didn't like too many calls, had a short fuse.

'I need someone here to watch the Hauptbahnhof – to report to me at the International when Tweed arrives. You got that? I'm now at the Hotel International . . .'

'You told me before.' Vollmer sounded impatient. 'I can't get anyone there before tomorrow. That will have to do . . .'

'I'm registered as Claus Kramer . . .'

'Noted. Don't make more phone calls than you need to. I'm busy. Tomorrow . . .'

There was a click. The bastard had rung off. Up yours. He pulled at his beard as he left the booth, fuming.

Forty-Seven

It was 6.17 p.m. as Tweed and Diana left the express at Lübeck. Tweed had suddenly changed his mind, decided to leave Hamburg by an earlier train. Butler watched them as they climbed the steps off the platform. Nield was already at the top of the flight, disappearing from view as he made his way on foot to the Movenpick.

Following at a gentle pace – to give them time to get a cab – Butler had the impression Tweed couldn't wait to reach Lübeck. Everything had suddenly become hurry-hurry. Walking out of the concourse on the higher level, he saw them climbing into a taxi.

He waited until their cab had pulled away before summoning his own. It was still broad daylight. Holidaymakers strolled back to their hotels for dinner. The atmosphere was warm and humid. Butler suspected Lübeck was at the end of a torrid day.

'It's like coming home again,' Diana said to Tweed, snuggling up against him in the taxi. 'Ann Grayle *is* in for a surprise when she sees me. I'm looking forward to that.'

'I thought you didn't like her.'

'It's a kind of love-hate relationship.' She smiled impishly. 'I like her, she hates me.'

The manager at the Jensen had welcomed them back, Tweed had registered, was just about to press the elevator button when Harry Butler appeared, carrying his case. Tweed ignored him but said to Diana in a loud voice, 'Your room number is 307, mine is 303 – so you can easily pop along to see me. Let's get down for dinner as soon as we can. I'm famished.'

Fifteen minutes later Butler walked into the large oblong-shaped room which was the restaurant. The place was crowded, had the jolly atmosphere of people enjoying themselves. They gave him a table by the windows at the end of the room overlooking the street and the river beyond. Tweed and Diana were at a table against the wall, chattering like magpies. A few minutes later he idly noticed a tall, heavily-built man with a blond beard and long hair enter accompanied by an attractive brunette. They were given a table on the far side of the room, near the serving counter and bar.

Newman slept for twelve hours aboard the sloop at Trave-münde. Ann Grayle had sent Ben to fetch some dry clothes, insisted that Newman took a shower, and when he came out wrapped in a bath-robe she sat him at a table already laid and presented him with a large bowl of steaming hot asparagus soup.

'It's from a tin, but you do look as though you need some internal central heating quickly,' she drawled. 'And here's a glass of whisky. Neat. Does everything suit His Lordship?'

Later, Newman had put on a pair of outsize pyjamas Ben had brought back. Grayle had asked no questions, typical of the discretion of an ex-diplomat's wife. After the meal he'd been taken to a bunk which he collapsed into, hardly able to keep his eyes open.

Grayle, a glass in her hand, had perched for a moment on the edge of the bunk, a wicked look in her eyes.

'Better if you sleep alone tonight, don't you agree? I'm not sure you'd be up to any sort of physical activity . . .'

That was the last thing he'd heard anyone say until he woke. Strong light was pouring in through the porthole above his head. He looked at his watch, expecting it to have stopped. Someone had wound it for him while he slept. Christ! It was noon.

He took Grayle out to a long lunch at a place on the waterfront. Again she asked no questions. As for Newman, he wallowed in the release from tension, the end of the need to look at everyone as a potential danger. Grayle talked about her past life in Kenya, mentioning Dr Berlin.

'I didn't even like him then. These do-gooders always bore the hell out of me.'

It was mid-afternoon when they wandered together along the waterfront. Newman pointed to the *Südwind*. The cruiser had a deserted look. He asked whether she'd noticed any activity on board.

'No, but I've been on a shopping trip to Hamburg. I spent several days there, so I don't know. The precocious Diana is noticeable by her absence. Must have found some new man to roll around with . . .'

It was after six in the evening when he left the sloop and called Park Crescent from a public phone booth. Monica came on the line and he heard the relief in her voice when they'd talked for only a minute.

'Where are you, Bob? Are you all right?'

'Lübeck. I'm OK. I desperately need to talk to Tweed.'

'I don't know where he is.' She paused. 'Where are you calling from?'

'Public call box. Chosen at random . . .'

'He's over there. Flew to Hamburg. Today. He was going to stay at the Four Seasons, but when I tried to call him an hour ago he'd checked out. No forwarding address – and he didn't even sleep there one night.'

'I'll call again, Monica. I have to go now . . .'

'Take care.'

'Thanks, but it doesn't matter any more.'

Newman put down the receiver, took out a cigarette, lit it and thought. Hamburg today. An unscheduled departure. The second trip to Germany. Tweed would be geared up, moving fast. Was he on his own? That was what worried Newman. Then he had an idea. He checked the directory, found the number of the Jensen, dialled the number. He recognized the manager's voice.

'Have you a Mr Tweed from London staying with you?'

'Yes, he's just arrived. You wanted to speak to him? He's having dinner. I saw him go in a few minutes ago. You want to speak to him now? Could you hold on a minute?'

It seemed an age before Tweed came on the line. Actually it was thirty seconds. Newman had checked by his watch.

'Who is it?' Tweed asked cautiously.

'Newman . . .'

'Thank God! Where are you calling from?'

'Public phone booth in Travemünde. Can I come right over? I can be there in fifteen minutes by cab. Are you alone?'

'No, Diana is with me . . .'

'You know what I mean.'

'The answer to your question is no.'

'Well, thank God for that. Book me a room if you can. I am on my way . . .'

'We're having dinner. Just started. Take your time. Are you in one piece?' The anxiety came clear down the line.

'By a miracle – several – yes. See you.'

On his way back to the sloop to tell Ann Grayle he had to go into Lübeck, Newman passed the local police station. An old building with a Dutch-style roof, it perched on the corner of the waterfront and a side street, St-Lorenz-strasse. Newman paused briefly, his eye caught by a poster. It was a reproduction of the Identikit picture of Kurt Franck. The poster was beginning to curl at the edges, taking a secondary place to other more recent posters of wanted villains. He stared at it for a moment before hurrying on.

'If I ever meet you again I'll know you,' he said to himself.

*

Munzel couldn't believe his luck. Sitting facing Lydia, he had glanced round the restaurant and there, on the far side of the room sat Tweed. With a blonde.

His mind raced as Lydia studied the menu. He glanced round the room again. It was packed. Some of them were getting very merry. Waiters ran backwards and forwards. The perfect atmosphere for what he had in mind. Lydia looked up from her menu.

'What are you thinking about?'

'Look. I've just remembered an important customer I promised to call this evening for a decision. I've left my notebook with his phone number back at the International. Mind if I dash back there? I'll only be fifteen minutes. Help yourself to the Beaujolais. Order your first course. OK?'

'Phoning a customer at his home? Will he like that?'

'He won't like it if I don't. He's busy all day at his factory. Fifteen minutes. No more . . .'

Munzel slipped out of the dining-room. He got lucky again outside the Jensen. A taxi was depositing more guests. He grabbed it. 'Hauptbahnhof,' he instructed the driver. This way there'd be no connection between himself and the International – if the police made careful enquiries afterwards.

'Mr Tweed?' The waiter seemed nervous. 'There's a gentleman outside who wants a word with you. He doesn't want to come into the restaurant.'

'Will you excuse me, Diana? I shouldn't be a minute.'

'Don't worry.' She waved her cigarette holder. 'I'll hold the main course for you.'

Tweed was puzzled. It was too early for Newman – and he'd have come straight into the restaurant. He walked out into the narrow lobby. A short stocky figure smoking a cigar stood near the exit. Kuhlmann. The man from Wiesbaden gestured towards the street.

'Let's take a short walk. They say walls have ears – although I've never seen walls growing them.'

'It had better be short. I'm in the middle of dinner.'

Kuhlmann led the way in silence past the diners at the tables on the pavement. Inside Harry Butler stood up, told the waiter he'd be back in a minute, saw Diana sitting by herself, changed his mind and sat down again.

'How did you know I was here?' Tweed asked.

'The manager phoned me. Don't blame him. I guessed it would be the Jensen when you came back. I leaned on him. No sign of Kurt Franck. Vanished off the face of the earth for about two weeks. Now you're back I've put out a fresh general alert.'

'Thank you. And Dr Berlin?'

'Still gone missing. You're not saying now you're back he's going to reappear?' Kuhlmann suggested.

'I'm saying just that. Not yet, perhaps. But soon, yes.'

'You wouldn't care to enlarge on that?' Kuhlmann suggested.

'No, I wouldn't. Any more of those ghastly murders?'

'No.' Kuhlmann stopped on a deserted section of the pavement to relight his cigar. 'You go absent. Franck goes absent. Dr Berlin goes absent. The murders stop.'

'You wouldn't care to enlarge on that?' Tweed enquired.

'Just a policeman's observation. If you need me, I'm at the local police station. Possehl-strasse 4. I'll write it down for you.' He did so on a small notepad, tore off the sheet, gave it to Tweed. 'If I'm not there, try headquarters at Lübeck-Süd.'

'I may need usc of a safe phone again . . .'

'Use Lübeck-Süd – as before. Always available.'

'And now, if you don't mind, I'd like to get back to my meal.'

'Just thought I'd let you know I was around.' Kuhlmann paused as they turned back. 'I just made a bet with myself.'

'And what was that?'

'Now you're back peace ends. I'm expecting everything to detonate any time. Enjoy your meal.'

Munzel closed the door of his bedroom at the International, turned the bolt. Taking a bunch of keys from his pocket, he unlocked a small metal box which he extracted from his back-pack. The inside was lined with suede, divided up into small compartments holding various plastic containers. He took out a plastic tube holding yellow capsules.

Holding the small tube in one hand he flicked off the top, tilted the tube, allowed one capsule to fall into the palm of his hand, recapped the tube. Child's play. He put the capsule back inside the tube. Mescaline. A hallucinogenic. One capsule and you were way out in space.

Leaving the hotel, he caught a cab from outside the station back to the Jensen. He sat down opposite Lydia shortly after Tweed had returned to his own table.

'This white wine is glorious,' Diana greeted him. 'Won't you join me?'

'I feel like something to pep me up. I wonder if I could get it here.' Tweed called over their waiter. 'I'd like a drink, a Margharita.'

'I've never heard of it, sir.'

'It's a mixture of tequila and fruit juice. At least ask the barman. I'll write it down for you.' He wrote on a sheet in his notebook, tore it out, handed it to the waiter.

'That will pep you up.' Diana gave him a certain look, her eyes half-closed. 'This could turn into an interesting evening.' She drank some more wine. 'And I'm getting tiddly. Darling,' she continued, 'you look a bit faraway.'

'I didn't expect to meet that chap who called to see me – at least not so soon. Doesn't matter, he's gone now.'

'But look what's coming.'

'Your Margharita, sir,' the waiter said. 'We have a new barman. From Italy. He knew the drink immediately. Enjoy yourselves. The main course will be a little longer . . .'

'Take your time,' said Tweed.

'And it's a proper Margharita,' Diana said, peering at his drink. 'It has salt round the rim of your glass.'

Tweed sipped, then took a larger gulp. He set down the glass and beamed, nodding his head with satisfaction. 'You may have to help me up to bed.'

'That I would enjoy.'

Across the room Munzel talked to Lydia and watched Tweed's table. He had observed the arrival of the drink. People, their meal finished, were leaving. Other guests, waiting at the entrance, were filling up the tables again. There was a lot of movement. He leaned forward and whispered to Lydia.

'See that chap the other side of the room, the one with a blonde?'

'The one wearing glasses?'

389

'Yes. I want to play a trick on him. He once beat me to a business deal. He boasts he's never been drunk.'

'Sounds a stuffy type . . .'

Lydia was merry but still in control of her faculties. She drank just a little more as Munzel went on explaining.

'He is. This is what I want you to do. For a joke.' Under the table he took the plastic tube from his pocket, levered off the top, tipped one capsule into his hand, replaced the top. 'Don't let anyone see this. Hold out your hand when I tell you to. I'll drop a capsule into it. Pretend that we're clasping hands, but don't squeeze it.'

'What's in this capsule?'

'Something harmless – but he'll be rolling like a ship in a storm. You leave the table, pretend you're going to the toilet. As you pass his table you'll have to create a diversion, then drop this in his drink . . .'

'No more instructions,' Lydia broke in. 'I've served behind a bar – as part of my hotel training. This will be fun. I'm ready.'

She reached her hand across the table, turned her palm upwards and he grasped her fingers lightly. She withdrew her hand, holding the capsule, stood up and moved slowly among a crowd of new arrivals. Alongside Tweed's table, she stumbled, put out a hand to save herself and knocked over Diana's half-full glass of wine.

'I'm terribly sorry,' she said in German. She swayed, put out her hand towards the toppled glass. Tweed looked up at Lydia. Her hand passed over his Margharita, dropped the capsule, picked up Diana's glass, mumbling apologies. The wine stained the cloth but missed spilling over on to her dress.

Lydia straightened herself with difficulty, walked on slowly towards the exit, apparently unsteady on her feet. A waiter rushed forward with a napkin, mopping at the cloth.

'Clumsy tart,' said Diana. 'She doesn't know when she's had enough.'

'Nothing on your dress?' Tweed queried. 'Good. You do look absolutely stunning.'

'Thank you, kind sir.'

She glowed with pleasure as the waiter refilled her glass, as Tweed gazed at her. She wore a black velvet evening dress with narrow shoulder straps. In the soft light from the wall lamps her beautifully-shaped shoulders showed to full advantage. She was also wearing jet drop earrings, her lipstick was a pale red, her nail varnish a pale pink. Very nineteen-thirties. Tweed lifted his glass, took several deep sips of the Margharita.

'And I've trimmed my nails,' she said, extending one hand.

'Why?'

'Because I'm learning to type, silly. You can't type with talons. I'm getting pretty good at it. And I've just about mastered shorthand – in English and German. That came easy. The typing's rather a bore. So mechanical . . .'

Across the room Munzel had summoned the waiter, handed him a one hundred-deutschmark note. 'I may have to leave suddenly – an urgent appointment. That will more than cover the meal.'

'There will be a lot of change, sir . . .'

'Keep ten per cent for the tip. I'll call back tomorrow for the rest.'

Tweed took another sip of his Margharita, put down the glass and blinked. He took off his glasses, rubbed at them with the corner of his handkerchief, put them back on. He blinked again.

'Is something wrong?' Diana asked.

'Excuse me. I'll be back in a minute. I'm OK . . .'

He walked rapidly out of the restaurant. Butler saw him go, saw that Diana was left alone and remained in his seat. Tweed pushed his way through the queue waiting for tables, headed for the elevator, pushed the button. His head felt very peculiar. He walked inside the elevator, pressed the button for his floor. The small elevator began to ascend. He blinked again. The walls seemed to be closing in on him. He stepped out, hurried to his room, key in hand. He had trouble inserting the key, turned it, pulled it free automatically and shut the door, then locked it. As he took his hand away his fingers dragged out the key, which fell on the floor.

He turned on the light, stared. The room seemed full of smoke. Something drifted towards him through the smoke, something floating in space. A naked cherub, an evil grin on its horrid little face, a pudgy hand stretched out towards Tweed. Christ! He'd been doped! That bloody girl had dropped something in his glass. He staggered towards the bathroom and the cherub floated backwards, beckoning him on.

391

Downstairs in the lobby Munzel asked the girl behind the reception counter to get him a pack of cigarettes. She looked dubious about leaving her station until he gave her the tip. The moment she'd gone to the bar he reached over, lifted up the box containing the registration slips, rifled through them. *Tweed. Zimmer 303.*

He thanked the girl when she came back, paid her, pressed the elevator button for Tweed's floor. Inside the elevator, the second the doors closed, he took out his bunch of keys, found the pick-lock. This was Munzel the pro, he told himself. The master of improvisation – improvisation of accidents.

Forty-Eight

Tweed was hallucinating. The tiled bathroom floor was crammed with naked cherubs, staring up at him, reaching up to him through the smoke with their beastly little hands. *Water!* He had to drink water – before the hallucinatory drug thoroughly polluted his bloodstream. He grabbed for the glass, knocked the soap on to the floor, filled the glass, drank it all down, refilled the glass, drank more.

Fresh air! The atmosphere was stifling. Sweat ran off his forehead. He staggered to the double windows, slipped on the soap, saved himself by grabbing the ledge. He threw open both windows. Below was a sheer drop of thirty feet, straight down to the tiled floor of an interior well. All windows overlooking it were glazed, like his own. Better get away – dangerous.

He stumbled back to the tap, filled the glass, drank more water. Something touched his shoulder. He jerked round. One of those hideous cherubs, floating in space. Dining-room, Four Seasons. Then the connection was gone. A horseman in hunting clothes appeared out of the fog. The horse reared up, crashed down on top of him. He felt nothing. A skull floated out of the mists, the skull of Harry Masterson, grinning hideously. He put out a hand, pushed it away, his hand feeling nothing, *pushing through the skull*. He turned away, grabbed the glass, refilled it. As he drank he glanced into the mirror. Oh, Jesus!

Hugh Grey's image, a head without a body, stared back out of the mirror, laughing madly. With a trembling hand he refilled the glass. He had a moment of clarity. The bloody paintings Masterson had shown him at his Sussex cottage. He forgot what he'd remembered a moment later. He drank more water. The stuff was running down his suit jacket. Get it inside you, for God's sake.

His own head was floating now. He couldn't see it – he could feel it drifting away from his neck. A vile sensation. He refilled the glass, drank greedily. Guy Dalby's head stared at him out of the mirror, catlick drooped over his forehead, an evil smile on his drifting face. Tweed's left hand reached out to the mirror. The image receded, vanished.

He felt his feet leave the floor as though someone behind was lifting him. Now he was floating in space, like one of those astronauts he'd seen on TV. Tweed hammered the glass he was holding down hard on to the area beside the wash basin. He heard, felt, the *thud*. Again his mind cleared.

The atmosphere seemed fresher. Air percolating in through the open windows. A logical thought. He sensed his mind was on a tightrope – midway between sanity and hallucination. Another logical thought. He drank three more glasses. Something touched his left hand. He looked down. A cherub with an outsize head gazed up at him, its hand touching his. Oh, no . . .

He stared down at the obscene thing. The vision was less defined, faded as he continued staring at it. He stepped back, slipped on the soap tablet and his foot skidded. He saved himself again by grabbing the edge of the basin with his left hand. Must keep away from those open windows – and the abyss beyond.

He was filling the glass when he glanced in the mirror. In his state of shock he let the water fill up the glass – run over the rim. He'd never had time to switch on the bathroom light. The only illumination was light filtering in from the bedroom. A figure loomed behind him. He saw it only vaguely in the dim light, the face of Kurt Franck. The face moved, was shown up in a little more light. He'd grown a beard. Tweed took a firmer grip on the glass and swung round. This was no hallucination. This was for real.

*

393

Franck had stepped out of the elevator into a deserted corridor. He checked the numbers of the rooms. He found 303 at the end of the corridor. He tried the handle gently. The door was locked. He inserted his pick-lock, fiddled, felt the lock slide open.

He went inside into a bedroom. The light was on. From the bathroom he heard the sound of running water. He turned to lock the door. No sign of the key. Too tricky to use the pick-lock. He'd want to leave quickly. He walked into the darkened bathroom.

Tweed was standing staring into the mirror over the wash-basin. Munzel noticed the soap smears on the floor, gleaming in the dim light, the open windows beyond. A perfect set-up. So many accidents happened in bathrooms. He stepped behind Tweed. Their eyes met in the mirror. Tweed swung round with surprising speed. He dashed the glassful of water into Munzel's eyes. The German couldn't see for a moment. In that moment Tweed brought the tough base of the glass down on the bridge of Munzel's large nose. His eyes watered – this time with real pain – but Tweed was too weak to have delivered the blow with great force.

'Bob! How good to see you . . .' Diana had half-risen from her seat, handbag tucked under her arm, when Newman walked into the restaurant. 'Tweed is here,' she went on. 'I was just going to find out what's happened to him . . .'

'Why?'

'He suddenly felt unwell. He went to his room. But he's been there a long time. I was going up to see him. And soon after he'd gone I saw a big blond German get up from his table over there and go out of the restaurant. From the back, the way he moved, in a great hurry. . . .'

'Tweed's room number?'

'Three-O-Three . . .'

'Wait here. Don't move.'

Newman, remembering the placid pace of the elevator, ran up the staircase. 303? That was the room Tweed had occupied before. He knew exactly where it was. He reached the third floor, raced down the corridor, tried the handle and pushed it open quietly, pushing it almost closed behind him. The sounds

394

came from the bathroom. He ran to the open door. Tweed was grappling with Franck, who had his huge arms round Tweed's waist, lifting him off the floor.

Newman, fresh from East Germany, took in the scene at a glance. The soap-smeared floor, the open windows beyond. He clenched his right fist, jerked his elbow back, rammed his fist forward, slamming a vicious kidney punch into the German. Franck let go of Tweed, doubled over, straightened up and started to turn. He slipped on the floor, skidded clear across the bathroom and his hands slapped down on the window ledge. He turned again and his feet slithered under him. He ended up half out of the window, his waist against the ledge, his long legs stretched in front of him.

He bent down, hauled up his left trouser leg, heaved out the broad-bladed knife from the sheath strapped to his leg. That reaction took a few seconds. Newman had crossed the bathroom, avoiding the skid-marks. He stooped down, grasped Franck by the ankles, elevated them and shoved with all his strength.

The German shot out of the window, disappeared. They heard his wailing shriek, cut off suddenly, followed instantly by a horrible soft thud. Newman peered out. Franck lay spread-eagled in the yard far below, reminding Newman of one of those chalk-mark silhouettes police left behind, showing where the corpse was found.

'Anyone see him go?' Tweed asked.

'Doesn't look like it.'

'Keep it . . .' Tweed had trouble speaking '. . . quiet.'

He fumbled for his wallet, got it out, dropped it on the floor. Newman picked it up as Tweed crept into the bedroom, warning Newman to keep clear of the skid-marks. He sagged on to the bed.

'Get Kuhlmann. Local police station. Possehl-strasse 4. Something like that. Folded sheet of paper. In my wallet. Tell him what happened. Discreetly . . .'

'I've found it. I'll get the number from the directory here.'

Newman made the call. He was put through to Kuhlmann almost immediately. The conversation was short. Newman put down the phone, came over to Tweed who had propped up a pillow and was slumped against it.

'He'll be here in five minutes. I'll just pop downstairs, see

Diana, stop her coming up. She was on her way when I went into the restaurant. Anything you need now?'

'One thing. Bob, get me a glass of water.'

Kuhlmann arrived with only one other man, a Dr Rimek, who insisted on examining Tweed while Kuhlmann spent time with Newman in the bathroom. Rimek, a humorous-looking man in his sixties, was thin and stooped and wore a pince-nez.

He listened while Tweed confined his description of what had happened in his hallucinatory experiences, nodding his head occasionally. Then he checked Tweed's pulse, blood pressure and used his stethoscope. He straightened up and grunted.

'What's the verdict?' Tweed asked in German.

'Tough as old hickory, you are. And you did just the right thing – drinking litres of water. I'd say it was mescaline, something like that, you were drugged with.' He looked up as Newman came back into the room. 'If that drink, whatever it was called . . .'

'Margharita,' Tweed said.

'If that drink is still on the table in the dining-room I'd like the glass for analysis . . .'

'I brought it up with me.' Newman opened the wardrobe and took a glass rimmed with salt from the top shelf. 'This is it.'

'Excellent.' Rimek took a wide-mouthed plastic bottle out of his bag, poured the contents of the glass into it, screwed down the top. 'I'll know tomorrow . . .'

'Phone the results to me,' Kuhlmann called out from the bathroom door. 'He'll live, I take it? Good. And, Rimek, not one word about this to anyone else.'

Rimek took a blood sample before he left. He paused at the door, staring at Tweed. 'Two days' complete rest. You don't have to stay in bed. Just in the hotel. Maybe a short walk tomorrow afternoon. No more than two hundred metres. Same the day after. And no alcohol for two days. I'll get off now.'

Kuhlmann waited until Rimek had gone, then lit his cigar and began talking.

'Before I call the clean-up squad – fingerprint, photographer, forensic, etc – we have to get our story straight. Newman has told me what happened. Now I'll tell you. You feel up to this, I hope, Tweed?'

'Go ahead.'

'You don't want any publicity – being who and what you are. Newman arrived soon after you came up here.' Kuhlmann jabbed his cigar at Tweed to emphasize his point. '*You* were never here. You were in the dining-room. You gave Newman your room key to borrow a handkerchief. He comes up, finds the door wide open, finds Franck rifling the room. Pull out a drawer in a minute, empty the contents on a floor. There's a struggle in the bathroom – where Newman found Franck taking a pee. Franck pulls a knife. That went down in the area with him. You've left the bathroom windows open – it's a hot night. Franck goes out of the window – slipped on the soap. That's it. Keep it simple. The local police chief is a pal of mine – I'll keep him off your back. I'm going to phone Possehl-strasse now.'

'How can you keep it quiet?' Tweed asked. 'Someone must have heard Franck – he screamed when he went down . . .'

'You'd be surprised how people don't hear things like that. The manager knows. I had a word with him before I came up. He won't talk. Hotel guests aren't keen on acts of violence. He took me into the area. There's a door under your window you can't see from up here, a door he locked and I have the key.'

'I'd better get out of here for the moment,' Tweed said.

'Definitely. Use Newman's room . . .'

'I think I can make the dining-room. I have a friend down there.'

'Better still. Your colour's coming back.'

While Kuhlmann was using the phone Tweed pointed to a drawer. Newman pulled it out, turned it upside down. Shirts, socks and handkerchiefs spilled on to the floor. He picked up one of the handkerchiefs embroidered with Tweed's initials.

'This,' he said, 'is the borrowed handkerchief. I'll give you mine – just in case some eager beaver searches me.'

'You might bring me some tissues from the box in the bathroom,' Tweed suggested, planting his feet on the floor, testing his strength before he stood up.

Newman brought the tissues and handed him one which he had screwed up. 'My handkerchief is inside that. If you don't mind keeping it.'

Tweed shoved it inside his jacket pocket and then started

397

using the other tissues to dab at his jacket front, drying out the water he'd spilt down it. Diana was bound to spot the dampness, to ask what had caused it. He took several steps round the room, then paced more briskly. His head had stopped pounding.

Kuhlmann put down the phone, said the team would be there inside ten minutes, so they'd better get moving. And he'd be back the following day to talk some more.

'They'll have trouble smuggling Franck out,' Tweed said.

'Oh, they'll scrape him up, cart the bits away.'

Forty-Nine

Tweed stayed up half the night in Newman's room, listening in silence to his account of his experiences in East Germany. Earlier he had gone down to the dining-room, assured Diana it was only a stomach upset. That covered the fact he hadn't felt like eating. Coffee, however, helped to clear his head.

He saw her safely to her room. As the door closed and he turned round he saw Harry Butler sitting in a chair close to the elevator, reading a copy of *Lübecker Nachrichten*, the local paper. He nodded to him and went to Newman's room.

'So,' he commented as Newman finished his report, 'you've had a pretty grim time . . .'

'And now we know Dr Berlin is a fake. The trip was worth it to find that out.'

'I suspected it. But suspecting is one thing, knowing is another. Lysenko must have trained an impostor all those years ago. It's creepy – their long-distance planning. I want this kept quiet, Bob.'

'You mean we don't tell Kuhlmann?'

'Definitely not. Nor that bastard Peter Toll, who sent you in. Keep it just between the two of us.'

'Why?'

Tweed stirred in his chair, drank some more of the coffee sent up by room service. 'Because if I'm right, if Janus is what I suspect he is, we face the most appalling scandal in London if this ever got out. The press would have a field day. Like the

Duke of Wellington, I'm feeling my way forward, tying knots in a rope. If I'm right, how I'm going to solve the problem God only knows. Janus is not only Lysenko's man in London – he may also be a mass murderer.'

'Janus? You've used that name twice . . .'

'The codeword I cooked up with Monica for the rotten apple sitting in my own barrel. Janus, like the January god. The man who looks both ways – to the East and the West.'

Tweed checked his watch. 3 a.m. He stood up, felt his legs were normal, walked into Newman's bathroom and quietly opened the window, gazing down into the well. Men in plain clothes were moving about. *Kriminalpolizei*. The body was covered with a tarpaulin. Through the open door beneath his own window he saw more men arriving, two carrying a stretcher. He shivered, closed the window silently.

'They're about to take Franck away,' he said, sitting down again. 'In the middle of the night. No one in the hotel will be any the wiser. Kuhlmann has been very cooperative – covering up the whole business, which is what I want.'

'So they won't know in Leipzig? They'll go on thinking Franck is still after you?'

'Exactly that. Also Pete Nield came over with me. Someone – as I expected – followed me from the airport. Butler followed them to an apartment in Altona. I have the address in my wallet. I'm giving it to Kuhlmann in the morning. He may find a way of neutralizing this character. He could just be the main link in the communications system Lysenko must have between here and East Germany.'

'And I caught sight of Harry Butler in the restaurant when I first arrived. You've brought over the big battalions.'

'I think we may need them. I sense we're close to the climax of this business . . .'

'Which I still don't understand,' Newman remarked. 'Janus is the traitor in the Park Crescent setup. Balkan is the controller of Markus Wolf's spy network in West Germany . . .'

'Lysenko has deliberately made it complex. I'm convinced their set-up is diabolically simple. I think Janus and Balkan are the same man. A stroke of genius on the part of our Russian friend.'

399

'But that would mean the same man – Janus in London, Balkan over here – is controlling both our network and theirs. Theoretically, he'd be fighting himself . . .'

'But only theoretically,' Tweed pointed out. 'He'd be in a unique position to manipulate my agents the way he wanted to. Lysenko had pulled off an unprecedented coup.'

'Had?'

'I'm going to locate Janus and destroy him – and bring down Lysenko with him.'

Tweed's expression was grim as he stood up again and went to the bathroom. He came back after peering out of the window.

'I can go back to my own room, get a bit of shut-eye. They have gone, taken away the body. We'll talk about how we'll go about it in the morning.'

Tweed was finishing his breakfast in the room at the back of the Jensen when Newman reappeared and sat down, looking at Diana who was inserting a cigarette in her holder.

'You should have seen the meal he's had,' she said. 'Five rolls, lashings of butter, tons of marmalade. Nothing much wrong with his stomach today.'

'I was ravenous,' admitted Tweed. 'But I'm a new man now. Time to get cracking. And where have you been?' he asked Newman.

'To hire a car. An Audi. I foresaw something like this. We ride everywhere today. No walking.'

'Is Tweed all right?' Diana asked.

'Last night Bob insisted on getting a doctor in,' Tweed said quickly. 'He diagnosed a mild bout of food poisoning. Silly quack said I shouldn't walk more than two hundred metres for the next two days. The trouble is, Bob has taken him seriously.'

'I should think so, too,' Diana agreed forcefully. 'When you eventually came back to the restaurant last night you looked really out of sorts. And you couldn't eat anything. By the way, you said you had an appointment this morning. I think I'll go shopping, spend some of my ill-gotten gains . . .'

Tweed looked up sharply at the remark, then cursed himself for his mistake when she replied.

'I was only joking. You looked quite severe . . .'

'Put it down to lack of sleep. Yes, you go shopping, enjoy

yourself. This afternoon we're going to Travemünde . . .'

'Can I come too?' she asked eagerly. 'I left some things I need on the *Südwind* – and I'm simply dying to see Ann Grayle's face when I tell her we've been to London. I can tell her?'

'Why not?'

Tweed stood up with Newman, glanced across to where Butler was lingering over his coffee. This morning he wore an open-necked blue shirt, cinnamon-coloured slacks and wrap-round tinted glasses. Even Tweed found him difficult to recognize; Diana certainly wouldn't spot him when he followed her.

'Where are we going?' Newman asked as he settled himself behind the wheel of the hired Audi.

'Lübeck-Süd police headquarters. Kuhlmann phoned before I came down to breakfast. He has news. But first we'll call in at the Movenpick. You drive past the Holstentor and I'll guide you. I want a word with Pete Nield, send him over to help Butler keep an eye on Diana.'

'Dr Berlin is back. I told you I had news,' Kuhlmann announced with satisfaction. 'That's only for openers.'

At Lübeck-Süd Kuhlmann had taken them up in the elevator to the locked room where Tweed had used the scrambler phone on his previous visit. Newman and Tweed sat at the table, drinking coffee from the canteen. Kuhlmann remained on his feet, waving his cigar, about to continue, when Tweed spoke.

'Where is Dr Berlin now? What time did he get back?'

'In his mansion on Priwall Island. Gates closed. Guards posted. Dogs patrolling the grounds. He arrived back at precisely 11.30 p.m. last night, travelling inside his black Mercedes. They brought the ferryman back to take him over – he has that kind of clout.'

'Any chance of a second raid on that mansion – if I wanted it?' Tweed asked.

'No chance. I got my backside paddled about that. Berlin has clout in Bonn. He's a friend of Oskar Graf von Krull, the banker. I can't even put close surveillance on that mansion any more. Unless, of course . . .' He puffed at his cigar. 'I was provided with iron-clad evidence of a crime. Iron-clad.'

'Not to worry. You've managed to keep the Franck episode quiet?'

401

'That I've managed. He's from the East. All his identity documents checked out – except the driving licence. The computer showed its owner died six months ago in a crash. And Peter Toll of the BND is on his way here – flying in from München.'

'I'd like to see him. As soon as he arrives,' Tweed said tersely.

The phone rang. Kuhlmann listened, spoke briefly, put the receiver down. He turned to Newman.

'They're ready to take your statement about Franck. Room 10. Ground floor. You can find your own way?'

'I can . . .'

'The statement should be as we agreed last night. Not one word more.'

He waited until he was alone with Tweed. 'I don't know where Newman has been . . .' He paused, but Tweed remained silent. '. . . but he's a changed man. Something has happened to him.'

'He's grown harder,' Tweed agreed. 'At one time he'd have punched it out with Franck. He didn't hesitate to jerk him out of that window . . .'

'Knowing he'd end up spread over the floor of that well like a mess of goulash. But Franck did pull a knife – and that's something else I wanted to tell you. In confidence.'

'Of course.'

'Franck murdered those blonde girls. That knife fits the murder weapon. We've got our psycho . . .'

'Are you sure?' Tweed frowned, startled.

'I'm always sure. The pathologist is checking it now. Is something wrong?'

'A major theory I had just went out of the window – the way Franck did.'

'What's your next move?'

'I think I'll go back to Travemünde – ask a few more questions. Those boat people who commute between the Med and the Baltic fascinate me . . .'

The phone rang again. Kuhlmann listened, told them to send him up. 'Peter Toll has arrived,' he told Tweed. 'I'll leave you alone with him.'

*

402

Toll started out bright and breezy, adjusting his glasses as he sat opposite Tweed, who stared back without any particular expression. Then Tweed let rip, castigating the BND chief for sending a British civilian across the border.

'He went voluntarily,' Toll protested. 'And where is my man, Pröhl? I've had a talk with Newman downstairs. He's given me invaluable information – about a changed code. And he was very concerned as to the fate of a girl called Gerda. That we may not know for months. We're having a longer chat later . . .'

'You are not. Newman went through hell behind the Curtain. He was almost caught several times.'

'I regret that. In future I check with you first. But I didn't know he was your employee,' he pointed out.

'He isn't. And I've phoned London – Pröhl is flying back to Germany.' Tweed stood up. 'I think in time we will cooperate well together. Let us say goodbye on that positive note.'

He was alone for barely a minute when Kuhlmann returned, sat down and crossed his stocky legs.

'I left you alone until he'd gone.'

'And how did you know he *had* gone?'

'There's a pressure pad under the carpet outside the door. Someone steps on it, a light is activated in another room.'

'Tricky little place you've got here,' Tweed commented. 'You were talking about Franck.'

'He had a beard. Long hair, too. But the main thing is the beard.'

'I don't quite follow you.'

'Explains something which had puzzled me. Why did Franck go underground for as long as about a fortnight? Now I've got it – he had to hide away while he grew that beard.'

'Say that again.'

'I thought I spoke clearly.' Kuhlmann looked miffed, then he nodded his head. 'Of course, you're still suffering from that mescaline – it was mescaline; Dr Rimek phoned me the results of the analysis this morning.'

He took the cigar out of the corner of his mouth. He spoke with slow, deliberate emphasis. 'I said, why did Franck go underground for about a fortnight? He had to hide away while he grew that beard.'

'I've been an idiot – not seeing it earlier . . .'

'Not seeing what?'

'Wait! You said Dr Berlin is back – did your man actually see him clearly inside that Mercedes?'

'No. I checked that. He has those amber-coloured net curtains inside the car. They were drawn. The chauffeur was driving. He saw a vague outline of a figure in the back, a man who wore tinted glasses – the type Berlin wears . . .'

'So,' Tweed pressed, 'he had no clear and visible view of the passenger in the back?'

'No.'

'I thought not.' Tweed's tone expressed deep satisfaction. 'I predict we won't be seeing Dr Berlin for about another ten days yet.'

'You wouldn't care to explain all this? No? I thought not. Incidentally, you'll be on your own from now on. I have to get back to Wiesbaden. I only stayed here to track down the murderer of those blonde girls. Thanks to Newman, case closed.'

Fifty

'Five hundred kilos of heroin,' Tweed said to Newman as they strolled along the Travemünde waterfront. 'That would cause havoc in Britain. Worse, in some ways, than a couple of atom bombs. Could you load that amount aboard a cruiser like the *Südwind*?'

'Yes, if you stacked it to the gunwales. Bit of an exaggeration, but it could be done.'

'Do you think that cruiser you saw approaching the *Wroclaw* was the *Südwind*?'

In the distance, wending her way among the crowds, Diana, wearing a cherry-coloured dress, was heading for the vessel Tweed had named. Behind her ambled Harry Butler, his blue shirt concealed beneath a white lightweight Marks & Spencer sweater. Pete Nield strolled on the opposite side of the road.

Butler and Nield had followed Newman's hired Audi in their own hired Fiat on the drive from Lübeck to Travemünde. Newman shrugged in answer to Tweed's question.

'There are so many of these power cruisers in this part of the world now. It could have come from a marina anywhere along the Baltic – here, Kiel, Flensburg. And don't ask me if I could identify the chap in the balaclava who brought his cruiser alongside the freighter. I couldn't.'

'Lack of evidence.' Tweed grunted. 'And now Kuhlmann is going back to Wiesbaden – although I think he's wrong. I can see Ann Grayle. Let's have a chat with her.'

As usual, Ann Grayle was smart as paint. She wore a cream linen V-necked sweater, a navy blue pleated skirt, court shoes and a rope of pearls. Her right hand clasped a glass as she welcomed them aboard.

'And how are you, Bob? Fully recovered?' She eyed Tweed with a dry smile. 'So, the claims investigator has come back too – with the delectable Diana. Sit down somewhere – and would you like a drink? It's a punch. I'd better warn you – it carries one hell of a kick.'

'Not for me,' Tweed said hastily. 'Perhaps a glass of orange juice?'

'I'll risk the punch,' Newman said.

'Ben! One glass of punch, one orange juice.'

The head of Ben Tolliver appeared again above the companionway, curious to see who'd come aboard, then vanished. She talks to him like a servant, Tweed thought. Grayle was at her most upper crust as she arranged herself in a canvas seat, crossing her shapely legs.

'This old tub is getting like Piccadilly Circus. I bet Bob didn't tell you he slept on board here two nights ago.'

'Really?' Tweed pretended innocence. 'I'm sure he found it to his liking.'

'And that's a dirty remark if ever I heard one. Piccadilly Circus, I said. I had the oddest visitor the night Bob came aboard – not thirty minutes before he arrived.'

'Who was that?' Tweed enquired.

'I don't know. Said his name was Andrews, but I didn't believe that. Nearly scared me over the side. All those bandages.'

405

'Bandages?' Newman interjected.

'Yes, like someone just out of hospital. Maybe he was. His whole face was covered in them – except for the eyes and a slit for the mouth. Said he was a reporter, asked me questions about Dr Berlin. Oh, things are livening up. The august Dr Berlin is back. I suppose he'll be meditating in his locked study.'

'He'll be doing what?' Tweed asked.

'Oh, didn't you know?' She paused as Ben appeared with the drinks on a silver tray. 'Ben, that tray could do with a good clean.'

'Then you'll be having a little job waiting – when you can get round to it.'

She glared as Ben served the drinks and disappeared down the companionway. Tweed had studied Tolliver as he handed round the glasses. The red complexion, the blue-veined nose of the hardened drinker. Whisky, probably. The tropics encouraged its consumption, the way of life he'd enjoyed in the 'good old days'.

'As I was saying,' Grayle continued, 'whenever he returns from one of his mysterious trips to God knows where, Dr Berlin locks himself in his study and meditates. None of your bogus *guru* nonsense which was popular not so long ago. He simply wants to be alone. Like Garbo, I suppose.'

'How do you know this?' Tweed enquired.

'He sacked one of his servants. A German who drank like the proverbial fish. He told Ben all about it in a bar one night. Shortly after that, he disappeared. Never been seen around since.' She raised her eyebrows, took a sip of her punch. 'A sinister disappearance some people said.'

'And what about this stranger with the bandaged face? Was he really English?'

'I'm sure he was. From his voice. Said he'd been in a car crash. Only superficial injuries, but mauled all over a bit. I'd have told him to leave – I pretended to fetch a handkerchief, left the drawer open, the one where I keep my gun. And Ben was aboard, doing something to the wheel. I have an alarm button concealed under the bunk I was sitting on. So I wasn't too bothered. And he intrigued me – his questions about Dr Berlin.'

'What sort of questions?'

'Had he returned to Priwall Island? Did I know him? When I said no – except twenty years ago in Kenya – he wanted to know his timetable. How much time he spent here. How long he was away. *When* he was away. In the end I told him I was a diplomat's wife, not a bloody walking encyclopaedia. He pushed off soon afterwards, limping back across the gangway.'

'He was lame? Could you describe him?'

'This is getting a bit much. No, I couldn't describe him. He said the strong light hurt his eyes, so I turned them down with the dimmer. About Bob's height and build, I think. He wore one of those floppy duffel coats, so it was hard to tell. That was the night the strange power cruiser put in here.'

'Strange?'

'Never seen it before. It moored at the landing-stage beyond the *Südwind*. It arrived a few minutes before this so-called Andrews appeared like a genie out of a bottle.'

'It's still here?' Newman asked.

'No. It must have moved off during the night. It was gone by morning. The *Nocturne*.'

Tweed froze, his glass half way to his mouth. He frowned, trying to recollect where he'd heard the name before. She misinterpreted his expression.

'I do know what I'm talking about. I was just going below when I saw it berthing. I used my night-glasses to read the name on the hull. *Nocturne*. I suppose,' she continued, 'as an insurance man all you know about is statistics. *Nocturne*, I said. Chopin composed them.'

'I have heard of Chopin . . .'

'Good for you. Oh, look whom we have here. We are honoured. How are you, Diana, darling? Care for a drink? You've never been known to say no.'

'You're looking marvellous,' Diana said as she came aboard.

'This old thing?'

'I meant the outfit, not what's inside it . . .'

'Really?' Grayle placed her glass carefully on the table, rose slowly to her feet, her expression icy, as Tweed stood up quickly, staring at Diana. Grayle opened her mouth, closed it without saying anything, and studied Diana before speaking.

407

'What's wrong? You're trembling.'

'I'm terribly sorry. That was unforgivably rude of me . . .'

'Something's happened?' Tweed asked.

Diana clenched her hands, took a deep breath. She looked at Tweed, then at Newman. She unclenched her hands, folded both arms across her breasts as though struggling for control.

'Could you both come to the *Südwind*? Something *has* happened.'

'Someone has been on board while we were in England. All my things have been searched. I'll have to wash everything – the thought of a burglar feeling my underclothes . . .'

'There's no outward sign of a burglary,' Newman remarked.

'Yes, but a woman can tell when someone has been rifling her things. They tried to cover it up, but I can tell. Things are not the way I left them. And, it's weird. They've put new locks on the cupboards I don't use – which are most of them.'

'Show me an example,' said Tweed.

'This cupboard, this one – and this one . . .'

The locks certainly looked new, and they were deadlocks – not what you expected aboard a cruiser. Tweed stared round the cabin. The storage space was considerable. And it would take more than a skeleton key to open these locks. He looked at Newman, who was checking the general capacity of the newly-secured cupboards.

'All the drawers containing your own property were locked?' Newman asked.

'None of them were. They don't lock. I'm packing all my things now.' She heaved a suitcase down off a shelf, placed it on a table, flipped open the case. She started taking her clothes out of a drawer, putting them inside the case. 'I'm clearing out. Could I stay with you at the Jensen? I'll pay for my room. You've spent too much on me already . . .'

Her hands were trembling again. Tweed put an arm round her waist, sat her down on the edge of a bunk.

'You need a drink. Where is it?'

'In that cupboard.' She pointed. 'Cognac, please. Just a little.'

Newman found the bottle and the glasses, poured a small

quantity into a glass and handed it to her. She took several sips, put the glass down.

'Thank you. Both of you.'

'You seem exceptionally upset,' Tweed observed, sitting beside her. 'Is it only the burglary? It doesn't look like a normal burglary.'

'It's those new locks. I've got to get out of here – away from Travemünde. He must be back.'

'Dr Berlin?'

'It's his boat.'

'How are you off for money?' Tweed asked, changing the subject.

'I'm all right at the moment. And soon I'll be able to earn my own living. In London I called a couple of secretarial agencies. I was amazed what they pay for a competent secretary. It's time I stood on my own feet. I'm all right now. Let me get on with the packing. I feel I must do something . . .'

Tweed stood up, asked Newman to stay with her, then walked back along the landing-stage to the waterfront. Butler was leaning against a lamp post, taking random shots with a camera. Tweed paused beside him, cleaning his glasses. His lips hardly moved.

'Emergency. Diana must be guarded night and day. She could be in danger of her life. The risk has increased enormously. Tell Nield. Arrange a roster between you – one on, one off. Then you can both get some sleep.'

'Understood.'

Butler had his camera raised, was snapping a large white passenger ship just approaching the narrows from Sweden. Tweed was turning to go back to the *Südwind* when a uniformed policeman ran across the road and spoke. Tweed thought he recognized the man from Lübeck-Süd.

'Mr Tweed?'

'Yes.'

'Chief Inspector Kuhlmann is on the phone. Wants to speak to you urgently. Can you come back with me to the station?'

Inside the small police station facing the waterfront, Tweed was given a tiny room on his own. He picked up the receiver lying on its side and stood, looking out of the window.

'Tweed speaking. How did you know I was here?'

'I had you followed. Chap on a motor-cycle. That's immaterial. Kurt Franck didn't murder those blonde girls.'

'I did wonder. How do you know that?'

'Pathologist's report after examining the knife. It's very similar to the weapon used, but it's not the weapon. They've checked it under the microscope. There's a minute nick in the blade – so small you'd never notice it with the naked eye. However carefully that knife had been cleaned traces of dried blood, human skin, flesh, etc. would have remained inside the nick. No traces. And the curve of the blade isn't quite the right angle.'

'So my theory becomes valid again . . .'

'The theory you won't tell me about?' Kuhlmann snapped.

'Because I'm not sure I'm right. It's become complicated again, grimly so. And I suppose if I asked you to search one of Dr Berlin's cruisers, the *Südwind* – rip it apart – you'd jump back a kilometre?'

'Ten kilometres. If *I* hadn't had friends in Bonn that raid would have finished me. And my job is to find that mass-murderer. Top priority.'

'You think you'll succeed?'

'They never did identify your Jack the Ripper.'

Ten days passed. Newman had the impression Tweed was in a passive phase, an opinion shared by Butler and Nield when the two men discussed their chief.

'He's waiting for something to happen, a development,' said Butler, who knew Tweed well. 'When it does, watch his smoke.'

At Tweed's suggestion, Diana spent a lot of time in her room at the Jensen, perfecting her shorthand and typing on a machine she'd hired locally. She never went anywhere near Travemünde.

Butler and Nield took it in turns to guard her. When she took a short walk in the town one of them was always close to her. Tweed had persuaded Kuhlmann to issue each man with a Walther automatic and a temporary licence to possess a firearm.

And Tweed's so-called passive phase was packed with activity. He phoned London and arranged for a Sea King helicopter to be flown to Lübeck. He also took a great interest in the local private airfield at Blankensee, a nowhere place out in the country sixteen kilometres east of Lübeck.

Butler, who held a licence to pilot a helicopter, drove Tweed to the airfield. Close to it they saw a sign pointing down a side road to the right. *Lübeck-Blankensee*. Turning down it they drove along the Blankensee-strasse, a long straight road bordered by trees and fields beyond.

The airfield was on their left, larger than Tweed had expected, stretching away towards the east. It was a lonely spot. The departure building was a single-storey modern edifice which carried a large sign above the entrance. FLUGHAFEN LÜBECK.

'No one about,' Newman commented as they walked inside. The entrance hall had a strange floor – paved with small pebbles. To their right was an empty restaurant which appeared closed. Tweed made for a noticeboard, glanced at it.

'Polizei – Raum 4,' he read out.

Inside Room 4 a policeman sat in shirt-sleeves drinking coffee with two men in flying gear. Tweed introduced himself and the policeman checked his identity and then said he'd leave them alone.

'You'll know these two gentlemen,' Tweed said to Newman. 'They flew us last year from the Swedish island of Ornö into Arlanda Airport. Bill Casey, pilot, and Tom Wilson, his co-pilot and navigator, plus radio op.'

Casey, a good-humoured man of thirty-one with sandy hair shook hands with Newman. 'With Tweed involved,' he said, 'my bet is this is a hairy one, too.' Wilson, dark-haired, about the same age, was more reserved, simply nodding as he briefly shook hands.

'Now,' Tweed said briskly, 'let's get down to it. You managed to borrow a Sea King?'

'She's out there now,' Casey confirmed. 'Getting her was a job. The papers I had to sign, but she's all yours. And the controller here has loaned me this chart.'

He spread it out over the table. Newman was surprised by the area it covered. The whole of the Baltic, continuing north to the Skagerrak – the vast body of water which entered the North Sea and the Atlantic – and Oslo.

'Exactly what we want.' Tweed was becoming very animated,

411

Newman observed. Action was coming. Tweed produced several Polaroid prints, laid them alongside the chart. 'These were taken by a colleague in Travemünde a few days ago – pretending to be a tourist, snapping shots at random. This power cruiser is the *Südwind*. Think you could recognize it from the air if it heads out into the Baltic?'

'If I can keep these prints, yes. Wilson will soon pick it up with a pair of high-powered glasses. From a distance.'

'Good. I wouldn't want the helmsman to know you were interested in him. There are two more very similar cruisers I want you to look out for. The *Nordsee* – and the *Nocturne*.'

'Half a mo' while I note those names down.' Casey scribbled in his notebook. 'How far do we follow them, bearing in mind we can only tail one if they take different courses?'

'Only one will head for the west, turning north through the Öresund between Denmark and Sweden, then on into the Kattegat and the Skagerrak. I need to know its ultimate destination when that happens.'

'It *will* happen?' Casey queried.

'I'm betting my whole career on it. Of course there'll be other cruisers poodling about along the coast. It's the one of the three mentioned which goes long distance I want tracked. Radio regular reports back to Lübeck-Süd police HQ. And on this bit of paper is the call sign, the waveband, etc. You address each signal to Kuhlmann – it's written down there. I understand you know German, Casey?'

'My second language . . .'

'Transmit in German. That's important – in case of interception from the other side. You sign off as Walter Three.'

'We brought over night-sight equipment as requested. How do we go about covering night and day?'

'Take it in turns to fly the chopper.'

'I told you it would be hairy,' Casey said to Wilson. He looked at Tweed. 'You've marked where the *Südwind* and the *Nordsee* are moored with crosses. What about the *Nocturne*?'

'She's disappeared. I think she may come back.'

'You do realize we're going to be pretty conspicuous?' Casey pointed out.

'I want you to be. More pressure on the target I'm after. The Sea King does have Danish markings?'

'Again, as requested.'

'So people – including those across the border – are going to think it's some kind of NATO exercise. The locals will soon get used to your patrols, hardly notice you. But for God's sake, don't stray over the border.'

'That thought had occurred to me,' Casey replied. 'And I think we'll get moving now . . .'

'Pressure?' Newman queried as they drove away from the airfield. 'On Dr Berlin?'

'As much as I can bring to bear. Head for Travemünde – I'm going to haunt that place, mingle with the boat people. The news will reach Priwall Island soon enough.'

'And I'm sticking with you. Butler and Nield have their hands full watching over Diana. You're after that five hundred-kilo consignment of heroin, aren't you? I thought so. But what makes you think it isn't already on its way to Britain now?'

'A remark Kuhlmann made the morning after Franck attacked me in my bedroom.'

'And, of course you wouldn't care to tell me the remark?'

'Of course.'

Fifty-One

'I've changed my mind,' Tweed said as they approached the turn-off point to Travemünde. 'Drive us back to Lübeck-Süd, first. I want to reassure Kuhlmann – he got me authority for the Sea King to use that airfield, to use their radio system. Then we'll drive on to Travemünde . . .'

Kuhlmann took them to the same locked room with the scrambler phone. As they sat round the table Tweed pointed to the phone.

'If I need to use that in an emergency and you're not here, could you arrange it so I'll be permitted up here?'

'My pleasure.'

Tweed told him about the Sea King now operating from Flughafen Lübeck. Kuhlmann said he'd also arrange it so all

413

signals from the chopper came straight through to him. The German lacked his normal aggressive bounce. Tweed sensed frustration but ignored it.

'There is one thing before we go,' he remarked. 'I'd have thought a fresh warning should be issued that our murderer is still out there . . .'

'Hell! That's what's getting me down. I've asked for just that action. It's been vetoed.'

'Who by?'

'The *Land*.' He looked at Newman. 'As you know, we have separate state governments who carry a lot of clout. I called Kiel. They called Lübeck. Kiel came back with nothing doing. I'm not even permitted to have new posters put up – Franck's have been removed, naturally. Schleswig-Holstein is one of the poorest states. Relies heavily on the tourists. They don't want another scare about a mass murderer on the loose. They say that pathologist's report isn't conclusive.'

'So we wait for the next killing?' Tweed said grimly.

'I've run out of leads.'

'I haven't.' Tweed stood up. 'We'd better get going.'

'Funny thing,' Kuhlmann said as he accompanied them to the elevator. 'We'd have trapped Kurt Franck even if he hadn't tried to kill you that night. An American girl, Sue Templeton – a blonde – who helped me a few weeks ago, got in touch with me the following morning. She'd seen him walk into the International. He had a room there, too. Nice girl, sharp as a tack and, like so many American girls, has lots of initiative.'

'On holiday?' Tweed remarked for something to say.

'Yes. She's still here. Spends most of her time out at Travemünde with her English boy friend.'

During the next few days Tweed reminded Newman of a spider which had woven its web, confident that sooner or later the fly would get caught up inside it. He wandered round the waterfront at Travemünde, spent time with Ann Grayle aboard her sloop.

They frequently saw Casey's Sea King, flying low over the area, once even crossing direct over Dr Berlin's mansion on Priwall Island. Grayle remarked on it, then hardly noticed when it passed overhead again.

414

At Tweed's suggestion Newman waited his opportunity, then invited Ben Tolliver to have a drink with him in a bar. The old Kenya hand accepted at once and they chatted easily together.

'Diana Chadwick?' Ben mused, in answer to Newman's question. 'She used to run a bit wild in what we called Happy Valley, but promiscuous? I wouldn't call her that. The trouble was Ann was competing for the attentions of the same man. It was that kind of world. Diana won hands down. You can't do that to Ann Grayle . . .'

'I was a farmer,' he continued after sipping at his Scotch. 'One of the few successful ones. Dr Berlin was a weird one even in those days. Kept to himself on that medical station he ran for the natives out in the bush. I always said he had grown that black beard to make himself look the part. Fancied himself as a second Dr Albert Schweitzer. Then he disappeared one night. We thought a wild animal had got him – they found bloodstained clothing. Next thing we hear, he's turned up in Leipzig. Not interested in women.'

'Diana knew him rather well, I gather.'

'Only one who could get near him. Helped him out with the nursing, fetching medical supplies from Nairobi. She has a way with men. I mean that in the nicest sense.'

'And now no contact? Between Dr Berlin and the rest of you?'

'Wasn't much back in Kenya. None at all here. Except for Diana. They go back over twenty years. Think I'd better get back, see if Ann's all right. She's Miss Bossy Boots – you must have noticed. But I rather like her.'

It happened as they were walking out of the bar which stood almost opposite where the Priwall Island ferry plied back and forth. Tweed kept a close eye on the ferry and now he stood quite still, a hundred yards or so from the landing point, his gaze fixed on the incoming vessel.

'Well, I'll be damned!' Tolliver exclaimed. 'That looks like Dr Berlin coming out of hibernation . . .'

At the prow of the ferry moving close in to the landing stage was a black Mercedes, its waxed body gleaming in the sunshine. A uniformed chauffeur sat behind the wheel; one passenger occupied the back seat. Tweed stood by himself at the edge of the road as the ramp was lowered, hands thrust inside his jacket pockets. The car bumped over the ramp, swung in his direction. Newman started running.

The Mercedes moved slowly at first. As Newman ran he saw the figure in the back behind the amber net curtains lean forward, as though giving an instruction. The car changed direction, suddenly accelerated, heading at high speed direct for Tweed.

'Look out!' Newman yelled.

Tweed remained motionless as a statue, staring straight at the dim silhouette of the man in the back of the car. People stopped, turned, gazed in horror. The Mercedes roared forward. Time seemed to stand still. Tweed himself stood still, hands still thrust inside jacket pockets, very erect, feet planted slightly apart. Oh God, no! Newman kept on running.

At the very last second the Mercedes swerved away. Tweed felt the force of its slipstream. His trousers whipped round his legs. The hush which had descended on the waterfront was broken. People began walking again, chattering, looking back at Tweed as Newman reached him.

'Are you bloody mad?' he gasped.

'He's cracking.' There was infinite satisfaction in Tweed's voice. 'At long last he's cracking.'

'What the hell does that mean?'

'I think – just in case anything happens to me – you'd better know more about this business.' He looked up as Casey's chopper passed overhead. 'That has probably helped. Now let us drive out into the country, have a walk where we can talk with no danger of eavesdroppers. Fortunately you've been thoroughly vetted, signed the Official Secrets Act. In fact, Bob,' he continued as they made their way to where Newman had parked the Audi, 'you are the only person I can confide in.'

They walked along the country road leading to the private airfield. The sun blazed down and Newman carried his jacket over his arm.

'You could talk to Butler and Nield,' he pointed out.

Tweed shook his head. 'I don't know how I'm going to solve this one – it's quite the grimmest problem I've ever faced. Let's take it step by step. Balkan is the codename for the master agent Lysenko is using to operate his network in West Germany.'

416

'I have grasped that . . .'

'Janus is the name I've given to the man Lysenko has planted inside my own organization in London. One of four men – Grey, Dalby, Lindemann or Masterson. All right so far?'

'Clear enough.'

'Janus and Balkan are the same man. It's Lysenko's master stroke. He must have infiltrated Janus years ago – and six months back I promoted him – whoever he is – to be one of the four European sector chiefs. The blunder is my responsibility.'

'How could you have known?'

'Irrelevant.' Tweed's tone was curt. 'I did it. But it gets worse. I'm now convinced Janus-Balkan is Dr Berlin . . .'

'Jesus. What put you on to that?'

'Two chance remarks – one by Diana, the other by Kuhlmann. When we attended Dr Berlin's party we stared at each other across a distance – while he sat on the terrace. Diana said maybe he – Berlin – had wanted *me* to see *him*.'

'Why would he want to do that?'

'Arrogance, supreme self-confidence, verging on madness. He was confident I wouldn't penetrate his disguise.'

'Disguise?' Newman queried, mopping his forehead.

'The beard, the dark glasses – above all the beard.'

'What about it?'

'We now come to Kuhlmann's chance remark after Franck went out of my bathroom window. He said he now understood why Kurt Franck had gone underground for about two weeks. He had to do that – *waiting for his beard to grow*.'

'So?'

'The same thing applies to the so-called Dr Berlin. Thanks to your hair-raising excursion behind the border we know he is a fake. And you told me Falken said he hoped someone would get Berlin because he'd betrayed a number of Falken's agents.'

'But the beard . . .'

'We know from Ann Grayle, from our own experience, that Dr Berlin stays under cover inside his study at the mansion on Priwall Island every time he appears – stays under cover for about two weeks. That's the time it takes him to grow that beard. That afternoon at the party I was staring at one of my own sector chiefs without knowing it – and I've still no idea which of the four it is.'

'If you're right you do have a problem. If you identify him and the world press gets on to it they'll crucify the Service.'

'It's even worse than that, Bob.'

'I thought we'd plumbed the depths.'

'I told you earlier about my visit to that psychiatrist, Dr Generoso. He talked of the tremendous pressure a schizo – a man leading a double life – works under. Philby used alcohol. Generoso agreed one form of release in extreme cases could be sadistic murders – the killing of those blonde girls. You see what I'm up against now?'

'Yes. It's pretty deadly. If Berlin is the mass murderer as well as one of your sector chiefs – and if the killings are brought home to him – the scandal that would break in London would be without precedence in history. Let's turn back to the car. I'm sweating like a pig – and not just with the heat. This is why you've been so secretive with Kuhlmann? You don't want him to solve the case . . .'

'I just don't know how to handle it. Yet,' Tweed admitted. 'And then we have a further complication. Lysenko is, I'm certain, in his most audacious mood. He's using Berlin to transport that appalling drug consignment to Britain as soon as he can. We have to stop him delivering that load of poison somehow. And a Drug Squad man in London warned me they're expecting it in the near future.'

'Hence the Sea King? To track Berlin's cruiser when he sets out for England?'

'Yes, partly. And to put more pressure on. It all hinges on pressure. That's why I said back in Travemünde I believed he was cracking when the Mercedes came at me. I think he told the driver to run me down, then changed his mind. The schizo side took over briefly.'

'Why change his mind?'

'I'd have thought that was obvious. He'd have been arrested, exposed to grilling by Kuhlmann, brought up on a manslaughter charge – at the least. His identity would have been blown.'

'So, we go on waiting, putting on the pressure?'

'Not for much longer I think – after what happened today. And I think the unloading point for that huge drug haul may well be East Anglia. Even King's Lynn. Significant your Polish captain, Anders, mentioned those places. He may have been trying to tell you something.'

'East Anglia? That makes Janus Hugh Grey, surely? Doesn't he live near King's Lynn?'

'Place called Hawkswood Farm. And that's not like you, Bob. To accuse a man on such flimsy evidence.'

'Flimsy?'

'Yes! They *all* know that area. They all pay periodic visits to Wisbech nearby – on the river Nene. The interrogation centre is there. You know that. And *all* four attended a party at Hawkswood Farm two years ago on July 14. That same night – early in the morning shortly after the guests had left to drive home – a girl called Carole Langley was brutally carved up and raped. A blonde.'

'That does rather tie it up,' Newman commented grimly. 'I take it the case was never solved.'

'You take it aright.'

'Then why don't you check with Monica on the whereabouts of all four men now?'

'Which is exactly why we're driving back to Lübeck-Süd.'

'One thing puzzles me,' Newman said as he climbed in behind the wheel. 'Who was that man with the bandaged face who asked Ann Grayle about Dr Berlin?'

'I have no idea. Let's hurry. I sense things are about to detonate.'

'Can I have a cigarette, Bob?' Tweed asked.

Newman concealed his surprise, offered his pack, lit the cigarette for Tweed, who'd given up smoking years ago. It was an indication of the pressure Tweed himself was enduring as they sat in the locked room at Lübeck-Süd.

Tweed had spoken to Monica and told her he would wait for a reply, giving her the number. He took short puffs in the way a man or woman unaccustomed to smoking does. The room was airless, the temperature high in mid-afternoon, all adding to the tension as the two men sat in silence.

The ringing of the phone made Newman jump. Tweed stubbed out his half-smoked cigarette, lifted the receiver.

'Yes, Monica, it's Tweed. You were lucky? You got through everywhere quickly. What results?' He listened for maybe a minute. 'I see,' he said. 'No, don't bother. Yes, Bob is OK. 'Bye.'

'No news,' he announced.

'I don't understand. Surely their deputies know where they are.'

'They don't. Not with Lindemann, Grey, Dalby or Masterson.' Tweed leaned back in his chair, clasped his hands. 'It's my own fault – I instituted the new system six months ago. Prior to that, every sector chief had to be available when London called. I thought that system made them desk-bound, sapped all initiative. Now they can go off without letting their deputies know where they are. They call back to their own HQ to check on developments – but don't have to reveal where they are. All four have gone missing.'

'So any one of them could be sitting in Dr Berlin's mansion on Priwall Island at this moment – having grown a beard?'

'That's about the order of it.'

Tweed looked up as the door opened and Kuhlmann came in, closing the door behind him. The German sat down with them at the table.

'No sleep for two nights. It's getting to me. I checked out that address you gave me in Altona, Tweed. Apartment is in the name of a Martin Vollmer. We're tapping his line.'

'Any results?'

'Yes. He phones a Flensburg number. I called Flensburg, got another tap put on there. Heidi Dreyer – the girl at the Flensburg number – calls someone in Kiel. It's a complex route. I've caused interference in the Flensburg apartment block. That way Heidi won't be suspicious. All the phones are out of action. I've broken their communication system. As you requested, Tweed. I can hold it no more than another three days.'

'That might be long enough. Thanks.'

'Expecting something?' Kuhlmann asked.

'Imminent,' Tweed said.

10.30 p.m. Travemünde Strand. Balkan was walking.

On the beach the air was still balmy. Sue Templeton checked her watch. Ted should be back soon with the wine. She stretched out her long legs, dug her bare feet into the sand. The American girl was making the most of her last week in Europe. She wore

420

a simple cotton dress decorated with a polka dot design. The beach was deserted at that hour. She loved the peaceful atmosphere, the sound of the sea gurgling.

She heard the slushing tread of feet moving across the sand, tensed, reached for her handbag and tucked it half under herself. Whoever it was, was approaching from behind her. She swung round, knowing it wasn't Ted. He ran everywhere.

She jumped to her feet, holding her handbag. The figure was silhouetted against the glow of light from the Maritim Hotel, the lamps along the promenade. Difficult to see. She shaded her eyes with her left hand. Her eyes narrowed. She drew back her right bare foot, dug it deep into the sand and kicked upwards, sending a sand spray into the newcomer's eyes.

She nearly escaped, but a hand grasped her arm, a leg looped round her ankles and she fell over backwards. Sprawled, she stared up and opened her mouth to bellow at the top of her voice. One hand closed her mouth, the other hoisted a broad-bladed knife as a body hit her prone form heavily. She fought back, clawed at his face, tried to knee him in the groin. Her raised knee flopped, lifeless. He had slit her throat from ear to ear. He hoisted the knife again, plunged it between her breasts, jerked it downwards savagely. Blood seeped into the sand.

Ten minutes later Ted Smith, her English boy friend, came running down the beach, holding a bottle of wine. He skidded to a halt, stared down.

'Oh, my God! No! No . . .!'

Part 3

The Janus Man

Fifty-Two

Newman and Tweed enjoyed a late and leisurely dinner with Diana at the Jensen. The restaurant was full and Harry Butler sat at the window table by himself. It must be his turn for night duty, Tweed thought. Nield would be over at the Movenpick, catching up on sleep.

He let Newman and Diana do the talking. They'd finished the dessert when Diana placed a hand over Tweed's. She winked at Newman.

'He's gone into a trance. He does that, you know . . .'

'Leave him alone,' Newman chaffed her. 'He's thinking. It doesn't come easy.'

The waiter came to the table a few moments later. He told Tweed a Mr Kuhlmann was on the phone. Tweed excused himself, went out into the lobby and said he'd take the call in his room. On the way up in the elevator he checked the time. It was midnight.

'That you, Tweed? Imminent you said. You were too bloody right. Blessed with second sight?'

Kuhlmann sounded disturbed, which surprised Tweed. The German was always so cool, detached.

'What's happened?' he asked.

'Another murder. Out at Travemünde Strand. On the beach. Almost the same place where the Swedish girl, Iris Hansen, was butchered. This one is something else again.' He paused. Tweed could have sworn he heard Kuhlmann gulp.

'Go on. I'm listening . . .'

'American girl this time. Sue Templeton. I knew her. She helped me track Franck. A blonde again. Of course. And I could hardly recognize her. That maniac had a field day this time.'

'Know when it happened?'

Tweed's voice was steady, almost off-hand. Inwardly he was feeling sick. Pressure. So Dr Generoso had said. Pressure will make him crack. And I've applied the pressure . . .

'Just about 10.30 this evening. What? No – no trace of the

425

killer. Hold on, Tweed. Someone's handed me a signal for you.' Brief pause. 'It's for you – from Walter Three. Signal reads, power cruiser *Nordsee* under way. Proceeding to north. Tracking. Signed Walter Three . . .'

'That's it? I must go.'

'They'll be talking about this latest killing in Lübeck now,' Kuhlmann warned. 'The victim's English boy friend who found the body ran back to the Maritim and blabbed all over the reception hall. And I must get back to the beach.'

Tweed paused half way inside the restaurant. A waiter was chattering to a group at a table near the entrance. He caught a snatch of the conversation.

'An American girl . . . cut to pieces . . . raped . . . spread all over the beach . . .'

Tweed walked down to his own table at a normal pace. Diana was sitting rigidly, her right hand clenching her napkin in a ball. Newman looked at Tweed with a bleak expression.

'Have you heard? Out at Travemünde?'

'It's beastly, horrible,' Diana burst out. 'Another poor blonde girl . . .'

Tweed put an arm round her shoulder, glanced across at Butler's table. 'Better get to bed,' he suggested.

He saw Butler leaving his table as he escorted her from the restaurant with Newman at his heels. They rode up in the elevator in silence. Diana unlocked her door, said Good Night, closed it. Tweed took Newman by the arm.

'We have to move fast. Everything's happening. Go over to the Movenpick. Wake up Pete Nield. Kick down the door if necessary. He's to get dressed, pack his case, pay his bill and be back here in ten minutes. Pack your own case. I'm going up to pack mine. I'll pay your bill. I want to be out of here in fifteen minutes. Now, I must have a word with Butler . . .'

'Where are we going?'

'Travemünde. I want you to drive there like hell. It's all exploding as I predicted. See you . . .'

He beckoned to Butler who had just stepped out of the elevator, took him along to his room and closed the door.

At that hour, with Newman driving, they made record time to Travemünde. At Tweed's instruction Newman parked the Audi near the police station. With Newman on one side and Nield on the other, Tweed explained as they walked along the waterfront.

'Nield, you're a qualified radio op. Are you rusty?'

'Hardly. I'm a radio ham in my spare time. That is, what spare time I get. Why?'

'Can you handle the latest transceiver aboard a power cruiser?'

'I'll give it a try.'

'What are we up to?' Newman asked.

'Heading for the *Südwind*. I've told you about the signal Kulhmann gave me. We're going to follow the *Nordsee* in the *Südwind*. I trust one of you can navigate at night?'

'I'll give it a try,' said Newman. 'What about the Sea King?'

'Casey's trying to track the *Nordsee*. My bet is it has Dr Berlin at the helm, that he's heading for the Skagerrak. His ultimate destination could be England. I think he's taking that huge drug haul with him. Lysenko's audacity has gone overboard. It does happen. A man holds a job too long – thinks he can get away with anything. Although, using Balkan is clever, I admit.'

'Who is Balkan?' Nield asked.

'Here's the landing stage,' Tweed said, ignoring the question. 'We have water to drink.' Newman was carrying a large plastic canister Tweed had obtained from the manager of the Jensen.

Tweed led the way, feet clumping rapidly along the planks of the landing stage, carrying his suitcase in his right hand. He was about to cross the gangway on to the *Südwind* when Newman rested the container on the stage and grasped him by the arm.

'Let me check. I'm armed.'

'You didn't take that Luger with you . . .' Tweed glanced at Newman. '. . . on your recent trip?'

'Of course not. I gave it to Toll. He put it in a safety deposit box at a local bank, left the receipt and a letter in a sealed envelope for me at the Movenpick. I collected it a few days ago.'

Newman opened his jacket, revealed the hip holster. A pro had once told him never to use a shoulder holster. 'Takes half an hour to drag the thing out,' he'd warned. Newman extracted

427

the Luger, took out the torch Stahl had given him and went aboard the darkened vessel.

Tweed glanced round. The waterfront was deserted. Lights showed in the portholes of some of the moored craft, including Ann Grayle's sloop. There was no wind, the air was stuffy, the sky above studded with enormous stars. Nield followed his upward glance.

'A clear night – should be good for radio transmission. And I'm armed, too.' He produced a Walther automatic. 'By kind permission of Kuhlmann. Harry has another one.' He looked at the *Südwind* as Newman reappeared.

'Come aboard,' Newman called out. 'All clear.'

'You go aboard,' Tweed told Nield, handing him his case. 'Get everything ready for immediate departure. I have a call to make from the local police station. Back in five minutes.'

He got through to Monica quickly. She sounded relieved to hear his voice. She's holding the fort all night long Tweed thought.

'I'm so glad you've called, Tweed. A message has just come in from Butler. Speaking from Lübeck Hauptbahnhof. Reads as follows. "Diana has flown the coop. Boarding the night express for Copenhagen. Arrives Copenhagen 0645 hours. Will leave any message Royal Hotel. Butler." ' Monica paused briefly. 'He sounded in a rush. Action this day, as Churchill used to say?'

'Very much so . . .'

'I'll sleep here. Good luck.'

Copenhagen? Why Copenhagen, Tweed wondered as he hurried to the *Südwind*. And why had Diana panicked? Newman had the engine throbbing as he went aboard and entered the wheelhouse.

'We can go any time,' Newman reported. 'This is going to be one hell of a chase. Berlin will be able to move as fast as we can. Want a cup of water?'

'Yes, please.'

Tweed extracted the packet of Dramamine he always carried for sea sickness, popped one of the yellow pills in his mouth and swallowed water. Nield, who was fiddling with the powerful transceiver, watched with amusement.

'It's calm as the proverbial millpond.'

428

'A glass of water wobbling on a table can make me feel very queasy.' Tweed used his pen to write on a notepad lying on the chart table. 'Here is the call signal, waveband, etc. Casey is operating on from the Sea King. He's Walter Three. Well, can you operate that thing?'

'You're joking? Give me a few minutes to get the hang of it.' He took the sheet of paper Tweed tore off the pad. 'I tell this Casey what when I make contact?'

'Everything. That we're pursuing the *Nordsee*. That we need regular fixes on that vessel's position and course.' Tweed glanced briefly at the chart Newman had spread out over the table. 'Where did you get this?'

'From that stack of rolled charts under the table. Very well equipped, this cruiser, for going almost anywhere. And as I told you earlier, we have full fuel tanks.'

'How long to reach Copenhagen?'

'Be there by morning.'

'That is,' Tweed amended, 'if he takes the eastern route through the Öresund. He could veer west and use the western channel between the Danish islands of Fynn and Sjelland . . .'

'Casey will be able to guide us – when I get through to him,' Nield said.

'Ready to move?' Newman asked. 'Right. Cast off, Pete.'

'I'll give a hand,' Tweed said.

'You'll feel queasy,' Nield said as he led the way down the gangway.

'Oh, do shut up!'

Nield waited at the stern while Tweed released the bow rope from the bollard, ran back on board and heaved the gangway on deck. Nield stared, surprised at his chief's strength. Then he dealt with the stern rope, threw it on board and leapt after it as the *Südwind* drifted away from the landing stage. Newman gently increased power, the cruiser moved out into the channel and he swung the wheel north – north for Copenhagen.

Tweed sat on the edge of a bunk in the large cabin, acutely miserable. He kept checking his watch. The Dramamine took full effect in half an hour. Nield appeared at the door.

'I've made contact with Walter Three. The *Nordsee* is heading for the Öresund. It's Copenhagen.'

Tweed shook his head. 'I think he'll proceed through the narrows and into the Kattegat. Can't Newman keep this thing on a more even course?'

'He's doing just that. Sea's calm. Lovely night for our cruise . . .'

'Do shut up!' Tweed repeated.

When Nield had gone he closed his eyes, but only for a moment. The pitching sensation seemed to increase. He looked again at the two new locks which had been forced open, the steel chisel and hammer lying on the bunk alongside him. He forced himself to his feet, went to one of the large damaged drawers, opened it. Empty. He checked the second drawer. Also empty. He took a deep breath and heaved himself up the steps to the bridge which was enclosed and roofed over. Newman was helmsman while Nield crouched over the transceiver with his headset.

'Damned rough, isn't it?' he remarked.

'Rough?' Newman stared at him. 'A trifle choppy, that's all. We're in the open Baltic. And Casey wants to know whether he should radio the harbourmaster at Copenhagen – get the *Nordsee* stopped and searched.'

'No! Under no circumstances. We must track him to the bitter end, find his ultimate landfall.'

Tweed held on to the gleaming brass rail at the front of the bridge. He was beginning to feel less ill. The Dramamine had taken effect. One every four hours, he reminded himself. The only way he could get through this traumatic experience.

The bow rose and fell gently, rose and fell. Tweed felt like spare cargo. He was nearly going spare at the thought of the time he might have to spend aboard this rocking tub. He was unaware of the passage of time, resisted the temptation to keep checking his watch. At one stage in their passage Newman lifted a pair of high-powered glasses to his eyes and gazed to the west. He scanned the horizon, his night sight excellent on the dimly-lit bridge. He handed the glasses to Tweed.

'Over there. The Fehmarn Belt. You can pick up the lights of the train ferry crossing from Puttgarden to Rødby.'

Tweed eventually found the lights. It would be carrying the night express to Copenhagen. It gave him an odd feeling to realize Diana was aboard. Thank God Butler had spotted her panic departure – which meant he also would be on board. His message to Monica had said they'd reach Copenhagen at 0645 hours. Long before the *Südwind*. Once the express had moved off the ferry it would thunder through the night. He became aware that they were changing course, lowered the glasses, looked at the compass. North by north-east. He glanced back at the stern, saw their wake curving in a wide arc.

'What's happening?' he asked.

'Look over there – the flashing light. Gedser lighthouse. Keep on our previous course and we run slap into Denmark. Look at the chart,' Newman said.

They were moving under full power now. Tweed had realized this when he saw the swift sweep of the wake, a blurred froth on the black Baltic. He groaned inwardly when he examined the chart. Only about a quarter of the way to Copenhagen.

'I think I'll take a brief nap,' Nield said, standing up off the leather-backed stool in front of the transceiver. 'Always kip when you can. Wake me if Casey calls . . .'

Kip when you can. The phrase recalled to Newman Falken's three basic maxims. Where was the German now? Where was Gerda? He pushed the thoughts out of his mind, concentrating on his steering. Newman and Tweed were alone for the first time since they'd boarded the *Südwind*.

'Is this legal?' Newman asked. 'Pirating the *Südwind*?'

'Doubt it. Is smuggling heroin – five hundred kilos of killer, legal?'

'You have a point. What do we do when – if – we catch up with Dr Berlin?'

'If I'm right, he has to disappear forever.'

'That's why you checked that I had the Luger?'

'We'll decide how we do it when the time comes. We can't afford the scandal. England can't. Mass murderer a senior chief in the SIS. Not on, Bob. I'm just not sure how we are going to accomplish the job.'

'Which is why you won't let Casey get the harbourmaster at Copenhagen to stop the *Südwind*?'

'I don't like it any more than you do. But it's the only way.'

*

They were off the east coast of the Danish island of Sjelland – on which Copenhagen stands – when Tweed spotted the navigation lights of the Sea King approaching high up. He glanced at the transceiver, went aft to the cabin and shook Nield who was sprawled in one of the bunks.

'Signal coming through . . .'

Nield came awake instantly, swung his legs on to the deck and ran up the steps. When Tweed reached the bridge he was sitting with his headset in position. He listened, made a note on his pad, acknowledged, took off the headset and went to the chart table, marking a cross.

'*Südwind* now here. Very close to entrance to Öresund.'

'Call back to Casey,' Tweed said sharply. 'Tell to keep the vessel under very close observation for the next hour.'

'What's the matter?' Newman asked, turning the wheel a few degrees. 'And I've been thinking. Why didn't *we* take the night express to Copenhagen with Diana and Butler? We'd have arrived in plenty of time to hire a boat and wait for Berlin to arrive.'

'Because of the signal Nield is sending. The *Südwind* may still turn due east, then move north up into the Swedish – even the Finnish – archipelago. Even with a chopper tailing him, he could have given it the slip. You remember those archipelagos? Thousands of islands and they're like a labyrinth.'

'Why would he go up there?'

'Because he may make another transhipment to another vessel. They've done that once – you saw it aboard the *Wroclaw*.'

'What type of vessel?'

'Maybe another power cruiser like this one, like the *Nordsee*. A cruiser called the *Nocturne*.'

'You have a reason for thinking that?'

'Yes. I've just realized who that man with bandages on his face – the one who called on Ann Grayle – is.'

Fifty-Three

'The cargo is well on its way. I've just received a radio signal confirming all is well,' Lysenko reported from his apartment in Leipzig.

'A signal from where?' asked Gorbachev in Moscow.

'From the shipper of the cargo to Rostock. It should reach its destination within the next seventy-two hours.'

'Any hitches?'

Lysenko hesitated briefly. 'None. Everything according to schedule.'

'You paused before you said that.'

Damn him, Lysenko thought. He doesn't miss a thing. He manufactured a sneeze. 'Sorry, I think I have a cold starting.'

'Keep me informed. It's not over until it has arrived . . .'

Connection broken. He never sleeps, Lysenko thought. He has the stamina of an ox. He hurried down to the darkened street where his car was waiting. Arriving at Markus Wolf's building, he took the elevator to the office after showing the guard on the entrance door his identity. Opening the door, he found another man who seemed to need no sleep. Behind his desk, Wolf looked up, stared at him through those square-shaped glasses which gave him a stern look.

'A problem, Lysenko. All communications with West Germany have been interrupted. When I told you earlier I thought it was a technical fault.'

'It might still be that. The West isn't as efficient as it likes to boast it is.'

'No. Something is wrong. The interruption has gone on too long. I'm worried. I sense trouble.'

'Why?'

'No word from Munzel. And what has happened to Tweed? I'm unhappy when I don't know where he is, what he's doing.'

'He can't do a thing.'

'I may remind you of that statement in the not too distant future,' Wolf rapped back.

*

It was broad daylight. The *Südwind* was proceeding at full power into Copenhagen harbour. Hours earlier Casey had reported that the *Nordsee* had moved on a course due north – into the Öresund, heading for the Kattegat between Denmark and Sweden.

Tweed had taken over the wheel from Newman during the night – to give himself something purposeful to do, to give Newman a chance to get some sleep. As he replaced Newman he had asked him about the forced drawers in the cabin.

'I did that while you were phoning Monica from the police station. Found a box of tools, selected two drawers at random, and levered off the locks with the steel chisel. Found nothing.'

'You expected – hoped to find?'

'The drug consignment. Seemed logical. That cruiser I watched being loaded from the *Wroclaw* could have been the *Südwind*. Why do *you* think Berlin had new locks attached?'

'Bluff. He's a clever swine. He hoped we'd think what you thought. Maybe wait and waste time watching for him to come back. What puzzles me is that was the moment Diana started to panic – when she saw those new locks.'

'Ask her – if you ever see her again.' He caught the expression on Tweed's face. 'Sorry, I didn't phrase that too tactfully.'

Newman reappeared as they approached Copenhagen, took over the wheel from Tweed. From the sea Copenhagen was a city which had changed very little with the passage of time – except for two high-rise buildings poking their ugly multi-storey edifices above the surrounding buildings. Tweed stayed on the bridge, guiding Newman since he knew the harbour well.

During the night they had encountered very little traffic in the Baltic. Now, under an overcast sky, the sea was alive with pleasure craft – yachts pirouetting in the slight breeze, small cruisers put-putting over the choppy waves. Newman skilfully threaded his way between them.

Nield sat by the transceiver, wearing his headset, taking down a message. He signed off, swivelled round in his chair and gave the gist of the signal to Tweed.

'A long one. Casey landed at Kastrup to refuel, took off again. He's having trouble tracking the *Nordsee* – too much other traffic afloat in this part of the world . . .'

434

'He hasn't lost it?' There was alarm in Tweed's voice.

'No. God knows where he's going. He keeps heading north. It's beginning to look like Oslo. He's proceeding up the west coast of Sweden, keeping close in among the regular traffic. He's off Gothenburg now . . .'

'Call back Casey,' Tweed said. 'Warn him to keep closest possible observation.' He was studying the chart. 'He's just reached the point where he could veer due west across the Skagerrak and into the North Sea. Ask for a further report within fifteen minutes.'

Newman had reduced speed considerably. They saw the hydrofoil which made regular crossings – taking no more than half an hour – to Malmö in Sweden. Elevated on its great skis, bow out of the water, it plunged over the sea as though gliding. Tweed continued to guide Newman who had reduced speed to little more than walking pace.

'What's the next move now?' Newman asked.

'I have to check two things in Copenhagen. Take a cab to the Royal to see if Butler left any message when he got off the night express with Diana. Then we go on to Lindemann's HQ near the Rådhuspladsen, find out where he is. And I can call Monica from there.'

'And after that?'

'I've really no idea.'

Nield received a fresh signal from Sea King when Newman was easing the *Südwind* along a wide channel past some grey-camouflaged warships. They were now deep inside Copenhagen and ahead the channel ended in a cul-de-sac.

'We berth on the starboard side,' Tweed instructed. 'This is where the Oslo boats sail from.'

Newman swung the wheel, crossed the channel, headed for the waterfront where ancient warehouses loomed behind a wide promenade. A huge fountain sprayed like an opening flower. Men and women strolled under the grey sky wearing raincoats. Behind the fountain loomed a magnificent palace. Tweed pointed to it.

'Amalienborg Palace. A beautiful place . . .'

Nield removed his headset. He handed Tweed the message and stood up, stretching his arms and legs.

'Casey reports *Nordsee* well north of Gothenburg. Moving

435

like the clappers, maintaining a northern course, hugging the Swedish coastline.'

'Then it looks like Oslo,' said Tweed.

Tweed asked the cab driver to wait outside the Royal Hotel, walked inside with Newman, leaving Nield behind in the cab. The layout had been changed since his previous visit. The reception area in the vast hall comprised a number of round tables supported by a central column. Perched on each table was a console with a girl in attendance. He picked a brunette, said he was expecting a message to be waiting, gave his name and waited while the girl walked behind the glass wall of a rear area.

'American reception technique,' he commented to Newman, waving a hand at the tables. 'The girl taps out your name for your reservation and it all comes up on the screen. The modern age.'

'And you prefer the old system? One long reception counter as they had at the Four Seasons.'

'It's more human. We'll all end up as machines . . .'

He stopped as the girl came back holding an envelope. She asked for identification and he produced his passport. When he had the envelope they walked over to a seat and sat down while he tore it open, took out a folded sheet, studied the hastily scribbled message and handed it to Newman.

'Good job we brought our cases with us.'

Diana took cab from rail station for Kastrup Airport. Booked one-way ticket to Oslo. Staying at Grand Hotel. Am following. 0730 hours. Harry.

'Why is it a good job?' asked Newman after absorbing the message.

'Because we have to move fast. It's Oslo again . . .'

'Almost looks as though Diana is joining Dr Berlin there.'

'And I was wrong about her. We'll fly to Oslo. Lindemann calls it the shuttle. Only a fifty-minute flight – planes leave here for Oslo all day long. Amazing service – and the flight is non-stop.'

'What about the *Südwind*? And Casey somewhere up there in the wild blue yonder?'

436

'We ditch the *Südwind*. Nield can take the cab back to the boat, contact Casey, tell him what we're doing, instruct him to land at Fornebu – that's Oslo Airport – and wait for us.'

'I've never been to Oslo.'

'You have a treat in store. Now for Erich Lindemann. We can take a separate cab. Speed is essential now.'

'Someone,' said Newman inside the cab on their way to the Rådhuspladsen, 'is going to pinch the *Südwind*.' He sounded envious. 'Superb boat. Equipped with everything. That transceiver, the most powerful Verey pistol – and did you see the fuel drums roped down at the stern?'

'I did.'

'That means the *Nordsee* probably has the same. They are twin vessels. Which means Dr Berlin could be heading for almost anywhere in Western Europe.'

'That had occurred to me.'

Tweed said no more until the cab dropped them at the entrance to Lindemann's HQ. It had been a short ride. He gave the driver a generous tip, glanced at the plate on the wall. *Export-Import Services North*. He ran up the shabby stairs, knocked on the door.

It was opened by a tall, severe-looking woman, thin, erect, in her late fifties. She didn't seem pleased to see him.

'Mr Tweed. I wasn't expecting you.'

'So I'm a pleasant surprise. This is Bob Newman. Miss Browne.'

'With an "e",' she informed Newman, looking even less pleased. 'I suppose you'd better come in.'

'Some place we can talk privately,' Tweed said. 'And where is Lindemann?'

'I really haven't the slightest idea. The inner sanctum, I suggest . . .'

Inner sanctum. Tweed groaned inwardly. She really was the embodiment of an ex-senior Civil Servant. She showed him into an austere and excessively tidy room. The only objects on Lindemann's desk were two telephones. Tweed walked round the desk, sat in Lindemann's chair. He could see that didn't please her. Short of time, he decided there was only one approach.

437

'How long has he been away? I'm in a hurry. I need direct answers. Please. And do sit down.'

'I usually require written authority before I report on Mr Lindemann's movements . . .'

'I'll ask just once more, Miss Browne, then you're on the first plane back to London. How long has he been away?'

'About three to four weeks. He left almost as soon as he returned from his week's leave.'

'Left for where?'

'He didn't say. He leaves me in sole charge.'

'So you must have some way of contacting him?' Tweed was convinced she was hiding something. He had a stroke of inspiration. 'Or has he contacted you? I must know.'

'Well, yes. He called me only yesterday. To ask if there had been any developments. I said no – it seems to be quiet at the moment.'

'Where did he phone from? Don't say you don't know. You have been here a long time. You know Scandinavia well. I think you must – do – know where he called from.'

Miss Browne fiddled with her long bony fingers, clasping them in her lap. She was making up her mind. Tweed stared at her in silence, began slowly drumming his fingers on the desk.

'He didn't say where he was, but I could hear voices in the background. I know the languages now. They sounded Norwegian. When he's in Oslo he stays at the Grand Hotel. May I ask – is my position at risk?'

'Not now it isn't. And I wish to make a phone call. Could I use this phone?'

'I'll give you a line.'

Alone behind the desk, he dialled Monica's number. She, at least, sounded pleased to be talking to him. 'You must be psychic,' she said. 'Not five minutes ago Kuhlmann phoned. He wants you to call him back at this number. Still Action This Day?'

'Yesterday. I must go now. Be in touch.'

He dialled the number he had memorized, which was Lübeck-Süd. Kuhlmann came straight on the line. He sounded grim and weary. Lack of sleep.

'Tweed, the pathologist has examined what's left of Sue

Templeton, that American girl. He found a lot of skin under the fingernails of her right hand. The poor girl put up a fight. Main thing is, the killer must have one hell of a scratch on his person – probably on his face. Thought you should know. Getting anywhere?'

'Thanks. And yes. Because of that, I'm in a rush.'

'OK.' Kuhlmann paused. 'Put a bullet through the bastard for me.'

'You are about to look down on the Ninth Wonder of the World,' Tweed said to Newman. 'The approach to Oslo Fjord. It's quite magnificent.'

They were flying at thirty thousand feet aboard the DC-9, Orvar Viking. At Kastrup Airport they had grabbed a late breakfast and then caught the flight by minutes. The cloud bank over Copenhagen had dissipated soon after takeoff. They flew up the west coast of Sweden.

Tweed had pointed out to Newman – and Nield who sat behind them – the Skaw, the northernmost tip of Denmark, stretching out into the Skagerrak. A flat, claw-like peninsula, it had a barren deserted look from that height. Newman peered out of the window as the machine began its long descent.

The pilot had made an announcement that the air was exceptionally clear, the view coming up rarely seen. Below on the azure blue sea Newman could make out tiny specks of white – the wakes of invisible vessels heading north. Was one of them the *Nordsee*, he wondered. Then he leaned closer to the window.

It was his first sighting of Norway. The most southerly of the islands guarding the entrance to the huge fjord came into view. Newman stared down, fascinated. They were like ragged-edged pieces of a jigsaw thrown down at random on to a gigantic table of blue ice.

The descent continued. The islands became larger, some covered with dense fir forest. Between them vessels plied their way northward, heading for distant Oslo. Houses began to appear on a few islands. Newman had never seen so many islands clustered together, drawn back from the main channel wending its way towards the Norwegian capital.

The aircraft flew on, dropping all the time, following the

course of the fjord. Suddenly they were lost inside a cloud like fog. They were flying very low now. Newman went on staring out of the window. He stiffened as they flew out of the fog. Just below rose a whole series of hump-backed hills, range upon range. It was quite different from what he had expected.

The plane swung in a vast arc, diving inside the fog and emerging without warning. The hills, covered with dense forest, looked to be too close. The plane climbed abruptly. Then the machine descended, flew across a stretch of water. 'We're going to end up in the drink,' Newman was thinking. The wheels touched down. The airport was located at the very edge of the fjord. Newman let out a sigh of relief.

'Marvellous,' crowed Tweed.

'Bloody marvellous,' Newman agreed.

Tweed wasted no time once they reached the exit hall. He asked for chief of security, was ushered with Newman into a small square office lined with green filing cabinets and occupied by a short well-built Norwegian in a pale blue shirt and navy blue trousers who rose from behind his desk.

'I'm Iversen, chief of security. Who are you?'

'Tweed. Special Branch. From London.' He slapped down a folder on Iversen's desk. 'I need to speak urgently to Captain Georg Palmer of Norwegian Intelligence. He's out at Huseby Gardekasernen – near Røa.'

Tweed took out his notebook while Iversen checked the folder and handed it back. 'Here's the phone number,' Tweed said. 'May I?' He took a pad on the desk and wrote down the number.

'I'll talk to him first,' Iversen said, picked up the phone, dialled the number and spoke in Norwegian, then switched to English. 'Yes, sir, your description fits him perfectly. I'll put him on the line.' He held out the phone. 'I can leave you alone . . .'

'Not necessary, thank you.' Tweed spoke into the phone. 'I am at Fornebu, as you'll now know. Just arrived. Need to talk to you, Georg. No, don't come to Fornebu. Can we meet at the Grand Hotel? In about a couple of hours from now? I have to check certain things first. Yes, I'm glad to be back. Look forward to seeing you again. 'Bye.'

He thanked Iversen and outside in the entrance hall they

found Nield waiting. He gestured towards the western side of the airfield.

'I found Casey. He's where the police choppers take off from. In the private section.' He fingered his small black moustache. 'I think you ought to talk with him. We can walk. The exercise will do you good.'

Tweed blinked as they emerged into brilliant sunshine. Newman took a deep breath. The air was crisp, invigorating. As they walked he looked towards the hills rising up behind Oslo. The air had a sharp, crystalline clarity, bringing the hills covered with forest closer than they were.

'I like this place,' he said.

'The pace is slower here,' Tweed said as he trotted briskly towards the Sea King he could now see. 'There's no place in Europe like it. In some ways, you feel you're living in the nineteen-thirties. In the nicest possible way. Well, Casey, what's the position?'

'The *Nordsee* is approaching the entrance to Oslo Fjord. About eighty nautical miles south of the first island.'

'How long ago was that?'

'One hour. We landed here, refuelled – so we're ready for a long flight if necessary . . .'

'Which it might well be,' Tweed agreed.

'Then we took off again, flew back down the fjord and over the Skagerrak. Just to make sure he hadn't changed course.'

'Which he could still do,' interjected his co-pilot, Wilson. 'South-west would take him out into the North Sea. And he had reduced speed a lot. For the first time since we tracked him from Lübeck.'

That was quite a speech for Wilson. And a shrewd point he'd made, Tweed was thinking.

'Has he spotted you, would you say?' he asked Casey.

'Bound to have done so by now. Not during the night – but there's so much traffic off Sweden we had to move in closer. Other choppers were around, but only one Sea King. Us.'

'Can you wait here while we drive into Oslo? Have you had a meal?'

'Easily,' Casey replied. He looked up at the sky. 'Night will be coming within a few hours. Maybe that's what he's waiting for. And we had an excellent meal at the restaurant. Go about

441

your business, Tweed. We can wait. You can always call the airport – they know where we are.'

'I am in a rush . . .'

They took a cab into Oslo and Newman stared out of the window, taking in the new experience. The highway followed the upper reaches of the fjord, giving views of marinas crammed with sailing craft and the intensely blue water beyond. Arriving at the Grand Hotel on the main street, Karl Johans Gate, Tweed bustled inside, carrying his case.

Newman paid off the cab and lingered for a moment with Nield, taking in the atmosphere. Tweed had been right. The pace was slower. None of the 'must get there yesterday' frenzy of London or New York.

Karl Johans Gate stretched due west. In the distance an elegant ochre and pale grey building stood on a small hill. The Royal Palace, Newman guessed. Across a park on another street an old cream and grey tram trundled through the city. The Norwegians strolled, made way for other people. Yes, I like this place Newman thought.

Inside Tweed was questioning the chief receptionist.

'We need three rooms with baths. You can manage that? Good. I'd also like the room number of my friend, Erich Lindemann.'

'Mr Lindemann isn't staying with us. He always does when he is in Oslo . . .'

'You mean he checked out today?'

'No, sir. Mr Lindemann hasn't stayed with us for the past two months.'

So much for Miss Browne and her knowledge of Scandinavian languages, Tweed thought. I'll bet she can't speak a word of one of them. But, of course – Lindemann is the linguist. He wouldn't want an assistant who could understand what he was saying on the phone.

'I have another friend who is staying here. Miss Diana Chadwick.'

'Now she *is* with us.' The receptionist glanced over his shoulder. 'Room 736. But she's out. Her key is on the rack.'

'Don't mention I enquired when she comes back. I want to surprise her.'

Newman and Nield came inside at that moment and registered. On their way up in the elevator Tweed warned them not to unpack, to be ready for departure at a moment's notice. He had just dumped his bag in his own room when the phone rang. A Captain Palmer was waiting to see him.

'Send him up, please. And ask room service to send up two pots of coffee.'

Palmer was a tall, thin, wiry-looking Norwegian in his early thirties. Dressed in a plain grey business suit, he shook Tweed's hand warmly, sat down and crossed his legs. He had thick sandy hair, a long nose and dark observant eyes with a hint of humour in them.

'Too long since we met, Tweed. I gather this is an emergency, so let us dispense with the greetings. What can I do to help?'

'A large power cruiser is approaching the entrance to the fjord. White colour with brass trimmings. Called *Nordsee*. I've had it shadowed by a Sea King, now waiting at Fornebu. If I send out my chopper again it might frighten off the man aboard from heading for his ultimate destination . . .'

'Which is?'

'I've no idea yet. I wonder whether you could arrange for at least one police launch from Sandvika to keep an eye on the *Nordsee*'s movements. It appears to be heading for Oslo, but I need to know any alteration in course. And discretion is the order of the day.'

Palmer shook his head. 'Not a police launch. They only patrol the fjord near Oslo. What we need is the Coastguard. They operate in the outer reaches of the fjord. I can make the call now from here. We should have one vessel watching your prey within thirty minutes. A more precise description of the *Nordsee* would help.'

'I'm not good on boats . . .'

Tweed called Newman in his room, asked him to come, and when he arrived explained what was needed. While the two men talked he phoned down to ask if Diana had arrived back. She hadn't. Palmer then took over the phone, dialled and spoke rapidly in Norwegian. He put down the receiver.

'A Coastguard vessel will be on station shortly. The commander will report to me personally by radio direct to my HQ. I will then call you if there are developments.'

443

'I believe you're supposed to make a report of all incidents?' Tweed remarked.

'That is so.' Palmer shook hands again and went to the door. He turned before he left. 'But then again, I often have the most extraordinary lapses of memory.'

The next few hours – while Tweed waited for Diana to come back to the hotel – were tense. Night fell and Tweed arranged a roster for dinner. While he ate with Newman and Butler Nield stayed in the reception hall, seated in a chair. The instructions Tweed gave were precise and surprised the others.

'She may already have her bag packed and try to leave when she knows I'm here. If necessary, you are to forcibly restrain her in her room. Then call me via reception.'

They ate in the Grand Café, attached to the hotel, a large and rather old-fashioned place which overlooked the main street. Newman looked round, fascinated by the other diners. He'd noticed some of them at their tables an hour earlier. He remarked on the fact to Tweed, who sat gently drumming his fingers.

'Yes,' Tweed agreed, 'it's like pre-war customs in England I've read about. Gone forever. People – the locals – come and sit here for ages talking. It's part of their way of life.'

'And you're bothered about something? Diana?'

'Diana, yes. It's getting so late. But also, no report from Palmer. Something has gone wrong. I sense it.'

'This has happened before at this stage of the game . . .'

'True. This particular game though is the most dangerous I've ever played in the whole of my career so far.'

They were about to leave the Grand Café when Nield appeared at the door and beckoned to Butler, who jumped up and walked over to him. They conversed briefly, Nield vanished in the direction of the entrance hall and Butler returned to their table.

'She's just collected her key and gone up in the elevator.'

'Then I'd better get up and see her.' Tweed's tone was so grim, there was a ruthless expression on his face Butler had rarely seen. Tweed stared at him. 'I'm going to grill the hell out of her. You and Pete had better come with me. Stay outside

444

her door – in case she tries to make a run for it. If she does, stop her.'

He walked straight out of the restaurant to the elevator bank, pressed the button, waited, stepped inside the elevator without a word. As it ascended Butler and Nield exchanged glances behind his back.

Tweed walked out into the corridor, checked the room number indicator, strode off to the left, turned left again and then right. He rapped on the door of 736. Diana, clad in a white sweater and a cherry-coloured skirt opened it.

'Tweed! How on earth did you . . .'

'We have to talk.' He pushed past her into the bedroom, closing the door. 'You have to talk – tell the truth. For the first time. Sit down.'

'When I'm asked nicely . . .'

'Sit down! Question number one. How long have you known Dr Berlin?'

She sat down on the edge of the bed, crossing her legs as she studied him from under her eyelashes. Tweed remained standing, hands clasped behind his back.

'Over twenty years. You know that . . .'

'The *real* Dr Berlin I mean. Hurry up. I'm short of time.'

'I don't know what you mean.'

'Why were you so scared out of your wits when you found the locks had been changed on the *Südwind*?'

'I knew it was a warning.' Her voice had changed. She had a lace-edged handkerchief she began picking at. 'I thought at first I wouldn't be able to get at any of my own things – until I saw my drawers had been left alone.'

'Who were you scared of?'

'Whoever had changed the locks . . .'

'How have you managed for money all these years since you left Kenya?'

'You think I've slept with men, don't you, Tweed?'

'No. So who gave you money to live on?'

'He did. He made me a regular allowance.' A vehement note came into her voice. 'I never slept with him. Not once.'

'I can believe that. So what made you worth the allowance?'

'I'm frightened. Horribly frightened.'

'Why?' demanded Tweed in the same brusque tone, 'did you

445

run out on me? Take the night express to Copenhagen, then fly up here?'

'Because I was horribly afraid – after I heard that American girl had been killed on the beach. I knew it must be him. I thought I'd be next. I'm a blonde. I have a girl friend who works in Oslo. I've had dinner with her. And Oslo seemed far enough away from Lübeck. I panicked. I want to start a new life. I'm sick of being a kept woman – even though I never performed the services a kept woman normally renders.'

'So, why did Dr Berlin keep you? As a witness? As one person who gave him credibility? One person who would say he was the same man as the Dr Berlin in Kenya? Do I have to drag it out of you, for God's sake?'

'No, not any more. You're right. I was his witness. When we first sailed from the Med to Lübeck years ago he saw me. How he knew who I was I don't know. Maybe from a photograph. Perhaps someone told him I'd known Berlin well in Kenya. I was on my beam ends for lack of money . . .'

It came pouring out now Tweed had broken through the dam. He still remained standing, showing no sympathy, not daring to risk stopping her flow of words.

'He invited me to his house on Priwall Island. I went quite happily – until I saw him in his study. I knew at once that he wasn't the man I'd known in Kenya. He admitted he wasn't. Then he put me a proposition.'

'Go on! Don't stop now.'

'You're being beastly to me. All right.' She sat stiffly as she continued. 'I had very little money – Ken, my husband, left nothing when he was killed hunting in the bush. It wasn't a secret – that I'd no money. He offered me a generous monthly allowance if I'd tell people he was the Dr Berlin I'd known in the old days. As you said, he needed a witness. I accepted.'

'What did you think this impostor was up to?'

'Oh, he told me some story – that he was the original Berlin's half-brother, that he wanted to carry on his charitable work, that he could do that best if he had his brother's reputation. For raising funds for refugees, things like that.'

'You believed him?'

'Not for a moment.' She was shredding the lace handkerchief. 'And he knew it, but he didn't care. He let drop a remark which

446

suggested he was engaged in some kind of smuggling. I thought, what's the harm? I needed the money.'

'Wait a minute.' Tweed produced a document from his breast pocket. 'Read that. It's the Official Secrets Act.'

'Why?'

'Just read it.' Tweed went to the door, asked Butler and Nield to come in for a moment. He explained they were witnessing the signing of the Official Secrets Act by Miss Diana Chadwick. When she had signed the document the two men left the room.

'Now,' said Tweed, 'you must know that Dr Berlin is not only an impostor, he isn't even German. He's English.'

'Yes.'

'Tell me anything you can about his real appearance – without that beard he grows every time he returns to Lübeck when he pretends to be meditating or some other rot. His habits.'

'He collects fine wines . . .'

'What?' Tweed let out the exclamation involuntarily.

'I said he collects fine wines. He even has a dozen bottles of Chateau d'Yquem in his cellar at his mansion. He says it's a good investment. And once I caught a brief glimpse of him without his beard just after he'd arrived. He had a loop of hair drooped over his forehead. Rather like Hitler.'

'A catlick?'

'That's right.'

'Now.' Tweed stared hard at her. 'While we were in England I took you round with me to visit four men in their homes. I watched carefully your reaction when you met them – and their reactions. I couldn't spot a reaction which gave any of them away. One of them is Dr Berlin . . .'

'Really?'

'Yes, really.' Tweed's tone was sarcastic. 'That was why I took you with me. And don't deny it. I checked how much money you had in your handbag before we visited my first suspect. Two hundred and fifty pounds . . .'

'How very gallant of you.'

Tweed took two steps forward, stood over her. 'You little fool. We are dealing with a mass murderer. And you are the only witness who can point the finger at him. How much do you think your life is worth? After we'd visited all four men

447

you had another four hundred pounds in that handbag. All of them had an opportunity to pass that money to you out of my sight.'

'What does my signing that document mean?' she asked quietly.

'That none of our conversation in this room can ever be passed on to another person. If it is, you can be prosecuted and sent to prison.'

'Charming. And to think I was once very fond of you.'

'You want to go to London, don't you? Start a new life, earn your own living? You can do that – once this horrible business is cleared up. You know who Dr Berlin really is, don't you?'

'Yes.'

'Who is he then?'

In a very soft voice, not looking at Tweed, she told him.

Fifty-Four

From his own room Tweed asked Newman to come and see him immediately. He had hardly put down the receiver when the phone rang. It was Captain Palmer of Norwegian Intelligence, a very apologetic Palmer.

'I am covered with shame and confusion, Tweed. And I am so sorry not to have contacted you earlier.'

'What's gone wrong, Georg?'

'We have lost the *Nordsee*. That is not entirely accurate. The Coastguard never even found the cruiser. It has been quartering a vast area – continuing after dark. What will you think of us?'

'The same high opinion as before. And now it doesn't make any difference. I know exactly where it's heading for. *My* apologies to the Coastguard for wasting their time.'

'You have time for dinner with me tomorrow night?'

'Next time, yes. I'm leaving almost at once. My thanks.'

Newman arrived as he broke the connection, waited for a few seconds, then began dialling Park Crescent. Newman stood by the curtained window while Tweed gave Monica very precise instructions, then paused as Newman gestured. He told Monica Newman wanted a word and collected his shaving gear from the bathroom while Newman carried on a brief conversation which he couldn't hear.

'We're leaving immediately,' he said as he emerged from the bathroom and Newman put down the phone. 'You're ready? Good. Butler and Nield are escorting Diana. They should be in the lobby waiting. We pay the bill, we leave.'

'Where for?'

'Fornebu.'

The lights were on inside the pilot's cabin aboard the Sea King as Tweed bent over the chart with Casey. Newman looked over his shoulder while Butler and Nield fussed over Diana, settling her in her seat in the passenger compartment.

'You think you can spot the *Nordsee* at night?' Tweed asked.

'Only if I have some idea where to look. We are equipped with the most sophisticated night-seeing devices – which is why the RAF kicked up such a fuss about my borrowing their machine. You must have gone up to PM level,' Casey joked.

Which was exactly the level Tweed had invoked, but he was careful not to confirm the fact. He took the blue crayon Casey was holding and made a neat cross.

'That is the airfield where you land. Time it so we get there close to dawn if you can.' He made another neat cross. 'And that is the point the *Nordsee* is heading for. You know where she was late this afternoon. What course would you follow?'

He handed the crayon back, Casey studied the chart for a few moments and then carefully marked a course. He shrugged his broad shoulders as he straightened up.

'That's only a rough idea. And we shall arrive there long before a power cruiser can make it.'

'All the better. I need to be there ahead of her.'

'And,' Casey decided, 'if we are to make your landfall at dawn, there should be no problem. If necessary, I can land at Esbjerg in Western Denmark to lose a little time, to refuel. We'll see how we go. Take off now?'

'The moment you're ready.'

*

449

Tweed was sitting alongside Newman, two rows behind Diana who sat with Butler. He woke with a start, realized he had dozed off. Rubbing his eyes, he stared in surprise out of the window. The first light of dawn was breaking. The Sea King was flying remarkably smoothly. Tweed put on his headset so he could talk with Newman who was wearing his.

'He must be very close. Shouldn't we go up and see Casey?'

'I just did that a few minutes ago. Another twenty minutes yet. No hurry. What happened between you and Diana? She hasn't looked round once.'

'I told you – I was going to grill her. Naturally, she didn't like it. She won't forgive me. All part of the job.'

'Pity. You two looked as though . . .'

'Drop the subject. Wilson is beckoning to us. We'd better get along there.'

He took off the headset and followed Newman. The vibrations of the rotors drummed in his ears, trembled under his feet. The pilot's view was spectacular. The North Sea was like a sheet of glass, deep purple glass. Ahead the coast of Norfolk curved in a great sweep towards the Wash.

'We're ten minutes from Langham Airfield,' Casey informed him, 'but that isn't why I called you. There's a power cruiser ahead which exactly fits your description.'

'That's impossible. He could never have got here as early as this.'

'It has a different name though.' Casey had handed over control to Wilson and he gave Tweed a large pair of very high-powered binoculars. 'See for yourself.'

Tweed stared through the lenses at the white cruiser heading in towards the Wash. He passed them to Newman and grunted. 'The clever sod. He fooled us. He never was aboard the *Nordsee*. One of his men was at the helm – probably that thug who was chief of security at his mansion. He had another cruiser tucked away in one of those marinas, a *third* vessel. He must have seen Casey's chopper flying over Travemünde and it alerted him. My guess is he left Travemünde hours earlier. Must have done to get here by now.'

'We could be just too late,' Newman commented.

'I'll have to drive like hell,' Tweed replied. 'Just so long as Monica has done her stuff.'

'This is some kind of private airfield at Langham?' Casey asked.

'Yes. Used to be an RAF station during the war. I hear that sometimes Prince Philip uses it – for flying in to Sandringham. I know the place. It's a bit disused.'

'Better get back to your seats,' Casey advised. 'And I'll take over now,' he told Wilson.

'Will the man in that cruiser wonder about us?' Tweed asked.

'Doubt it. I've just seen two more choppers. They supply the oil rigs. Part of the scenery round here.'

Tweed stirred restlessly in his seat, peering out of the window. He caught one glimpse of the cruiser, heading direct inside the Wash, leaving behind an arrow of wake on the sea. The purple was changing to blue. The machine tilted and he lost sight of the vessel.

'What did you talk to Monica about on the phone back at the Grand just before we left my room?' he asked.

'Nothing much. I wanted her to get me something. It's been a long trail,' Newman remarked.

'Full circle – back to East Anglia.'

They were across the coast now. The machine descended and turned rapidly. Tweed clasped his hands to keep them still. The Sea King dropped vertically. Beyond the window the ground came up to meet them. Newman leaned across Tweed to look out.

Disused. Langham Airfield was certainly that. He could see grass growing up through a concrete runway. The machine landed, the rotor beat slowed.

Tweed was the first to alight. Newman followed and was surprised at the size of the airfield. It was wide open country. From beyond a distant hedge he heard another sound as the rotors ceased turning. A gobbling noise. Must be a turkey farm nearby.

'We're very close to Blakeney,' Casey called down. 'A nice little resort.'

'Thanks for the ride.'

Newman ran after Tweed, who was heading for a group of three cars parked on the edge of the field. A Ford Cortina, a Volvo, a Fiat. Monica climbed out from the Cortina as Tweed

451

arrived. The air was crisp and fresh off the sea and she was muffled in a scarf and a camel-hair coat.

'The Cortina is yours. Keys in the ignition,' she told Tweed. 'Are you all right?'

'Yes. Take Diana back into town. Drop her at Newman's flat.' He turned as Newman arrived. 'I forgot. Diana has been using your flat. Hope you don't mind?'

'Charge you a stiff rent.'

'I have to do this one on my own, Bob. Who needs the Volvo?' he asked Monica.

'Bob asked me to have it here on the phone from Oslo. Monty the guard and George the doorman drove two of the vehicles. I left them at a crossroads nearby. Thought you might not want them to see you.'

'I'm leaving now.' Tweed climbed behind the wheel of the Cortina. 'What's the Volvo for, Bob?'

'Me. Maybe I've had enough. Time for a holiday.'

He had a strange smile on his face as he waved Tweed off and turned to the Volvo. Monica opened the rear door, showed him two petrol cans with screw caps stacked on the floor. To keep them stable she'd packed foam rubber between and around them.

'That's what you asked for. Each one is almost full. Not for me to reason why – there are garages everywhere if you need to tank up . . .'

Tweed took a country road, the B1388, to Little Walsingham, turned along the B1105, and at Fakenham joined the A148 for King's Lynn. He pressed his foot down, trying to gauge how long it would take the power cruiser to make landfall. It was going to be a close run thing.

His face had a set expression. He knew if he thought about it he'd feel very tired. The fresh East Anglian air blowing in through the window was sharpening him up. How the hell am I going to manage it? he kept asking himself. There was hardly any other traffic on the road. He had the world almost to himself. He overtook a large furniture van. Smithers of Edmonton. He wondered about that van.

Approaching King's Lynn, he turned on to a side road which would avoid getting tangled in the one-way maze. He crossed the bridge over the slow-flowing Ouse just south of the town.

Ahead stretched the flatlands of the Wash. A thin veil of mist hovered on the horizon. He had moved on to the A17 now. He began to keep a careful lookout for the side turning to Hawkswood Farm, the remote house perched near the edge of the Wash.

Near Sutton Bridge he swung off the A17 on to a turn-off towards Gedney Drove End. He was now driving along a very minor road, elevated above the surrounding countryside but with an excellent tarred surface. He stopped for a moment, reached for the Tupperware canister of water Monica had shoved into one of the pockets facing the rear seats. He prised off the lid and drank greedily. His mouth was dry – dry with fear. Through the window came the faint sound of the whispering grasses swaying gently in the fields below.

He clamped down the lid, shoved the canister back inside the pocket and drove on. As far as he could see there was no sign of life. Not a human being, not another vehicle. In the distance he could see the long single-storey building which was Hawkswood Farm. Again no sign of life. No smoke from the chimney. No car parked in the driveway.

Tweed pulled in at the entrance to the track leading to the dyke. Switching off, he pocketed the keys, got out and began walking rapidly towards the farm. The breeze flapped his trousers. Somewhere behind him he heard the purr of a car's engine in the distance. He ignored it, concentrating all his attention on the farm.

He opened the picket gate carefully so it wouldn't squeak. His rubber-soled shoes made no sound as he walked up the path. He tried the handle of the front door. Locked. He took out his bank cheque card, eased the plastic sheet between door jamb and lock, heard it click.

He turned the handle again carefully, pushed the door open slowly, listened. Taking a few paces into the living-room, he stopped. On a side table stood a large and heavy glass mortar and pestle. The noise of gushing water came from the half-closed kitchen door. He took several cautious paces forward, peered through the gap between the door and the wall on the hinged side. He blinked at the macabre sight.

Standing with his back to Tweed, in front of the sink, a man was shaving. He had removed the right-hand side of his black beard, exposing a long scar where Sue Templeton must have clawed at him. He was about to lather the other side. He turned off the tap. He reached up with his shaving brush and paused. Tweed never knew what alerted him. He dropped the razor, reached inside an open drawer, grabbed a broad-bladed knife and swung round. He had taken two or three paces towards the living-room when Tweed began to run, snatching up the heavy glass pestle.

He ran out of the front door, down the path and turned on to the road in the direction where he had left the car. Behind him feet pounded on the road. Tweed ran full tilt, the pestle grasped in his right hand like a relay runner's baton. His pursuer was gaining on him. He increased speed. The fresh air he gulped into his lungs helped. He reached the track which led to the dyke, turned down it. Beside his Cortina a Volvo was parked. He ran on down the track.

The dangerous stretch came when he arrived at the end of the track, climbed the little rise and went down the other side. He began to run along the narrow path leading to the dyke, which rose like a frozen green wave in the distance. Tweed only caught a glimpse of it. He had walked this way before, knew the risk. Behind him he heard the steady pounding of other feet. He kept his head down, placing his feet carefully, avoiding the hard tufts of grass which could bring him sprawling in a second. He'd never climb to his feet again.

He was getting out of breath, keeping his mouth closed as he evaded the treacherous tufts. Then he got his second wind. He increased speed a little, aware that the gap was still closing between himself and the man behind him. He was sweating like a bull with the effort. Sweat ran down his forehead, dribbled from his armpits. He reached the foot of the great dyke.

He scrambled up the inner side, reached the top, slithered down the far side. The vast expanse of the Wash spread away before him, well beyond the marshlands and the creeks. He had a brief view of a power cruiser moored to the landing-stage which had been reinforced with fresh timber. He was very close to the area he remembered, the patches of sand, the sinister acid green grass which seemed to float on top of the ooze. He turned at bay, breathing hard.

A man was charging down the outer side of the dyke, the

454

ugly-looking knife grasped in his right hand. Still a macabre sight, half a black beard remaining on the left-hand side of his face, Hugh Grey stopped, eyes glaring wildly. Not really sane.

He moved towards Tweed, expecting him to turn away, to try and run. Tweed did the unexpected. He moved in close, brought the pestle down savagely on the wrist of the hand holding the knife. Grey dropped it, looked surprised and in that moment of indecision Tweed moved again. Grey was standing with his back to the marshy verge. Tweed lifted both fists, hammered them with all his strength into Grey's solar plexus. Again the look of surprise. He toppled backwards after stumbling a few paces. He sprawled across the surface of the ooze. He tried to sit up. His feet and legs began sinking first, disappearing rapidly. The ooze sucked him deeper. He was only half in view, from the waist up.

He panicked. Placing the flat of both hands on the mud, he tried to stop the suction hauling him down. He screamed obscenities at Tweed, then began pleading for help. Tweed stood without moving, silent, breathing heavily. The hands disappeared. Grey tried to haul them out, couldn't. The mud closed over his forearms. He let out a strange bleating noise. Nothing intelligible. Only his neck and head showed now. He stared at Tweed. He opened his mouth and took in a gulp of mud. The head sank slowly out of sight. There was a brief disturbance. Ripples and bubbles where he had gone down. Then the ooze settled to its normal smooth surface.

Tweed picked up the knife, tossed it into the quagmire. It landed on its point, disappeared in seconds. Tweed looked towards the cruiser and Newman was standing on the deck, watching.

Tweed and Newman were lying down on the landward side of the dyke, peering over the crest at the cruiser. Newman had released the mooring ropes and the vessel was drifting very slowly away from the landing stage as the tide went out.

'So, it was Hugh Grey,' Newman said.

'Yes. Diana told me. How did you get here?'

'Thought you might need a bit of assistance. I drove along the coast road, the A149. I saw you take that side road from

455

Langham Airfield and guessed I wouldn't be far behind.' He
held a Verey pistol in his right hand. He extended the index
finger of his left hand. 'Taste that.'

'Heroin . . .'

'And that cruiser is stacked to the gunwales with the stuff.
A carpenter had even cut out special compartments to store it.
It was under the deck planks. Everywhere. And it had much
the same equipment as the *Nordsee*,' he added, raising the
Verey pistol. 'You've seen its name?'

'The *Seebeck*. Dr Berlin – Hugh Grey – did have a third boat
hidden away. What are you going to do?'

'I've emptied several of the fuel drums – again, like the
Südwind, it had plenty of spare fuel. I tumbled a couple down
the companionway into the main cabin. It's drenched. And you
see those two petrol cans perched on top of that locker? One
is half-empty – I spilt it around. That is the trigger for my little
atom bomb. Five hundred kilos. Regrettably, even in the Drug
Squad there could be men who'd sell their souls for the money
that lot would bring in. I do wish Gorbachev could see this.
Keep your head well down, for God's sake.'

The *Seebeck* had been caught up in a strong current, was
now drifting faster at least thirty feet from the shore. Newman
took careful aim with the Verey pistol, his target the cans of
petrol. He pulled the trigger.

Nothing much happened. There was a sizzle. Then Vesuvius
erupted. A roar like thunder swept out across the Wash. The
bow of the vessel headed skywards, trailing a tongue of flame
like a Cape Canaveral rocket. It exploded into a thousand
pieces. Followed by the main detonation. Tweed guessed the
fire had reached the drums toppled into the cabin. Amidships
the *Seebeck* came apart, blasting seawards, scores of fireballs.
A plume of black smoke ascended vertically. The relic of the
stern crackled. Flames spread round the rim. A third explosion.
The stern soared out over the sea, ascending at an angle of
about forty-five degrees. It blew up in mid-air. Fragments fell
back into the water, hissed, disappeared. For a short time the
sea had boiled where the *Seebeck* had drifted to, then it calmed
down. There was a sudden silence. Gulls wheeled away inland.
No trace remained of the cruiser.

'Grey went up with that,' Newman said. 'We saw him standing on deck just before the explosion. Technical hitch. They'll never find enough to work out what really happened. And I saw your tussle with Grey. I had my Luger ready. Just in case. You led him here deliberately.'

It was a statement. Tweed nodded, climbed slowly to his feet and brushed rubbish off his suit. 'That had better be what we tell them,' he agreed. 'And yes, I led him here on purpose. A mass murderer, a traitor. He had to disappear. The scandal would have destroyed the Service. We've done the job.'

'I do believe we have.'

'Except for driving back to the farm, making sure there are no traces of the beard he'd half-shaved off in the kitchen – things like that. His problem was he couldn't shave it off in Lübeck, and since he's had no chance until he reached the farm. Too busy steering that cruiser. Must have had stamina – the stamina of a madman. I suppose we'd also better call the police.'

Epilogue

Tweed was alone in his office when Harry Masterson came in. He gestured for his visitor to sit down in the chair opposite his desk and stared at him for a minute. It was Masterson, the irrepressible Harry, who broke the silence.

'I heard about the tragedy up in Norfolk. Poor old Hugh. I suppose it wasn't a time bomb?'

'That we'll never know. The Forensic people are going barmy. Can't find enough of the wreckage to tell what happened. The risk of the game. I wanted to ask you something. What were you doing in Lübeck – walking round all bandaged up and asking a lot of damn-fool questions?'

'I suppose I might as well own up. I had a hot tip – from one of my best informants inside the DDR – that Dr Berlin was also someone high up in London. So, I hared up there to check it out.'

'And what about the *Nocturne*? It was seen – by a highly reliable witness – berthed at Travemünde.'

'I am in the shit. Might as well own up to everything. A pal of mine brought it up to Lübeck from Chichester. You see, I needed somewhere I could hide out. I didn't trust a hotel. I sailed it from one marina to another along the Baltic while I went on checking out this Berlin character.'

'Must have cost a fortune – the *Nocturne*.'

'Oh, it did. Trouble was I never thought anyone would believe me. Remember that holiday I took in Monte Carlo? Walked into the Casino one night for a lark. Won a fortune – probably because I wasn't really trying. Pocketed the lot, bought myself the *Nocturne* – and a Porsche. Never been inside a casino since. Once in a lifetime. Don't push your luck.'

'You were in the wrong territory, Harry.'

'I know. But at that last meeting you did lay it on pretty thick that Dr Berlin was what you wanted to know about. Ask for something, you're liable to get it. Sorry – if that helps.'

'You always wanted Germany, didn't you?'

459

'Truth is, I can't stand the Roumanians and Bulgars.'

'I'll think about it. And I have Bob Newman waiting to see me.'

Tweed was standing by the window when Newman came in. He had a wan expression when he turned round and ushered his guest into a chair. Newman studied him as he lit a cigarette.

'Diana has found herself a flat. She has also found herself a job. She doesn't waste much time.'

'Give her my congratulations when you see her.'

'Not a good idea.' Newman paused. 'She doesn't want to see you again. I argued, got nowhere. I'm taking her out to Waltons for dinner tonight. And I made my statement to the police about the Norfolk business. They weren't too happy. As you suggested, I told them to contact you and that shut them up. Case closed.'

'Don't worry about Diana. She needs a new start in life. I am also very grateful to you . . .'

'Nonsense. My experience inside the DDR may come in useful one day. And I'm sorry about Diana. I thought maybe you and she . . .'

'Forget it. I'm very tired.'

'And Kuhlmann might like this back.' Newman laid a Luger on the desk. 'I've got rid of the ammo. What about Dr Berlin – the German end?'

'Kuhlmann is handling that. I had a long talk on the phone with him. He's spreading the rumour Berlin has returned to Leipzig. End of story.'

'See you, then . . .'

Monica came into the office after Newman had left. She found Tweed sitting at his desk, writing out a letter. Placing a file on his desk, she caught sight of a sentence.

'My God! What are you doing?'

'Writing out my letter of resignation. I committed a major error of judgement – when I chose Hugh Grey.'

'But that's buried . . .' She paused. 'Sorry, that was not a very well phrased comment. You solved the problem brilliantly.'

'And I created it.'

'I phoned Paula Grey as you asked, and she's at my place. I told her you were holding an important meeting out at Hawkswood Farm. She seemed glad to come. Last night – over a pot of tea – she broke down. Told me she saw Hugh drive off after his birthday party two years ago. Later she found drops of blood on his shirt. That's why she put Portman, that private investigator, on his track. Did you suspect it was Grey?'

'He was my prime suspect, yes. Little things. We all live by habit. I noticed the countryside close to Travemünde was very like East Anglia – I think that was why Grey chose the port as his base. Nostalgia for home surroundings. Later – after Newman told me about the huge drug cargo – I recalled the reinforced landing stage at the edge of the Wash. The clincher was the *absence* of something. Grey knew he was being followed by Portman and never reported it to me, which would have been his normal reaction – in case it was the opposition. He didn't *dare* do that – it could have led to Grey himself being put under close surveillance.'

'And what about that weird episode when Diana caught him unawares at the mansion on Priwall Island? When she saw him before he'd grown his beard and he had a catlick over his forehead. Rather like Hitler I think you said?'

'My guess is he only had seconds to act – but he had fast reflexes. He combed his hair down over his forehead – so if she ever passed on his description to the wrong person they would think it sounded like Guy Dalby – which it did. Hugh had to be a very clever villain to achieve what he did.'

He finished writing, read through the letter, then placed it on his desk and leant back in his chair. Monica reached forward, picked up the sheet, folded it and put it inside her handbag.

'I haven't signed it yet. What are you doing?'

'Sleep on it,' Monica advised.

'I was going to.'

'For a week. If, at the end of a week, you still feel the same way, I'll give this letter back to you.'

'I won't change my mind . . .'

'Of course not,' she replied. 'And now, just for once, I'm going home early.'

Tweed was left alone, sitting at his desk, staring at the wall map which showed the border between two worlds – East and West.